OPERATION CONDOR

OPERATION CONDOR

WITH DEATH AND LOVE

DANIEL NUCHOVICH

SEAWORTHY PUBLICATIONS, INC. • MELBOURNE, FLORIDA

Operation Condor
With Death And Love

Published in the USA by:
Tablet Publications
(An imprint of Seaworthy Publications, Inc.)
6300 N Wickham Rd.
Unit #130-416
Melbourne, FL 32940
Phone 321-610-3634
e-mail orders@seaworthy.com
www.tabletpublications.com

Library of Congress Cataloging-in-Publication Data

Names: Nuchovich, Daniel I., author.
Title: Operation Condor : with death and love / Daniel Nuchovich.
Description: Melbourne, Florida : Seaworthy Publications, [2022] | Summary: "Operation Condor was a cruel campaign of political repression and state terror involving military operations, dictatorships, and assassination throughout South America. In the country of Uruguay, it imposed an authoritarian government dedicated to the capture, jailing, torture, and killing of all opposition. Thousands of workers, students, dissidents, and politicians were prosecuted and eliminated. The bloodshed was horrendous. Others were kidnapped, tortured, and killed in allied countries, or illegally transferred to their home countries to be executed following Condor operations. Then in Uruguay, a young medical student, Daniel Blum, distraught by the kidnapping and murder of his beloved girlfriend, and seeking revenge, conceives a risky plan to find the assassins. Oblivious to the danger, he enters the morgue claiming an interest in forensic medicine where, between corpses and autopsies, he succeeds in befriending some of the detectives, winning their trust, which allows him to enter the main police center. He succeeds in obtaining training in the use of firearms, but he finds himself powerless and unable to advance. He then manages to help a friend to escape capture by the dictatorship and this draws him into a secret underground organization. Using newfound resources and alliances he works to solve the murder of his girlfriend and the kidnappings and murders of other young students. Then he meets a young woman who becomes his companion and lover. With her at his side, he attempts to solve these mysterious murders while avoiding being crushed between the powerful opposing forces of the dictatorship and the opposition"-- Provided by publisher.
Identifiers: LCCN 2022046281 (print) | LCCN 2022046282 (ebook) | ISBN 9781948494632 (paperback) | ISBN 9781948494649 (epub)
Subjects: LCSH: Operación Cóndor (South American countersubversion association)--Fiction. | LCGFT: Historical fiction. | Novels.
Classification: LCC PS3614.U76 O64 2022 (print) | LCC PS3614.U76 (ebook) | DDC 813/.6--dc23/eng/20220927
LC record available at https://lccn.loc.gov/2022046281
LC ebook record available at https://lccn.loc.gov/2022046282

Dedication

This book is dedicated to Ana, my wife and friend.

It also dedicated to all those who lost friends and relatives under the brutal boots of the Uruguayan dictatorship

Preface

This book was written using Dr. Blum's historical work, archives, documents, military records, statements, and photographs. It describes his involvement with the dictatorship and the risks he ran. It is based on real facts and actual events. Some names and locations were changed to protect the individuals involved, however many of the events, names and places are described as they occurred. Although written as a novel, many of the descriptions were taken from horrible incidents caused by this military despotism, and they can be found in many archives and documents.

During the early 1970s, Uruguay writhed under the cruel boot of a military dictatorship which was part of the Operation Condor. The country was overwhelmed by terror, dirty war, abductions, and death squads. Most of the events occurred as they are described in this book and are supported by the research, data gathering, interviews, and document reviews done by the author. Most descriptions can be confirmed through Google search, Wikipedia, The Guardian, YouTube, Uruguayan and Argentinian newspapers, and even The New York Times and BBC archives.

Chapter 1

Monday marched past midnight. The din from the streets had calmed down and the city of Montevideo, Uruguay turned to the night quietness. The aromas of the evening slowly entered through the window and mixed with the strong odors of the room.

Daniel Blum squeezed the wound a little more. He took a step toward the window and inhaled, trying to guess the details of the street, the smells of the pizzeria on the corner, and the diesel smoke of the taxis that were passing by. The night nestled in, barely any voices pierced the black air, and there were already few taxis running.

There's not much movement, he thought. *Bad sign.*

After the initial suffering, the pain had finally calmed down. Daniel waited a little, took his hand off the wound, and sighed relief when he saw that it was no longer bleeding. He looked at the clock leaning on the peeling wall. "Two o'clock in the morning already," he told himself, wiping blood from his hands with no concern. A small clot had stuck to his wristwatch, and he wiped it on the curtain without thinking. His fingers were getting sticky already from the drying blood.

He began to assess the situation. The bleeding caused by the blade had been alarming, but despite the initial damage, the wound had been disinfected and stitched, and the bleeding had waned and finally stopped. It was an ugly, painful cut, and it took him a long time to stick the edges together and sew them well. One of the arteries had been cut and it had taken a while to control. The condition required a transfusion.

He felt like smoking to calm his nerves a little. A scream distracted him. He looked at the clock again. "Six more hours until eight," he sighed and yawned, thinking about what to do next. He wrapped the piece of skin he had to remove and then removed his gloves and threw them all at the trash bin where various colors of gauzes draped, all stained with blood.

He rearranged his clothes and checked his white coat, saw that his sleeve was stained with blood and began cleaning it. The stain was fresh and was coming off easily.

He assessed the situation again while leaning on the wall. He could see some bloodstains on the floor and a bigger one at the foot of the stretcher. He didn't like it. He was sure that nurse Matilde was going to get angry like in the previous case, with that wounded girl, and yell at him to clean it. He'd better get out of there.

He swiftly washed the patient's thigh with hydrogen peroxide and then with alcohol, spread the wound with antibiotic cream, put clean gauze on it, and wrapped it up. He adjusted the drip of the transfusion and ordered the patient, "You stay in the hospital until tomorrow, do not touch the transfusion tube and stay still until Matilde comes."

"Yes, yes, thank you," the wounded man answered.

Daniel squeezed him on the shoulder to cheer him up, gave him a smile, and went to rest for a while. Some coffee would do him good. Yes, coffee with sugar is good at that time of the morning. He gave instructions to the patient, called the nurse to give her the directions, and went to the break room.

Matilde came in despair.

As he walked away, he heard Matilde muttering: "But Daniel... once again! You littered the floor again, but... I'm not your maid!"

Daniel didn't want to argue again. He went to the restroom and later to room number five, which the students used as a break room. Interns, doctors, and students used that room in the emergency department as a resting place as it was just outside the front door. From there, they could see immediately what cases were coming in. It was an old room, as old as the hospital itself, with green walls and peeling paint, old metal tables and stained chairs, scattered stinky ashtrays, some dead roaches in one corner, chunks of pizza filling the trash bin in the other, but it had two advantages a little unusual for what the hospital was: the tap water worked, and the electric sockets worked too. Sitting there, the practitioners would drink coffee, smoke, chat, eat, and disentangle a bit from the bustle of the Emergency Service of the Hospital de Clínicas, the largest hospital in the city of Montevideo, Uruguay, a huge medical palace, old, vast, dirty, and full of smells. Fascinating.

Daniel sat down. He stretched his back and arms. He soaked some cotton in a glass of water and started cleaning two stains of blood from his coat. He raised his legs and leaned them on the chair. He examined his trousers. Luckily, no stains. He loved those smuggled corduroy pants that he bought from an American cargo ship.

He lit a cigarette and enjoyed his first breath of smoke while the smell of tobacco was mixing with the smell of chromium mercury, alcohol, and vomiting coming from room number four. The Emergency Room had calmed down, another bad omen. He didn't like it when the emergency area was too quiet. It could be the calm before the storm.

He looked at his watch. 2:20. Claudia brought in some coffee.

"Is this fresh, Claudia?"

"Yes, Daniel."

"Sugar?"

"Yes, Daniel, yes," she replied. "Just stop staring at the door."

"Sure." he said, looking at her.

"You make me nervous."

Claudia was a good girl, a student, and his companion when he was on call over the last eight months. They had prepared for a couple of exams together. She stood tall and slim, her lush black hair mostly covering a flat chest. She had a big mouth, strong lips, and an amiable smile. She would sit on that chair, when she could, in between cases, drinking coffee, smoking dark tobacco cigarettes, and study. Under her partially open coat she wore a thick colorful shirt and had the quintessential stethoscope hanging from her neck.

"That last suture was very well done, little Danny," she continued. "Are you going to be plastic?"

"No, Claudia. I told you that when we talked about the specialty we're going to choose." He answered, passing a cigarette.

"Yes, thank you," she said "Oh, but this is a light tobacco cigarette. Too light for me. Mmm... well, give it to me anyway." She took the smoke and drew on it hard. "Been to the medical department already?"

Daniel didn't answer. He didn't feel like talking, and Claudia talked a lot.

They smoked a little. Daniel went through his clothes a bit more, looking for possible bloodstains like a tick searches for soft skin.

"Ah, and Tamara... you hear anything about her?" asked Claudia. "You call her?"

"Nothing... no." Daniel suffered every time she asked him about that impossible woman. Tamara had left him one more time about three weeks earlier. "No. I don't... I don't know."

"Why don't you call her instead?"

"Cause I—"

"Call her and... and... so you can stop feeling like that."

"Just leave it."

"Listen. Tamara could... I mean...she..."

"Alright, leave me alone with that, Claudia!" he replied, as she tried once again to remove the sting of bitterness Tamara had left in his mind. It was the third time that she split, and Daniel had finally realized that although she loved him and had cried as she said goodbye, they had such a tumultuous relationship that they had to finish it.

"Don't ask me anymore about Tamara," asked Daniel. "It is... It's just that it..."

I'm sorry," replied Claudia, feeling guilty for having said her name. "Well, Daniel. I didn't know that... hmm... well... excuse me—"

They remained silent. They looked a little more at the peeling wall. Claudia remained silent, gave him some of her coffee, and patted his back as if she were apologizing.

"Well, Daniel, and what did Dr. Ramirez say about the class?"

"Nothing, Claudia," he said to her reluctantly. He checked his robe again and saw that the stains had come out.

"Like nothing?" she continued. "You *did* talk to Ramirez? Mmm, Daniel? What did he tell you?"

"That the class will be given again, late morning. Warn the others."

"Oh, well," said Claudia. "Thank you." Dying curiosity rose in her face. When no longer able to stand it anymore, she put her glasses on as if for her next question. "Tell me, Daniel, what happened to her? Why the obsession with that woman? You know I'm your friend. Talk to me a little, yeah? Don't get like... like..."

"Leave me now, Claudia!" said Daniel with an impatient voice. "Please leave the matter. I told you..."

"What... what went wrong? Why is it so painful? You had other girls before."

He looked at her, attempting to explain. He couldn't answer it. The emergency door suddenly opened wide and banged against the wall. It startled Daniel and Claudia. Paramedics and police stormed in, carrying a traumatized man into one of the rooms. Screams and commotion cluttered the air. Daniel left the cigarette and the coffee and got up.

"But what...?"

"Stay here, I am going," he said. "It's my turn."

"Don't get in trouble, Daniel. Count to twenty before entering. Did you hear me?"

"Yes. Yeah, I heard you."

He went to room number eight, the trauma room, but it overflowed with nurses, police, and paramedics and he couldn't get in or see anything. He stood outside. "One... two... three..."

He waited. The paramedics, a nurse, and two police officers came out.

"What a disaster," said one police officer.

"Four... five..." Daniel kept counting.

"Did you see how young?"

"What a pity, no?"

"Six... seven... eight..."

"Poor guy. A shot like that. What a mess."

Daniel reached ten, took a deep breath. "Eleven... twelve..." and went in.

The nurses bustled about.

"He's dead," said one nurse. "Dead," as she took off his clothes by cutting them with scissors.

Daniel put on gloves and was ready to help.

"Lift that leg, Daniel," said the other nurse.

He obeyed.

"Take off his shoes," she said.

Daniel took them off.

A slim, pale body. Cold. The flaccid flesh. Dead. Daniel could feel the absence of life.

He was a young man. He had a lot of blood on one side of his head. *Another one,* thought Daniel.

The curtain opened and Dr. Perez-Cabrera, the surgeon on duty, entered the room, with his loose coat and smell of tobacco, and behind him Dr. Millan, tall and bald. Between the two, they checked the entire body out; examined front and back, side to side, head to toe.

"Hmm...one shot in the head," said Dr. Millan. "Nothing more."

"There are no needles or blunt force trauma," said Dr. Perez-Cabrera. "But there seems to be something unusual."

"Yes, as in the other case," a doctor said, angling an examination light.

"Hmm... yes. Look. Stains of gunpowder, there, you see.

"Suicide."

"What a pity. Such a young guy."

They all searched each other's faces.

"Yes, or maybe he was killed." continued the surgeon. "Who would've done it? Hmm... he was about twenty-five years old?"

One more dead, thought Daniel. *Another suicide.*

He saw cases like this in the emergency room, and this case was no surprise. For one thing or another, they brought dead young people there almost every night. Asphyxiated, drugged, shot, stabbed, car accidents...a grab bag of reasons. There, at the Hospital de Clinicas, death was part of life. While Daniel remembered the first two dead people he had seen, he realized that he had already seen so many that he had lost count a while ago.

However, something was unusual this time, and the two doctors were uneasy with the sight.

"Listen to me," said Millan. "This is *not* a suicide. This..." he squinted and leaned in, "Hmm...yes, I think they killed him."

"Shh, speak low," said the nurse. "Remember..."

The two doctors zipped to silence. Thinking.

There wasn't much to do, anyway. Daniel was going out of the room, but he stayed when he saw two detectives heading his way. He saw two more detectives and one police officer through the front door, like watching from the distance, looming. Something seemed different in this case, but Daniel didn't know what it was. A certain intrigue was floating in the air.

Two detectives then another entered the room and closed the curtain. One wore a long brown jacket, a dark shirt, and a horrible tie, as was the usual. The other wore a flowered shirt. Daniel saw that they had grim faces, and they were frowning, so he took two steps back. They signaled one of the nurses to leave and talked with Doctors Perez-Cabrera and Millan.

Daniel looked at them but moved his face to the side and down so they wouldn't pay attention to him.

"And what do you think, MacLagan?" Millan said.

"Yes, this is the third case," answered the detective, who was carrying an enormous weapon like a mortar.

"We have a problem."

"Suicide?"

They looked at each other and shook their heads from side to side.

Dr. Millan scratched his mustache. Daniel took a slow step back.

"What...?" said the other detective, who was also carrying a weapon. "No, it's not a suicide."

"They brought him from a military barracks."

"But then... what...? is it an execution?" said Millan. "Like the other case, eh?"

"Executed by the dictatorship."

A short, thick silence suddenly hung in the air. MacLagan wiped the blood with his handkerchief as he looked at the other detective. They said something with their eyes. Perez-Cabrera looked at them both curiously, knowing what they were thinking. Daniel looked at the four of them, trying to guess what was going on. The silence was stark. Perez-Cabrera squeezed Dr. Millan's arm and mumbled a few words.

Something dense hung in the air.

"What do you want me to say?" Dr. Perez-Cabrera asked in a low voice.

"What you already know." said the detective. "Which is a similar case. Look, see? See? Handcuff marks on the wrists and ankles."

"Ah and look here. See?"

"Oh, gee..."

"Mmm, yes, I see. From where?... but from what base?....another victim of the army?

"Doctor," the detective nodded and blinked, "That is not to be talked about."

"We don't know. We don't know why, and we don't know from where, but surely, they are..."

"Shhh, wait, this is..."

"We don't know, but he could have been a junior member of the communist party or... or related to the Tupamaros. Yes. Therefore, I think..."

"Yes; surely," said the other detective.

"But..." Perez-Cabrera said, "they would have been tortured, and look, not a mark, not a cut. In this case it seems like something strange is going on. Are you sure?

"Killed by the military?" asked Dr. Millan. "But you can't..."

"It seems to be the third," said MacLagan. "I'm going to call the technicians to make the identification of the body. Keep it quiet."

"No, wait, MacLagan, look, it's the fourth case. Do you remember that girl?"

"Oh, yeah. Clearly executed."

"They executed him too," said the nurse. "Don't you see? A young boy gunned down like this by those assassins."

"Shut up!" said MacLagan. "Quiet please, don't you make any noise or comment about this."

For a while they all stood still again, again in silence, looking at the body with respect, as if trying not to know what they already knew.

In that moment, when turning around, detective MacLagan saw Daniel in the room's corner trying to disguise himself as a wall, holding his breath, and praying that he was not seen.

"But who is this?" he shouted, pointing at Daniel. "Who are you?"

Daniel's heart stopped. They were going to kill him.

"Ah, he's a student." said Dr. Millan. "Daniel, what are you doing here, eh...?"

Daniel went pale. His tongue stuck. He couldn't answer. Fear stabbed him in the gut, pushing him deeper into the peeling wall. He was a witness and will be eliminated.

"Don't make a stupid face." shouted the detective, suddenly frowning. "Eh, what are you doing here?"

"He was helping," interjected the nurse who had stayed. "Don't scare him like that, poor thing."

"Listen to me, Daniel," said MacLagan, opening the jacket and showing his weapon. "I don't know why you are here, but I warn you: you weren't here and heard nothing. Do you understand me?"

Intimidated, Daniel swallowed at the site of the revolver and knew that his life was changing. That MacLagan looked like a mafia envoy. He had a mean face and a sour odor. With a dark shirt, hair combed back, and a long jacket, he was scary. He had the look of someone who had killed people.

"Yes... yes... I understand," he said, trying to sneak away, while smelling the stench of the weapon mixed with the scent of cheap cologne that came from the agent.

"Oh, oh," said the nurse. "Don't scare him like that, MacLagan, he's cute. Don't be mean to him."

"Yes, leave him," said Dr. Millan. "He's just a student."

"Hopefully studying Advanced Silence," MacLagan quipped.

"Stay there and don't move," the other detective gave the order.

"And shut up, did you hear?"

Millan and Perez-Cabrera put their fingers to their lips, signaling for Daniel to keep quiet. The nurse made a funny face at him. The four of them continued talking and exchanging opinions while Daniel's gaze went from the pressing eyes of the detectives to the lifeless eyes of the dead man. The bloody hole in his head was still dripping.

His lifeless face seemed to wait for one of the four men who were there to give him a magic touch to regain the life that had left him. *So young*, Daniel thought, *He's younger than me.*

"You must clean him a bit for the technicians," said a voice.

"For what?" said the one with the flowered shirt in a low voice. "You don't see that it's another political murder and we won't be able to investigate it."

"Shhh, don't talk about that," MacLagan said nervously.

"But...you know well that—"

"Stop. You must follow the rules. Clean it up a bit."

"Yes, but...no, wait, I don't want to erase the marks. Hmm...wait, no, better don't clean anything for now. Let's take some pictures. Isn't there a camera here? Where is it?"

Daniel thought of the camera he had back in his bag.

"No. We don't have any," Millan said, putting his chubby hands in the pockets of his large robe.

Daniel froze.

"There isn't any camera here in the emergency room," affirmed the nurse.

"What?" said one of them. "They don't have a camera... What a shame."

"We always need a camera," asserted MacLagan, scratching his chin.

"Hmm... eh... eh... I have one," said Daniel, raising his hand a little, immediately sorry for having spoken.

Silence. All four looked at him in surprise and anger, for having opened his mouth. Daniel shrunk to the wall and prepared to be bitten.

Coming out of their surprise, the agents looked at each other approvingly.

"How come you have a camera here?" asked the surgeon. "You can't bring cameras here."

"It is that doctors Carvajal and... and... and the *Russian* Sepansky asked me to... to bring it two days ago to take... to take photos of skin flaps and sutures and... and I thought... because of photos of the flaps... and... and I thought..."

"Oh yeah?"

"And what kind of camera is it, Daniel?" Perez-Cabrera asked with a mocking tone. "One of those birthday party cameras... The kind you use for children?"

"Ha! one of those pocket cameras?"

"No. It's not that kind of camera," Daniel answered. "It's an Asahi-Pentax."

The detectives nodded, impressed with the expensive-sounding name.

"With three lenses, 35-150 lens, filters, and 400 ASA rolls. And I have a flash with triple speed."

"Ha! Look at this baby boy..." said Dr. Millan. "Showing off. Making himself look like a man."

They turned to each other approvingly.

"Well, bring it over."

Daniel didn't move.

"Well..." said MacLagan, "go out and bring it here without talking to anyone." He paused too briefly. "Did you hear? Hit it, quick."

"Ah, just stop scaring him, MacLagan," said Dr. Millan. "It's okay, Daniel, relax. Go and bring it here."

Daniel left quickly, went to the desk of the head nurse, and asked for his bag, which she kept under lock to prevent theft. He returned to room number eight and showed them his camera.

"Prepare it," said MacLagan. "For each shot, you take one with flash and one without flash; you hear me?"

They had Daniel take several photos of the impact zone, from various angles, and then of various parts of the body.

The two doctors looked on without speaking, a little surprised that Daniel knew how to interpret the orders of the agents and was so skilled with his camera.

"Okay, it's done," said the agent in the floral shirt. "Good." He held out his hand. "Give me the roll."

"What? No! The camera and the film are mine."

"Shut up," Agent MacLagan said. "What you have in your camera is police evidence. Give me the roll!"

"No!" said Daniel, getting defensive and running towards the door. "It's mine!"

"Come here, Daniel," shouted the detective in the floral shirt. "Give it to me!"

"Don't be daring, Daniel" the surgeon shouted. "Give it to him. But..."

"No, I will not!" Daniel said with a quivering lip while also sticking out his chin and lengthening his neck, knowing that the doctors would protect him if things got worse. "They are going to damage the camera and the film."

The tension grew in the air. Daniel held the camera under his coat and was attempting to leave from the side of the curtain.

"Give him the roll, Daniel!" asked Millan loudly.

"Just give me the camera roll, Daniel!" screamed MacLagan.

"It's mine!" he answered, breathing hard, with his adrenaline kicking, opening his eyes, and straightening up with a bit of courage. "I will develop it and will then give you the *photos*."

"Oh no, you won't!"

"But..." said the nurse. "Just, just— but Daniel, just give it to them, before something happens to you."

"No."

"You are talking to the police."

"But this beardless idiot..." said Detective MacLagan, full of anger. "Who do you think you are, stupid?" He paused then tried to reason. "You're going to spend the night in a cold cell at the police station. Is that what you want? Give it to me now and none of this ever happened. You know quite well that this is criminal evidence."

The officers' anger increased as Daniel stood upright with his arms behind him, holding the camera under the coat and facing them. Daniel's attitude surprised them, and the doctors did not understand how he had the courage to face them. In a moment of silence, it was clear to Daniel that he would not be doing well. The aggressive energy of the two agents was greater than what he was trying to display. He was going to lose.

"Well, that's fine!" he exclaimed, with a challenging voice. "I roll up the camera roll, take it out and give it to you. But I have photos there that I need."

MacLagan glared at him. Daniel rolled back the film. The other detective took a step toward Daniel, but one of the doctors held him.

"Don't look at me like you don't know what I'm talking about—" stated Daniel, loudly. "I have photos of mine here. I need them."

His cocky attitude surprised the four men.

"Ah, yes? Well, you come tomorrow after five o'clock to the police headquarters, third floor, and the roll will be returned to you, developed, with your photos." He paused then added, "And be grateful that we let you keep the camera."

"Yeah," affirmed the other detective. "And that we let you go free... this time."

Daniel handed him the camera roll.

"Ungrateful!" Daniel said to the detective, already coming out of the initial scare and recovering his personality and attitude. "Without me you would not even have this evidence. So, this's how you thank me, eh?"

"But shut up, you fool." Detective Pranchin, the one with the floral shirt, yelled at him.

"Don't lose the roll, I need those photos." Daniel rebuked aloud, knowing when to be daring.

"Get out of here, rude little boy!" MacLagan yelled, veins swelling on his forehead.

"Don't be insolent," Millan barked at him. "Drop it. Calm down. Just drop it."

"Oh, but... everybody calm down, Daniel, Detectives MacLagan, Pranchin," asked the nurse. "There's a dead body here."

"You are a—"

"Yeah, shut up, Daniel," warned the nurse. "Don't dig yourself any deeper."

"You better go, Daniel," said Millan, patting him on the shoulder.

Daniel left the room oscillating between furious and scared. He went to the corridor. Claudia was there.

"I came to rescue you before they kill you," she said. "Or they will cut off that long nasty tongue of yours."

Daniel looked at her without answering.

"Go to sleep before you get into more trouble," Claudia added.

Daniel stayed there. He didn't want to go.

"But what possessed you to get into trouble like this, Daniel? Just go now... just go to sleep."

Daniel went to the break room, made some tea, smoked a cigarette, calmed down, and went to the student dormitory, where he was greeted by a lull tide of snoring. Raul was in Marta's bed, lying with Rosa, Marta was in Daniel's bed, Alberto and Luis were in Raul's bed, all of them lying down with clothes and coats, as one sleeps when on call. The bathroom light was on and there were chocolate wrappers and cookie pieces on the floor. He pushed Marta towards the wall and laid down next to her. Marta smelled good, and luckily; she wasn't snoring. He unbuttoned her coat, covered her a little with the blanket, removed the stethoscope from her neck and put it along with some other items on the floor. He put the camera in a bag and hung it next to the bed. He unbuttoned his robe and covered himself with the blanket. He smelled Marta a little more, bringing his nose close to her hair, and leaned his head back, preparing to sleep. As soon as he put his head on the pillow, images of the dead guy came to him. *Who was he?* he wondered. Poor boy, so young. *Was it a murder?*

At half past seven Marta elbowed him to wake him up. He got up, washed his face, and brushed his teeth, drank the coffee Rosa gave him, ate half a cookie that Raul shared, gave a cigarette to Luis, and went to class.

"Don't forget your bag," Marta reminded him.

"Thanks and Claudia?"

"Sleeping. Leave her. She was up all night."

He spent the morning moving from class to class on the eighth floor of the Hospital de Clinicas, examined patients and talked with two professors about a case of pulmonary hypertension. He left at twelve, quickly went down the street, crossed to the cafeteria, hurried down a piece of ham croissant, and took a taxi to the medical school to give his daily anatomy class. The traffic crawled along the streets congested with cars, but he didn't care. He liked Montevideo; he liked the city. He arrived at the School of Medicine, went down to the basement, put on his long, crossed dissector's tunic, and grabbed his dissection box. Daniel was an assistant professor in the Anatomy Department and had two groups of students assigned to him, whom he taught while dissecting cadavers that were treated with formaldehyde.

His students gave him no problems, luckily, seeing his tired face, knowing that he was coming from the emergency room after being on call. Daniel helped his students to dissect the armpit region in a corpse that luckily was fresh and without the usual excess of formaldehyde, and then told them about the branches of the brachial plexus, while he struggled to keep his mind calm and away from the knowledge that he would have to go to the police headquarters and face the lions alone. *They are going to skin me alive*, he thought. *But I must rescue that roll.*

Two hours later he snuck a brief break in front of the corpse while eating chocolate that a student gave him and smoking a cigarette that another student passed him. They talked about movies to distract themselves a bit. He later dissected and explained the anatomy of the abdominal wall to the students and told them, "We'll open the belly tomorrow. Bring some cologne."

At five o'clock in the afternoon, he took a taxi to the police headquarters, there on San Jose Street at the corner of Yi Street. The gray street and the litter on the pavement did not seem to herald anything good. At the entrance, an ugly and hairy gorilla wrapped in a police uniform asked him where he was going. Daniel explained, and the ape showed him to the elevator.

He went up to the third floor, identified himself to another uniformed ape and said why he was there. They showed him to a large office. A few minutes later, three of the detectives showed up, including two from the night before. A police officer and a tall guy with a mustache walked in through another door. All of them were bearing arms, and they were smiling and swearing. Each sported a sarcastic smile, except for the dry MacLagan. They had done what Daniel feared. They had seen certain photos that had been on the camera roll and that he wanted to prevent them from seeing. *Crap*! thought Daniel, *I'm in trouble.*

"So, skin flaps, huh?... plastic surgery, hmm?" said Pranchin, the agent in the floral shirt, which today was a different shade but same pattern. "Hmm, what a selection of scientific pictures you had. Wooow!

"Nice medical science, you immoral!"

"Yes, anatomical *cuts*, eh?" said the other.

And they brought out the photos of Carmen that showed her good physical virtues. They made comments while laughing. Daniel flushed with shame and outrage.

"Gee, her breasts look... scientific."

"*Mammary glands*."

"Huh?"

"Mammary glands I think they're called... you know,... scientifically."

"Uuuuuhh...and this one of the lower areas. Ooh là là!"

Daniel was frozen.

"Yeah, and her bikini is a medical wonder," said another agent. "You really took your time to study her."

The office was packed full of old desks, piled high with papers and folders. The agents wore dark shirts and the classic ugly ties that never seemed to fit them, except Pranchin in his ugly floral shirt.

Where did he get that ugly shirt from? thought Daniel. The scent of ink, cigarettes and dirt hovered in the air, mixed with the smell of old paper and cheap cologne.

"Please... it's Carmen," said Daniel. "Carmen."

"Oh, sorry, oh, we didn't know it was *Carmen,*" said one agent, with the face of one bitten by chickenpox, laughing even more, "Oh, oh, it's Carmen. Listen everybody."

"Hey guys, show respect. It is *Carmen,*" yelled Pranchin, grinning ear to ear.

There was a brief silence, where all looked at each other. The MacLagan guy was standing there, in a long coat, serious, gray, looking at Daniel with half-closed eyes, as if angry, and evaluating him with disdain.

He's thinking where to shoot me at, thought Daniel.

Smells of coffee, rancid pastry, and a feeling of antipathy and scorn also hung in the air. A ceiling fan in the background screeched. They all carried guns.

I shouldn't be here, thought Daniel.

"Ah, ah, it was the Carmen from the surgical photos, oh yes, excuse me sir. Voluptuous, the girl, eh?"

"But what scientific *flaps* does Carmen have?" said a fat agent with an actor's face, contributing to every easy double entendre and cheap cliche in the book.

MacLagan kept looking at him without speaking. *I'm sure he's still angry,* Daniel thought. *He might throw me in jail and have some criminals take care of me.*

"She... she is a friend," said Daniel. "It's... she's... it doesn't matter."

"Ah, yes... degenerate." One of the agents rebuked him. "Pervert!"

"Please."

"Gee... but this beardless man is a rascal."

"Is that what you do with your camera, little pervert?"

"I'm not!" protested Daniel, aloud. "No. It's Carmen, Carmencita, from the Casa El Ensuenio located by Convención and Canelones. It is one of the brothels of the South District. I do... I take... I took pictures there."

"What?"

"Casa El Ensuenio?"

"Listen to me well, Daniel," finally MacLagan spoke, aloud, angry. "The next time you attempt to talk to me like you did in..."

"Shh, shh, MacLagan, calm down," said Pranchin. "Hold your nerves. Hey, he's just a kid."

"Yes, calm down, man," said the chubby agent. "Don't get mad."

"But you two don't know how this little crappy boy raised his voice to me there, in the hospital," MacLagan protested.

"Well, okay, I mean, look, you're not his father or a saint," said a tall agent with a big mustache who was in the background. "So don't scare him for fun."

"Okay. Regarding the photos. Does your mommy know?"

They all laughed.

"Ah, ah, and did you take the photos before or after?"

"Or during...?"

Daniel was not laughing.

"Well... before and after."

Silence. They looked at each other.

"Ah, but what a naughty little boy," commented the chubby detective from the back. "He's not as dumb as he seems."

"Ah, ha, ha, and how much does she charge you? Eh?

"Nothing. She doesn't charge me a thing. She is a friend. Can you give me the negatives, please?"

"She doesn't charge you? But..."

"No, she is... she... eh... please, the negatives."

"Okay," spoke MacLagan. "Yes, here, these are your negatives. We cut the others and they stay here."

Daniel took the envelope. The agents stopped laughing. Something strange was in the air. Who was this student?

"And these other photos?" asked another of the detectives. "Where is this?"

"They are all shots at the same brothel, of the wall, of the paintings, that's the concierge. That's Carmen's friend, Lucia, with the two bikinis that Carmencita made for her."

"They're nice photos." commented the one in the floral shirt. "Why are some of them brown?"

"It's sepia," answered Daniel. "I use special filters to give a sepia look. Can you give them to me now?"

"Ah, and these shots? They look good up close, almost like the pores are visible. What is it?

"They are macro shots. Made with a special lens."

"Hmm... interesting. And why is she naked in some photos and dressed in different clothes in others? And some in different bikinis?"

"So, I can show them, or... or she can present them, to different agencies; or to companies."

"Agencies? What agencies?"

"Marketing companies, ladies' shops, clothing manufacturers, and what have you."

"Why? Why would you...?"

"Yes, why would you do that?"

"I am trying to help her."

"Help her?"

"Mmm... I see," MacLagan asked with a serious face. "And who is that Carmen again? Who *is* she? -

"She's a teacher in the Paso Molino neighborhood and wants to be a model. These photos will help her TO GET A BETTTER JOB. I'm preparing a folder for her so that she can present it to various agencies later. Some pictures I take myself to agencies. May I go now?"

"She's a teacher and a prostitute? How come?"

"Mmm... well... life is difficult for all of us, right?"

"And how... eh, how are you going to help her?" asked the chubby guy as he approached, curious.

"I'll see. I will try. I mean... I'm trying. I'm going to help her get out from the mud."

"From the mud?" agent MacLagan asked. "What mud?"

"From the mud of poverty. I'm putting together a good catalog for her. I am sure it will be very useful to her."

They all fell silent. Daniel's words took them by surprise. They looked at him, trying to absorb his words. A few long seconds went by.

"And you...? You take photos? I see that you're knowledgeable. You take courses?"

"Yeah. Did you take courses? Training?"

"Yes, of course I did."

"But... why are you helping her? With everything you can do in the world. Why help someone like her?

"Eh... Uh, I don't know. I just did it."

"And how did you... eh... how did you meet her?"

"Ha! Do I need to tell you that? You're a grown man; and a detective. Figure that out."

"You... you..."

"Yes. May I go now?" Daniel turned toward the door. "Ah, and hey, can you tell me what you know about the boy from last night that—"

"Shut up!"

"That can't be discussed.

"Okay."

"Do you hear me?"

"I told you last night not to talk or ask about that. You know that our hands are tied. We cannot investigate it."

"But... you are... you are..."

"You don't need to remind us of who we are!" yelled MacLagan, veins bulging again.

"But-but they killed—"

"But nothing! Be thankful you're alive. Shut up and go away."

They gave him the photos. He thanked them. They didn't move, only stared.

He was going to say a few sarcastic words of his own, but in that place, there was a smell of weapons and crime, and he kept his thoughts to himself. He looked at them and turned to go. He was afraid that they would insult him and make him feel bad, but no one said anything. They had fallen silent again. Daniel walked away slowly. When he was by the door he turned around again. The detectives stayed there, looking at him, thinking who knows what. He looked at that group, Pranchin in the floral shirt, MacLagan the unsympathetic man in the long coat, the chubby guy with the actor's face, the agent with the big mustache in the background, and another agent who was writing in his notebook. He examined them slowly. There was something strange, mysterious like, in that group. Something not violent, not criminal, perhaps intriguing and that no longer scared him. Daniel didn't know what it was, but something occurred to him. He took two of the best photos of Carmen, the ones that showed her the most elegantly, and returned the photos to them. He placed the photos on the table and left. Almost at the door, he turned around again and looked at all of them. He saw them staring at him, absorbed in their thoughts, in silence and without moving, like they had realized that there was something intriguing about him as well.

Daniel went downstairs and out onto the sidewalk of San Jose Street. He walked aimlessly, kicking the litter and the dry leaves, while his adrenaline was dissipating. He stared at display windows and shops, dodging dog poop, looking at the people passing by. It had all been an unusual experience, he concluded. He turned to Plaza Libertad and sat on one of the benches practicing one of his favorite entertainments: daydreaming while watching people go by.

The year was 1974, and the brutality of the Uruguayan dictatorship was emerging. Personal freedom was dwindling while social repression was increasing. As a student living in his own world, oblivious of the social danger that the country was falling into, Daniel didn't even realize that he had taken a step into a red circle.

Chapter 2

"So, I left," Daniel said to his friends, sipping coffee at the coffee shop. "What was I supposed to do?"

It was Thursday. Daniel was meeting his old friends at the Chez Pinieiro coffee shop on the corner of 21 de Septiembre Street and Ellauri, in the Pocitos neighborhood, one of the finest areas of Montevideo, Uruguay. A noisy place, full of people, and aromas of coffee, pizza, and cakes. His friends had already called him several times to talk to him and to cheer him up after Tamara had left him. They knew that the separation from the girl had left him heartbroken and sad, and they wanted to give him some friendly support and advice.

Busy waiters passed by carrying pizza and croissants to one table or coffee and beers to another.

"A murder!" said Manuel. "Gee... and then you at the police headquarters. How horrible. What a mess."

"Yes, looked like it was a murder," added Daniel. "A boy like that, our age, executed. Why executed?"

"Yes, how terrible," added Ernesto. "This military dictatorship is killing people."

"Yea, but this is Uruguay, my friend," said Manuel. "And hey, we are in Montevideo City, under a dictatorship, and those things do happen."

Manuel, his soccer and photography partner, had gone to take a course in Spain and had brought him a book on photographic techniques. The two shared a passion for photography and every so often they went on photo-trips through the city of Montevideo, armed with their cameras—Canon and Asahi Pentax—taking pictures of streets, people, and gardens. They had taken many photos while training together.

Alberto, from the University of Economics, was also there.

"We must catch up, Daniel," Manuel said, encouraging him. "We need to go out as before, to photograph people, landscapes, and parties."

"Yes, yes," Daniel answered "I added two new lenses to my Asahi-Pentax camera. I will be ready after next week."

Pablo and Carlos, agronomy students, were also there, sipping coffee. Ernesto and Pepe listened to them while drinking beer and nibbling on pizza. They were all intrigued by Daniel's obsession with Tamara and wanted to cheer him up and criticize him at the same time.

"Three pizzas!" shouted a waiter. "Table two."

"Coming up!" said the cashier.

Another waiter passed by with two cups of coffee and a tray of ham and cheese croissants. The place was busy.

It was 1974, and things had gotten worse. The military dictatorship was imprisoning any suspicious citizens. They didn't just catch known communists or members of the Tupamaros Revolutionary Army. They were catching anybody they wanted and even torturing people for no reason. The streets bustled with soldiers and jeeps.

"Yup and it seems that there are more dead young guys like that one," Daniel added. "However, they can't be investigated. Even if it happens in military barracks, as seems to be the modus operandi."

"It's the dictatorship," added Ernesto. "They are like this and there is nothing that can be done about it. Hey, get me another coffee."

"He's right," said Carlos between sips of his coffee. "They catch them, they torture them, make them sing, and then kill them; just like that. They kill them!"

They knew it. Those deaths were occurring, and they couldn't be investigated. There was nothing the police could do since they could not confront the army. It was a military dictatorship; the generals held the power and that was it. Neither the army nor any military barracks were going to allow the police or detectives to stick their noses in their affairs.

Uruguay had not always been like this. It used to be a very rich country after World War II and was even called, *the Switzerland of America*. However, the politicians sank the economy. Corrupted, careless, and incompetent, the presidents of the National Council, the Blancos, and the Colorados Batllistas, mismanaged the economy while it was slowly sinking.

"Yes, for sure. Both Blancos and Colorados wrecked the economy."

"Ha!" said Pablo. "And the supposedly *educated* middle class kept voting for them."

"Shame on all those politicians," said Ernesto. "For what they did to their own country between 1953 until 1968. They bankrupted Uruguay almost as if they did it on purpose. Gee... to their own people. How could they let a country as rich as ours tank like this?"

"Oh yeah? Blame the Uruguayan people itself who kept voting for them and didn't care. Those politicians did it with the complicity of the middle and upper classes."

They kept talking about this. Where was that great Uruguayan culture? The people of Uruguay prided themselves on their great educations. How could it be that they continued voting for them?

The collapse of the factories resulted in a permanent decline in income. Still, the politicians didn't care. The various social sectors, workers, public employees, farmers, and business trade unions fought for better salaries amid an inflation that nothing seemed to stop. All of this was right in front of the politicians' eyes, yet they didn't care. Unemployment and hunger grew, and an economic failure of this magnitude detonated an inevitable social crisis with street parades and protests. Human rights went to hell as the repression of a blind government grew.

"Yes, Alberto, that's the way it was."

Daniel has read about it.

"Those incompetent politicians," stated Ernesto. "Both Colorados and Blancos totally disregarded the outcry and miserable life of workers and poor Uruguayan people. They were deaf to the cries of the unemployed and the hunger of farmers. They didn't care about their own people, and this fomented violent conflicts."

"Yeah! That's why the Tupamaros revolt came to exist."

"We all know it," remarked Alberto.

The Tupamaros were all intellectuals and thinkers, who couldn't face that misery anymore, who couldn't stand still while the people were starving and suffering, while the corrupted government didn't care. They organized themselves as a fighting group, the Tupamaros National Liberation Movement.

"Yes. That's how it all started."

"No. No. No. It all started *way* before them. The Tupamaros didn't cause the socioeconomic mess of this country. They were a response. Just a knee-jerk reaction to all that."

"Yes. I know, I know it wasn't just like that," Pepe concurred. "However, I could never agree with them. They chose violence."

"Pepe, there was nothing else to choose *from*," replied Daniel "Nobody was listening."

"Violence, Daniel, don't you see?"

That was how it happened. The collapse—misery, lower wages, unemployment, and hunger—was the root of a growing national tension. The Tupamaros National Liberation Movement was a group of students, intellectuals, professors, and highly intelligent professionals who reacted against all that and fought for a better Uruguay. They stood up against injustice, and attracted trade union members, students of all kinds, and people of middle class and poor socioeconomic status. However, the mind of Uruguay was divided. Many stated that the Tupamaros were right, and that they were a product of the huge injustices and the terrible economic inequality. However, other members of the society denied that and were blaming it all on the Tupamaros.

"Hey, I know this quite well," said Alberto scalding his tongue sipping a fresh cup of coffee. "The Tupamaros would never have emerged unless it had been because of the economic disaster. *Because* of it. All caused by traditional parties. It was *all* the politicians' fault, both Blancos and Colorados."

"Yes, I agree."

They kept silent for a moment. They knew it. The fight had been terrible. The confrontation between the Tupamaros, the police, and the army had been and remained fierce. The Tupamaros managed to steal a lot of money, guns, and explosives, then they attacked police stations, the media, and even kidnapped the British ambassador. They carried out some assassinations and even killed an American agent. The response of the military dictatorship had been horrendous, and activists, trade union leaders, university professors, students, and anyone who might have said anything against the dictators were being abducted, tortured, and made to disappear. The people of Uruguay grew scared.

"The shootings have been horrible and—"

"They did what they had to do."

"Well, they didn't have to emerge so violently," replied Pepe. "They should have done it democratically. They could have created a political party and allowed people to vote."

"They couldn't. Politicians had it all set to keep power, and the careless middle class supported them."

"I don't think so."

"Yes, I *do* think so," added Pablo. "I agree. Now they blame the Tupamaros Revolutionary Group, but things weren't like that. The great Uruguayan people are unaware and blind that the real cause was fifteen years of corrupt government that plunged the country and pushed it into bankruptcy and disorder. It was not the Tupamaros who sank our economy."

"Yes, that's true. Careless and incompetent politicians destroyed our economy. Then when poverty became overwhelming, the only people who got up and fought against it were the Tupamaros."

"You are right, of course, but this created an anti-Tupamaros repression which gave the military a chance to grab the power, give a coup d'état, lead us to these hard times, and to this very volatile social situation."

"Horrible."

It was well-known. It was because of the politicians that the army and the Joint Forces took power. Because of them, Uruguay was going through extremely hard times.

They kept silent for a while, absorbed, thinking about all the things they just talked about and about the dead man that Daniel had described. A waiter passed by shouting his order for steak with fries. The bar was upscale and lots of patrons enjoyed the food and ambiance. Lots of noise. Napkins on the floor. Carlos and Ernesto got a beer each and lit a cigarette while they looked out the window watching cars go by.

Changing the subject, Daniel told them about his experiences in the emergency room of the Hospital de Clinicas, the things he learned and how much he liked it. He lit a cigarette and continued telling them about his position in the Anatomy Department, his students, the corpses, and his anatomical dissections.

"Ah, but you're a professor."

"Nerd!"

"Shut up."

"Corpses? That's horrible."

"That sucks Daniel!" said Pablo. "And... and you open them up? Horrible. You realize that suddenly your life has been filled with death, and blood, and... and..."

"Oh, oh, Daniel," said Carlos. "You're walking in a path with lots of death and little love, as your neighbor says."

"Are you referring to that girl?" asked Pepe, entering the main theme. "What's her name? Eh...Tamara, yes? That love affair you had, is it because of her?

"Oh, yes, the Tamara affair, yes, but don't get on the subject," Pepe warned Carlos. "Don't poke his wound."

There was a bit of silence. Daniel looked down the street. He didn't want to be asked. Ever since Tamara had left him, he had been left with a hole in his chest. He loved her.

"Mmm.... perhaps we should talk about her, Daniel," added Pepe. "That woman was not good. You know it! We were worried about you.

"Luckily, you finally managed to leave her."

"No. She left him.

"Oh, shut up."

"You've got to get out of that drama, Daniel," Carlos criticized him.

"Well... how is she? I mean, how does she look?"

"Don't you know, Pepe?" replied Pablo "Don't you know what kind of woman she was?

"A danger! A danger for this dummy."

"Yes. A dangerous woman. Tell him, tell him."

"Hey, she is beautiful. Too big for you, Danny boy, but she is gorgeous."

"Do you want to know, Pepe? That Tamara, she was that big, brown-haired woman you saw him with downtown. Remember?"

"Oh, mommy dear, but she was bigger than you, little Danny boy, and she was... hmm... she was..."

"Yes, said Pablo. "Um *robust*, eh? Tall. Big. Breasts like... like a—"

"Hey, shut up!"

"Sinner!"

"Who wouldn't miss those boobies!"

Daniel didn't want to get into the topic. Several times Pablo and Carlos had warned him to leave her. "That woman is a problem for you," Carlos had told him. "You are playing with a time bomb," Pablo warned him repeatedly. "You told us yourself that she was half Tupamara and that she helps them. Are you crazy? Your hot head is endangering yourself and your family."

"What were you doing with such a big woman?" asked Pepe.

"Loving her," answered Daniel "That's what I was doing." He looked off down the street. "Loving her."

"Uuuuuhh...here is the romantic lover. Fool."

"Pig!"

"But... what a psychological hook you had with her, Daniel," asked Pablo "That was a bad relationship, silly."

"So I've heard," said Daniel, still looking down the street at a flock of pigeons waddling around looking for crumbs.

"Let it go, Pablo. It was his first love. Nothing hurts like that first one."

"Hmm... you were like a baby attached to a tit, man," Pablo added, with a little snarl. "And a dangerous tit, and you know it well."

"Pablo! Pablo! Shut up *now*."

"No. I won't. I won't shut up. The best thing that could have happened to you is that woman leaving you, Daniel! You had us worried sick about that dangerous relationship with that big woman of yours.

"Yeah, now, Pablo, leave him alone!"

They kept silent while cooling down. They took more sips of their drinks and talked about soccer, photography, the coup d'état, and the military dictatorship. They decided it was time to leave and continued their chat outside.

"Hey. Good luck with your Tamara."

"Yes, good luck with that beast, lover boy."

Daniel walked slowly toward his house on 21st of Septembre street, remembering that woman who until recently had been his. Tamara. What a woman. How much he adored her. He smelled his hands. It seemed to him that the smell of Tamara's skin was still there. He imagined her in the cafe, he imagined her in bed, loving and arguing. What a turbulent relationship. What a difficult woman. Losing her squeezed his heart like a vice.

He entered his house full of melancholy, greeted his mother and his neighbor Marisa and went to his room to study. Hours later he said good night and went to sleep. He saw Tamara dressed, he saw her in the shower, he saw her in her green dress, he saw her in the hotel they frequented. And he saw her by his side. "Tamara."

That night he had visions just before he fell asleep, but he didn't worry; they would appear from time to time. This time he thought there were visions of her, but no, it was like of a man. *A man? Who is he?*

Chapter 3

The next day, he went for a walk, then went to a coffee shop.

The images of Tamara came back to him.

What am I going to do now?

The waiter brought him coffee and a slice of pizza, told him something and left. Daniel began to think, he had to collect his thoughts. Ever since Tamara had left, he felt an emptiness in his soul.

"Give time to time," Carlos had said. "Don't buy into the lie. Love is bad, Daniel, we talked about it before."

"Yes, and your obsession with Tamara is worse," Pablo had told him. "An evil obsession."

He tried to leave those thoughts and focus on what he saw the day before: that basement.

He couldn't focus. It was one of those days when the memories of Tamara flooded his brain like a tsunami.

Yes, he thought, *it was an obsession.* An obsession that had torn him apart and now was pushing him. He began to remember. *Tamara.*

It had all started the year before, in his first year of medical school. He met a lot of new people and had made a lot of friends. There, when he had only just begun his contact with the leftists, they argued about things they had read in certain books and articles that Daniel did not know. Leaving the world of high school and entering medical school was a culture shock, where a world of innovative ideas and knowledge revolutionized his existence.

He kept remembering. He had become fascinated with conversations, chatting with fascists, centrist-democrats, and socialists, and it was thus that he suddenly found himself discovering books of all kinds that detailed historical suffering, endless exploitation, the evolution of capitalism, the imperialism, and the concepts of the eternal class struggle. He discovered Marx, Engels, and even read the Little Red Book of Mao. There, in those corridors, in those smoky rooms, his social and political awakening began. There, at that time, without knowing it, his course began to change. Without realizing it, the skin of his adolescence and his twenties started fading, began to peel off and fall away because of the socio-cultural, liberal, and academic environment with which he was in touch, and a new mind, more restless, more curious—and more lustful—developed.

He discovered that political culture had a special advantage: girls on the left were more liberal, and they improved—from bed to bed—his education. It had been a year of cultural and carnal evolution, and Daniel was a fast learner. He discovered that removing a woman's bra was more interesting than the smuggling he did as a teenager. Feeling safe, having eaten from many dishes, slept on many beds, enjoyed many breasts, knowing there would be no woman to tie him up, he went to a political meeting at the main campus of the University, and it was there, discussing political issues, that he met Tamara Marcketowitch, a cute, strong, and big girl, with a freckled Polish face, the daughter of wealthy local merchants. He knew she wasn't for him, because she was very big and tall, but he stared at her because there was something interesting about her, although he didn't know what. He listened to her talking with several of her friends and realized that she was intelligent, very intellectual, and communist, very communist, and very pro-Tupamaros. Moreover, he realized he was looking at her face when she was talking, instead of at her breasts, which was very unusual. "What an interesting woman." A challenge. He got into the conversation, and they chatted for a while.

She's not for me, Daniel thought, *that is clear, but she's interesting and... fleshy.* He had noticed the shaking of her chest when she raised her arm, and he became interested.

When he saw Tamara go out to the patio to smoke, he followed her, spoke to her for a while, invited her for a coffee the next day, and she agreed. *Ha! she fell into my net,* he told himself.

He knew she was to be taken to bed a few times and that's all. Just a few-and-through type trysts. *Some good carnal enjoyment and that's it.*

They met at the Sorocabana Cafe. Daniel was wondering why he asked that big girl out. *Geee...she's too big for me, why did I even bother?* Then she showed up wearing a black tight shirt, loose brassiere, and thick-framed glasses, three factors that turned Daniel into a cannibal. To make matters worse, she gave Daniel a kiss upon arrival, a kiss which poisoned him. They talked about something, but Daniel already wanted to roll out of there. He needed a corner so he could sink his fangs into her. Leaving the Sorocabana, they took Cuareim

Street towards Soriano, until they reached Paraguay Street, in the area where the street became darker. Daniel had bad intentions, and when he got there, he made her get off the sidewalk, so she was a bit lower, and in a fraction of a second, he knew how to catch her off guard and kiss her repeatedly. He squeezed his hand under her bra and thought it would be some action to control her and take her to the love-motel that was nearby and that he knew well. But he couldn't do it this time. A hot magnetism invaded his body and Daniel was left without plans and without defenses. There, on that same street where several of his victims had fallen, he couldn't do anything. A feeling of something new grew on him. A spiritual attraction. A connection. He then took her home by taxi and didn't even touch her.

He returned home, dumbfounded.

Two days later she called him to come to her house to have tea. "Just a tea. And let's talk."

Daniel showed up a bit uneasy, a bit concerned, and a bit with dubious intentions: he didn't know whether to attack, or not. Tamara was lovely, her freckled Polish face, her thick lips, the lower of which she bit when pondering something, combined with dark green eyes all gave her a mysterious air. Hesitating and not knowing if the stars would help him that time, he started to talk.

They enjoyed the tea and the dialogue until they got too close to each other. He looked at her for a few seconds more, enjoying the presence of that enchanting woman, and kissed her. Something very spiritual flooded him in that moment. He waited, then kissed her again several times and decided to advance. It was a delight to kiss her and feel her in his arms. He released the bra and then undressed her slowly while caressing her body. Her skin was warm and soft, with a kind of magnetism. They made progress slowly, hugging and cuddling with affection.

That night he felt for the first time something that was not the satisfaction of a conquest or the sexual glory of triumph, but a gratitude for something new that she had given him and that he still did not understand and that he later discovered it was called... *love.*

Daniel couldn't explain it. It was a new feeling, a rejoicing of two minds that met, souls that communicated. He spent the next day thinking about her. There was something very charming and different about that woman that was not erased from his mind. He felt something that went far beyond the sexual encounter. Yes, her breasts were wonderful, but there was something behind them, there was a heart, there was warmth and feeling and... and... *That never happened to me.*

They started seeing each other two or three times a week. She used to find him in her Citroen and on purpose she put on the black shirt. "You like it, huh?" They did not waste time with coffee or toast, but visited different motels in the city, where they hastily undressed and ate each other as if with delayed hunger. However, after those initial feverish encounters, they became more and more companions. They went to the movies, went for walks, and promenaded through the city. They even went to a dark tango bar in Old Town, where they danced to typical music until after midnight.

However, as he got to know her and loved her increasingly, Daniel realized that she was not for him and began to think that surely, she also realized that he was like a baby to her, younger than her, shorter, and less mature. She was inches taller than him and three or four years older. She was Christian and somehow involved with the Tupamaros, which made the relationship a bit dangerous. She was too much of a woman for him, and he knew it. The relationship got uncomfortable, and Daniel decided to cut it off. He spoke to her and explained it all, and she agreed. She cried, but she agreed. There, in the café on Avenida Brazil, they kissed, and they parted.

Daniel had been left with a bit of melancholy about the separation, which soon became sadness. So three weeks later he invited her to the cafe at 18 de Julio and Artigas Boulevard to chat in front of the city obelisk. Half an hour later, he was with her at the Montjui love-motel where they made love with a hunger that took a while to satisfy. Drenched and tired, they lay staring at each other until they fell asleep. The next noon they went to another motel, and at night to another. They were trying to fill the three weeks of emptiness they had.

Passion devoured them. They couldn't stop caressing each other. On occasions, in the love-motels, he would ask her to get dressed just so he could undress her again. "You are a pig." "I know."

Daniel was in love. Tamara was his first great love. They went out for many months, walking, going to the University Cinema, and the Cinema Club, sharing, going to the street market or to the park. They loved to walk through Sarandi Street in Old Town, and through 18 de Julio Avenue. She liked to love him, and he loved to love her. However, he was worrying again about how the relationship was turning into something else, something dangerous. He knew she collaborated with various people from the Tupamaros and had friends considered dangerous for the times they were living. Daniel had to face the reality that he was running a certain risk with her, especially considering that she was a communist, very Christian, very tall, and active with the Tupamaros operatives. She was bigger than him, too. *Geee...* Everything made her a forbidden woman for him.

They talked about trying to prepare themselves. The inevitable moment came, and as she was stronger, it was she who finally made the decision. She spoke with Daniel firmly, and right there, this time with great sorrow, the thing was over. The two shed a tear but stayed tough. "It is better this way," Daniel told her, disconsolate, and she answered him, "Yes, Daniel, it *is* better this way," and got into her Citroen and left. Daniel had remained standing there on the sidewalk, alone and hurt, watching her go away.

He didn't know that he would never see her again.

Chapter 4

As the days passed, Daniel tried to cram his pain aside. He had met other girls, but Tamara had been his first great love. He had tried to analyze his feelings for her but could not explain them. It was like a powerful magnetic force that attracted him to that woman. *Your forbidden woman, Daniel.* A woman linked to danger from whom he could not separate. That same force now created an enormous void from which it was difficult for him to recover.

Daniel returned to his routine of courses and classes. He channeled his anguish into curiosity and thirst for learning, which made him devour books. He went to libraries and bookstores and spent his weekends studying.

Having joined the Department of Anatomy as an assistant professor, he had improved his life with cadavers and dissections, and he convinced himself that the sadness would one day go away. "Tamara."

He taught anatomy in room B, on the second floor of the School of Medicine of the University of Uruguay. This was a large, old room, with only two cold tables, and a corpse treated with formaldehyde on each one. He had two groups of about twenty students, each at the dissecting table, and he would teach while showing the different anatomy sections.

He dedicated himself to teaching, learning, and getting more books, so his study hours increased. His social life dwindled and his outings with friends diminished, but his steps forward to knowledge and his foray into teaching made up for it. At the same time, when he could, he visited other libraries and expanded culturally by reading medicine and anatomy but also all kinds of books, such as politics, sociology, and even science fiction. His life had started to change.

His students were all kinds, rich, poor, middle class, from the city, and from the country. There were girls and boys, and their friendship was growing over the weeks. They brought food, pizza, and croissants to eat while they dissected. On the days when they opened the abdomen and then the intestine, Daniel told them not to bring food and to bring more cigarettes, because that day they had to remove fecal matter and it was a bit unpleasant.

When Daniel recounted his activities at dinner, his mother could only reproach him.

"Your world is corpses, Daniel," his mother would say. "It's... it's horrible what you do."

"Ay Daniel, Daniel, your life is a path of many deaths and little love," his neighbor Marisa said, laughing.

Estela, the neighbor from across the street, would ask him, "And how were the dead today?" and laugh.

Usually, he was in class from eight in the morning until twelve, at the Hospital de Clínicas Medical Center. And from there he would eat something in a hurry and then go to anatomy and give his class from two to five. After class, he stayed chatting with some students or with the other dissectors, smoking a cigarette or having a coffee. Sometimes they drank coffee or ate a piece of cake while dissecting a corpse.

"Ah, but how scary, Daniel," Estela would say when he described his activities. "How can you eat next to a dead body? But by God... this is heresy."

"Oh, I can't even hear that," said the Spaniard lady next door. "It is a... it is a profanity. You are walking with the dead."

"Oh, but what kind of child have I raised?" his mother complained. "All those corpses and... and... not a girlfriend. What kind of a son am I raising?

However not all the dead were the same. There were the dead and there were the other dead. The corpses that were dissected in anatomy were for Daniel like pieces of dolls in formaldehyde, a strong type of alcoholic compound designed to preserve the corpses without rotting. It had a very pungent smell and would turn human flesh a brownish color. A body prepared in this way could last for weeks in the open air. Every student, after the initial impression, would just accept those bodies as mannequins, vestiges of what had been a human being, and would build a mental wall against any feeling about their lack of life. However, the corpses in the morgue were fresh reflecting only the absence of life; they smelled bad and caused, even to anatomists, a displeasure. That was why almost none of the professors from the anatomy department came down to the morgue. They felt the anatomy rooms were teaching rooms, but that the morgue was the death room. For this reason, almost none of them used the spiral staircase at the back of the department, which connected the anatomy area with the morgue that was two floors below. That staircase was for them an unpleasant image and a connection that they preferred to ignore. It was an old staircase, with worn white marble steps, which would go down for miles into the depths of the earth where it was connected through an infernal door to the morgue, also known as the Forensic Institute. It was a bit distressing to pass near the place where the stairs led into the bottomless world of hell. As a warning to mortals, an old sign that said "Morgue" was nailed to the beginning, and an arrow pointing down announced that whoever would go down there might not return. To make matters worse, a smell that mixed rottenness and disinfectant hung in the air at the top of the stairs. That smell was a warning to those in doubt and showed that these were, literally and figuratively, the stairs of death. Daniel knew what the sign and the smell foreshadowed. "No one who descends the world of the dead can pretend his life would be the same."

Daniel passed through the corridor looking at that staircase that undoubtedly led to hell itself and repeated Dante's words to himself that whoever went down there would lose all hope. Its dirty and aged steps, its metal railing painted ancient green, invited lost souls to submit into the depths of morbidity and horror. On one occasion he had stood at the edge of the staircase smelling that strange smell that came up from there, imagining corpses and victims still moving and begging to return to life while being opened and chopped and sawed during autopsies. He had never dared to go down. Goose bumps came to him, and his mind was invaded with fear when he passed near there. Yet he also had a growing curiosity toward that unimaginable horror, a morbid attraction toward the terrible vision of death. He was apprehensive, but at the same time it had an attraction that he couldn't explain. Something was calling him from down there. He did not know if what he felt was a call or nothing more than that attractiveness that men felt in front of the weapon with which they were going to kill themselves. When he would feel like that, he would go to the patio to smoke and think but could not draw any other conclusion: death was calling him.

As he was dissecting a knee, one day, he noticed the joint was way too dry to show the ligaments, tendons, and cartilage. He asked Juan, who was an assistant to the chairperson and a technician in the forensic department, if he could bring him a nice knee, fresh, and cut to show the students the menisci and ligaments during class. Daniel had befriended Juan, whom he frequently treated with cigarettes and chocolates.

"Sure Daniel, my friend!" he answered. "No problem." He put a chocolate drop in his mouth and chewed and swallowed. "Yes. Go down to the morgue around three o'clock to get it, I'll prepare it for you."

"Eh... but I... Juan, I just—"

"Yes, yes, no problem, come! I'll wait for you. You go down the white staircase and take the corridor to the left after the staircase. Don't take the corridor to the right because... uh... it doesn't matter. Turn left and continue down the corridor."

Daniel froze, knowing he couldn't refuse the invitation. He knew at that moment that at three in the afternoon he would have an appointment with death. When he went to give the class, his nerves cut off his words, and he dedicated himself to observing the dissection of the students and smoking. He reproached himself for having asked for the piece, even thought of playing sick and escaping early, ducking down the street for a smoke and coffee at the street cafe. But he stayed. *How can anybody escape from death itself*? He knew within himself that the day and hour of the confrontation had arrived. He also felt that Juan was obeying certain hidden forces that had sent for him. *What is calling me*? *Who wants me to go down there*?" he thought. *For what*? He went straight to the patio to smoke another cigarette, but he couldn't think.

He went back to the dissection room. The students distracted him with greetings, questions, and pieces of cake.

It was two forty-five, and a heartbeat reminded him that death awaited him. He lit another cigarette. He tried to calm down, but his nerves tickled his stomach. *Why did I have to ask Juan for that knee*? he asked himself.

The minutes expired as his heart raced. He was smoking nervously. He told the boys that the emergency room had been terribly busy the night before and had left him without sleep. He moved away from the group of students and leaned back on one of the tables.

Two fifty-five...

Two fifty-six...

How scary.

His mouth went dry.

He looked at the clock, two fifty-seven. His skin got colder.

"Oh."

Two fifty-eight. His thighs got hard, his legs turned into wood, and they didn't want to go. The rest of him didn't want to go down that spiral staircase either. He looked around without seeing as his pulse pounded in his temple. He had seen fresh dead people before, on his rotation in the emergency service. They were bodies that until a little while ago had life and talked and thought and did things. In them, the absence of life and the presence of death were more obvious, cruder. And if they had been operated on or injured and their inner flesh showed, it was even worse. Those memories combined in his mind with the smells he had perceived, the blood and guts he had seen in surgery rooms; the mental jumble created anguish.

Then... the hour. The world came to a standstill. The sounds and voices disappeared.

The encounter with death had arrived.

Three o'clock.

He told the students that he would be back in a bit and slowly left the room, walking with a statue's legs. He went down to the first floor where the Gestapo was waiting for him to put him in the gas chamber, took the main corridor and approached the staircase. He didn't want to think.

He gathered courage and began to descend the spiral staircase of worn marble white as bone that led him to a gas shower where he would cease to exist. His legs weren't faithful, and he had to cling onto the railing. As he descended, the documentary images he had seen about World War II barrel-bombed his mind, and he could almost see the Jewish violinists playing their sad music as Nazi officers pointed their Luger pistols at him, forcing him to march. On the walls were images that moved and asked him not to continue going down. Twice he thought about stopping. Once downstairs, he stopped in front of the metal door as he caught a foul odor seeping through from under it. The malodorous screams of the dead warned him not to enter. He held the handle in a skeleton's hand, startled at the thought of entering. After a moment of hesitation, he opened the door of death itself and entered the morgue.

A nauseating smell fell on him, and Daniel knew it was the invisible spirit of the dead trying to drive him away. It was his last warning. Daniel stopped, frozen, his skin all prickly. He leaned against the wall and composed himself. He was in a narrow corridor that to the left led to another wide corridor that continued to the front. There was another corridor to the right, but Daniel knew he shouldn't take it. *If Juan, who knows me, said no, I'd better not go there.*

He concentrated and managed to eliminate his fear. As he turned into the corridor on the left, he could see a gurney where a dead man lay and seemed fresh, partially covered by a sheet and with a tag on his big toe that confirmed his death with a number. *The unlucky number,* he thought. There was the smell of decomposition and disinfectant mixed with the unmistakable stench of the non-living. There was another gurney beyond and then another, each with an unlucky one. To his right were two cold rooms that only the Devil himself knew what they contained. He continued walking slowly down the tiled corridor with dark green walls, passing the cold room and the laboratory on the left. Some laboratory workers greeted him without paying attention. He could not go back, nor did he have the courage to take another step, especially seeing that a few meters away the corridor opened into a larger room wherein stood five inclined marble tables, two of them with a coffin on top and one of them with an uncovered corpse

The initial shock was slowly fading away and a special attraction was pushing him forward. *Is it fate? Curiosity? What am I doing here?*" his every thought pleaded.

Three people, perhaps doctors, perhaps students, perhaps demons, were working busily, dismembering the inert body of what had been a woman. *She is not moving,* thought Daniel. *She's just holding her breath waiting for them to finish.* Dark old blood dripped from the woman to the floor. The guys raised their heads and greeted him with friendly gestures, a courteous welcome to the beyond. In his imagination, Daniel saw the woman turning her head, looking at him, and begging him to save her from these butchers. Nausea punched him in the stomach.

A dead man, partially covered with a blood-stained sheet, moved his head towards Daniel and muttered, *Please, tell them to let me go.*

A dirty dark-blooded hand from one of the doctors beckoned him. A voice said, "Hello!" They welcomed him into hell.

He answered the greeting without speaking, fearing that his voice would reveal the fear that was affecting him. He walked slowly, while the butchers bragged that they had found what they were looking for, put it on a tray and went to the laboratory, leaving him alone to face his fate.

"Ah Daniel... here you are," said Juan. "Come, come... ah... it's your first time here, ah... well. after what happened... poor guy... Did you meet him?

"Eh...? Who?"

"Ah, he wasn't a patient of yours, of course, I got confused with another assistant, mmm—Bermudez! yes. But... come and I'll show you."

One-eye Juan had only one eye. The other he had lost it was said, in a tango bar, for stealing a woman from a criminal who later waited for him outside and beat Juan nearly to death. He was taken to the emergency room, was admitted, and was lucky enough to leave three weeks later with his life, but without an eye, half of his right ear and three fingers. Slim, silver-haired, polite, Juan was a genuinely nice guy.

Next, and with the same gentleness and grace that a confectioner shows his delicacies, he showed him room by room and even opened the rooms where corpses were piled up just as he had seen in photos of the Second World War. He showed him the coffins and opened one of them so that Daniel could enjoy the moment a bit more. There was a man inside, pale and shrouded as with a layer of white icing. Horrible. Then he took him to the patio from where he went out to the street and explained that that was the official exit from the morgue, but that he could use it whenever he wanted, and even exit the medical school from there.

"Yes, you could go in and out of the medical school from that gate, as others do, as it is connected to the main headquarters via the marble staircase."

"I see. Yes." Daniel enjoyed his first breath of fresh air, the air of the living, since his first steps down the icy white marble.

"Smoking can be done without a problem, but you shouldn't speak out loud, let alone make jokes or sing when the relatives are waiting for the coffin in the yard," Juan said. "Trust me," he emphasized with eyes both privy and apologetic.

"Yes. Yes."

"Ah, and if there are relatives in the yard, especially if they are crying, do not go out with the tunic on, nor with gloves, because they are easily upset by the visions those garments foment. Be gentle."

Daniel lit a cigarette.

"Ah, also, yes, if there are relatives in the courtyard, he continued, "make sure that, when you leave, you greet them politely and say a few words of compassion. Remember that they are in a lot of pain and any good word will be well received." He drew from his cigarette and then cautioned with a two-fingered hand, "And do not hit on the widow or the daughters as Domínguez does, because that is not right."

"Domínguez?"

"Yeah. One of the detectives that comes this way. The chubby one, with an actor's face. You'll meet him."

"Is he from the police headquarters?"

"Yes."

Hmm... Domínguez.

Then One-eye Juan took him inside, and without much explanation grabbed the saw and the other instruments of the inquisition and put them between the feet of the unfortunate woman. The victim's abdomen remained open, and Daniel could see that the liver and pelvic viscera had been removed. Dried blood was dripping from the dead woman's nose and mouth, and her face was too pale. *This woman talked and ate until two or three days ago, she had—*

"Don't look at her too much, Daniel," Juan told him. "I can see it in your face."

"See—"

"You are philosophizing."

It was his first direct encounter with a fresh dead person in the morgue, and they were both in rigor mortis.

"A knee, a knee..." One-eye Juan brought out a tray and proceeded to slice open the thigh flesh with a butcher knife. He spread the muscles about four inches above the knee and then worked on the calf, slicing tendons and muscles like butchering an animal for a feast. He separated the quadriceps from its bone attachments, being careful to leave the fascia intact. Then separated and cut the hamstring muscles and left them hanging by their tendons. Blood and juices were dripping from both sides, so he had to stop and irrigate the area. "Ha, she's a bleeder," he said as he pulled and removed the artery. "But, but hey... see? This is beautiful." His knife sliced to the bone, increasingly delicate now, like preparing the cut to be served to a tribal king. Then he turned on the electric saw, cut the tibia and fibula about five centimeters below the knee joint and then the femur from above with great skill. Yellowish pasty marrow dripped from the edges, mixing with the dark blood. "Mmm... you're lucky." He then took the piece, drained it, washed it, and cleaned the dark wine-colored blood that was still dripping. "Just died yesterday evening. Fresh. All yours." He wrapped it in a plastic bag, cleaned it a bit more and said, "Mmm, good piece."

Daniel's heart did not beat anymore, and his lungs did not breathe during all that macabre moment when he was part of the partial dismemberment of a human being. Mesmerized and stiff, he could not react. He was going to ask the cause of her death but could not speak.

When Juan saw him, he started laughing. "You're green," he said, "breathe, Daniel, uh, breathe!"

Daniel didn't want to take the bag—his eye lasered onto a piece of gore that dangled from one of the severed tendons. That knee belonged to someone who was not already gone.

"Well, well," continued Juan. "Wait until I wash it a little more." He took the bag to the sink, took the piece out, washed it again, removed the gore, took a clean bag, put the joint inside, and gave it to Daniel with pride.

"Can I get you something else?" he asked like a drive-thru cashier. "An elbow? A hand?"

Daniel shook his head, and took the bag, thanked him, and left, scared stiff, while Juan laughed.

"Have good dreams tonight," One-eye Juan said.

Daniel fled from that place feeling disgusted and knowing that he had been an accomplice to a sacrilege. He scaled the white bones of the spiral staircase again like a thief, knowing that the eyes of the dead were looking at him and accusing him of having stolen something that should not cross to the world of the living. *I will pay for this*, he told himself while restless spirits clamored from the pit to return the piece. Shadows moved on the walls. Death itself tried to dig its claws into his back to stop him.

Haunted by ghosts, nauseated, he returned to the world of the living, walked through the corridor, gave the bag to the students, and told them he was coming back in a bit. He went back down to the professors' break room, took off his tunic, left it in the teachers' room, and left the school through the main entrance for a breath. He went outside to a nearby bar, sat outside, ordered a tonic water and a coffee, and smoked a cigarette.

"Are you OK?" asked the waiter. "You look sick."

"Yeah, yeah, I'm fine," he replied. "Just a bellyache."

He stayed there for half an hour, meditating, and calmed down. He tried to erase from his mind what would never be erased. He tried to look past what could not be unseen. Then he returned to the class, where they dissected the stolen knee and were able to see well the menisci and especially the structure of the ligaments and the cartilage. He explained the tendons and the joint dynamics and later placed the knee in the formaldehyde pool.

Later, when he took the bus to return home, the accusing eyes of those who were traveling pointed at him. Several of the passengers looked at him, knowing that he had been where he shouldn't have tread. He got off midway and walked home to burn off his adrenaline. He knew he had crossed a line.

That night Daniel had visions at midnight, images of people. He did not know if it was a product of being on the threshold of the dream, or his imagination, or whether it was something else, like some energy that he did not understand that was coming to him with a message. "They are the dead.... " he told himself, "But they want to tell me about something. What are they... visions?" It was like a nebula with shapes. As had happened before, he accepted those images without understanding why. He was still thinking about that when he fell asleep.

The next day he woke up knowing that he had crossed a threshold and that Juan had been the pretext for a greater inner force that wanted him to go down to the morgue. *But why?* he wondered without knowing. *Why?* He sat down and thought about it. Had he opened a gate he shouldn't have opened? He erased that thought, but he knew he had to get rid of his fear and those ideas. *I must get over this.*

That afternoon, when he left the dissection class, instead of going out through the main entrance of the school, he went down the infernal spiral staircase to the abyss of the dead, again, with the intention of going out of the morgue to the street. Disgust, dread, and the things he saw in his imagination haunted him. Souls and spirits were trying to make him go back. Three SS Nazis were at the door welcoming his return to the gas chamber. He had to focus on gathering his strength. He walked down the corridor to the left with tight buttocks and inadvertently looking back, feeling that he was being followed. He walked out of the morgue onto the street, sighing, "I can't go on like this," he told himself. One-eye Juan was outside smoking.

"Aaahh! Feel better now?"

"Mmm... yes," Daniel replied then paused. "No. Not yet."

"You're acquainting yourself with the morgue and this exit, eh? You're going to feel better now. You'll see."

Yes, he thought, *I'd better get used to it.*

"You'll get used to it. This is an important step you've taken."

"Why? Why...?"

"You'll see. You will discover it alone. Nobody forced you down here. You and only you did it for some reason."

"Reason? What reason?"

"I already told you. That is something you'll discover in time."

"I don't understand."

"Never mind," said Juan while looking at the sky. "The important thing is it's a good day to start. The weather is very nice."

"Yes," Daniel replied, looking at the sky as well, wondering what Juan was referring to.

A dark bird flew over the area and settled on the wire of one of the poles. Three more birds followed.

"They're crows," said Juan. "Those damned crows! Always around here, especially when Domínguez comes to the morgue. Gee, I hate them. Dr. Maggiolo says cries of the dead attract them. I think it's something that has to do with Domínguez and one day I'll tell you about it. They are ominous."

"Yes... crows," repeated Daniel. "I don't like crows." He stared at the birds chattering and sighed. *Damned crows*, he thought.

Daniel left. He took the bus and again felt that strange sensation that all the passengers realized he carried the smell and the mark of death, but in reality, no one looked at him or noticed him. He went for a walk around the city center, checked several stores in 18 de Julio Avenue, had a Fanta at the Lancaster Bar, looked at the people passing by, and wondered whether they would realize that he was coming from the center of human carnage, but no one paid attention to him.

Chapter 5

As his anatomy classes became more complicated, Daniel needed different anatomical pieces for teaching purposes. He had his own class and was responsible for his student's learning. Slowly, he noticed that his responsibility and dedication were rewarded and that he enjoyed his anatomy classes very much. He soon understood the didactic advantage of teaching certain parts, such as knee, elbow, ankle, and hand, using fresh pieces, so to provide better, more detailed knowledge to his students, he began to visit the morgue more frequently. He asked one of the technicians or one of the forensic doctors to cut the chosen piece, and that's how he began to interact with the professionals and doctors who swarmed there.

As his visits to the morgue, part of the Forensic Institute, became more frequent, his relationship with the people who worked there became more friendly. Guided by his eternal curiosity and astute knowledge of anatomy, he began to witness and sometimes even assist in autopsies with the doctors he knew, giving them a hand in their tasks. It didn't take long to find Inspector Pranchin there and then Officer Domínguez, the chubby detective with the actor's face who recognized him from when he had visited the police headquarters and greeted him with a handshake. "Oh, wow, but it's the Carmen kid himself."

"Hey, hi Carmen kid."

He didn't like to be called that way.

He also saw the unfriendly MacLagan on a couple of occasions, whom he had seen that bitter night in the hospital and who greeted him in a very formal way, with his harsh manners and gray face, looking angry. *He's going to punch me one day. I can tell.*

Sometimes the big man with the wide moustache that he had seen at the headquarters also came, a certain Martinez, with a dry and constipated face, who did not even look at him. There was something in those four that made them different than other detectives and police officers. Was it the relationship between them? Their looks? Was it their behavior? What was it with this group? In those times of harsh dictatorship, so full of hated police officers and injustices, when the street and its people hated the uniformed, those four created another kind of feeling. *What could it be?* he thought. They seem harsh, but they work in a manner that doesn't emanate aggressiveness. *Who are they?*

Other inspectors, police officers, and agents came frequently to the morgue as part of the forensic and police investigation of various deaths. Daniel still did not understand what different divisions and departments each of them belonged to or what functions they fulfilled in the various stages of the crime investigation, nor did he understand what difference there was between detective, inspector, and commissar. *But who cares?*

Daniel also didn't understand the difference between the morgue and the forensic institute, or why there were representatives of the judiciary department and even attorneys and legal assistants. *What are they doing here?*

Daniel went about his business, watched, chatted, helped, got his usual pound of flesh, and left. He had learned to be careful about which autopsy he was entangled with, since he did not want to be in one in which the body was dead for several days because he could not tolerate the putrid smell of rotting flesh. He learned that if the abdominal wall had a large green spot, or if the abdomen was swollen, that match was not his and he would strategically withdraw and disappear. He also discovered that certain crime victims had fresher bodies because an autopsy was necessary as part of the investigation and had to be done promptly. It was interesting to see the details of how one or more bullets or stab wounds had damaged the organs, resulting in the death of the victim. Soon, he began to check out books on forensic medicine and autopsy techniques from the library, which he read as a hobby while learning important details of forensic work.

His presence in the morgue became a common event, and since he knew a lot about photography, several technicians and doctors asked for his assistance in taking special and detailed photos of several of the pieces and even in preparing slides for their classes or pictures for the judges.

Many of the photos were taken by the technical police officers, who brought their own camera, usually a Canon. If there was a lot of work, Inspector Pranchin would sometimes take the camera and take photos too, although his photos were not that good. To make matters worse, one day the Canon didn't work well, Pranchin struggled with it and broke it. After the shouting and blaming, they sent a police officer with Juan to get Daniel from wherever he was teaching. They went upstairs, took the corridor, and found him.

"Daniel, we need you," yelled Juan, interrupting the class to the astonishment of the students

Daniel froze in his surprise. "Gee, what did I do?"

"They got you," said one of his students. "This is it for you."

"They're going to silence that big mouth of yours once and for all," said another student.

"Ha!" said another of the students. "They're going to make you swallow your liberal ideas."

There was a commotion among the students.

"Hey, hey, shut up all of you!" demanded Juan. "We need his photographic skills. Quiet all of you! Now, Daniel, come down."

He went down, apprehensive, and took care of the photographs that were needed at that time. They got him another Canon and told him to use it. "No," he said with the air of a frustrated artist. "Not like this." He changed the lens and the film and applied his technique. Once developed, his photos were well received and, thanks to his technique, his relationship with officers and personnel from the Police Headquarters improved, and Daniel, without knowing it, was advancing further into the red circle.

One day, two of the forensic doctors, after chatting with the police officers, asked him to bring his Asahi Pentax the next day. "We'll give you a locker and only you will have the key." Thus, Daniel brought his photographic bag with the Pentax, several lenses, a short tripod, and special filters, and took photos of several crime cases with high sensitivity film to absorb the details. He prepared photos and slides for professors and technicians, but seeing him there, several detectives and notaries asked him to take photos here and there of bullets, stab wounds, suicide cases, autopsies, and human remains, which they then used for their reports. The photos were always perfect; he did a good job on them. This assistance from his part opened several doors and allowed him to meet many people. He was helping without the intention of getting anything in return, but he felt within himself that this was, at that moment, part of the natural path he was taking.

One thing led to another, until on one occasion, they asked him to take the photos to the police headquarters. Daniel did not want to do it. He hated the idea of entering again in the cave *of those torturing sons of bitches* and tried to make excuses, but he had no choice but to do so because it was a favor. He had been asked by Dr. Maggiolo, who was a friend of his uncle. Daniel put the photos in an envelope, took the bus and went to the police headquarters on

San Jose Street. *I shouldn't have come.* Feeling shaky before reaching the door, he explained to the uniformed gorilla at the entrance where he was going and was told to go up to the criminology division. He went up, while an aroma of guns, cigarette smoke, old paper, and coffee surrounded him. He entered the hall, gave the envelope to a certain Gomez, and left without saying hello or goodbye. He left the headquarters with the disgust of having been in a sewer. *This is one of the nests of the animals who oppress and kill our people.*

However, that feeling did not last long, as he later understood that in that headquarters were policemen, detectives, inspectors, and deputies in charge of all kinds of crimes and that the really powerful oppressors were the Armed Forces and the ones called Joint Forces, the bloody arm of the dictatorship, whose headquarters were somewhere else. Besides, curiosity and fascination of being in a forbidden and dangerous place were changing his brain cells. Therefore, and on several occasions, he continued to take pictures and reports to the police headquarters, talked to several agents and detectives and slowly got used to dealing with them. His disgust for the place dwindled. Something about it was interesting, and he started to be interested. *Why would I like it? What is it? Where am I going with this?*

Thus, he began to interact with agents, officers, notaries, and legal and judicial assistants for one reason or another. Dry and shy at first, he realized that the policemen were not biting him and that the plainclothes officers did not smell any of his left-wing ideas nor were they going to strangle him in the corridors. Consequently, he softened up, and even from time to time, if the mood favored, he managed to smile. He even began to return a greeting or two. On occasions, officials and representatives of the Judiciary took him to the notary to certify the photos or to speak with the judge. There, nervous and scared, afraid that his liberal ideas would be detected, he had to explain anatomical and pathological details to officers of the technical police and representatives of some special services, or to the judge who did not understand who Daniel was or what were his functions.

What am I doing here? he asked himself. *Where am I going with this?*

Chapter 6

In the morgue, he had met Doctors Maggiolo and Echeverry, directors of the morgue and the Forensic Institute, who performed teaching autopsies to instruct students, inspectors, doctors, and technicians. They would gather around the corpse for the academic feast and listen to them with devotion. The session sometimes ended with a couple of photos taken by Daniel and chunks of flesh or organs that other professors would take with joy. Dismembering a fresh corpse was a welcome opportunity for many.

There were some things, however, that left Daniel worried. Night things. On several occasions, as it happened before, after having witnessed an autopsy of a crime, some hazy images, very vague, appeared to him at night, late, when he had gone to bed. As it occurred before, he just didn't pay much attention, but now some of those images were sharper, although they were barely visible. Again, Daniel didn't know whether they were the gloom of a dream, or if it was his imagination, or if they had been created by something, but the idea came to him that they could be related to the dead people he had seen that day. *Is it possible*? he wondered.

The idea of having in his room a portal to... *a portal to what? another dimension...?* seemed ridiculous. No. For sure they were part of his susceptible imagination. *Yeah, that's what it is*. However, the idea that they were something sent by someone or as a call to something, some mission, purpose, or quest, did not disturb him because he would soon fall asleep. He had no clear explanation to that and preferred to think that they were the product of fatigue. *What else would they be*? He didn't have an answer. He didn't want to talk about it with anyone.

He went on with his studies while days passed by, until he was faced with a series of questions.

"Why are you involved with such disgusting things, Daniel?" his mother and his neighbor Marisa asked him, disturbed, when he told them the things he was getting involved with.

"Where do you want to go with all that?"

"You are going in the path of your life marching with the dead and the executioners at the same time. Do you realize that?"

"What are you doing?" asked his mother.

"Anatomy, corpses, the morgue, and now the police headquarters, Daniel," Manuel said. "Daniel, but Daniel, what's wrong with you? What is it that calls you to go that way?"

"Holy Mary Manzanita, Danny boy," complained the Spaniard woman next door. "Your path is not right; you are walking with death but without love."

When he heard those comments, Daniel had doubts regarding the path he was taking. *Am I following one of the many paths of medicine*?" he wondered. *Or have I strayed from my path*? *Where am I going with all this*?

As days went by and while he was still thinking about those issues, one day Dr. Maggiolo and Dr. Etcheverry, directors of the morgue and the Forensic Institute, saw him withdrawn and thoughtful and took him to their office.

"Well, Daniel, I see you managed to get in this place," said Etcheverry. "No, no, don't explain it to us. We've seen others. You're not the first to come here because the dead called."

"I don't... I just—"

"Wait, wait, Daniel, listen," Maggiolo said. "We're not criticizing you. We also heard that call, many years ago.

"It's something that cannot be explained."

"It's the call of the dead."

"What? but I just—"

"Hey, wait, listen, the question you must ask yourself is if this is a temporary adventure, as it has been for others, or is this a path that you're taking without knowing exactly which way to go."

"Hmm... I know that—"

"Look, Daniel," Dr. Etcheverry spoke to him. "Every year we choose one of the students here to collaborate and learn at the police headquarters. It's an auxiliary position, without pay and without fixed hours. It's to give the opportunity to those who are interested in advancing in what may interest them."

"Oh me... I-I am—"

"No, no, don't answer us now."

"Maybe you don't have the answer you're looking for either."

"Explore the field and your environment and discover the roads.

"Your roads."

"Discover your way, your path."

"Here, a hand will always be given to you if you need it."

"Yes, thanks," said Daniel, calmer, the calm that comes from knowing someone else understands. "Thank you."

"And one question," interrupted Maggiolo. "Do you know about the DEMEM?"

"The what?"

"The DEMEM."

"No. No idea. What is it?"

"It's a special office in the Department of Justice. It is in charge... eh... well, you'll find out. Keep your ears and your eyes open and you'll see."

"But I don't go to the Department of Justice. I just never—"

"Not yet. Not yet."

"What do you mean, Dr. Maggiolo?"

"We live in very difficult times. Somehow you stuck your nose in the police headquarters, and we keep that in mind."

"In mind for what."

"Nothing," answered Etcheverry. "Nothing. We'll talk later. Go, now."

"We all must take care of ourselves," said Maggiolo.

"And we'll take care of you."

"Good luck, Daniel."

Daniel waited a while. One of the technicians came with some photographs of the man stabbed the previous day, then the notary's assistant came to sign the photos and authenticate them. They put them in an envelope and gave them to Daniel, who took the bus and went to the police headquarters. He greeted the gorilla on duty at the entrance of the police headquarters and went to the third floor. The three agents he knew were not there, so he knocked on the door of Officer Martinez, the head guy with a mustache and a constipated face and gave him the photos. He was about to leave when Martinez stroked his thick mustache and told him to turn around and sit down.

"I want you to tell me something, Daniel. What are you coming here for? Look at me, for chrissakes. What brings you here?"

"I came to bring the photos."

"An agent could have brought them or one of the boys," Martinez said with a very serious but almost sympathetic face "Why you? Why did *you* bring them? Do you want something from this place? This is the police station, man, what do you want?"

"I... I... no, they gave me the photos and they told me to bring them here. They asked me."

"We see you interacting with other officers and we—"

"Well, they asked me to take the pictures and give statements. What could I—"

"There is something else on your mind. What is it?"

Martinez was staring at him. Daniel was looking at the floor, not knowing what to say. The room was quiet, but bings of the elevator and clacks of typewriters could be heard from the other side of the corridor. Someone in the distance asked for a coffee. The minutes passed. Daniel looked up, examined the old folders that littered the desk and looked at Martinez, who was huge and armed. *If he gets mad, he shoots me on the spot,* he thought.

"What are you looking for here?" asked the mustached officer. "You're searching for something, aren't you?"

"No. This was not my decision. They told me, as they did before, to bring the pictures. I couldn't say no."

Martinez didn't say a word.

"What else?"

"I don't know," said Daniel. "I don't know what else to tell you."

He had no other answer. Worried, he closed the door, went through the hallway, then downstairs and to the street. He nodded at the gorilla and went for a walk.

He walked for a while, without paying attention to the people passing by. Half a block later he thought that some good guava pastries would help him think. There was always a reason to eat those baked goods. He went into a bakery and asked for a guava filled Danish and a piece of cake.

"Hi, is it guava?"

"Well senior, it has quince and guava both."

"Yes, I'll take them."

While walking and eating, one of the answers came to him: Explore the field in front of you, study the roads. *That's what I'm going to do*, he said to himself. *I'm going to explore the path in front of me.*

Suddenly he stood up, pastry in hand, feeling goose bumps, he felt the answer approaching him. What answer?

He felt a stomach upset, threw the pastry into a garbage bin, kept walking, and felt that there was a confluence of events that was preparing him for something. *For something that is coming*? he thought and kept thinking. *But what*?

The next day, just three blocks from that same bakery, another drama was being uncovered. At dawn, next to the garbage dump on the corner of Soriano, three cats were scraping the garbage bags, opening them while scavenging for food. Frequently the neighbors of the place threw out the garbage and left some food for the poor cats. One of those cats, when moving one of the bags, exposed a woman's leg. The white skin was stained with dried blood. The cats stood still, looking at that body that seemed asleep and meowed a bit, maybe bragging to his friends or maybe trying to wake the woman who was partially covered by bags. Two women who had gone for a walk stopped in shock when they saw the leg and for a moment stared at it in silence. One of them took a stick and moved some of the bags. When the body was exposed, they put their hands to their mouths in distress. The naked body was beginning to glow with the sunlight. The freckled face was that of a tall, pretty woman, and her straight light brown hair spread through the trash. A red rose was opening from the side of her head. They had shot her. One man and then another stopped to look. It was horrible.

There was something peculiar in that contrast between the beauty of that woman and the hideous emptiness of death that her body reflected.

More people came and joined them. The whole scene was horrible and sad.

Men and women stood there, hypnotized by the macabre scene, looking at the dead woman. A man took a few steps, took a stick, uncovered the woman, and removed some of the garbage that was on top of her. She had been a pretty woman, freckled-faced, tall, and shapely, and she was still beautiful in her death. With tears in his eyes, the man stepped back as if hypnotized.

A police car passed by and radioed headquarters. A half an hour later the corpse was lifted. Men and women made the sign of the cross in the air, or across their chest, then went home to call friends and relatives.

The inert body of the woman was taken to the Hospital de Clinicas where she was pronounced dead, but where it caused consternation among doctors and students when they saw that such a woman had been murdered. "Another one murdered," protested a doctor. "The military animals did it," said another doctor. Some other doctors who were able to see the body commented about her beauty, her long silky hair soiled with garbage, the single shot on the side of her head, and the sadness they felt after seeing her.

Several students hung a sign from one of the hospital windows that read "KILLER DICTATORSHIP" and even went outside screaming "Murderers!" The screams outside the hospital grew and more people joined screaming "murderers, assassins!" Police and soldiers came. There was shoving, pushing, issuing of threats, but in the end the body was loaded into an army truck and was taken to the morgue. Once there, the outrage of forensics staff and agents at what had clearly been a cold-blooded murder caused a stir that continued with the arrival of many students and professors from the medical school. They did the autopsy with precise detail, placed her in a coffin, and notified the funeral company. Outside, in the patio of sorrows, family and friends were engulfed in pain, desperation, and tears. They all hugged each other, crying with the hope that the irreversible claw of death could somehow release her.

Graffiti tags with *Assassin Dictators* sentiments bloomed through the city.

There was more shouting, stones thrown at cars, and a march was already beginning when four army trucks showed up, dispersed the people, and took the body of the woman and her relatives to North Cemetery.

Two soldiers were posted at the door of the morgue for twenty-four hours to ensure that things settled down.

The restlessness quieted down. Or it seemed to be quieting down.

In fact, it did not settle down and the army had to spread through the streets to impose 'peace,' pushing and arresting students and workers who were marching in the streets screaming, "Dictators are killing our children."

No one told Daniel that the body had been identified as Tamara Marcketowitch, and fortunately, he was not there when she was brought in. But eventually, with all the rioting going on, he found out and felt a paralyzing anger and devastation when he reviewed her file. He didn't go to classes for several days and just sat in his room.

It was in those days that Daniel, like many other students, learned of the disappearances and murders of many other young people, victims who appeared here and there with holes in their heads. It was not known how many. The press, complicit, said nothing.

Daniel knew that her case would not be investigated. Nothing could be done in a country controlled by the guns and boots of the generals. Something changed in him during that time.

Chapter 7

The morgue was a world of people. Officers, agents from the headquarters, students, detectives, and doctors from various departments all interacted there among the dead. It had a large room in the front where the five stretchers surrounded a central table, white and semi-inclined to facilitate drainage. The floor was made of large, gray tiles, arranged in a small slope, which kept the dripping liquids from stagnating as they spiraled towards the sewer. The stretchers and table were cleaned every day with disinfectant and deodorizer. To the right of that death room, a door led to the patio, the *Courtyard of Sorrows*, where stood two old benches to sit on. A large tree slumped in the corner. From that patio, one could cross and go out into the street through the gate. Ambulances, funeral cars, police cars, army jeeps, and crowds of bereaving people entered and left through that large gate at any given hour of the day or night.

There, in that Courtyard of Sorrows, the relatives and friends of the dead often gathered, serious, sad, sometimes impatient, sometimes crying, while they waited for the dead to be released and to be taken by the truck from the funeral company. It was an obligation to greet the family members when one passed by and sometimes say a few good words of comfort if there was distress. Therefore, the door that led to the patio had a small window with lattice where one could see and have an idea of the environment outside. If there were a lot of people lamenting and crying, better not go out there and take the door at the back instead. If things were not that serious, and many friends and relatives were smoking, those in the morgue would go out and talk a little with people and ask for or offer cigarettes. Many went out in civilian clothes, but those who were going to wear coats had to take them off and put on one of the clean ones that were hung next to the door under a sign that read, *Do not go out with a stained coat. Put on this clean one before you leave. Be nice.*

Three of the officers—Domínguez, Cabrera, and Castro-Aronceda—would look to see if there was a worthwhile woman among the relatives of the deceased, as they were like tigers preparing for a meal. They knew how to help those who suffered. They knew that the relatives who were there looked at those who came out of that den, with or without a tunic, as if they were messengers of the gods, capable of moving in and out of that dimension that separates life from death, and that they could go out and enter hell and the kingdom of heaven then return to earth as they pleased, as if they were untouchable demigods. These beings, especially the enchanted ones, had special powers and could say horrible things, but they could also give holy blessings with their eyes and words. They, those demigods, could decide if the dead went to heaven or hell, and they could have a word with God to let the deceased enter his kingdom or even with the Devil himself so that the punishment would not be severe. During their pain, the relatives knew well that these demigod men were the last contact their loved ones would have with human life. Shaking hands with them was a blessing and listening to them was receiving messages from beyond. Daniel felt that when he spoke to them, he got goose bumps. There, in that Courtyard of Sorrows, looking at the relatives of the deceased, he felt that they were contemplating him with the last hope of an impossible miracle, praying to themselves that death would not be as eternal and that perhaps the life of their loved one would resurface. After the first encounters of this type, Daniel was emotionally affected. He asked the forensics and detectives and they explained it all to him.

"It's not what you think, no, and you should know what counts here, Daniel," Cabrera told him with a hand over his heart. "You need to think about what they feel, do you see? When you speak with those grieving relatives, you always must bear in mind you're a divine messenger and you must behave as such."

"But if..." Daniel tried.

"Shhh, listen," Domínguez said. "Look at this place. Look where you are. This is the morgue, and it is just by the gates of beyond. That's the way things are. This is how people see it and feel it."

"This is the Courtyard of Sorrows, Danny," added Cabrera. "The anteroom of death."

"Keep in mind, Daniel," continued Domínguez, "that in that horrible pain they feel, any good word or gesture does bring some relief. Kindness can be healing."

"Don't treat the event according to what you know, but according to what they feel. Hmm?"

"Yes, yes, that... yes, I see."

"The relief is part of your mission. Never hesitate to provide relief."

Daniel felt animated when he heard those words. He started to go out with them into the Courtyard of Sorrows and listen to what they said. When they said something like, "He's already in a better place, he is finally free, everything will be fine for him, we know," it was giving the grieving family a divine message, then they all cried gratefully and shook hands. When they said, "She will never suffer again, our Lord has welcomed her," or "She will never feel pain again," or "Let's alleviate our pain knowing that she is now with our Lord," people cried and hugged them. Some women would hold their hands while crying. Daniel couldn't avoid his feelings and every time felt a squeeze on his heart. Those events saddened him. To make matters worse, and since he was new, he was often sent to do it and to confront the bereaved ones alone. They knew it would have a great effect on him. "It's your mission," they argued. Daniel would go out, feeling a heavy stone on his chest, and would confront the family of the deceased by himself. When he said his words, people would become emotional. Some shook his hand, others whimpered, bending their knees, and accepting the blessing, while others cried a lot and hugged him full of pain. Sometimes he would be hugged by a group in a circle, all crying. He would hug them back, sharing their anguish. He couldn't avoid feeling their deep and hard pain and he would be left troubled for several hours, affected by the emotions of the people. "Hey, it is part of your learning," they told him. "Accept it."

Sometimes, in the beginning, the encounter would be too disturbing and emotional, and the painful moment would be too much for Daniel to handle, and he would start to cry. The officers who commanded him, already immune to death and pain, hardened by life, would see him returning from his mission with his sad silly face, very affected by the event, and burst out laughing when they saw him so distraught. Daniel would come back, enter the morgue anteroom, and sit with his long face, facing the floor, while agents and doctors clung to the tables in silent laughter. Then Domínguez and Cabrera would come to pat him on the back and calm him down. There he would be, sitting in the morgue, in the company of officers, coffins, and corpses, feeling overwhelmed, until he would feel better. Here and there, a sip of whisky or rum would help him recover.

There were times, however, especially in the beginning, when Daniel was not used to it, when the pain of the people was too great and the moaning and crying affected him too much and he would stay there, frozen, with a hand on his face to hide his sorrow and his tears. Then Domínguez, Pranchin, Cabrera or one of the others would come out to rescue him. They would hug him or carry him inside, sooth him with coffee, cigarettes, a sip of alcohol, and some affectionate slaps. "It's like that, Daniel, life comes like this. Death is just part of our lives."

"Yes, Daniel, you are on a very special threshold, and this mission and these messages must be done."

It was horrible, but Daniel didn't get mad because he knew they weren't doing it meanly. The jokes and laughter were part of everyone's defenses to maintain sanity in that underworld.

However, he soon understood that for Domínguez and Cabrera those missions sometimes had a different meaning. They were womanizers.

If among the relatives there were some women who seemed worthwhile, Domínguez, Cabrera, and some other detective would put on their clean coats and go out on a secret mission. They would give the indicated words and would start a relationship that often continued later at the wake or at the burial. Domínguez was interested in the breasts and face of the women, while Cabrera was more of a hip and butt guy. For many of these women, sleeping with these demigods was a blessing and an opportunity to redeem the one who died or place him or her in grace with God. It was not sinful, on the contrary. The demigods repeatedly assured them that the deceased would be well cared for in the kingdom of heaven, or that he would have some beneficial consideration in hell. Often, these women would be granted blessing after blessing, in different hotels, assuring that their loved ones would be well for eternity. When these two agents told of their misdeeds in the usual hotels and love-motels, Daniel would be amazed by the lack of consideration towards the women they took advantage of and could not understand how they continued to date them. These women even picked them up in their cars.

"How... how can you...?"

"It is a liberation, Daniel, and you are too young to understand it."

Daniel tried to imagine a recent widow, overwhelmed by heartache and grief, naked in a hotel, being mounted by a detective, yet becoming happy and delighted because of how she was helping her deceased husband. He had to erase that image from his brain. It was too much. The image of a teenager sexually abused by two policemen who promised her that her mother will go to heaven suddenly invaded his mind. He just blocked the thought.

And the daughters...? What if you see a daughter... a teenager?

"Ay, ay, Daniel. If it is too young, nothing happens, but... you know... some of those teenagers look really...

"Yea, they are appetizing," added Domínguez. "Let me tell you how..."

"What? Shhh... I don't even want to know."

"Leave him alone, Domínguez."

No one ever criticized these adventures nor was there ever a woman who complained, on the contrary, they sent gifts, desserts, and homemade meals to the people in the morgue and to the officers of the headquarters thanking them for services provided. Some even sent letters and thank you cards. Daniel was very surprised by all this and couldn't understand it.

One day when he learned of one of the cases, he said, "But it can't be, Domínguez, it can't be. You slept with the poor widow while her husband's body was still warm."

"You are too young to understand it" said Dr. Bermudez, who was nearby and had listened.

Domínguez told him the next day, "What better relief for a widow, Daniel? Right? What better relief for a woman overwhelmed by the pain of having lost her father or mother than a person like me, making her forget her pain with phenomenal erotism, assuring her that her lost family member will be fine for eternity? "

Daniel watched them and listened to their stories as if hypnotized, especially when they recounted the details of their fiery encounters. He decided not to comment but was intrigued.

~~~~~~

Here and there Daniel learned of other cases of young men and women who had been murdered just like Tamara. The inspectors mentioned other cases, but they prohibited Daniel from talking about it.

"It's the dictatorship," he heard some of them say. "Those guys from the army and the joint military forces are a bunch of brutes, heartless murderers... and yet, they are Uruguayan."

"Yes, Uruguayans killing Uruguayans. Cannibals!"

Some murders had occurred after the ransom payment was made. *How scary,* he thought, the military was executing students and at the same time stealing money from their parents, asking for ransom. *What an injustice.*

Daniel already knew they were killing young people. Several of his friends from the hospital commented on other boys and girls who had been brought to the emergency room by ambulances or patrol cars. They were all young and all with a bullet hole in the side of the head. When that happened, people from the army or the police came quickly and took the body and did not allow questions. Many doctors were outraged, but there was nothing that could be done. *Yes, that's the way things are in the military dictatorship of this country,* he told himself. *Nothing can be done.*

"But ransom? Why?" a doctor asked. "What is this ransom thing?"
~~~~~~

One day Daniel asked himself, *But how many teenagers and young men have been killed like this after paying a ransom?* He had no answer.

Another day he asked Domínguez about it, who took him aside and again said, "Daniel, Daniel, please, you can't talk about that." Domínguez was good and friendly, but that was a subject that should not be discussed. "Don't touch this topic, Danny boy."

However, the deaths of that boy he had seen, and Tamara had not been isolated cases; there were more; many more. Moreover, in the morgue, Daniel found out that those murdered young men and women were a tragedy for the families, and he saw how a large crowd gathered in the Courtyard of Sorrows when that happened. There were shouts, screams, accusations, and protests in the courtyard and in the street, and several times police or army personnel came to disperse the people and cool the situation. Police cars or army jeeps were often seen at those events. Relatives were said to shout that they had paid ransom. They yelled things like "We paid, and they killed him anyway. Murderers!" "Sons of bitches, they made me pay, and they still killed her! Assassins!" With that, the idea was formed that it was the executors of the dictatorship that demanded ransom from the poor parents.

Days of horror mounted.

Daniel tried again to talk it over with Domínguez and then with Cabrera. "Do they really kidnap young people and ask for ransom?" he asked them.

Again, they took him into a corner and with a very harsh voice told him, "You can't talk about this!" and "We don't talk about this because they can kill you. Or... any of us, Daniel!"

"Daniel, Daniel, listen to us." Cabrera remarked. "This is Uruguay. We're under a horrible and cruel dictatorship. People are being imprisoned, disappearing, and murdered. It happens often and there is nothing we can do about it. Nothing!"

"Nothing!" Domínguez added. "Don't put your mind into that. Do not ask. Don't speak about it. The same can happen to you."

"But... but you could..."

"We could? Against whom? Daniel, some detectives have been killed too."

"What? How come?"

"Just like that, naïve Danny boy, some detectives and agents who tried to investigate this have disappeared."

"Disappeared? Do you mean—"

"Shut up. Just shut up."

They all kept silent.

Daniel ended up getting scared and asked no more questions.

The facts were clear, faced with a disappearance or a murder of that kind, there was little to nothing that a normal person, a detective, or even a sub-commissar could do without data, without witnesses, without help, or without power. Even if there were a witness, and even if there were some information, nobody could stand against the mighty strength of the joint military forces of the dictatorship. It was the reality of that time. Many people disappeared and relatives could not do anything or find out anything. They had to put it aside and get on with their lives. That's how he understood it. They knew there was a jail somewhere in the countryside, paradoxically called Freedom Prison, where many prisoners—political and non-political—were taken, and where they were tortured and even killed, but that place was inaccessible. For their part, the police could not do anything about a murder if agents of the dictatorship were suspected of being involved. They could not even request anything from the jailers of that prison.

It was also horrible to hear some army people telling others how proud they were that those actions were being taken. *What's in their heads*, thought Daniel, *how can they talk about it with arrogance*?

"This is the Nazi-Uruguay," a classmate told him. "They feel superior, they follow orders with satisfaction. They feel good about torture."

"Shh...," said another classmate.

"No one else's here..."

"These walls have ears."

"Listen, Daniel," said the first classmate. "Be careful. Uruguayan Nazis are torturing and murdering their fellow Uruguayans. It's a shame. Those soldiers, those policemen, those officers, are Uruguayan men, neighbors! And they hurt their own countrymen without compassion."

"Yes. Uruguayan animals who feel they are chosen and justified to imprison and kill their neighbors."

"Shhhh...stop guys! Shut up."

Among all that, there was something else that caught his attention. The nightly visions seemed a bit more intense, especially if he had been in the morgue that day or had found another young person dead in the emergency ward.

What are those images? What relationship do they have? he thought. *What's in my room? What's next to my closet? No. It's got to be my imagination when I am half asleep. Yes.*

Chapter 8

Monday. Another weekend was left behind. Busy with his courses, his emergency rotations, and anatomy, several days passed until Daniel returned to the morgue. He was leaving the emergency room one day at seven in the morning when a secretary told him to call home: "Doctors Maggiolo and Etcheverry want to talk to you," his mother told him.

He called the number he was given and made an appointment. He went to class, then left early, and took a taxi home to get some sleep. He was falling asleep standing up. He ate a bite and took an hour's nap. He got up, got dressed, and went to anatomy. At five o'clock in the afternoon, he entered the morgue.

Dr. Etcheverry came over, put his arm around his shoulder, slapped his face like an uncle does, and said, "Hi, little Carmen kid."

"Gee, they told you, eh?"

"Yep," the doctor said. "You're the new campfire story the veteran *elders* at the station tell new recruits."

"Great..."

"Come, let's have some tea."

They went into the office and closed the door. Dr. Maggiolo was there, reading. The three of them sat down and talked a little about the morgue and its problems, Daniel's studies, and general things. They served him a cup of Earl Grey tea, "our favorite, Danny," and lit cigarettes. Maggiolo got up and locked the door.

"And Daniel...? Did you find out anything?"

"About what?"

"At the headquarters."

"I got in there, yes, but what do I need to find out?"

"Did you find out about the DEMEM?"

"But that's in the Department of Justice. I didn't have the time to go and—"

"Yes, you did. They saw you there."

"But—"

"People who know you, saw you there."

"Perhaps we should explain to you about the Medical Forensic Department and the DEMEM," said Maggiolo.

"Yeah, sure."

"Did Martinez question you? And MacLagan?"

"Yes. Both. They made me sweat."

"I thought so! As expected," Maggiolo said. "We're in difficult times and suddenly you appeared poking your nose over there. Well... good. I suppose you are realizing that things are more complicated than it seems, right?"

"Where are you guys going with this?" asked Daniel. "What *things*? Am I supposed to do something there?"

"I know. I know. It's a... it's a bit more complicated...," said Maggiolo. "You probably thought that if you stuck your nose at the headquarters everything would be clear, eh? No, no, it won't be like that. There are things, eh...many things, that...hmm...need to be searched."

"Searched? What?"

"They need to be found," added Etcheverry, fiddling nervously with a fountain pen. "Look... hmm... there are things that people don't know or don't want to know."

"Pranchinetti is a very good guy and Martinez is a genius, but... so what? They must take care of themselves; they must be careful. They can't do anything. We are in a tough dictatorship."

"What? Do anything about *what*, Dr. Etcheverry?"

The professors kept silent. Daniel looked at them thinking, *what's going on here*?

"What is it that I need to do there? I just take the pictures... what are you suggesting here?

"We know you take pictures, Daniel, but there's something else."

"What?"

"We must go to the basics," Maggiolo said.

Etcheverry took off his coat and hung it up. The room had green walls, a green as old and dark as blue spruce, and was filled with books, old and new. To the side, on a small table, was a kettle with hot water and a coffee maker. The center table was wide, with many scattered papers, three dirty ashtrays, and pieces of a camera. On the side wall there was a small sink with four cups waiting to be washed for a long time. A small counter held a box with pipes, matches, and photos of family and friends. There was an odor of morgue mixed with the aromas of coffee, burnt cigarettes, and old furniture.

Maggiolo lit his thinking pipe and fell silent. Daniel threw the tea into the sink and got some coffee. Etcheverry gave him a piece of his chocolate.

"There's something we wanted to tell you," Etcheverry told him. "Pay attention."

They both spoke to him, explaining and insisting that if he wanted to start participating in the field of forensics, he needed to have a plan. They told him that it was necessary for him to learn all about the morgue, and about forensic medicine and its relationship with the Department of Justice and its Medico-Judicial office, and that it was time for him to begin to understand the operation and administration of that place and its connections.

"Looks like you have chosen a certain path, and we want to help you advance in it. If you want to advance in it."

"Yes, yes. I suppose I do."

"We will help you. We know how."

"That's your... eh... that's your official path. That official path... which is... well..."

"*Official* path? What do you—"

"Shhh... wait. Your progress at the police headquarters and your possible entrance to the Department of Justice seems to be the path you are interested in. We can help you with that."

"And we can help you with the DEMEM too."

"But what is this DEMEM and why is it so...?"

"Wait, wait, you must know this well," said Maggiolo, sipping his coffee. "This must be clear. This is the foundation that allows you to advance on the other plan."

"*Another* plan?"

"Your forensic path, as we can call it, is part of the whole plan. We—"

"You will need to do it. Whether you leave or decide to stay and follow your plans, *you've* got to do it," said Professor Dr. Etcheverry, touching Daniel on the shoulder in a friendly way.

"I've got to do what?"

"Step by step, Danny. If you want to do something in forensic medicine, DEMEM is the door."

"Okay, but where are you going with this? Yes, I would like to take that forensic path, yes, but... I don't understand."

"We know that" said Maggiolo, nervous, looking at the other doctor. "We need to move on to bigger words."

The two doctors looked at each other.

"Look, Daniel," Doctor Maggiolo said, cleaning his pipe. "It will be better if you understand how all this mess works. We would like you to do the training course in the Department of Justice, so that you understand its relationship with our department and our relationship with the Police Headquarters, with the Technical Police, the Ministry of the Interior, and other state agencies. Did you hear me well?"

"Yes....Yes, sure. I get it. Yes, but what else are you *not* talking about?"

"Always too clever for your own good!"

"You will understand as you make progress. Go to the Department of Justice to learn things well. Talk to Berta on the second floor and bring her this letter. And don't make a mess there, you understand?"

"And here you have the list of people that you must contact there. When you leave, I'm going to call some of them. They will be waiting for you. You're going to have to take a course."

"A course? But I don't have the—"

"Ssshhh...listen. You must understand this. In the future, if you want, you can enter DEMEM."

"Yes, yes, thank you Dr. Maggiolo, but I still don't know what DEMEM is."

"You will find out pretty soon."

"That is the first part of what we had discussed. But without this part, Daniel, the second part can fall apart."

"You are not obligated," Etcheverry added, holding his arm. "It's not an obligation. Ah, you also must know that you will go through a learning stage in the police headquarters. You already know that. You are already doing it, even if you don't realize it."

"If you do things well, that's how you would enter DEMEM. Go and talk to Berta."

"Yes, yes. I'll do that."

"But dress well when you go," said Etcheverry who was Director General of the Forensic Technical Institute. "Don't look like a butcher. Be respectful and don't talk back."

"Yes, DEMEM is a serious place."

"Yes, Daniel," Maggiolo said. "Your education and training are requirements for you to continue advancing."

"I just... I just don't see why. I want it, yes, but what's behind all that? What is that other thing you don't dare to tell me?"

"You will understand it better later. It needs to be done. It is not going to deter you, but rather help you advance."

Daniel kept silent for a moment.

"Well, is it clear? Now let's go to the next matter.

Finally, thought Daniel.

Maggiolo put down his pipe. The other doctor poured water for the tea, loosened his tie, and sat in the other chair. They were both serious and looking at each other like trying to find the right words.

"And about what we are going to tell you, you can't tell anyone, not even your mother, and I never told you. Do we agree?"

"Yes. Yes."

"Remember well, none should know," insisted Etcheverry. "After our initial conversation, in which we raised certain possibilities of finding out certain things... we... we were seeing that several factors have come together in you. You showed up around here like a nosy fox looking for something, and before we knew it, you already put your fingers in every corner. Wait, wait, don't jump. I'm not accusing you."

"Yeah, continued Maggiolo. "And before we knew it, you were in autopsies, involved with pictures, statements, smoking with the detectives, and exploring the police headquarters. You really have ants in your pants, unless... unless..."

"Unless what?"

"Unless you are looking for something."

"*Me?* What am *I loo—?*"

"Ssshhh... wait. I don't need to know that... yet. We've been watching you. We needed someone just like that, and we were already halfway... eh, discouraged. I mean, disappointed. Then... well, you showed up, and we watched your comings and goings, and with great surprise we found out that you had been involved in investigations with your father, until he was killed in the Capurro neighborhood. Well, we... eh... we found more about you."

"That's a bad neighborhood."

"What?"

"That neighbor—"

"What did you find about me?"

"It doesn't need to be discussed now."

"Yes. Good. Keep me in the darkness, sure!" answered Daniel and rose.

"Wait, wait, don't get upset."

"Cool off."

Daniel sat down. They waited. They lit cigarettes.

"We know, Daniel, we know about you," said Maggiolo. "And we know that your dad changed your last name to protect you."

"Please, please..."

"Ssshhh, now, we won't tell anyone."

"But listen. Yamandu and Martinez showed us your records, and from there we know it all.

"Those idiot bastar—"

"You think they're stupid there? They know everything about you."

"Damn it! And... did you see my police record too?"

Etcheverry laughed and said: "You think that those in the headquarters are blind?"

"There's a reason it's called your *permanent* record, Danny."

"We saw pictures of you," said Maggiolo. "You like to get in trouble, eh?"

"That blond was a beast, little Danny."

"Oh, gee... please!" voiced Daniel, throwing his hands up. "Why? What the hell are you doing this for? Besides... most of them are lies!"

"Yes, sure Daniel," Maggiolo interrupted him. "Sure. Yes. They are all lies. Are you going to tell me that the smuggling and the whores are all a big lie? But are you taking pictures of whores? What the hell...?"

"No. Only of some, more than anything of Carmen, because I—"

"Aaaahhhh, of Carmen, yes, sure. And that Susana?"

"And Liliana...?"

"Wait a minute, they were models, not whores."

"Sure. Sure."

"I did it because they were... they were... To help them!"

"Oh, shut up, Danny. We may be geeky doctors, but we're also grown men."

"Who knows how many of those you took to bed with the story of being a photographer."

Daniel, face flaming red, kept silent. *How did they find those pictures*?

"Of course, of course, you did it out of the pure goodness of your heart," Etcheverry emphasized. "Sure. Well, let's leave the subject. We can really see your goodness."

"What do you mean, Etcheverry?"

"Nothing. Nothing."

"What about the smuggling? Did you also do that out of um... goodness?" Maggiolo asked. "And what about the Salvo Palace parties? How roguish you went with that, man... but, don't you have a conscience? You want me to continue? Do you want to talk about Carmen, Zulma, and her friends? Do you want to talk about the times they pinched you for smuggling?"

"Nooo," Daniel groaned standing up, half cornered and embarrassed. "No, hmm.... Why do you dredge this up now? Why are you accusing me?"

"Quiet brother, we're not accusing you," Maggiolo said.

"We are not accusing you, Daniel."

"But why do you rub it in my face like that? I was younger, and friends took me to..."

"Younger? It was just a few years ago."

"I'm good now. I don't..."

"We know. We know. You were able to do it because you knew that if something happened, your father, who was deputy commissar at that time, would get you out of trouble. You felt protected. If it hadn't been for that, you wouldn't have done certain things. And I'll tell you more, about the minister's party in the palace you shouldn't have done it because—"

"A minister son of a bitch, Etcheverry!" Daniel yelled. "He deserved that. That great party he made..."

"Ssshhh, ssshhh, mister gun powder, don't blow a wad. We are not accusing you, but rather telling you that we've done our homework too."

"Listen to us. Hey, calm down."

"Well... well..." Maggiolo continued. That simply and clearly shows us that you have a special talent to do certain things and that somehow neither we nor Yamandu nor Martinez understand. You fall standing up like a cat."

Daniel kept silent.

"We don't want you to get upset, Daniel. Well.... Don't you want to enter the headquarters and to try to investigate something there?"

"But—"

"Listen, Daniel, Daniel, listen a little."

Daniel was silent. Nervous.

"Calm down, hey."

"I want... I want..."

Maggiolo sat down, then got up and made a tea while sighing.

They lit cigarettes. Etcheverry opened a small window to clear the smoke.

"Listen, stubborn! It's not only what you want. There are other things. There are other people."

"What things?"

"People! There are other people whose children were killed."

Maggiolo left his pipe in the ashtray and said, "Remember what you heard about the kids that are murdered after a ransom money was paid?"

"Yeah."

"Remember you asked us about it. You wanted to know."

"Yeah..."

"And you found out that it's forbidden to investigate. Hmm?"

"Yes. But how many? I only knew about... how many were murdered?"

"Many."

"So many."

"We don't know the number. But would you dig into this?"

"Dig into what? Aren't you going to help me? We are talking real murders here."

"Of course, we are talking real murders, Daniel! Dozens of them."

In a few words they explained to Daniel about the many young men and women that have been murdered after a ransom was paid. There has been no political or ideological reason for that. No jail records. No investigation had been possible.

"There's something important that you must understand. Beside what you know, there were others who were killed that way. You know of just a few. We know there were many."

"Damn!"

Daniel got up, stretched his legs, and sat down again. He didn't speak for a while as the two doctors looked at each other.

"Well then... then what?" asked Daniel.

The doctors were nervous as they were trying to share with him some information.

"Listen to us, Daniel. What would happen to that land-like-a-cat quality that you seem to have if... eh... if it were focused and... and helped... and... dedicated to find the cause and origin of... those deaths?" Maggiolo said staring at him.

"You got yourself into the police headquarters, you could find what others couldn't."

Daniel got goose bumps. ***What***? he told himself. Was he being given a mission?

"Do you visualize it?"

"You got in there already."

"You really care?"

"You really want to do something about the murders?"

Daniel could barely think or talk. The images he had seen in Tamara's hospital file flashed though his head. "What? What do you mean?"

"What you heard."

"Me? But I'm just a—"

"A student, sure."

"We know."

"Yes, a student," said Maggiolo. "But we also got a hint that you are looking for something there, aren't you?"

"Me?"

"Yes, you. You're trying to find something at the police center, aren't you?"

"Buh... but..."

"Aren't you, Daniel?"

"I'm just... I don't want to..."

"Aren't you, Daniel?" yelled Maggiolo. "Aren't you already looking for something there, slippery Danny boy?"

Daniel stood up, angry.

"Do you really care about justice?"

"Do you?"

"Yes! Yes!" he screamed. "And I will..."

"Ssshhh... shut up."

"Calm down."

"Sit down. Don't raise your voice."

"Calm down. Calm down. We don't know for sure what you are looking for and we have the idea that you're not going to tell us, but we do know that you were checking the police headquarters looking for something. Yes or no?"

"Okay, yes."

"And, if we are not mistaken, you did find something. You found a secret area, a forbidden room, haven't you?"

Daniel kept silent.

"Well, have you or not?"

"Okay, yeah."

"Alright. Alright. You did find the place. Do you know what's in there?"

Daniel kept quiet, thinking.

"It's one of the things I'm trying to find out."

"The room with bars and two blue beret soldiers loaded with machine guns at the entrance?"

"Yes. That one."

"That's the informatic center. Everything that enters the headquarters, and anything coming from other police stations or radio communications is sent there. Every crime, every death, every robbery, everything. From there it goes to the main information center of the terrible Joint Forces and the military command.

"Every death, Daniel. Every crime, every disappearance, every arrest."

"Every kidnapping. Every one of those who were shot and everyone who came back alive."

"It's all in there."

They all looked at each other.

"We don't know what you are looking for, but I can tell you that access to that room could be very revealing. It could have information about the boys and girls that were murdered."

"So why don't you look at the records?"

"What records? They're gone. No records. Someone made them disappear."

"Someone inside the headquarters?"

"Yes. We think so. And we don't know who or how many are involved."

"Hmm... I see," added Daniel.

"Again, we don't know what you are after but entering there may help all of us."

"Sure," said Daniel. "If the bullets don't stop you."

"Sure."

"But, what if Yamandu or Martinez or some other detectives go there to investigate?"

"They're not allowed to even enter the corridor that goes to that place. No one at the headquarters is allowed near that door."

"Yes. Two agents tried a few months ago, and they disappeared."

"Damn! But this is—"

"Now the question is how to enter; and even if you enter, how can you find what you and we are looking for?"

Daniel froze at his intelligent gaze, hoping to understand. *They are throwing me to the lions*, he thought.

"Hmm? What would happen, Danny?"

There was a little silence. Daniel began to understand and the skin on his back prickled. He held his breath.

"What would happen, uh...?" Etcheverry said. "Hmm... eh? If instead of you alone there were other people who could help you from the shadows?"

Daniel froze again. He felt like he was being pushed into a tunnel and opening a door to something, but he didn't know what. He felt an electricity in his mind.

"Hmm?" repeated Maggiolo. "What would happen, Daniel, eh?"

"I will disappear too."

"No, no..."

"I'll be found dead in a garbage dump, for sure."

"Oh no you won't."

"Not if it's done right."

Daniel's imagination exploded into images. *Shit*! he thought.

"The thing is, maybe... maybe.... If we help you climb higher, if you're smart, as I see you are, you might find yourself on occasions... uh... in special situations where you can use your desire to find out what happened. Others could help you and what you can find out could help many."

"Maybe thousands, Danny."

"Do you understand this... eh?"

"Yes, I'm getting it."

"That's the way, Danny boy, let us help you so you can help many others," Etcheverry emphasized. "You wouldn't be the only one, see? Do you get that?"

"Yes, I see, yes. They will use my body for target practice."

"Look, Daniel," said Maggiolo. "You already saw that on your own you could not advance much, eh?"

"Okay."

"Are you agreeing?"

"Yes."

"I imagine by this point you've realized that with just entering the headquarters you do not find out anything you're looking for. You probably thought that when you entered there, you'd find clear clues, specific data, and even a little sign that reads, 'This is it', eh?"

"Hmm... yes."

"And you saw that you couldn't find out anything. You met people, you stuck your nose in various places, but beyond that you didn't learn anything new."

"I thought there'd be..."

"Yes, yes, you thought, you thought. But you saw. Without help and without a plan... and without someone who knows," explained Etcheverry, "your curiosity and your audacity will not discover anything."

"Right."

"Are we in agreement?"

"We are going to help you, but you must cooperate with the help," continued Maggiolo, "play ball and not act unfriendly or get stubborn, do you hear me?"

"You must be part of a cog and not a lone ranger, as Dr. Fierro calls you."

"Yeah, I understand, yes... yes," said Daniel. "Oh, do you know him?"

"Of course, we know him," Etcheverry continued. "And if you wonder why, why of all this, suffice it to tell you that those you saw dead were not the only ones. We know very clearly what that means. We were touched by the same evil."

The pain of that phrase hit right into Daniel's forehead. The two teachers looked at Daniel with the big eyes of bossy bosses but looking from one to the other he could see a hint of pain behind their eyes and tears forming while they remembered something painful. He had no need to ask for details, they could be guessed from their looks. He could see that the two of them were remembering things that happened to their loved ones. He could feel their secret pain. He was silent, respecting their memories and the images that assailed them. A shiver crawled up his back. There was more than pain in the mind of those doctors.

So, it's about something else, he thought. *How many more*?

After a while, wiping his eyes and nose, Maggiolo spoke in a softer voice. "Do you understand what I'm talking about?"

"Yes, Doctor Maggiolo, I realize it."

Maggiolo sat down. There was a long silence. They all looked at the floor.

"Look, Daniel," said Maggiolo. "You're going to need help, you may need a team, and you're going to need power. Without that you will not advance. And we... eh... we're going to do something about it."

"Huh? What do you mean?"

Maggiolo reached into his pocket and pulled out a key chain. Etcheverry did the same, and they both put something on the table. They were two key chains, with an attached string made of red and gold filigree. The keys were big, like 4 inches long, brown, rusty, and held three little pieces of metal with carvings on them. He was able to see that one had the image of a compass with a letter G, and another had a cross. He stared at the keys in amazement. Those were occult symbols. *What's going on here*? he thought, *why are they showing me this*?

They all kept silent.

A symbol thought Daniel. *The badge, another symbol. The crosses, the compass, the letter G. What's this*?

This indicated that these two professors were part of a secret group that was organizing something in the shadows.

"That is the way you will have access to power... are you understanding?"

"Yes—well... no," answered Daniel. "Not understanding, not the whole thing."

"Power, little Danny."

"I realize."

"But nothing. We said nothing. You didn't see anything."

And they placed their keys back in their pockets.

"We didn't say anything about that. We didn't talk about this; do you hear me? Secrecy is essential."

"Some of us Uruguayans know that we must do what we must do. Certain malevolent forces have been launched against our country, and from the quiet corner we're in, we must make some adjustments."

"But no one can do it alone, Daniel. Those keys tell you that there are certain people in this country who understand that certain barriers must be put aside to do what must be done."

"But you didn't see anything."

"Not a thing. I didn't see anything, I know. But... am I supposed to have something like a mission? A task?"

"Shut up," Maggiolo added. "First understand that whatever is done, it should not be done alone."

"This is bigger than one person."

"Bigger than you."

"You cannot and should not do it alone, without help and without power."

"There's no remedy, Daniel. We must do what we must do, but nothing should be done by the lone action of a hotheaded individual."

"Yes, Daniel, it's an opportunity!" Maggiolo said. "And... and... it will be a mission if you want it to be, and here there is no obligation. There is nothing we can say to compel you to do so. Only your sense of justice, your natural curiosity, your ability to stick your nose in, combined with a computer center, could solve that enigma that has already taken the lives of many people. But remember... I didn't tell you anything because that's not what we talked about."

"But speaking boldly and clearly, why doesn't Martinez or the others find out?"

"We already told you. They must take care of themselves. If they do something, anything, to find out, those in the fearsome Joint Forces would find out and get them out of the way or make them just disappear. That's one of the reasons MacLagan is so nervous with you. He feels that you may open a can of worms—force him to investigate something that could get him, and you, killed."

"We don't know who is behind those disappearances in which they ask for ransom. Are they soldiers? Officers? Police? Officials?"

"Maybe officers of the dreadful Joint Forces?"

"We don't know. Maybe it's people from the ministry. Or commissioners, or... or... sub-commissars."

"We've already dealt with others, and it didn't work out. Whoever they are, when someone investigates, they vanish, nothing is found."

"They disappear."

"No idea?"

"Now, do you understand, Daniel?" Etcheverry continued. "If they know that we are searching for them, they'll vanish. You must do it without anyone knowing, and that's why it must be someone from the outside."

"But I... I'm a student... a student."

"We already know."

"And Joan of Arc was a peasant girl."

"Nobody forces you, but there are desperate people who need help."

"I hope you realize that you don't have to do it if you don't want to. No one is going to know. But someone from the outside, stealthy and without shame, who already comes with impulse, and—and... if we bring him closer to the information center, then he will not create suspicion, and maybe he will find something."

"Hmm... I see," answered Daniel.

A silence fell over the room.

Daniel mentally chewed on what they told him. "Hmm... Interesting," he finally said.

"But here we only talked about your courses," Etcheverry said.

"Yes. Here we only spoke of courses in the Department of Justice," said Daniel. "Nothing more. I didn't talk about anything else." "Yes. Good. It's okay. What do I do now?"

"Now we need a plan. And you're going to need help and power."

"Who? *Someone*?

"We already know who. There are two of them, Berta, the assistant director of one of the Justice Departments, and the other is Martinez's niece. But don't let that info escape you."

"Two women?"

"Yes."

"Please don't try to sex them up, Danny."

"Very intelligent and smart, possibly smarter than you think."

He stood there with a nervous chuckle, shaken by everything he had just understood, and with goose bumps. A very particular emotion came to mind. "Who's Martinez's niece? What's her name?"

"Gina."

"Gina?"

"Yeah. She knows about all this. With her we can communicate more freely and with her we will draw up plans. She will give you intellectual help."

"So where do I find her? What do you know, how much do you know about—?"

"Yeah, yeah, leave it there. She's gonna find you. You'll understand. But be very careful, you can't talk to anyone—Martinez or anyone else. Not with your mother. First go to the judiciary and talk to Berta."

"Hmm..."

"And don't be a pig with any of them, you hear me? They're nice women."

"We know, ha! We know quite well what a pig you can be, but respect Gina, eh? She's there to help. Keep your distance."

"Their ideas will serve you well. Ah, by the way, you will also meet Lourdes, she's to be respected too."

"She's got a body like the kinda models you like to photograph."

"But don't touch her."

"Yes, good. Eh... but... Gina, Lourdes, what is it with them?"

"You'll see."

"Just restrain yourself. Show good manners."

"Yes, okay."

"We agree?"

Daniel looked at the coffee pot, then at the wall, and then at the table. He looked up and saw them both, looking at him not with bossy faces but with worried faces. He suddenly understood many things. In the face of the death of loved ones there was nothing that could be done or said, but certain people were organizing something.

How many? Daniel thought. *How many has this dictatorship killed? What is the extent of the damage that those brutal animals in uniform have done? How many have they killed?*"

He took a deep breath. *Uruguayans killing Uruguayans, how can it be?*

"Yes, it's okay, I realize that... yes, understood," he finally replied.

Daniel was silent, sitting. Then he stood up, approached them, and silently shook their hands, making them understand that he had understood well what he had to do. At one point, it seemed that they could not control their emotions. They stood up, and each one gave him a hug and shed a tear. Daniel left the room with teary eyes and already knowing that, suddenly, he had another path in life. *What did I get myself into... again?*

He understood well what they told him. And he also understood that he was getting into something of which he had no idea. His emotions calmed. He began to ponder as he walked and climbed the white staircase of death. From the walls of the staircase, the voices of the dead whispered warnings to him. Inaudible screams of Nazis and victims of the holocaust warned him that he was entering another red circle of death and seemed to scream warning messages. There were voices from the past, but there were voices from the present as well, restless souls of those who were assassinated. His heart beat faster, he grew anxious, something was approaching. He held the rail and started to sing aloud to ward off that feeling and hurried his steps. He needed to do something about these stairs. *They shouldn't control me.*

He got to the corridor, left his coat in the Anatomy room, and went for a walk down the avenue. *What have I let them get me into? What path is this? Where does it lead me?*

He had no answers because he knew there were no answers. Nothing is done because nothing can be done. Some Uruguayans have decided to do what must be done.

He went home but could not go up to his apartment. Something made him feel restless. He went to Biarritz Park around the corner, sat on a bench to smoke and waited to calm his mind. *What's going on here*? Apparently, there's an organization... an organization? Why that key, why the badge? What do they have to do with it?

The park was nice and quiet, but Daniel's thoughts didn't leave him. A warm wind moved the leaves from side to side. Some tennis players passed by. A dog barked in the corner. Daniel couldn't clear his mind.

He realized he needed to know more.

I am getting in the middle of something, and I don't know what it is.

A woman passed by and greeted him. A man with two dogs was across the grass. The park was relaxing him but not giving any answers. He stood up and started to walk.

Chapter 9

A few days later, things were different. Daniel's attitude changed.

Nobody noticed, nobody knew about it. Only him. *I am going to do it.*

He knew that bad feelings between him and Martinez's group might hurt his plans. He needed them to be on his side. Maggiolo and Etcheverry had instructed him well.

He entered the police headquarters with the right foot and determination. The gorilla at the entrance already knew his face and let him in. Daniel went up to the third floor and reported to the investigation office. The detectives were not there, and he went to Martinez's office. Daniel knocked on his door.

"Come in," Martinez said. "Ah, it's you.

A smell of coffee and cigarettes hovered around the desk. Martinez had a huge gun on his side, with which he looked even bigger and even his mustache looked thicker. He was wearing a light green shirt and a ridiculous blue tie. He dressed as they usually dress: horrible.

"What do you need?" asked the chief.

Lieutenant Rodolfo Martinez Carlotti, who was simply called 'Martinez,' officer, commissar, chief detective and director of the department, chief manager of one of the criminology divisions, member of the general staff, smoothed his large mustache, cleaned his glasses, and looked at him with an aggressive curiosity. A tough guy.

Be careful, Daniel, the words of Maggiolo sounded in his brain. *No missteps. Be careful with what you say.*

"Yes, here I bring the pictures of the murdered banker."

"Very good," Martinez said. "Leave them there, on the table. And listen to me Daniel, I got the call from Professor Etcheverry at the morgue. I also got a call from Dr. Maggiolo. They told me they chose you as an assistant. Are you sure this is what you want to do?

"Yes. Sure, yes. They told me that every year they choose one, so..."

“Does it have to do with what we had talked about?” asked Martinez, combing his mustache with his fingers.

“Yes, sir,” he lied. “I’m going to work as an assistant. Yes.”

“So what? How did Etcheverry choose you?”

“Well... I—eh— the one who proposed and chose me was Dr. Maggiolo. He told me that... that if I had an interest in forensic medicine that... well. He told me that last year they chose an assistant who...

“Yes, but he didn’t last long.”

“Oh yeah? Okay. The doctors explained to me that other students—”

Martinez leaned back in his chair. He lit a cigarette. “I know well what you’re doing...” he said while blowing cigarette smoke, “and what you have been doing... but this is a far more serious role.”

You don’t know anything, Daniel thought.

“Accompanying detectives and officers while they investigate a crime scene and taking photos of the scenes themselves can be a very disturbing experience,” continued the officer. “You’re not made for that.”

“Yes. I understand, but—”

“That goes beyond being an auxiliary or... or an assistant. What’s up here? You’re a medical student, your path is to become a doctor, why’re you going to waste study time involving yourself with police issues? You don’t think...”

“I wanna do it,” said Daniel, very sure of his false words. “It’s a field that attracts—”

“Let me continue talking. Don’t you think that as an assistant you are getting into strange things?”

“Is that I—”

Martinez softened his face. “You know, I was an interrogator once. For the military. I can tell if—”

“I’m not sure what you’re—”

“Tell me, what’s the truth?” asked Martinez with harder eyes. “Why do you want to get into the headquarters...? What’s going on?”

The door opened. MacLagan slid in. “You again,” the agent said. “What’s he done now?”

“I was just bringing the pict—."

“Oh yeah? What else do you want to tell us?” MacLagan said, opening his long jacket and showing his weapon, a gesture that Daniel had noticed he liked to do to intimidate. “What are you looking for here?”

Daniel had already read something about MacLagan. William Jeremy MacLagan was of a British family but had changed his name to Guillermo. He was rough, and it was said that no one who called him “Guille” or “Willy” should expect to continue living. As tall as a cypress, as tough and arid as the side of a mountain, he was always armed and smelled of gun cleaning oil mixed with that awful English lavender. *This guy must be a very constipated man to be like this*, thought Daniel. *A hard poop guy, dry as a Brit, who must hate his own guts*. The guy had three favorite weapons, but Daniel only knew about one of them, the silver Beretta 38 Special, with an extended barrel for better aim and longer range. Daniel knew that several criminals had gotten a taste of his bullets. When doing street affairs, MacLagan liked to open his jacket and allow the silver glow of his gun to show through as a message. Nobody missed that convincing detail. Brown hair, combed back, bad eyes, aggressive blood. He drank tea instead of coffee. In the street, dogs barked at him, and cats looked at him suspiciously.

"Nothing," Daniel lied, hardening his mind and face, and making an innocent expression. "I don't know what else."

"Keep your face inexpressive and your butt tight," Etcheverry had told him. "Convince them."

"You're sticking your nose in around here," MacLagan said in an executioner's voice. "Are you looking for something? Speak."

"Nothing... I am learning," Daniel said aloud. "What did you expect? *I have to fight back*, he told himself.

"Speak."

"MacLagan is going to be one of those who is going to give you problems," Etcheverry had warned him. "Talk to Martinez like we told you, talk to him well, he's a righteous man. But Guille... he's tough and suspicious of everyone. Control your words."

"Whatever you do or say," Maggiolo had said, "resist the pressure."

"We saw your police records, Daniel, we know who you are, and we know about your father. What do you want to find here, brat?"

MacLagan called him *el mocoso* instead of brat, probably to flash his street creds and/or to show he was not British.

"What?"

"Don't say *what*, and don't raise your voice again. We know a few of the things you were involved with in the past. We know of your felonies, kid, we know you also studied detective science.

Silence.

"Shit... I didn't expect this."

A silence fell upon the room and lasted a long time. Daniel was feeling diminished and scared, but suddenly he remembered Dr. Maggiolo's words: "Whatever happens and when it happens, remember what you're doing.

Remember. In those moments when you feel desperate, remember, remember why you are doing this." That gave him strength. He took a deep breath and mentally prepared himself to continue the inevitable confrontation. The two officers tried to calm down, they lit cigarettes and backed off.

"What... what about my father?"

"We know who he was and why he was killed in the Capurro neighborhood. He was always searching; he was always sticking his nose in. You have his blood, and you are as nosy as he was. What are you looking for?"

The two officers were irritated; they looked at Daniel thinking while he looked at them. He viewed these two as masters in recognizing hidden truths, who after having questioned a thousand criminals would know well when someone is hiding something, very surely had realized that he was hiding some information.

Several minutes went by. All three calmed down. Daniel started to stare at Martinez trying to make him understand that he couldn't talk with MacLagan present. They both looked at each other, knowing what they knew, understanding something.

The silence continued. A bad feeling hung in the air.

The noise of voices and typewriters pressed through the door. The hairs of Martinez mustache looked like needles. The smell of MacLagan's lavender was mixing with the smoke of their cigarettes. The air was thick.

Daniel had been instructed by the two forensic doctors about the possibility of this encounter, and perhaps this was his only advantage. "Don't jump, Daniel," Etcheverry had said, "let them talk and voice their anger."

They all waited.

Daniel was nervous. "You are going to be nervous, Danny," Maggiolo had told him, "But keep your mouth shut."

Domínguez and Pranchin came in and Martinez told them the purpose of the meeting.

"Listen to me well Daniel," said the chubby Domínguez with his actor's face. "What real reasons do you have? What are you hiding?"

You will never know, thought Daniel.

The detectives were getting restless. Something just didn't make sense. But Daniel had foreseen that moment and had prepared the half-truth that he was going to tell. Maggiolo and Etcheverry had warned him well. He put on an impassive face as he began to unfold his story.

"Yes. Okay, I will tell you, but first—"

"Speak."

"I have plans," Daniel answered. "But I don't like to talk about my plans."

"You *don't like*?" yelled MacLagan, nervous about how Daniel spoke. "What kind of filthy plans do you have?"

"Why can't you tell us?"

"Because I don't know if they will be fulfilled later."

Martinez and MacLagan looked at each other like they were about to lose their patience. Sparks shot out of their heads. MacLagan's anger made him sweat, and he removed his jacket and swung it to the hook on the door the way a matador swings a red cape.

"What do you mean?"

"It is... well... hmm..." Daniel continued. "The photographic laboratory is part of the technical police, which is part of the Investigations Division. There, analysis and expertise on criminal acts are carried out. The important thing for me is that it is part of the CID, the Criminal Investigation Division of the headquarters. That division and the leadership itself are commanded by the chief executive officer, the general commissioner, and captain Yamandu Solano Boresky, who in turn are part of the Police General Staff.

"Ha! You were sticking your nose in, huh?"

"You call him *The Russian*, right...? Because he looks like Stalin. And that—"

"Shhh... shut up, Daniel, don't repeat that, if he hears you, he will kill you."

"And... and... and be careful because the Russian hears through walls."

"Yes. Good. Okay. And that General Staff depends on and is linked to the Ministry of the Interior."

"Where did you learn that from?"

"I— I... I stuck my nose in.

"Ah! look at this guy."

"Where's this going?" asked Pranchin

"That technical photography, which is part of the National Directorate of Technical Police, links the Ministry of the Interior and the Judiciary Power. The technical photograph division uses people from two directories."

"Aaaahhhh."

"So?"

"That, in addition, medicine in this country is controlled by the Ministry of Public Health."

"You're confusing us," said Martinez.

Yes, I know you're getting mixed up, thought Daniel.

"And so what with that?"

"That there is an office in the Justice Department that few know about and it is called DEMEM, Department of Medical Establishment of the Ministry of Health, which has multiple functions, including supervising criminology activities, liaison with courts, connections with all police divisions, inter-ministerial relations, contacts with different boards of the general staff, with the army, with the National Directory of Technical Police, which links with the Ministry of Public Health, the Ministry of the Interior and also..."

"Oh, oh, quite a connect-the-dots lecture."

"What are you talking about? What is all this?"

"And what do you want with that?"

"That there is a branch of DEMEM here at the headquarters and in four ministries, including the Ministry of the Interior and the Ministry of Public Health, but the central office is at the headquarters of the Judicial Power, located four blocks from here, at the Libertad Square."

"Well, I don't know about those things," said MacLagan. "But... so what? Why do we need to know that?"

"In the future, I want to enter the DEMEM," said Daniel, who was careful how to give the information he had gathered in his mind.

"Tell them about DEMEM," Maggiolo told him, "Convince them about that." Daniel had practiced those phrases in front of more than one mirror.

"Is that your goal?"

"So... but are you—"

"Is that it, then?"

"Yes," said Daniel. "And you cannot enter there by contest or exam. You enter through relationships and personal recommendations."

"How come?"

"What?"

"That to enter the DEMEM it's not a matter of passing an exam. I must relate to high up people and make myself known."

Everyone remained in silence. They couldn't contradict him; Daniel had the story well prepared.

"And you want to enter the headquarters so... so they begin to know you, to begin to relate, eh?"

"Yes, that's the way. Help to be helped later. Networking. That is my goal."

"And why don't you do it through the Ministry of Public Health?"

"Because it just doesn't work that way," Daniel continued. "I could become a professor, or a chair in one of the medical departments, wait thirty years, and still, it won't open any of the DEMEM doors for me. However, if I do the right things, and do them well, perhaps that's the edge I will need. So, you can give me a kick in the butt and throw me out of here, or you can allow me to continue on my way. I promise not to make any disturbances."

"But why don't you go straight to the Judiciary and become a volunteer there?"

"No! First because it is very boring. Second because I would have to take a course, study some notebooks, and pass an exam and other complications to enter... *if* I enter. It is much more difficult to climb over there."

"How would you know? Who told you?"

"I am nosy snot, remember?"

"Did somebody tell you all that?"

"Yes, I stuck my nose in over there already."

"Uuuuuhh... And who helped you find out and learn all this?"

"Dr. Maggiolo and Dr Etcheverry."

"So, the big shots of the morgue... and from the Forensic Institute? Hmm... I see."

"Yes. Them."

"Aaaahhhh."

Again, there was silence. Daniel waited. He had no intention in revealing his plans.

"And... but... and how do *they* know all that?"

"Because Dr. Etcheverry is Deputy Director of DEMEM. And who do you guess is Secretary General?

"Who?"

Daniel didn't reply but looked at MacLagan sideways.

"Dr. Maggiolo," said Martinez.

"Aaaahhhh."

"Because..."

"You're smart. You little rascal, you are something."

"And have you been calculating all this like that?"

"No, Domínguez. Things turned out like this. I don't know why I got into the morgue; I don't know why I got into anatomy. Things turned out that way."

"Are you going to do the course for the judicial?"

"Yes, but they only give the course to those who are recommended. I already asked to do that course, but they said no. I have to find a way to get in."

They kept talking, kept asking questions, until the subject was exhausted, and Daniel got up to leave.

"Well, I'm going. If later you decide something, then let me know." He stayed still and did not speak anymore.

MacLagan and Martinez looked at him without quite understanding. Intelligent as they were, they sensed and felt that there was another reason or reasons why Daniel was there, although they knew that this was not the time to inquire. Something just didn't add up. Daniel looked at them, knowing what the two of them were thinking and knew that it was time to leave. He got up and went to the door. He got to the street, breathed fresh air, and this time he went for a walk on 18 de Julio Street to distract himself. He knew that the step he was taking and the steps he was going to take were risky, but he had thought about it a lot and was not thinking of changing his course. He knew that if he did not take that step, he would regret it forever. He planned to take it by lying to whoever he had to.

He reached 18 de Julio Street and started to walk among the thick crowd. Men, women, and couples were passing by. The shops offered beautiful clothing, the aromas of the coffee shops were inviting, a street vendor was selling ties and watches, another was selling magazines. A kiosk added aromas of hot chocolate and newspapers. He loved walking among the crowd and feeling his senses stimulated. He reached Plaza Libertad (Freedom Square) and sat on one of the benches to watch passersby. The hot peanut guy was near there yelling "Hot peanuts, hot peanuts, come and see how Daniel gets in trouble."

"To hell with this guy," he thought.

"Hot peanuts! Come and learn how Daniel lied to the detectives!" yelled the man. "Hot peanuts."

I don't like this peanuts guy, thought Daniel.

He got up, crossed Freedom Square, and got a chocolate bar at the kiosk.

Chapter 10

With his comings and goings to the headquarters, taking photos, writing reports, and giving sworn statements, Daniel got to know other inspectors as well as thieves, prostitutes, and criminals. He met several other inspectors and sub-commissars. There was a sub-commissar inspector, however, who he had met already and who was called officer Gomez, and who they called, "Urine Gomez," a very nice guy. Daniel had talked to him occasionally but didn't think it was prudent to ask why they called him that. *Urine, gee, why would he be called that?*

He continued with his duties—hospital, anatomy, morgue, and police headquarters—while getting used to his routine, when a new problem faced him. Unexpectedly, the David Lewinsky situation fell into his lap and diverted him from the path he had set out.

And just like that, Daniel jumped from corpses to problems.

One Saturday, when he went to a talk at the Hashomer Hatzair Club, the Zionist organization to which he belonged, he ran into a problem. David Lewinsky, a longtime friend, was wanted by the armed forces. Not that he was clean. Daniel knew that he was cooperating increasingly with the revolutionary group Tupamaros and that this was going to happen sooner or later. Even his sister Dorita knew. But Lewinsky, an engineering student, highly intelligent, and a great lover of science fiction like him, stubborn as none, continued with what he considered "a historical commitment."

"It's my responsibility, Daniel," he had told him a year earlier. "The Tupamaros are the only ones who dared to fight against the political corruption and are now fighting against this dictatorship. They fight for freedom and against social injustice.

"Listen, David," he had told his friend, "Getting too close to them can burn you."

"No, you listen, Daniel. The National Liberation Movement of the Tupamaros is the only political movement that does something against what President Pacheco Areco did. That man suppressed freedom of speech, treated poor people like slaves, enforced a state of military emergency, and repealed all constitutional safeguards.

"Stop, David. Your family..."

"Oh, shut up, Danny, wake up. That government imprisoned political dissidents, used and still uses torture and... and brutally represses liberal demonstrations. It is killing the people, Danny. That's why I secretly—"

"They are and have been a left-wing urban guerrilla group, David. Many of them have died or been imprisoned already."

"Yeah yeah..."

"David, listen to me. Bullets fly in all directions when there's a confrontation."

"They fight for freedom and equality; for a better Uruguay; for salaries and health care and... and social justice for everyone, not just for a select few."

"Listen, I know you're right, of course. I'm not against you. But the Tupamaros movement is engaged in political kidnappings, armed propaganda, and assassinations. They are armed communists. What do you think your collaboration can bring?"

"A free Uruguay. This country belongs to everybody, not just a few. Having your kids eating supper every night and go to school every day is not communism, it's just being human."

They didn't make any progress with those arguments. David was very stubborn and very socialist. No argument would make him change, so Daniel continued along his own path.

Now, great ideologist and great socialist, David, was locked in the basement of his uncle's house without being able to see the light of day. *A small personal price to pay*, he might say. But houses of several family members had been searched looking for him. Three of his relatives were harshly interrogated by the army Joint Forces. They were after him.

"They are after his head, Daniel, and they are going to find him," said Dorita, his sister. "I don't know what to do... they are going to kill him! Ay, Daniel, I must do something... he's my brother."

And so, unwittingly, this new situation fell into his hands thanks to Dorita, David's bigmouthed sister.

And what a sister that Dorita. Of medium height, dark brown hair, large and very Jewish nose, thick and sexy lips, some enchanting breasts and with hips that invited action. He had dated her a few times in the past, seeking perhaps comfort, perhaps something else. They had met at a class on Zionism organized by the Hashomer Hatzair social club and Daniel had liked how argumentative and informed she was. Initially he did not want to pay attention to her because she was his friend's sister, and he did not want problems. However, the second time he saw her in the Hashomer he noticed that she had made a very serious and fatal mistake: she had come with glasses and dressed in a dark blue Lacoste shirt, tight, and with a very loose bra, which allowed visuals of a certain abundance in her front. To make matters worse, she put on a very good perfume, Opium, and that increased her attractiveness and her bad luck. Daniel couldn't ignore those details. Her firm breasts softened his brain and triggered sparks of lust. He tried to resist her, he did the best he could, but his flesh was weak and an hour later he invited her to go for a coffee. They went to a café in Pocitos neighborhood where they chatted for a couple of hours and then went for a walk. By the time he realized he had made a mistake and that he might not be able to control himself, it was too late. He decided to take her home and make the effort to hold on and say goodbye without touching her, but she had also made up her mind to not miss the opportunity. Without Daniel knowing it, she had taken him to the door of her aunt's house, who was in the Piriápolis Resort at that time. She invited him inside in a very innocent way to have some tea, Daniel hesitated, *A tea, Daniel, nothing else.* As they entered the apartment, Daniel felt that he was entering a danger zone. They savored the infusion in silence feeling an inner fire that grew. Daniel couldn't believe that his mind and body were so possessed and focused on just one thing. His mind raced thinking of the world of warm surprises he could find under that shirt. He wanted to kiss her slowly, he wanted to do everything slowly and just start with kisses. And perhaps see each other another day. He wanted to wait and then see how things were going to develop, because, after all, she was the sister of a friend, and the sisters of friends deserved respect and are not to be touched. It was one of the laws of the street.

However, suddenly, perhaps pushed by his slowness and determined not to let that moment pass, she took off that blue Lacoste, and stayed there, close to him, with her glasses, her aroma, and her warm body. Daniel stared at her, flushed, still in his amazement, while the image of her breasts produced bursts of blood in his brain and sparks between his neurons. He kissed her, quietly and slowly, knowing that there was no hurry, and then lowered the straps of her blue silk bra and slid it down past her elbow. He was astonished admiring her attractiveness and feeling the intensity of her growing aroma. Dorita shone like a sun while Daniel freed her from her clothes and looked at her as the beautiful woman she was. They embraced, sharing each other's heat, enjoying the contact of their skins. They took the time to love each other with care.

What a woman Dorita Lewinsky was. Enchanting. Lovely. The passion of that night ignited a relationship that lasted several weeks, in which they did not tire of getting intimate and discovering each other in the love-motels of the area. They also delighted themselves in cafes, confectioneries, and went to the movies, and two of the tango bars that Daniel liked, although she was not good at tango. Sometimes she would bring a cake to the hotel.

However, Daniel had to leave her because she was very possessive, she wanted to go out every day without caring that he had to study, and she did not like at all that he taught using corpses. "You've got necrophilia," she said, "you like the corpses more than me, wash yourself with detergent before touching me, did you hear me?" And she hated that he went to the police headquarters. To top it off, she was not interested in dancing or reading, and, even worse, she implied that she was looking for a firm boyfriend to marry, which made Daniel very nervous. Very nervous. Even worse still, she came to his house, became close to Lila, Daniel's mother, and several times she tried to fix his room and make it neater. The situation became critical when one day Daniel returned from anatomy. "Ah, hi Daniel," his mother said from the kitchen. "Dorita is in your room, reading." Upon entering his room, he found her naked from the waist up and Daniel had to dress her in a hurry and tell her that with her mother at home, no. "There will be no games of this kind, Dorita."

Those signs did not bode well, and Daniel saw a possible pregnancy coming through *carelessness*, so he opted for a cordial escape. He talked to her and explained to her his feelings and other stories, and they separated but stayed friends.

Luckily, she was not hurt because she understood that he was not what she was looking for. "Besides, I don't like that there are so many corpses in your life," she said, "and way too many policemen." However, later, every so often, she would call him when she was alone and needed comfort, or he called her when he needed a breast to drown his despair. They knew they could count on each other.

So here was Dorita telling him about her brother.

"Daniel, they will catch him sooner or later..." she said crying. "What can be done? "They are going to kill him."

She would come to his home after hours, lay in his bed and cry while Daniel and his mother felt saddened and impotent confronted with her pain. They knew, too, that he would be caught, tortured, and sent to the Freedom Prison, perhaps never to be seen again.

Daniel did not know what to say, nor did he know how to help. He was sure that the end of David could come soon, as those things were happening often.

Poor David's body would be found in some garbage dump... if they found it at all. *Poor David*, he thought. The idea that his friend was going to get caught sooner or later, and that he had no chance seemed horrible to him. Daniel had known him for years; he knew his parents and his family.

What if there was a way? he thought.

No, he concluded. There was nothing that could be done.

"Daniel," Dorita cried, "they are going to kill him. The dictatorship is going to torture him to death. He's my little brother... my only brother."

It was terrible to see her crying like that. But how can she not cry?

They went for a walk, he tried to console her, but there was no consolation. Daniel didn't know what to do. "There is nothing that can be done. How scary this whole thing is."

"They are going to kill him like a dog," she cried. "Worse. We don't even kill dogs like that."

There was no way out. Poor David. Poor family.

What if there was a way? he thought when he came home, meditating. "*What if... what if...?*"

He tried to sleep but couldn't. He rolled over in bed. He tried not to see the nocturnal visions, which seemed more intense that night. He sat. He was sweaty. Talked to himself. Thought. He remembered something. Sometimes life puts you in unusual circumstances so that you do something unusual... *What? Who the hell said that?* he said to himself. *Ah, hmm... it had to be that old man of the temple*. Bernstein, the rabbi. He decided to go talk to the old man.

The following afternoon he entered the Vada Ir Synagogue on Canelones Street—an old building, full of old prayer books and even older furniture, one of the favorite temples of the European Jews that had come to Uruguay escaping from the Nazi wave. The rabbi's wife glared at Daniel and said, "Why don't you leave him alone?"

"I need to talk to him."

"Again...? leave him alone, Daniel, let him rest."

Rabbi Bernstein was at his desk studying a chessboard. Daniel greeted him and sat down.

"Yes, just enter without asking permission, stupid boy" he said. "Didn't they teach you to knock on the door? Hmm, oops, you have a wet dog face."

"Yes, I have."

The rabbi put the game pieces together and said: "Start playing and talk to me. I can see something is wrong with you."

Daniel began to tell him what was happening, while moving the pieces. He told him about the hospital, the anatomy class, the morgue, the headquarters, and David and Dorita. Rabbi Bernstein listened to him with increasing attention. The room smelled of old books. A Torah roll was open on another desk.

Daniel moved a pawn and later the bishop.

"No, leave that bishop alone. Tell me Daniel, didn't it occur to you that the dead were not going to lead you to anything good?"

Daniel put down his bishop and moved the knight.

"Your life is a sea of dead people, Daniel. And every time you come is even worse."

"I'm afraid so."

"You entered the red circle. No one made you enter or pushed you to enter. You entered of your own free will. Do you remember what we had talked about?"

"Yes, I remember, but... it's not like that, it's just..."

"And you also went out with Dorita. You hammered the nails in your own body."

"Good...well..."

"And in the street, Daniel," the rabbi insisted, "haven't they ever told you in the street that common wisdom that if you mess with a friend's sister sooner or later there will be trouble?"

"Well... we—"

"And... and... especially Dorita. *Dorita*, Daniel! Please. With Dorita! Stupid boy! She puts her breast on a hook and you go and take a bite like... like.... But did you grow up in a basement?"

"Well, she's good... and I thought that—"

"It's like you and I never had a conversation. You can't sleep with whomever you want. I see you thought that out very well. You thought that with your groin, boy!" The rabbi's bishop swallowed Daniel's horse. "You want coffee?"

"Hmm... I didn't see that move coming," Daniel answered. Then, knowing that Bernstein's coffee was horrible, he added, "No thanks, I'm okay."

"Are you still having your night visions?"

"Here and there. Sometimes I see people at night, but I don't know what they want."

"Who are they?"

"Who knows."

"Only in your room?"

"Only in my room."

"You must have opened a gate somewhere."

"What gate?"

"It's too complicated."

"Well, I didn't."

"Maybe those visions want you to get out of the police headquarters."
"Maybe..." Daniel said, shaking his head unconsciously.
"By God, Daniel. What are you doing there with those butchers?"
"I'm... I am working on my path. Two professors have advised me."
"A path...? Hmm...And the morgue has to do with that?
"Yes."
"And your visions? Didn't they get worse with all that?"
"Yes. More of them come to me now. I don't know what to do about it. I don't understand why."
"Hmm... I guess one day you'll know. Maybe they will tell you how to improve your chess. You would have to play more often. Mmm... or maybe they want to tell you that you should not sleep with your friend's sister."
"Oh, please."
"Hmm... and now you're at a crossroads, again. I don't know how to solve this. There's nothing in the Torah that helps you... nor can it help David." He also had to know he would get in trouble. "And stop playing, I see that today your chess is a disaster."
The rabbi thought for a while, then said, "Those visions are coming from beyond. You better know that."
"Beyond what? What do you mean...? Maybe I'm imagining them."
"You're not."
"So, what are they?"
"Gee, I don't know. I figure..." The rabbi paused then finally said, "Nothing... forget it."
"But what can I do? I mean, with David."
"You mean besides no longer plowing his sister's field?"
"Come on..."
The rabbi chuckled then straightened up. "I don't know Daniel. I don't know how to help him... nor how to help you. But... but... hmm... I'm afraid of what might happen to him. It scares me."
"Me too."
"Daniel, look at yourself! Corpses, morgue, police headquarters and visions. What... what does that suggest to you?"
"I don't know. I don't know whether there is a connection there."
Bernstein sighed, shook his head, and reclined in his chair.
"But there's one thing that... eh... I don't know... something worries me about... about the things you told me. I don't think you like the dead so much, but rather... hmm.... How to say it? It's like something leads you down a path and you don't realize it. I don't know. It's that... it's like the dead aren't your goal

but part of your path... eh... like they are on the way to reach a certain goal. Something like that."

"I don't know... yes, maybe. Hmm... I don't know either."

"Listen to me, Daniel. There are people who stay their whole lives in the same house, on the same corner of the same neighborhood, and don't care to know anything else. And there are others who go out, move around, eager to discover other things and live in different places.

"What do I... what are you telling me?

"I don't know. I don't know. But knowledge is a fickle friend anyway. What we know today is meaningless tomorrow. Meaningless or wrong. You're going to get into something, and I don't know what it is. Perhaps your visions will clarify it for you. You're like... like you're going into something, but I see the path you've already traveled, I see a path, but I don't see where you're going in it."

"I feel lost, Rabbi, with the David situation."

"Me too, but I tell you what I told you before, that sometimes life places you in unusual situations allowing you to dare doing unusual actions."

"I remember that, but I don't know what to do about it."

"No? Good luck then."

Daniel stood up. Looked at the books while thinking. He didn't know what to say. After a short while he said goodbye to the rabbi, got out of the room and headed for the door of the synagogue. As he was leaving, he saw the rabbi's wife again who told him, "Happy now? Now, leave him alone. Let him rest."

"I needed to talk to him," Daniel replied.

"Well, you already did, you screwed up my day, now go away and don't come back."

"If you could understand..."

"I don't want to understand anything coming from you. Out."

He walked down Canelones Street. He felt disturbed. Two blocks later he saw the door of the El Ensuenio. He thought about Carmen, how has she been? He went inside.

"Carmen is busy, Daniel, she is with a client," he was told, "you wanna wait, or can you come later?"

Daniel turned to leave.

"Lucia is free if you want..."

"No, thanks." He decided to keep walking.

Daniel took Soriano Street, had a coffee at the bar by Soriano and Rio Branco. He then went home. He couldn't study. He watched television until bedtime, then he laid down, but half an hour later he sat on the bed, *What if there was some way to help him... in an unusual way*? What if there was? How? *How could I help David*?

He laid down and tried to sleep. The haze of an image appeared to him. It was shaped like a man. "No," he said. "Not today. Leave me alone."

He went to the kitchen, drank some water.

Something unusual? Unusual... Like what?

The he went back to his room. After a while three more images showed up in a haze. They were barely moving and had their hands on their heads.

"But what do you want?" he asked in a hush. He got no answer, then he fell asleep.

In the morning he got up, had coffee, and went to class. He was thinking most of the day about what to do. If they catch him, he's going to end up like the others, dead. What to do...? *What unusual thing can I do?*

"Oh, Daniel, they are going to kill him," Dorita cried. She was right, they were going to kill him.

What if I ask for advice? But who? Who could advise me? Nobody, nobody.

At midmorning, while in class, the secretary of the floor came to tell him to call home, that there was a woman crying there.

"Damn, you did it, Daniel!" voiced Claudia. "Your smarty-pants impregnated somebody."

"But why's she crying?" asked another student.

"Wouldn't you be... look at him!" replied Claudia to waves of laughter. Then she said to Daniel, "Good luck, you atrocious animal."

"Shut up, Claudia."

The call was from his mother. Dorita was in his room crying. "What did you do to her?"

"Let her cry. There's nothing I can do."

Claudia had come with him and had heard part of the dialogue.

"Let her cry?" said Claudia. "That's all? The poor thing is asking for help... and you.... You're a monster, Daniel!"

"Who's with you?" asked his mother. "Ah, the other one, eh? That's why Dorita is crying."

"No, no, listen, it—"

"Tell her!"

"Tell me what? Who is she?"

"Shut up. No, not you. Mom, I'll call you later."

"But Dorita..."

Daniel hung up.

"You and that Dorita," said Claudia.

"Ssshhh, Claudia, it's complicated." He pulled his hair. "I don't know what to do."

"Well, as a man, you should go and give her some support. Maybe you should marry that Dorita, be considerate, it's your child after all. Be responsible, and maybe..."

"What? What do you think happened, weirdo?" said Daniel, then he started to describe the problem with David and his sister Dorita.

"Oh, oh, I'm sorry. I misunderstood. Gee... the situation is just horrible."

"I know. You see?"

"Yeah," said Claudia, bowing her head. After a moment she looked back up. "What are you going to do?"

"I don't know. The reality is just there's nothing I can do."

"I wish I could help."

"Sit here with me. Help me think."

"No," said Claudia. "Honestly, you attract problems. They come to you out of nowhere, like fruit flies on bananas. You are not going to involve me this time."

"Claudia, I need to talk about..."

"No, no. You're dangerous. Bye."

He didn't know who to talk to. There was no one to get advice from. His thoughts mortified him. *A friend is going to be tortured and killed and there is nothing I can do.*

He walked in the street thinking, barely aware of the passing cars.

Worried, apprehensive, he decided to go talk to Martinez, the section chief at the police headquarters, thinking that perhaps he could provide some idea of what to do. He went to his office, nervous and scared, and began to tell him how much this boy worried him and to inquire whether Martinez could give him an idea of what to do.

Martinez cut him off, angrily. "Are you an idiot?" he shouted at him. He lit a cigarette, blew the smoke out hard, then added, "We don't talk about that; we don't talk about these things, Daniel."

Silence.

"I told you and the others told you too," said Martinez, with furrowed brows. "We don't even speak about those things. We all tried to give you hints about keeping your mouth shut and nose out. Even MacLagan, for Christ sakes!"

"But um... I'm just—"

"Get out of my office. But... damn you are crazy!"

Daniel realized his mistake, he shrunk, fell silent and left the office, very worried. He decided to leave in a hurry and go outside to calm down and think.

It was a mistake to try to talk to Martinez. *Gee...what a mistake.*

He did not know what to do and worse, he was already scared for having told it to a strong officer of the headquarters. He didn't even want to wait for the elevator and headed for the stairs. Yet when he was going down the stairs, Martinez came, seeming bigger and meaner than ever, approached him with his Jews-eating face and said in his ear, "Tomorrow, five pm, corner of Colonia and Tristan Narvaja. Don't even talk to your family," and went off saying "not even to your mother!" and ran a finger across his neck from side to side, as if to indicate that if he said something, they would cut his throat. Daniel was left with weak knees, not understanding much, nervous, knowing that he had gotten into serious trouble. *I'm dead*! Once in the street, his voice echoed in his mind saying, *You don't talk about those things... not even your parents.* He was already in trouble, again, and a cramp in his belly was predicting a bad outcome. He felt that one doesn't come out clean out of this. *What did I do? They're going to kill me on that corner.*

"You don't talk about such things," MacLagan had once said.

What did Martinez mean by that?.... umm.... Martinez...? *No, it couldn't be.*

But who was this Martinez? He knew very little about him. He knew that he was not a weakling, but a very brave and mysterious man. "He's a real macho," Pranchin had said of him. "Martinez can be very cruel," they had told him, "Take care of yourself and be very careful, Daniel." Domínguez had warned him. "He's a scary man, Daniel," Urine-Gomez told him.

He imagined himself lying in the street, shot, with his blood and his life running away. *Horrible*, he thought.

Now... what to do?

At night, lying down, he didn't have any answers. The next morning, he asked himself what would happen on that corner. *They'll just shoot me there*, he told himself. In the head like the others. Probably won't even get out of the car. *They'll shoot me from the window.*

And even if they let him live, Daniel figured that if the dictatorship system finds out, he'd lose everything, his studies, his career, his job, his future, everything. *Everything*. He was very worried.

For sure they'll put me in the trunk of a car and throw me to the dogs, he thought. His mind did not rest.

"Morning news, morning news, a handsome medical student riddled with bullets was found at the intersection of Colonia and Tristan Narvaja Streets," he said aloud, holding an air microphone to his face, "Young Uruguayan Jew shot dead." His mind did not rest. He had a stomachache, *Oh no, another one, not now.*

When the time came, standing there on that corner, confused, not knowing what was happening, Daniel felt that he had ants in his pants and a snake in his belly. He was looking at the windows of nearby houses for a sniper. A woman passed by, then another, and then a man with a puppy. What to do? Who was he waiting for? My executioner? he wondered. *Young student stabbed in the street*. His belly started to hurt again. A man with glasses passed by holding a map of Montevideo with a confused face and asked Daniel for directions on how to get to a place in the downtown area. Daniel had to try to calm his mind and connect the words, but when he was explaining, the man gave him a slip of paper with two phone numbers and said that first they needed four passport photos of the boy and his complete information. "When you get them, call those numbers for instructions."

"Color of his hair? Long or short? Wears mustache?

Daniel explained.

"He must change. He must change. Change to very short hair, very blond, remove the mustache, earring in one ear. Four photos. He warned the boy must stay where he was, not to move. "He should not even breathe; did you hear me?" He told Daniel that he couldn't talk to anyone, "Anyone! Do you get it?" They would *kill* him. "Tread very carefully. He can't even tell his parents." And he added that the responsibility was all Daniel's and the risk too, that he should not make a mistake, that the plan was that with new identification David would leave Uruguay as a tourist, to tell the boy not to say anything to anyone, and added, "and now go and keep walking like nothing happened here, go ahead. Leave. Go. Then he added aloud, "Thank you very much for the instructions," speaking in a grateful way and smiling.

Daniel saw him leave and later getting into a large black Mercedes Benz half a block away while he kept walking half crazed with fright. Sweat ran down his shirt. It took him several blocks and two trips to the bathroom to calm down.

Crap!... and now? he thought. *What have I gotten myself into?*

He called Dorita, met her in a cafe, and told her what happened. She looked at him with amazement, without understanding but grateful. "Do not ask me. Don't say anything."

She asked many questions that Daniel couldn't answer. He told her that all this had scared him a lot, that there was danger, to hurry up and take all possible precautions and to not to talk about it with anyone. "Don't use the phone." Then he went home.

The next day his mother came from the street market saying that a neighbor who worked in a bookstore had given her a book that he had ordered. "That guy was so nice. Said the book is for you."

The book was tied with a thread. Daniel opened it. A small envelope peeked from inside, he saw the photos, and a piece of paper with data. *David was now very blond.* He went to the bar on the corner, where he was welcomed by a cloud of rum and gin that costumers were enjoying, called the number they had given him, was told to go out for a walk along Tomas Diago Street in half an hour.

Three blocks from his house, a car passed slowly and a woman inside said, "Daniel?"

He approached her, gave her the envelope saying out loud, "I'm going to buy the barbecue and then I'll go there," and continued walking with hard buttocks and his heart beating fast. The trees spied on him, and the passing dogs suspected him. A passing man looked at him with accusing eyes. *They all know, even the dogs.*

The following day, when he was in class at the Hospital de Clinicas, a doctor came and gave him a CASMU medical magazine with an envelope. He told Daniel that the boy had to be very well dressed, with a very elegant jacket and expensive pants. "Has to look like an elegant rich man, perfumed, with an expensive suitcase," and that he was leaving with the TTL bus to São Paulo in two days, to say goodbye to his parents only. "Only to his parents, no one should know anything," Also no one makes any telephone calls, "Forbidden to use the telephone," that they should not speak to anyone, that each person notified multiplied the risk, and gave him the tickets and other details. In Sao Pablo, members of the organization were waiting for him, and they would give him passage, money, and safe harbor wherever he wanted. "Listen to me well," the doctor added, "one mistake and they kill him." And then he turned around and left.

Daniel stayed there, standing, feeling that he had suddenly entered something he did not know about. He had thought that by passing the photos and giving the data that would be the end of his intervention in the matter. Yet it was clear that there was an organization, and that suddenly he, inevitably, was already involved with it. If he backed off, the boy could be caught and perhaps killed. If he continued, he would become even more linked. *Ay.* Nazi executioners would soon catch him and dismember him to teach others a lesson. His heart stopped and connected with his guts. A cramp brought bad news. Daniel went to the bathroom, where, sitting there, he tried to meditate and find a way out, but the options were clear. If he failed, David could lose his life. There wasn't much to think about.

Claudia walked down the corridor and said, "You look like you got into one of your moods. I'm leaving, don't talk to me."

"Listen, Claudia."

"No. I know your face."

He called Dorita, nervous, and told her to come to the hospital with the excuse of seeing a relative of hers who was recovering. She came by taxi and went up to the ninth floor where Daniel was waiting for her. He gave her the tickets and all the information, including the new identity card for her brother with a different name and surname, blond in the photo, and explained the plan. He explained about the TTL bus plan and told her not to talk about it with anyone because it could cost her brother his life. He stressed the need for absolute secrecy. He told her that he would see her in two days at the TTL bus station.

Dorita turned pale, she asked many questions that Daniel could not answer.

"No more questions!"

She wanted to hug him, but the shock held her back. She leaned against the wall, tearing up.

Daniel told her that he would call her the next day at her house asking for her aunt, if she said good things to him then it will mean that everything was going well, if not, to let him know quickly. "Be very careful, Dorita, things will be in your hands."

She left amazed and trembling.

Daniel tried to continue with his routine as best he could, but at night he didn't sleep because of fear. The images moved faster and were brighter. He took his pillow and went to sleep in the living room, "So maybe now you'll leave me alone," he told the images.

The next day he tried to teach his anatomy class in a normal way, but he was anxious. He smoked, looked out the window. He had to open the abdomen of the cadaver, something that in general he found attractive and interesting, but he opened it quickly and badly, moved the omentum and intestines to the right and to the left, then again to the right, from one side to the other, nervous.

"Are you looking for something in those guts?" asked a student.

"Hey, did you lose your keys in there?" asked another student.

"Eh?" he replied before coming back to present. "No, nothing. I slept badly again."

"Surprised to hear you slept at all," another student said.

That afternoon he called Dorita from a pizzeria.

"Ah, hello, hi, and... How is your aunt?"

“Oh, thanks for asking,” she said. “Yes. She is much better, yes. She is improving, yes. Thanks. Yes.”

That evening, he had a silent dinner at home. His mother couldn’t understand why he was nervous, so he had to give some excuses. He ate some of the spinach pie that his neighbor Estela had prepared for them, then he went to bed. Images came again, but he was too nervous to pay them attention and asked them to leave him alone and let him sleep.

Chapter 11

The following day, after two hospital meetings, he left early and went to the bus station, nervous all the way. There were the two huge blue buses there with *TTL logos*. There was a police guard and an army guard inspecting documents. He waited. He lit a cigarette. *What happened*? he wondered. *Why aren't they coming*? People and cars passed from right to left. The policemen were standing as if they knew they were waiting for a special victim. Two of them had machine guns and nervous faces. *Oops, and now?*

Minutes were passing by. Nervousness was in the air. *This is not going to work.*

Even the guards were nervous. *They know.*

David was nowhere to be seen.

The plan failed. He was caught.

After a while, a noisy family appeared, with a blond son very well dressed and carrying some expensive bags, wearing a silk scarf. His father got out of the car right in front of the policemen and started warning him about the women of Brazil and about not getting a sexually transmitted disease.

"And don't eat what you don't know."

The guy was happy, and everything seemed fine, and no problem was going to occur.

"Don't spend your money on women," the mother warned him aloud.

The policeman next to him smiled and raised his index like agreeing with his mother.

At that moment, one of the soldiers carrying a machine gun called the officer who was inside. The officer came out and started talking to the soldier. Two more soldiers came. David was happy, unaware, smiling a few feet from them, and mixing with other people. The officer began asking questions and reviewing documents. Some people got worried and started moving to both sides.

Something was going on. The soldiers were nervous.

Apparently the officer was alarmed by something. He made gestures.

Another soldier came and spoke on the radio.

That's it, they found out.

The officer started pointing at people. A woman was resisting and screaming. A man was taken inside. An upset officer approached David. The seconds ran. Something had happened. The officer talked to David, aloud, demanding something. *Oh, they're going to grab him.*

But the soldier that approached him took a woman next to him by the arm and led her inside while she screamed. A man was pushed to the ground. There were more screams outside and inside the TTL station. Several policemen became nervous, but the scene quickly calmed down and they continued their routine check. Daniel's heart leaped out of his chest and immediately connected with his guts. *Gee, not now.* They went through David's documents, but he didn't even look like anyone who might even seem like who they were looking for. David looked at Daniel from a distance, moving his eyebrows and winking. He said goodbye with a nod, got on the bus, and after a while the big TTL bus left and disappeared. Daniel was left with goose bumps, legs made of ice, a racing heart, and crampy guts. *Whoa. What a scare.*

Mission accomplished. Uuuuffff!!

When the bus had left, and Daniel could move and breathe, he ran to the bathroom at the TTL station. *Ay, that spinach pie,* he thought while sitting. When he came out, Dorita approached him with her parents and her family, they looked at him without saying hello but with tears in their eyes that reflected everything they felt. Daniel saw in their looks how worried they had been that David would be arrested and die tortured by the dictatorship and how relieved and grateful they were. They made him tear up. That David, who was for him nothing more than a friend, but was for them their only son and brother and the light of their eyes. He was their life and their hearts beat for him. Their fear, their pain and now their gratitude were enormous and were reflected in those tears of relief and joy. Daniel stood there, frozen by the emotions of the moment then couldn't hold himself and hugged them. They remained like that, in silence, crying, for a while, hugging each other. More tears. Kisses. Farewell. And they all left.

Daniel watched them leave, slowly recovered, and started to walk.

In the middle of the block, a young employee came running with an envelope in his hand. "Sir! Sir! Your receipt, sir! Your receipt and your key..." He gave Daniel the envelope. Daniel put it in his pocket and kept walking. Near the bus stop he put his hand in his pocket, *Receipt? Key?* he thought. *Why did I get it and what key?*

He took the envelope out of his pocket, where he found a long brown key attached to a piece of thick thread made of golden and red fine strings. *Damn. What's this*? A key ring was holding a large brown key and three small round pieces of metals with the same engravings he had seen before, the cross, the compass with the letter G, and now he saw that the third one had the Star of David; same as Maggiolo and Etcheverry showed him. He was mesmerized. He looked around. *Are they here*? He stood there wondering, *were they involved with this*?

With the key there was an attached TTL receipt that had something written on it:

1. **Remember a favor repays a favor.**
2. **Be careful what you ask for because I can give it to you.**

Gee... What's all this? And this message... what's it mean?

He examined the key; it was old and innocuous and did not indicate anything. It was not a padlock key or a modern key. It was a long, half-rusted key, the kind that was used to open gates long ago. He looked at the thread that held the key and examined the red and golden filigrees. How weird. What key could it be? Key to what, for what. What would that badge be? Daniel did not understand and was tired of trying to understand. *It's got to be a mistake.*

He started walking again and suddenly had goose bumps, like a chilled breeze comes in the night after a long hot wait. *No, this was not a mistake. It's a message.* A note, the thread, the key. It was sent to him by the one who had organized the escape from behind the curtain and indicated that he knew him... and that he was now somehow in debt to that organization.

Then yes, there is an organization here, he thought. *And they know who I am.* He knew right there that he had gotten himself into something big, too big, and into which he should not have gotten. *But I had no choice,* he said to himself. Had he not acted, David would have ended up dead.

He imagined himself being judged: *Sorry Mister Judge, I did it for David.*

Oh yes? Well kill the Jew with an ax then! shouted the neo-Nazi judge.

Oh... he fretted inside himself, *what did I do?*

He stayed the rest of the afternoon as if floating in his thoughts. That shitty thread, the key. What was happening here? Martinez... could he be linked to that? He had no answers, and he knew that under the circumstances, it was best not to ask questions or find out anything.

As before, he had no one to talk to because he could not talk to anyone=; Not even to his parents, his friends, or his uncles. He did not know of anyone who could answer his questions.

So, he went about his routine.

He did not dare to go to the headquarters for several days. He didn't know how to face Martinez or how to deal with the whole situation. How to deal with that mustached guy if one owes him such a favor? *What will he ask me in return?*

But a few days later he was asked to take some photos to headquarters and give an affidavit. Commissar Martinez passed him in the corridor, he saw him but did not even greet him, as was customary, giving him a message of silence. There was nothing to talk about. Daniel swallowed hard, loosened the knot in his gut, and went about his business.

As he left the police headquarters, a strange sensation came to him knowing that he had crossed an invisible line and had entered another field of which he knew nothing. This must be part of the red circle that Rabbi Bernstein was talking about. He walked, kicking dry leaves and sticks in the street, avoiding dog poop as per usual in Montevideo, and went to Freedom Square, one of the main squares of downtown, where he sat on the steps to watch people go by. *What is all this?* he thought for the millionth time. *What did I get myself into?* People passed by without looking at him, a child greeted him, couples passed by chatting. From his left came the smell of coffee from one of the cafes facing the square, and from his right the smell of hot peanuts from a street vendor. *Not this guy again.*

"Peanuts, fresh and hot," shouted the man. "Here! Here! Hot-hot little peanuts! Come and check Daniel's key! See how he got in more trouble!"

I don't like this guy, Daniel told himself. He looked around. The aroma of peanuts was attracting him, but the guy was making him nervous.

He decided not to get peanuts. He kept walking. The peanuts guy looked at him. *He knows.*

Chapter 12

Two or three days later, Dorita called him to invite him for dinner. She picked him up dressed in high heels, a tight dark green dress, loose bra, and plenty of bad intentions. Irresistible.

Daniel lived in a big apartment building and was waiting downstairs. As usual his mother, Marisa and two other neighbors were there chatting when Dorita got out of her car. They knew Dorita, and they realized she was coming with sultry ideas. They made some comments that made Daniel feel embarrassed.

"Shut up all of you," he replied. "Rest your tongues."

Dorita gave him a big kiss and greeted the speechless women. She took him for a dinner of prawns in golf sauce and bottle of Asti and from there straight to the Carrasco Inn, where she didn't let him remove her dress until *after* they made love. She then scratched his back to relax him and devoured his body with lust and fire. Daniel was carried away by the circumstances, and thanks to more Asti, he dedicated himself to loving her all night. She told him that her parents and family wanted to give him something important for what he had done.

"Dorita. I want nothing. There can be no payment. It is a matter of conscience."

"But... Daniel—"

"Dorita. How much can your brother be worth? How much can the life of a human being be worth? You see? There is no gift or money that can pay that."

She got teary and Daniel too.

"Dora, Dorita, your brother David is priceless. There is no gift that can give me more than having done what my conscience dictated and now having a clear mind. That peace in my mind and in yours is the best reward.

Her eyes filled with tears, and she started to cry. She cried for a long time, hugging a pillow, releasing the stress and panic she had felt for too many days, thinking her brother would die. He just hugged her and let her empty her pain, reassuring her and caressing her body until she calmed down. Later, in the shower, they took their time to appreciate each other.

He returned home at nine in the morning. Dorita got out of her car and hugged him, kissing him, and rubbing her body against his.

"I will always be in your debt, Daniel."

"We are even."

She got in her car and drove off. Daniel gave her a wave and a big smile as she left. When he turned around, he saw the morning battalion of neighbors, Estela, Marisa, and the Spaniard woman from next door, who were in full morning patrol, looking at him, smiling, and half astonished.

"Holy Mary Magnolia," said the Spaniard neighbor. "Look at you. Were you two wrestling?"

"Is she also your therapist, eh?" Estela said. "Does she always dress like that for um... *therapy*?"

"Did she forget her bra, or she only wears it before therapy?" asked Marisa, laughing.

"So, you went back to her? Hmm? Is there a marriage?"

"A shotgun wedding?" Estela asked, laughing. "Umm... an expecting belly?

"What an indecency."

He looked at them, wondering how they managed to stay up to date and how much time they would spend on the street. He went to sleep. He was already feeling much better. Dorita was good and helped him cleanse his soul a little.

When he woke up, it was already three in the afternoon. That Sunday night he had to be on call in the emergency room. He had traditional Sunday tortellini for lunch and sat down to watch television with his mother. Then they went for a walk together and at eight o'clock he was already in the emergency ward of the Hospital de Clinicas. His first case was a heart failure, which he handled with the doctor on duty. He opened a couple of abscesses and calmed a lady with migraine. With another patient, what appeared to be diverticulitis ended up being an appendicitis, and he went to the operating room with the surgeon. From there, the night was charged with fractures and small injuries, so around four in the morning he went to the sleeping room. Claudia was in his bed. "Lie down here and don't snore," Claudia told him. "And for god's sake don't start talking."

"Claudia, you've got to listen to..."

"Just shut up."

He fell asleep.

Daniel liked the emergency room rotations. He would see interesting cases, and there was always something new to learn. Heart disease, pneumonias, and all kinds of digestive diseases came through there. Traumatized, shot, dead, and alive, they were everyday bread. There were all kinds of wounds to stitch up, and he loved that. He sewed legs, arms, and scalps. He helped surgeons with complicated wounds, assisted orthopedists in fixing fractures, intervened in deliveries and cesarean sections. They discussed the complicated cases that arose. It was a great pleasure for Daniel to be there, and a great experience. In his classes he learned theoretical medicine, and in the emergency ward he put it all into practice.

Two or three days a week, his workday in the emergency ward was long. He would usually sleep between four and seven in the morning, dressed and wearing his coat, sometimes with Claudia, sometimes with Marta or Liliana; when he woke up one of them would give him coffee and a piece of pastry or cake. On Thursdays it was his turn to bring something, so he would bring croissants and Dobosh cake to share with everybody. They were all nice to each other.

From the night in the emergency room, he would go to class in the morning, then get some fast food at noon, and from there to teach anatomy in the School of Medicine. After that, a quick visit to the morgue where sometimes they would wait for him with certain autopsy parts to photograph. He would complete a couple of reports while eating a piece of cake that they saved for him, drink a dirty coffee, and then take the bus or a taxi to the police headquarters to leave the photos, maybe sign a statement or talk to one of the officers or agents. On occasions, when he left the Anatomy Department, he would go down the white staircase of death, already immune to his ghosts and Nazis, and he would go out into the street through the door of the morgue where a plainclothes policeman, or an inspector, or an officer of a funeral company did him the favor of taking him to the police headquarters after they stomped out a cigarette or crumpled a coffee cup. If he was told by the agent they'd take him home later, he made up excuses to avoid it. He did not want his neighbors to see him arriving in a police car and even less in a hearse.

A few days later Daniel met Pranchin in the corridors of the headquarters, who told him:

"Hi, Carmen kid. We were already missing you."

Pranchin was smiling at him. He was a good guy, with a good face and an easy smile, the kind of guy you'd loan money to and not wonder if he'd pay you back, or the type to loan you money and not want anything in return. Skinny, long-nosed, disheveled, he was always wearing ugly floral shirts, a wrinkled suit, and an ugly tie, badly knotted, and that never matched. His full name was Julio Donnatto Pranchínnetti, but he was called Pranchin, and he was an inspector officer for the homicide division as well as sub-commissar of the second criminology division. He was of Italian blood and that's why he got along so well with Martinez. It always seemed like he had slept with his clothes on. Sometimes he wore a small hat or beret to cover his bald scalp. With a half-smoked cigarette hanging from the corner of his mouth like it had been glued there since his teens, he looked like a homeless poor man who did not give away his great intelligence, his medals, or his enormous experience in solving crimes of all kinds. He had quite a brain, full of culture, books, and movies trivia, and he knew every corner of the city.

Domínguez was an inspector sergeant in the criminal surveillance department, but at the same time he was one of the officers of the CIC, the Criminal Investigation Center of the headquarters. A man with power; Daniel found him to be a nice and friendly individual. He was a very sweet guy, a little chubby, with slightly curly black hair. He was well groomed, always wearing nice, clean, and ironed shirts. He always smelled good and said he bought his cologne at the pharmacy at Rio Negro and San Jose. "I only use French colognes and imported condoms," he said. He looked like a movie actor. He was at the same time very Christian. "I am a man of God and women," he used to say. His specialty: recent widows, as Daniel found out. "They are the ones who are most in need, Daniel," he said. "Death is horrible. Many of those women, those daughters, suffered greatly with the death of their loved one. I release them, I help them. I know they need someone like me to free themselves from their anguish, something new to hold onto while letting the old one go." Then he proceeded to describe to Daniel and Cabrera the most intimate details of his love affairs. "However," he remarked, "on some occasions, if it is needed, I go through the sacrifice of helping one of the daughters..." He blew out smoke and leaned in. "Of course, if she's not *too* young," he added smiling. Daniel was again speechless when he heard that, while officer Cabrera laughed all the way. No one had the stomach to ask him how young was too young.

There was something very peculiar about that Domínguez. Every time he went to the morgue, several crows would perch on the trees and columns that surrounded the Courtyard of Sorrows. Their screech was typical. "Look," One-eye Juan told him one day, "you would think they were always there, but they leave when Domínguez is gone."

"Those crows are the spirits of the women that Domínguez screwed up," said Juan. "These are things that you don't know... and you won't understand.

That degenerate Domínguez is not the good guy you see. He has done bad things with many women and that is why—"

"What? What'd he do?"

"I'm not going to be the one to tell you. But the crows know, and one day they will take revenge."

"But what? What?"

"Leave it now. I don't like to talk about it. But... but you just don't use women like... like... Ah, just forget it."

Using his visits as an excuse, Daniel was learning a few things from the headquarters, such as where the technical section was, where the files were, and where was that mysterious section called Interpol. He was also realizing that the deputies and officers of the headquarters did not relate to the Joint Forces of the army, they stayed away from them and in no way considered themselves part of the repressive apparatus of the dictatorship.

Those Joint Forces were a combination of special trainees from the army and police department. They carried special uniforms, special pistols, were more aggressive and they considered themselves superior. They were part of the armed branch of the dictatorship. They would not respond to the chief of the police center since their main command was the General Command of the Joint Forces located in a fortified section of Montevideo. Nobody messed with them.

Daniel also met one of the chief deputies of the police headquarters, a certain Captain General Yamandu Solano Boresky, who apparently had a lot of power there. He was a tough, dry, serious man, who was rarely seen. Tall, broad, and with a mustache thick as Stalin's, this Captain Yamandu Boresky was head of the Homicide Division, the Criminal Investigation Department, and one of the main leaders of the headquarters command. He was a member of the General Staff and chief of Martinez's section. He stood and puffed out huge, with banana bunches for hands and bear legs, the son of a Russian mother who was said to have fought at Stalingrad and had been a beast.

"His mother killed Nazis, Daniel," Domínguez told him one day. "Go figure. That old woman killed Nazis, and some say she did it with her bare hands... imagine that."

"Ha! Yes, they say she did that alright," added an agent. "It's scary just to think about it."

"Scary for him," Domínguez said pointing to the other agent. "And his own mother was a semipro wrestler."

A couple of chuckles bubbled up.

That must be why Yamandu looks like Stalin, thought Daniel. He's got like an air of that dictator, and that must be the reason behind that hard face and those penetrating eyes.

"Take a look, Daniel," Pranchin told him one day. "Flies don't fly near Yamandu. You be careful."

Daniel also met Officer Stachenko, a son of Russians. *That must be the son of a bitch who made me nervous just by looking at me*, Daniel speculated. With that child-murderer attitude and that butcher face, like all Russians. The brutality of the Russian military was well known.

"Take care, because Stachenko and the Russian Yamandu are friends."

That was not good news. *Gee, two Russians in this place,* he thought.

Neither of them spoke to him since they looked at him with antipathy and gave clear signs of not wanting to see him in that place. *Sure. It must be because of my Jewish face.*

Chapter 13

Daniel learned a lot at the police headquarters, and discovered the different divisions, including the office of the Police General Staff and other secret rooms. He found everything very interesting and realized that some functions of certain offices were fascinating. He took the opportunity to find out why they called Gomez *Urine-Gomez*. "Because he is always calculating how much a person urinates according to their size and complexion," Cabrera told him, "And then he looks at you and says 'ah, today you must have urinated half a liter,' says it even to women on the bus, so we just don't like it."

"Yes," Domínguez emphasized, "and if he sees you just when you left the bathroom, he starts asking you questions about how much you peed and what color.

"He's a nosy guy. Very smart, yes, but he's a tough guy to deal with."

However, everyone admired the enormous wisdom that this Gomez had. "It's an encyclopedia, this guy. He knows everything."

"Also, this *Urine-Gomez* is a loving guy. Once a week he brings pastries from the Hamburg confectionery for everyone."

Daniel met a lot of people at the headquarters and got in touch with other agents, some of whom already knew him from his photographic work. He discretely interacted with the people from the different divisions, trying to guess if someone was talking to him about something related to the information center. *Will they give me an indication*?" he wondered. In one of the offices, he saw the Russian officer Stachenko again, a man with a dreadful face. Some said his name was Wiktor and others that his name was Boris. Not much was known about him. *Gee... this guy's uglier than an ogre's wart*, he thought. He just didn't like his looks or his face, Russian *dog, who knows how many Jewish girls you and your family have killed or raped, you damned Russian,* he kept thinking, remembering what the people of that country did in World War II.

In the end, he decided to go to visit Urine Gomez, who was having coffee with *Whiny Susan*, with the excuse of the photograph.

"Why do they call her *Whiny*?"

"Ah, Daniel, too many nickname-reveals in one day kills the kidneys," Gomez emphasized. "Hey, listen, by this time in the afternoon you must have already urinated three times and at least two hundred milliliters each time, yes? Tell me, share those details, I am your friend," he added with sweetness and great sympathy. "Was it yellowish or light?"

"Eh, yellowish, of course, but—"

"Do you shake well?"

"Oh, shut up, Gomez. And... hey, can I ask you something?"

"Oh, oh, here he comes with his questions again," said Susan. "I've got a headache already."

"Yes, go ahead," said Gomez.

He asked them various questions about the subdivisions and Urine explained it to him. The next day, just as an unimportant thing, he asked *Whiny* Susan to show him different offices, about which she complained but agreed to do it anyway, and so he got to know several areas such as the Logistics Department, Central Crime Office, Technical Center, the INTERPOL and even the Central Informatics Division, a huge office at the end of a corridor on the first floor full of computers and with a very restricted entrance. "You are not allowed to get near that door," Susan warned him. The antechamber of this information center had bars and two starchy, blue-dressed officers, with blue berets, armed with submachine guns between the bars and the door. They were sitting and had a telephone next to them. Three bayonets were hanging at the wall. A sign at the wall read, *Do Not Approach*. Susan and Daniel turned around.

"Yes, Daniel, they might be delighted in poking some holes in whomever tries to get in there."

"Oh, they are..."

"You can't even take this corridor, Daniel," Susan said. "See the red lines in the wall? They're a warning."

"Dangerous, eh?"

"Yes, Danny boy. They told me to warn you. The guards have orders to shoot."

This is it, Daniel told himself. *Now I know it for sure.*

"Who told you?"

"I don't know. From there, once inside, you can find a staircase that goes straight to the basement, which has a door on the ground floor, she said. "We know it from years ago, before it became the Information Center of the Joint

Forces. We know that both levels are full of computers and archives. At the lower level, outside, three or four blue berets watch the entrance. They have heavier machine guns, and guess what?"

"Grumpy attitudes?"

"Grenades!

"What!?"

"They told me to tell you that too, funny boy."

"But *who* told you?"

"Nobody, I didn't say anything, I don't know, I'm just showing you around," she said looking at him firmly with penetrating eyes.

Daniel understood. *Damn it*!

Susan was very nice.

Underground floor? he thought. *If this is an entrance to the basement room,* he thought, *one could also enter from the basement area. There must be a second door....* What would be in the basement? What could be in that room? However, he was disappointed to see that the entrance of that computer center was forbidden territory, and with aggressive soldiers guarding it. He later asked Urine about that place.

"The army doesn't allow anybody in there," he told him.

"Why?"

"Those computers get all the information from this headquarters and all the police stations and are linked with those of the army and those of the Joint Forces. They are even connected to the radios of our patrol cars. That room is totally forbidden. Only people from Interpol with permission from Yamandu or above can enter."

"Interpol?"

"Well... hmm... there's Interpol and there is another Interpol. The ones allowed there are the other ones, the Joint Forces' Interpol, see? Although we've also seen some strange-uniformed officers entering the place."

"The army and Joint Forces? Both?"

"Well, yes and no. Hmm... you should know. The dictatorship took the very best of the army and the police, trained them well in special ruthless management centers, gave them darker uniforms and more modern weapons, and those are now the Joint Forces, the special army of the dictatorship. But shhh... we shouldn't be talking about it."

"Come on, Gomez."

"Shhh... just keep in mind that the officers of the Joint Forces are the Uruguayan Gestapo. Yes. Now shut up."

"But... gee... now I see... sure... we have a Uruguayan Gestapo here. For sure they behave like that."

"Ssshhh... don't raise your voice."

"But... what about the room?"

"All the information gathered by all police departments and Interpol goes into that room. Gee... they even get inputs from agents in high schools, factories, therapy groups, and the university. From there to the command center of the Joint Forces. Stay away from that place, don't get in that corridor, and don't repeat what I told you."

"Dangerous, eh?"

"Ssshhh... I guess there are things you don't know. The Joint Forces are the armed strength of the dictatorship, they are like a SWAT team but much larger, like a Gestapo I told you, with a lot more people, and broader authority. You've seen them. They have darker uniforms and wear either a helmet or a blue beret. They are very aggressive and... well, they are a bit more complicated than..."

"What do you mean?

"Listen," Urine Gomez continued, lowering his voice to a faint breath. "They have several branches. They have the branch you know about, but they also have the plain clothes branch that behaves like a paramilitary command, executing violent ops and making it look like it was civilians, including assassinations and attacks on certain institutions. They also have their secret police."

"Hey, this is like in the Nazis time."

"Yes. Sometimes they attack people or institutions looking like Tupamaros, creating the justification for further attacks and assassinations.

"This is terrible."

"Shhh... yes, false flag ops. This is Nazi Uruguay and Uruguayan Nazis control the street and the society. If necessary, they do operations using the paramilitary squads. Heard of them?"

"No. Well, they were talking about them in the halls of the medical school. I thought they'd be..."

"You need to get those thoughts out of your brain, and soon. There are things you better not know... or even suspect you know."

"Crap! So, what else is in that room?"

"I told you. That room, with nearly a dozen tentacles, gathers all the information from every police station and the Interpol and communicates it to the head of the giant octopus."

"Giant octopus?"

"The Condor, Daniel."

"The Condor...? What Condor?"

"The Operation Condor. Hey, I shouldn't be talking to you anymore. Go!"

Daniel stood firm.

"I said—"

"No, Gomez. Tell me. What operation? What Condor, Gomez?

"The Operation Condor is the inter-dictatorial center. It manages and coordinates the South American dictatorships. It provides money, training, and weapons. Go and find out. Get out of here. Just go!"

"What?... inter-what?"

"Ssshhh... listen. I don't want to talk about it. Lower your voice. I thought you knew. Uruguay is part of the monstrous Operation Condor, which unites us with the dictatorships of Chile, Argentina, and Brazil in a common front against the communists. Ah, Paraguay is also in. Ah, and Bolivia. It's a cleansing campaign."

"Cleansing?"

"Elimination, Danny."

"But... are you telling me—"

"No! I didn't say anything. I'm just showing you around. We're talking about urine and vitamins. Now, get out of here. You make me nervous."

Daniel left through the corridor. He left the headquarters with some weight on his chest and some questions in his mind. *Condor Operation*?

Condor?

He went home.

At the headquarters he would raise his antennae, trying to understand that secret computer center. *There's a hidden basement*? He was intrigued. *What would there be in that area*? Where do those stairs lead?

"Gomez... could you go in there?" he asked another day, recalling that he had been told that the staircase of the information center descended right there.

"No. Not allowed. I told you this is not a subject to talk about."

"But... what's in there? A vault?"

"Come on, let me show you," Urine Gomez replied.

He took him to the first floor and from there, down a staircase, they went to the ground floor, took the administration corridor, and went to the basement. *Oh, so then the stairs of the second floor don't go there*, thought Daniel.

That basement was a big jail system, divided into smaller cells. Gomez showed him the different sections of the prison, the central corridor, the middle fortified desk with four special agents in dark uniforms carrying machine guns, the side corridors, the minor crimes section, the major crimes area, the cells of the mentally altered and psychotic, and the warehouse to receive and store

God knows what accoutrements of torture and murder. With the help of another officer, they went through a fence and then behind bars. "Even fleas don't pass through here without being controlled," the officer said. "There's no way forward for you except back where you came from."

"What a control," said Daniel, "and... are they like this twenty-four hours a day?"

"Longer if they had their way," said Urine.

"Yes, and Saturdays and Sundays," said the officer.

"Hey, hmm... that place, what is it?" he asked.

"What place...?"

"There..." said Daniel, pointing to a large area with a security door in the background like a looming iron curtain.

"Ah, that's a cell," the officer told him. "It's not part of the prison. That's the lower gate of the informatics section, it's full of files, communications equipment, computers, and only special army service officers go through there. We're not allowed there."

Okay, thought Daniel, *am I getting closer?*

Chapter 14

A few days later Daniel woke up knowing that he did not know how to advance. Suddenly he realized that the field was too big and the problem too difficult.

I have to talk to them, he told himself upon leaving his afternoon anatomy class. *This may end up being too dangerous.* He went to the morgue. The professors were gone. He then went to the street to find a taxi. A police patrol car approached him, *Oh, what now*? The officer knew him.

"Listen to me, Daniel, they're waiting for you," he said. "Go over there, to the other side, and continue straight until you see a Mercedes Benz."

Curious, Daniel walked to where the agent had directed him. *Here they will screw me up*, he said to himself. *They're going to grab and beat me. What have I done?"*

There he went, intrigued and nervous, with a guilty conscience for things he remembered, to meet a large Mercedes Benz two blocks from the college. He had seen that car before. The driver was lying in the car and when he saw him, he said, "Hello, are you Daniel?"

He said, "Yes."

The driver got up and opened the back door and said, "Please..."

When he got into the car, the driver closed the door and walked away. Inside was an old man, very well dressed, combed with hair gel, and smelling of foreign cologne. His imported alpaca jacket was hanging to the side, and Daniel saw that it had a green emerald on the lapel. He also had a ring with an emerald the size of an eyeball. He greeted him by name, speaking in a pleasant way. He spoke like those people who were above the law, who were much higher than money. He told him that there was something Daniel should know about a certain person he had recently met, and that perhaps they had something in common. Daniel felt like he was in a cave, thinking about the bad things he had done, and it was hard for him to react. The man told Daniel to calm down and explained how he and his organization had managed to get his friend David out of the country. Daniel was amazed.

"You?"

"I imagine what you're thinking," said the guy. "Who am I, what do I want, and how are you going to get out of this... right? Well, listen for a moment to what I'm going to tell you."

Daniel tensed.

"But no, don't be nervous," the man said, while extending a calming hand. "Didn't you like the gift of a fake ID and credentials for your friend David? Didn't you feel relieved, at once, to get the necessary documents and tickets to save his neck? See...? I am not against you; I am not your enemy."

"You? Did you fix everything?"

"Yes. Well, not just me, my... *organization*, let's say. They were waiting for your friend in São Paulo. They put him up in a hotel and gave him the choice of which destination he wanted to go to. He left to wherever he chose and arrived safe."

"Thank you, very much, sir."

"But everything was done well. We did it well because we already have experience. Congratulations are in order to both of you, because you grasped the rules of the process from the outset."

"Both of us?"

"Yes. You and that Dorita. Nice girl, Daniel."

"Rules...? What rules are you referring to?"

"Speed and top secret. Yes."

"Yes?"

"Yes. Once it is decided to remove a person, it must be done as quickly as possible and in the greatest silence. Speed *and* secrecy. Sometimes you do not have to say anything to the passenger until the last moment. There are times that even the parents should not be told, you never know who is going to brag about whom or who is going to call whom."

"Yes, good..."

"Good. I hope you are calmer. I suppose you received my little note on the matter of favors."

"Yes. That means you surely have plans for me, right?"

"I will explain that later. You must acknowledge that you are a complicated individual, eh?

"Well... yes," he said; and thought, *what does he know about me?*

"Listen to me Daniel, your life is a jumble of books, deaths, classes, anatomy, study, cinema, and women, although with more than one you really threw yourself into manure. On many occasions you were a hotheaded fool." The man lowered his head but kept his eyes on Daniel, knowing in objective moments he would agree with that statement. "Besides, what you did at the Salvo Palace party and by smuggling things are just stupid mistakes."

"Don't make me feel uncomfortable."

"No. I don't want to make you feel uncomfortable. But... how did you do those two things?"

"I don't like talking about it. It was before entering medical school."

"Oh, yeah? You did that knowing what you were doing. That one in the palace was... and with the *Minister...*"

"Please."

"How you stuck your nose in the seventh police station was something that..."

"Not now, please."

"Good, good," he said then changed subjects with his face. "Listen, Daniel, I want to tell you something, but before starting I had to tell you that getting people out of harm's way is just one of the many tasks of our organization. We do things silently, secretly, and only with reliable people. We already know you, and we know that you are trustworthy. It may be time for you to move on to a next stage."

"What stage...? I'm not at any *stage*."

"You are. By getting mixed up in the Lewinsky escape, you got into something."

"No. I did it to make him a—"

"Ah, yes? Did someone force you to get in or did you get into it alone? Nobody forced you."

"No. I just did it...."

"Listen to me!" said the emerald guy. "You just need to know that there *is* a stage, but about which I will not explain. And you got into that stage by your own will."

"Fair enough, sir. But then, who are you?"

"At this moment it doesn't matter so much who I am," he answered. "You will know in due course. What is important is that you understand some things. The first is that you cannot talk about what you did with friends or anyone. The secrecy and the silence must continue."

"I get it."

"Good thing, because not everyone understands it. I want you to know that although our organization is vulnerable, if you break our trust we can fight back. It is important that you understand that detail. Nothing that has anything to do with that Lewinsky getaway can you discuss with your mother or even close friends. With nobody! You never know who is going to secretly brag about it and with whom."

"Yes. I get it."

"With nobody. Did you hear correctly?"

"Yes. Yes. I get it."

"Do you understand that we could destroy you if you open your mouth or do something against our organization?"

"Yes. Yes!"

"The second thing is that you are now part of our gear, and you must accept it and help when we need you, such as the doctor who came to speak to you in the hospital that time, or the man from the street, you see? All silent gears. Everyone has his own life, but they give us a hand at certain times. Are we in agreement?"

Daniel was silent, remembering those people.

"Do we agree?"

"Yes, yes. However, if according to... But... this is... you don't tell me who you are or what you need of me... or what kind of organization you have... everything is kind of confusing. What type of gear do you want, one who blindly accepts what every joker on the street tells him, who doesn't ask any questions and is as gullible as a schoolgirl? I... I don't... how about some explanation?"

"Don't worry so much!" the man chuckled. "I already told you that we need you. You will understand other things in due time."

"But... why me? Why me? All I did was give a hand to a friend in distress. I didn't sign up or become a member of any um... *organization*. I did not ask to join anything. Why now all this?"

"Just like how I got my first kiss, because that's how it happened!" the old man with the green emerald said aloud, half annoyed now. "Because this is how things happen. Because that's how you appeared, and because that's how the... it doesn't matter."

"Why? I am asking you why?"

"Well, okay, and because you are also at a very special crossroads between the Uruguayan Jewry, the Jewish leftists of your community who we don't know how they trust you knowing that you help those at the police department, the leftists, and the Bolsheviks of the university who we can't understand how they can respect you being you're a contradictory Jew with a loose tongue, and those of the police headquarters who we just can't imagine how they accepted you with that long hair like a woman and your twisted leftist ideas. We also can't figure out your position in the school of medicine and why the students respect you when they know what you are. Yes, just like that."

"Hmm... I see."

"Ah, and because we can control you with your secret. There you have it!"

Shit, Daniel told himself with a hidden hard swallow. *He has painted my life. Who is this guy?*"

"Think about it. You've gotten where you've gotten without anyone inviting you. You're in places where we wonder how you got there, how did you get in. Oh yes, by the way, how *did* you get in?"

"That's *my* business."

"Oh, *your* business. You want me to be the dumb schoolgirl it seems. Don't you know how to stay in a quiet corner watching television? You're some lucky guy, I tell you. And see? I know well about your past. A lucky mess."

"Oh yeah? Who... what would you know?"

"Are you stupid?" he asked. "I know about your records. Do you think I don't know several of the commissars and officers of several police stations? and the captain of the division, that Russian? The Russian with the big mustache... Boresky."

"Yamandu. They call him Yamandu. They told me that if you call him like you said, he gets very angry."

"Yeah, I know, I know. Did you see how he looks like Stalin? Ha! when he goes to the beach, people move away." The man cackled out a mocking laugh.

"Yes, he has a bad face," said Daniel. "Hmm... yes."

"Well, since we're on the subject, what the hell are you doing at the police headquarters?"

"Those are my things."

"Oh, sure. You're there for a reason, sure. What are you searching for there?"

"You're the big man with all the eye-in-the-sky secret info about everyone, why don't you—"

"Hey!" the man said, raising a clear and cold finger.

"Nothing," said Daniel, stepping back from the boundary he almost crossed. "I'm getting acquainted with people who in the future might allow me to enter the DEMEM, the Medical Department—"

"I know what it is. But what? Are you kidding? I know how you participated in investigations in the Capurro neighborhood when your father was deputy officer there. I read about it. I know very well why your father retired from criminology, and I know about the bullet he got as a going away present."

"Just... just leave the subject."

"You were involved in investigations then and for sure you are doing it now. What did you find there at the headquarters? What are you looking for?"

"I told you... can you leave me alone with that?" Daniel replied, and thought *if this old man has contacts, could he help me?*

The old man looked at him, thinking, knowing that Daniel was hiding something.

"Well, what do you want?" asked Daniel, trying to change the subject.

"There's something about you, Daniel, that instills confidence, and maybe that's why, and because of your innocent and childish face, it's why they accept you everywhere, and that's why we need you on the street, and that's why I have to stay in the gloom. Look let's leave it there. It's okay? But we're going to need you."

"I already feel bad about all this. Don't you understand that I'm just a student who did a friend a favor?"

"You mean you relied on us to do your friend a favor," the man said, and Daniel lowered his head. "Don't feel bad. This isn't a trap. You're going to have a mission. Don't feel bad, because favors with favors are paid, and the one who favors does, favors receives. And the one who does favors without asking for anything, receives a payment in some way."

"How... what did you say?"

"That. You heard it right."

"So, this means that at any time you, or some envoy of yours, locates me and corners me to do something, help someone, or get me into something I shouldn't, then maybe I'll be in danger, and maybe the danger would be bad, huh? Why don't you go and pick someone else? How do I know my life isn't going to be in danger?"

"What do you know...?" The old man smiled and admired the faceted emerald in his ring. "You're like the person terrified to fly in an airplane but screams down the busy highway in a car every day."

"Yeah but—"

"Well, listen to me, Daniel. You've already gone alone; your life has already been in danger, and this wasn't the first time. Have you noticed that? You. You alone. You and only you were the one who knocked on our door asking, no *begging* for help. You."

But why...? Hmm... the danger you are asking me—"

"No Daniel! No, Daniel! Nobody wants you to be in danger. If you're in danger and something happens to you, our goal is destroyed, because by wanting to alleviate a problem we did more harm than good. And look around this chaotic economy and corrupt government... you don't think there is plenty of danger afoot every day? But if something happens to you, we couldn't forgive ourselves. Our plans sink, and the opportunity is lost. So, with us you are probably *safer* than facing the chaos all on your own." The man polished his ring on his lapel. "In addition, we already have others, but we want *you* inside. Our organization is linked to other personalities of the military governments of Brazil, Argentina, Chile, and other countries, who also remain in the gloom."

"Ah, they are international? They're not a strictly Uruguayan group then?"

"Yes, we are an organization that operates in several countries, separated into groups and units. Each unit has its people and its... let's say... its collaborators."

"Your "agents collaborateurs," eh?"

"Yes. That... you could say that."

"That's what you want from me. Let Daniel be an agent collaborateur, huh?"

"Something like that."

"And what is the name of that organization? I don't want to feel like I am helping an international criminal organization that controls people, just uses assets like the CIA does, then throws them to the wolves when done."

"Wait, wait, don't make assumptions."

Daniel was silent. He didn't know what to say.

"Yes, we live in a horrible dictatorship, with all the chaos," Daniel continued," and the people you ask me to help seem to represent the machinery of that dictatorship."

He quieted for a moment.

"I'm going to tell you, Daniel, that as a young man," said the emerald guy, "you are a local and you are unable to see the big picture of what is happening." The man's face washed over with empathy and reason. "You cannot and should not judge whether the dictatorship is bad or good since little Johnny is hungry, or that little Susan was tortured, or that the workers on the corner have nothing to eat. No, Daniel! you must look at everything globally. Do not forget that the organization and the statements of the Communist Fourth International Convention affect us all. All of us. Only Operation Condor can stop that invasion. Only Operation Condor can reverse the damage they have done and allow us to live in freedom."

Whoa! thought Daniel. *What's he talking about? Again, that Condor word*?

"*Condor*, did you say? *Operation* Condor?"

Yes. A great campaign."

"Is that Condor campaign the one that gets people out?"

"Oh, no, Danny, more than that. I mean your friend David, that was just a little humanitarian excursion. The Operation Condor is much more than that. It is a very strong and necessary inter-American organization. It is designed to unite us and organize us in times of danger. Thanks to its necessary struggle, the communist guerrillas are being defeated.

"How? Eh... but we have the Tupamaros, and..." bumbled Daniel, "And they have been revolting against the injustices that exist in Uruguay. Are you going to tell me that they are wrong? That this *Operation Condor* is set to destroy them?"

"No, no, don't start arguing about those Tupamaros, Daniel. You're in over your head—politically and socially speaking—like a boy who romanticizes pictures of forests but gets lost in the woods. And yes, you *are* wrong. I know that what President Battle and the Colorado Party did against the rich Uruguayan economy has no forgiveness. I know the history and I know very well how the corrupted leaders of the Battle political party sank a country as rich as ours, and I know well that the Tupamaros movement is a response against what they caused. Yes, I already know all that. But that does not justify that those criminals, who are nothing but vigilantes, would call themselves saviors. Did you hear me? Let's not get into that."

"What do you mean? It is justified. It is a violent response against oppression and—"

"What oppression? When the Tupamaros started there was no oppress—."

"There was! Oppression by the politicians who controlled the country and the police! Financial oppression over the lower classes who could not get out of poverty. The oppression was..."

"What? Who brainwashed you?" yelled the green-emerald man. "The Tupamaros are part of the communist wave that is expanding through all of South America. They need to be stopped and this operation is doing it."

"Hmm... no, things are not that way," replied Daniel. "Now it's like—"

"Now nothing. Besides the mess they caused, the Tupamaros haven't brought a solution or put ideas on the table, and they have given a hand to the international communist party to infiltrate the country, so they must be taken out of the way. They are also linked to international Marxism. Especially considering that they are linked to Cuba, to Russia, and to the Fourth International, from whom they've received weapons, money, and instructions. That's why we must get them out of the way, see?"

"Kill them...?"

"Get them out of the way, I said. I didn't say by killing them, unless... Well, we are in a process. And we are in this Operation Condor, which is well organized and doing things well."

"Organized? Organized to break heads and torture? Into killing people. Is that what your Condor organization is about?"

"Ssshhh... oh, oh, wait. Do not think that way. Easy, easy. Don't jump to conclusions. Pacification does not mean extermination, silly lost boy. The advance of communism is horrible, horrible! That Marxist wave trying to invade South America is terrifying and what they could do is horrible. You look at the dictatorship as a violent reaction against the hunger cry of the poor, but I see it as a necessary reaction by Uruguay to stop the advances of the international communism that infiltrates our country, and I see the governments of Brazil, Chile, Paraguay, and Argentina integrated in the same reaction, in a joint plan, in an integrated idea, a Pan-American idea that goes beyond borders. An excellent program. That is the Condor, see? An InterAmerican, international operation. Fabulous. Ah, and Bolivia too."

In a moment of insight, Daniel asked him: "So... so Operation Condor then... it's a Pan-American idea, right?"

"Yes, it is, but it's more than just an idea. The Condor operation is a great Pan-American program that has been underway for a long time. It is a strong organized response, military, and inter-American, against the communist tsunami that seeks to invade and destroy our continent. But be careful, you can't talk to anyone about this. You don't have to agree politically, but heed this, please. Be careful!"

"But... I was told that this organization controls paramilitary groups in Latin America."

"Who told you? Well, yes, sometimes... sometimes we must use them, yes. Let's not talk about that, okay."

"They said it in the university. Those on the left know it. The Condor strengthens dictatorships, doesn't it? Operation Condor uses paramilitary squadrons to assassinate those who complain."

"Well... yes, of course. So, it should be. They must. It is a necessity. However, wait a minute, they don't just go and assassinate innocent people. No! They just neutralize communist guerrilla operations. It needs to be done."

Daniel froze, overwhelmed. *Oh, damn it, what have I gotten myself into?* All of that sounded too big and dangerous to keep asking and screwing around. Better to get out of all that. He kept thinking.

Who is this man? Who am I in front of? Daniel asked himself. *What did I get into?*

But at that moment, suddenly, a brain spark made him see an opportunity. Could it be? A chill ran down his spine. Could this be the opportunity to get the power he needed? He took a deep breath. What had the rabbi said? "... that if life gives you the opportunity, take it." Could this be the opportunity to find out certain things? But... how *not* to get in? How *could* he get in? *I don't want to get involved, no, I'd better go.*

Daniel felt that he could not miss that opportunity. *But what kind of opportunity? to put myself in danger?*

He remained quiet and looked out the window. The old man adjusted his shirt.

They waited. He was trying to find the right words.

This is it; I can't miss this chance.

"To all that," Daniel said, "now a new thing adds up." He tried to reach the old man with pity. "Something new that I have found, still more manure on my path. Like if all that wasn't enough, now they are kidnapping boys and asking their families for ransom. The military or the Joint Forces are doing it. And they still go and kill them. Everything has gotten worse in front of me, and it has touched me very personally."

"Yes. I have heard about it. It is part of the process. But it doesn't happen that way."

"Yes. They take boys and young women, ask for ransom, and then kill them."

"No, nooo... it's not like that, it's not true, no!! "

"Yes, they kill them."

"No," said the old man. "They only capture those who get into communist messes and with the Tupamaros. Drop the topic. Don't speak without knowing. A boy speculates aloud. A man sees clearly before moving his tongue. They only arrest people when they are required by the current system of justice to be processed properly. Invading their homes and taking them away for trial or questioning is part of this necessary process against crime."

"In some cases, perhaps yes. But others are returned or killed after parents paid a ransom. Do you understand? They ask for ransom and then they kill the victim."

"No, no, I refuse to accept it. It is not like that. Do not talk with your dirty mouth about the fair process of controlling subversion."

"It's true!"

The old man cleared his throat, straightening his hair, looked at the window.

After a long pause the old man said, "No one is asked for ransom here, do you hear me? Neither parents nor anyone else, and I know it very well. Don't get into that topic, Daniel. Where did you get that from? Who told you that? Did any of those communists pass you some gossip? Spreading propaganda as truth makes its own manure."

"No. No. I saw it myself in... in... in the morgue and in the hospital. You would have..."

The old man with the emerald was silent and stared out the window. His lips moved as if he were talking to the door.

Then Daniel told him about the cases he saw in the Hospital de Clinicas and in the morgue, and the cases he was told about by classmates and other doctors. "It's true!" he finished.

"I don't know what to tell you," said the old man. And he remained silent.

There was a long silence while the old man thought.

"Look... look Daniel, okay. Let's do this. I'm going to find out. I promise you I will investigate this. But I already tell you that you are still confused."

"I am right. You don't want to accept it."

"And what do you want?"

"Well... well... don't just accept it. Find out, find out, do some research, and then... and then, if I'm not right, throw it in my face."

The old man, very serious, kept silent.

"Would you be able to do something good and do some research?"

The old man kept quiet. Daniel froze, looked at the floor and looked at his hand, thinking.

"Look, I'm telling you because I know."

"I do not know what to tell you. We are part of a larger organization, where they don't tell me everything I need to know. There is... well, there is... there is a street fight at lower levels where there are deaths and injuries from both sides, and it is possible that—"

"No. I saw them. They are not shot to death anywhere, no!! They have a bullet at close range. On the temple! Execution style."

The old man stared at him, kept silent. It was a while before he spoke.

"Well, well, Daniel. Do not freak out. It's okay. I'm going to try to inquire. Well, I just... I just can't promise that I can inquire, but... I will do my best."

They both kept silent for a moment.

"In the meantime," said the man, "well, I need to know if you would be available."

"Available?"

"Listen to me. Operation Condor helps many people, but neither I nor my people can intervene in the pitched battle between the military dictatorship, the Tupamaros, and the communism that infiltrates Uruguay, Brazil, Paraguay, Bolivia, and... well. And there are people who drop dead."

"Yes. I accept that."

"But let's get back to the main issue. You saw how we helped you with your friend David."

"Yes, I understand, you tell me that the system to remove him, protect him, provide him with money and false documents, provide him with a contact abroad to help him, was... was it all part of a system that is in turn part of the Operation Condor and works in other countries?"

"Yes. I see you understood. Yes, thanks to that, your friend was saved."

Daniel was silent for a long time. *Here I will have to barter. If I help him, I might be able to find out something,* he thought. He got nervous. One voice in his head told him, *don't get involved, danger*! while another voice said, *don't miss this opportunity.*

In the end he spoke without looking at the emerald man. "Look... I can't erase from my mind that my friend is safe," he said speaking softly and calmly. "I can't help but feel grateful for what you did. I don't know what to do or how to do it, but I will play the game. I will give you a hand with what you ask, if you give me a hand with what I ask."

Silence.

"I will do what you ask me to do," Daniel clarified in a low voice. "If you help me find out something that is important to me."

"What help are you referring to? With what and how do you want me to help you?"

Daniel was silent.

The old man settled into the seat and twisted his body a little towards Daniel. "What are you looking for, Daniel? So then yes, eh? You are investigating something, eh?"

Daniel kept silent for a few seconds, trying to find the words, then explained his problem and what he was looking for. He told him what he was searching for at the police headquarters. He had to stop a few times to catch his breath. When he finished, he fell silent. The old man was silent, still, and looking at him with disbelief. Daniel waited.

Cars were no longer passing by, and the birds got stuck in mid-flight. The air stopped flowing. The world froze and the clocks stopped.

"This is very serious, Daniel. Very, very serious."

The two of them were silent for a while longer, looking at each other.

"What in God's name have you got yourself into, Daniel? You, little boy, are more lost than I thought."

"How can I avoid doing it?"

Silence.

Daniel talked to him a little longer and explained his goals.

"Well, fine!" said the old man. "Don't do anything until I find out more. Stay quiet. Do nothing. Just walk away and don't talk about this with anyone or even with your mother. Think about everything I told you. I'll see what I can find out."

"Yes. Please."

The man waited, turned his head to the window.

"You are a scoundrel, Daniel."

"I know."

"I didn't expect this."

"I figure."

"Keep what I told you a secret. When we need you, if we need you, you will know. Take care. Take good care of yourself, especially at the headquarters. Those walls have ears!"

"Yes."

"In the meantime, remember this, fight for yourself, and not for someone else's team, you dummy. We will contact you. Take this number, keep it in a safe place. Very surely, I will let you know with another person, and you'll know who that person is by something they are going to give you or say. Remember, don't say anything, or talk about it with anyone."

"Goodbye, Daniel. Maybe you need to go somewhere to think about it. Go to the Piriápolis Resort for a few days." He handed Daniel some folded bills.

"Sure. Bye."

He opened the door and rousted the driver, "Joaquin! Come on... let's go."

Daniel got out of the car. The old man closed the door, opened the window a little, and said aloud to him "I see that we chose you well, you are more alive, a better person, and more awake than I thought. Don't waste yourself, Daniel! Don't be so sentimental and so stupid, silly Danny.

The car left fast.

Daniel needed answers.

No. I need to focus on my goal.

Chapter 15

The next day he went to see Pereyra.

Professor Jorge Pereyra Bauza, whom they called *The Pocho*, was a good friend. He had been Daniel's literature professor in college. He didn't like being called *Pocho*. Tall, thin, half-bald, with short curly hair, he was extremely cultured. He always spoke gesturing. He was from the left and hated Argentine politicians, the military and "This horrible dictatorship."

"Yes. It's the Sephardic Key, with... with... wait... The Star of David *and* a cross? I don't get it. It doesn't make sense. Go and ask your rabbi."

He went to talk to the Rabbi.

Sofia, Rabbi Bernstein's wife, was near the door and she already gave him a bad look and made an ugly face when he came in. Daniel took her inhospitality less personally this time, assuming she treated all guests this way.

"Enough, Daniel. Oy vey! It's time for you to leave him alone. Let him rest.

"But I need—"

"You need? *You* need? This world is not only about you, foolish boy. Leave the poor man alone. You and your stories and problems and—"

Daniel greeted her and went into the rabbi's study.

"Hi Rabbi Bernstein, how are—?"

"Oh, Daniel, Daniel, what did you do now?" Rabbi Bernstein said when he saw him arrive.

"Rabbi..."

"Every time you come here you break my heart with something else, something more horrible than the previous. Chess?"

"No, not now. It's something else."

He sat near the ancient rabbi's chair and showed him the key with the small shield. Bernstein took them in his withered hands and caressed them carefully.

"Who did you steal this from, stupid boy? What did you do? Did you open a coffin and snatch it from a poor dead man?"

"No, no. I didn't do anything, Bernstein. Nothing. It was given to me."

"Gave it to you? *Gave*? These things don't happen, Daniel. These keys are not just *given*. Not to anyone, especially not a piglet like you. I know you. Who did you get it from? What's going on here?"

"I told you. I did not—"

"Daniel, these things don't happen like that. What did you do this time?"

Then Daniel told him how they gave it to him and when. For years he had been telling the rabbi things that had happened to him, seeking his advice, therefore the old man was not surprised by what he was saying.

"One day you're going to scare me to death."

"Well, I came here seeking your advice. What do you think?"

"That the next time I see you coming, I better hide."

The room smelled of old books and disinfectant. There was not much light. The rabbi had a short gray beard and a musty smell.

"Ah, don't talk to me like that. It's just that things happen to me. You know I'm not bad but interesting."

"Yes. Yes. Already. You get more *interesting* by the day."

"Good, yes, good and bad."

"If you get any more interesting, I will die from a heart attack when you walk in the door."

"Rabbi—"

"Look, Daniel. The thread represents the filigree of the city of Toledo in Spain, you see, those colors are typical, they represent and remind their belonging to the city of Toledo, and also reminds of the horrible Spanish repression. The key is a Sephardic symbol, and it is the key that many of them kept for centuries since they left Spain chased by the Inquisition."

"Uh..."

"Yes. When those people escaped from the Spanish Inquisition, they locked their houses and kept their keys, hoping to return one day. It was horrible what the Spanish people did to the Jews, and these symbols are to remember all that... and... and to feel united to those people and to that past."

"After all those years?"

"Yes. But Spanish anti-Semitism was and continues to be strong, and they could not return. The anti-Jewish fury of the Spanish people has been great, and it still is. Spanish people continue to be racists."

"But that happened a long time ago."

"It's still fresh in those families."

"And the Spanish government?"

"They continue to be anti-Semites there in Spain. Look, Daniel, Germany has done the impossible to be forgiven, with compensations, payments, etc. And today one looks at Germany with different eyes. But Spain? What has the monarchy, or the Spanish ministers done to cleanse the Jewish blood that soaks their history? Nothing!"

"Gee... I assumed..."

"The spirit of the Inquisition still floats in the air of Spain. Nowadays."

"Well, but... but going back to the subject of—"

"Oh. Yes. So... oh yeah, it's a very strong Sephardic symbol, Daniel. The key is a symbol of their belonging, of their origin in Spain, of the betrayal of that country, and of the bitterness and pain that they have experienced because of Spain. The key reminds them of the savagery of the people and the Spanish government that humiliated them and took their belongings."

"Was Spain that horrible?"

"Horrible. And it still goes on. Spanish anti-Semitism continues. The Spanish donkeys continue to blame the Jews for nailing their Christ to the cross. Damn! When will they accept that Jesus Christ was a Jew like us?"

"Hmm... and the other?"

"The shield, that plate, is more complex. You see here the compass and the angle ruler, see here? It's called a square, and it has the letter G, yes, you are right, it's the symbol of the Masons."

"Are you referring to Freemasonry? What is that organization?"

"It is a fraternity, it is something like a philosophical institution dedicated to promoting social processes, I don't know. Nor do I know what the G actually means though I've heard lots of peasant speculation. But I tell you that the origin of Freemasonry dates back centuries. There is something mythical, something medieval and sacred in its origins, something powerful but positive that remains invisible. They are strong, but they are dedicated to good."

"But who are they?"

"I don't know well. They secretly meet and organize a guideline to maintain justice and governmental sanity as best as possible."

"I see. And the crosses?"

"Hmm...the crosses, this one and this one, you see, they represent a branch of the Catholic Church. This all represents something... hmm..."

"What something?"

"Something strange. It's like all this... I don't know... it's as if this represents a kind of union of Sephardic, Freemasons, and Catholics in a single fraternity. And I guess for some purpose, or for some reason. Come on, Daniel, tell me again, tell me the truth, how did you get this?"

"From... from...nobody. It was given to me. I told you how."

They looked at each other.

"I can't say, Rabbi Bernstein. I can't talk."

"Oy vey!! I see...you really got yourself into something. Can't you spend some time without getting into trouble, stupid boy?"

"Please..."

"This is... hmm.... this is something that..." stammered Bernstein. "I don't know... this is unusual. Only a common, important, severe, and fundamental purpose could unite these three groups. Yes, yes, something connects it. I don't understand why or for what."

"But so, what...? I mean, how do I take it?"

"It is supposed that something like this should not have fallen into your hands, since this must be a secret. A thing like this is not given to someone without expecting something, without having a certain degree of confidence, without..."

"Because of what it means?"

"Because... because... it's like I gave you the keys to my house, or as if your neighbor gave you the keys to his car so that you keep them for an emergency, you see?"

"Hmm..."

"Yes. These symbols imply a relationship, a trust, a secret... perhaps the secret of something great that cannot be seen, but that exists as... as... as I would say invisible, yeah that."

"Some secret union?"

"Something like that."

"What are you talking about?"

"I'm talking about what's in front of you and you can't see it. Some union of hidden forces against evil."

"Oh, gee... don't start."

"It's the eternal fight, Daniel. Good against evil. Don't you see the two sides?"

"Too complicated. I don't think so, I just don't..."

"Daniel, don't you see the two sides? Don't you understand this?"

"What else?"

"I don't know. Maybe... Hmm... maybe as a message... uh... like they communicate that they're sharing something with you. And what are you going to do with that? Eh, Daniel? Don't do anything wrong. This... hmm. It's like they are telling you that they're with you... like they are part of you."

"It's strange, Rabbi."

"Yes, very strange."
"And creepy."
"Whomever gave this to you gave you a message: he's powerful; he represents some union of secret forces; and he is on your side."
"Ah, Rabbi Bernstein, stop... you are talking... this is your fantasy."
"Sure, sure, Danny, too complicated for you."
"I am just a... a..."
"A student. I know."
"Yes, I don't... I don't know," Daniel said as he got up. "I must think about it," he said leaving. "Thank you, Rabbi Bernstein, thank you."
"Oh, every time you go, I get worried. Daniel, stupid boy, listen, if they have given you the keys, this may be because they need... I don't know... maybe... Look, you better go."
"Yes bye, Rabbi," he said goodbye upon leaving.
The Rabbi turned around, raised his right index finger, and told him in loud voice: "You will be facing those forces soon enough! Remember this: you will need some power and some help from the angels."
"Oh, gee. Angels? What angels?"
"The angels from behind the shadow. They will help you."
"What?"
"Nothing. Just go. Before your stupidity spreads to me."
"Tell me more."
"Bye, Daniel. Go now."
Daniel took a deep breath. When he reached the door of the temple, the old Sofia gestured for him to leave.
"Don't come back," she complained. "Every time you get in trouble, why do you have to come to bother him?"
"Look, madam, what is it that—"
"A nuisance."
"What happens—"
"What happens is that you're a nuisance! let him rest in peace, Daniel."
He left the synagogue. *What a bad bitch this is,* he thought, and he began to walk down Canelones Street, then went up Andes Street and continued through San Jose. He walked and thought, but the more he thought, the more confused everything seemed.
He had no answer.
He got up the next day, decided. Perhaps it helped him to make up his mind that he felt he belonged to something great, although not visible.

Chapter 16

He had to go to the Department of Justice to talk to Berta and that Gina. Daniel entered through its main gate, as they had instructed him, and went straight to the office of the Director of the Supreme Court of Justice. Once there, a doctor in charge of something from the departmental prosecutor's office received him with a handshake and took him to the General Directorate of the Administrative Services of the Judicial Power. It was a large office, decorated with tiles inside, and where another director of something and his secretary were waiting for them, where he met Berta.

They walked him through confusing corridors with old doors, showed him ugly offices, explained administrative things, and gave him the manual on bureaucracy.

"As you can see Daniel, the General Directorate of the Judicial Branch has many officers which include architects, engineers, the planning division, the legal division, and the Forensic Technical Institute, totally controlled and dependent on our Judicial Branch, and whose director is Professor Doctor Etcheverry," explained Berta, the secretary, who was also the deputy director of the planning division. "Are you seeing this...? And within this institute is the Department of Medical-Forensic of the Ministry of Health, whose director is Professor Doctor Maggiolo-Cruz that you know, and who is linked to ministerial offices. We call it the DEMEM."

"Oh yeah. Yes."

"Well, the office you see there is the DEMEM, did they tell you about that?

"Maybe a little."

"Well. You can't get in there. Under their mandates are all those forensic doctors you've seen at the Morgue, which is our dependency and does not belong to the school of medicine as you probably thought."

Berta continued explaining details of the place and the Department of Criminological Medicine, the technical office, and the Laboratory of

Toxicological Chemistry, all of which fall within the judiciary. She bored him with more information and after giving him two other manuals to study, she introduced him to his "right hands," Lourdes, Jose Pedro, Gina, and Maria del Rosario, who would be training him.

So, this is Gina, thought Daniel. Berta said goodbye and left. Daniel greeted the four politely. Maria del Rosario was very beautiful, with teeth, breasts, and lips of ideal size. *Big, yes*, thought Daniel. Gina had a bad look, and he didn't like her. *Is this the Gina they told me about*? She didn't even look at him.

The four of them were dressed in long gray coats and had dry boring faces. They sat in one of the rooms with a large desk and two blackboards, and the four started explaining their two manuals and gave him another one to read. Daniel tried to look at Gina to see if she would give him at least a smile, but nothing, she wouldn't look at him. *Hmm, she's dry and not interested*, he thought. *It's like she doesn't look at me on purpose. Would she know me from somewhere*?

The session on bureaucracy lasted more than two hours, and each of the four talked to him about boring things, each more boring than the last.

The booklets he was given were read in three nights, three trips to the bathroom, and three bus trips. He went back four days later for more boring instruction. He wanted a way out of that, so he confessed that his schedule was a problem because of his anatomy classes and his student hours, and that he would not be able to meet the requirements. Gina neither looked nor talked to him, and she looked like she was kind of upset. *She shouldn't be that way*, he thought, *it's very impolite*.

They went to consult Berta and another sub-director. They agreed to give him the opportunity to meet them after hours and give him some classes in a cafe, since the Judicial closed at six. They met two days later at six in the evening at the coffee shop in San Jose and Yaguaron. Rosario couldn't come, but Gina was there. *Is it her*? Lourdes was dressed without a coat, with a light brown dress, and with a wide belt and sported her two elegant bulky breasts, which captivated Daniel immediately. Gina however did not captivate him because she had a negative attitude; she was dry and did not pay attention to him. *Hmm, for sure it isn't her*, he thought.

"Always remember that you're in class," Lourdes clarified from the beginning. "So, pay attention."

Lourdes and Jose Pedro then explained some things to him over coffee. It was boring, and he just couldn't take it. *This is not what I am here for.*

"Do you understand that? Forensic doctors are dependent on the Department of Justice, and work in the Morgue. Are you paying attention?"

They gave him two notebooks to study and talked about meeting two days later at the bar at San Jose and Rio Negro for the next class. Daniel didn't want to take those booklets and made a disinterested face.

Daniel was bored. *Pity me. Please, no more booklets.*

"Listen well," Gina said with a strong voice, giving him another notebook. "These are things you must know well! Forensic belongs to the Judicial, while the Department of Legal Medicine depends on the medical school. Read this notebook well." She began to explain the premises of the Judicial Power, its different centers, how they are managed, the management of the Morgue and its relationship with Headquarters.

"Yes, yes," Daniel nodded, agreeing to something, anything.

"You see?" she added. "The autopsy is not simply gutting and dismembering a corpse blindly diving into anything. Did you hear me, Daniel? Listen, Listen... the autopsy must follow a defined method and be carried out... but are you listening?"

"Please. You know well why I contacted you, and it is not for this."

"Quiet, please. Three of the advisers of the Department of Legal Medicine are officers of the headquarters and one of them is deputy commissioner, MacLagan, whom you already know. MacLagan also has links with several of our offices and with offices of the Hospital de Clinicas, Maciel Hospital, the Morgue, and the courts. The booklets will show..."

"Oh, please!" said Daniel with a face that showed lack of interest. "Enough of those booklets."

After that, Gina neither spoke nor looked at him. It was as if the very presence of Daniel irritated her. With her large teeth, wicked mouth, and her hair pulled back, she seemed interesting if not for her antipathy.

Maybe she knows me from somewhere where I did something bad... or... or she might be a friend of one of the girls I met, Daniel thought.

The girls kept teaching. Daniel was absentminded.

But will she be the one sent by Maggiolo and Etcheverry? And why is this chick so dry?

He looked around. There were all kinds of people in the bar, some eating pizza, others just smoking and drinking coffee. The lady next to them was chatting with her companion while she ate breaded veal. A man was slowly savoring hot espresso.

"Again, I tell you, Daniel, don't forget that you're in *class*," Lourdes clarified, as he began his whining.

"Do you hear us at all? Eh Daniel! Are you listening or not?"

"Yeah, yeah," he answered, getting half heated. "I'm learning! But... how much...?"

"That's up to you."

"What do you want me to do?"

"Try not looking at our breasts!" Gina said in an aggressive voice. "It's not comfortable."

Daniel was surprised and ashamed.

"Well... yes, sorry, oh, yes, that's fine," he said turning red with embarrassment. "Sorry."

"Don't be so basic," said Lourdes. "It's a matter of education."

"These classes are important."

"Yes. I know. Sorry."

"I'm leaving!" said Jose Pedro. "You can't do anything with this guy. He's not interested in anything clothed. Bye. Bye."

So, Jose Pedro left.

There, in the cafe, between toasted croissants with ham and cheese, vermouths on the rocks and coffees, they talked for a while more about what he had learned in the notebooks. As they spoke, Daniel's mind wandered, running away. He couldn't concentrate. A murmur of voices and napkins dominated the air. A girl passed by with a bouquet. One couple entered and another left. A while longer and Daniel's boredom disconnected him from the class and made him look at the prohibited areas of those two young women.

"Stop that," yelled Lourdes.

The people at the other table seemed to know what was going on. The lady of the breaded veal looked at him while she chewed. A passing waiter looked at him and raised his eyebrows in warning. *Shit*, Daniel thought.

A cake was brought to the table and Lourdes began to eat it reluctantly, irritated. Gina lit a cigarette and made a face like she wanted to leave at once.

"You are... you..." Gina said. "These classes aren't going to work!"

More people came to the café, sat here and there. Daniel fell silent as the aroma of fresh coffee, freshly sliced ham, and hot sandwiches mixed with the smell of cigarette smoke.

They didn't speak for a while, and Daniel didn't say anything. There was tension in the air.

"Is something wrong with you, Daniel?"

"Nooo, nothing," he answered, worried. "I'm fine." *What to do now?*

The ladies looked right through him, stared at him like some curious lab rat with a terminal disease they didn't want to contract, then refused eye contact.

What am I going to do? he thought. *I've got to stay but I don't like it, and nothing is happening with this Gina connection.*

The class ended without finishing, and Lourdes got up and said while leaving, "I can't stand this."

Daniel and Gina stayed there, in silence.

It's not her, he thought. *That's not the Gina I was told about. I'm not moving forward. This is a waste of time.*

He took a deep breath, looking at Gina for moments. She forced out a last drag of smoke and stubbed out her butt, shaking the thick ashtray.

Daniel made a deep sigh and lit a cigarette.

On the next table, the lady eating veal parmigiana looked at him like saying, *Stupid, you'd screw up the rain."*

An old couple was drinking tea and knew well what was happening.

The waiter came to pick up some dishes.

They both kept quiet for a while, looking at each other, intrigued, upset, trying to calm down after the bad meeting.

"Something's wrong, huh?"

The order yells of waiters and the chat of the people died down. Gina's face seems to heat up the whole room.

"What type of upbringing did you have? You don't know how to relate to people with respect?"

"Yes, it is that you... you and..."

"Let's go."

Daniel got up.

They got out and started walking aimlessly without speaking on 18 d Julio Avenue.

"They told me that you can help me."

"I don't know. Usually, I only help those not terminally stupid."

"Okay..."

"I don't know if you deserve help. You deserve more a slap and a course on etiquette."

"Gina, I— in those classes I was learning, besides... besides... it's normal, yes! normal that a young man like me would look at women's breasts."

She stopped again and looked at him, vividly upset. "Not in the imbecile way you were doing it. You were like... like taking our bra off with your eyes, like you've never seen a pair."

It's true, he told himself. *They are both well-blessed by mother nature.*

She put her hands to her face. "Brrrrrrrr...why am I talking to you?"

Daniel waited. Things were not going well.

"Please, Gina, let's walk."

"God, I knew times were tight, but they can't now be recruiting dudes as stupid as you."

As they walked, Daniel apologized several times.

Then they stopped talking, they waited and then began to talk about what had happened. Daniel told her something about what he had done. Gina stressed that it was not just his personal problem but similar problems of many other people. She took a few deep breaths.

"You have to stop facing it as your private problem and assume it as a problem of many people whom you must help," she said. "If you are interested in helping."

"What? What are you saying? But... but... how many people are you talking about?"

"A whole nation, fool."

"Okay, okay."

She stopped and looked at him with sad eyes and drew a deep breath then sighed. "Many, Daniel!" she said. "There's a lot of pain out there."

"Yes—I—"

"A lot of pain."

"Who? How many are there? What has been happening that I don't know?"

"Well, the thing is if you want to know that and if you want to help."

Daniel approached her a little and said, "But, how do I? What do I do now?"

"Learn. Listen. Understand this horrible situation. What you know of those who were killed, about those young men and women, it is just part of the total number, the greater suffering. There are many more... *many* more."

"How many? How large is the problem?"

"Large. And what you heard about the requests for ransom is also true."

"How many cases like that?"

"Many, Daniel, innumerable. We don't know the precise number. We need help."

"We? Who *are* you? Who is *we*?"

As they stood there, a small breeze brought Gina's body scent to Daniel. It was the smell of a woman, an animal woman, *The smell of meat,* Daniel thought. He then looked at her with a particular interest.

She looked at him, realizing the lust in his eyes, and got angry again.

"Get out," she yelled. "They sent a boy to do a man's job."

"What...?"

"Don't approach me with that wolf look. Listen, I'm leaving. With you it is impossible to speak."

"But no," said Daniel, separating. "Wait. Gina, wait. I need to know."

"Need to know? Need to know what? You're tiny little part? I'm trying to explain to you the big picture, how the dictatorship is killing young people en masse, while you are salivating while looking at my nipples, animal."

Gina went down to the street and stopped a taxi.

"Allow me to come with you. We need to talk."

"Talk to your fist," she yelled at him. "Or go and get your fever out with that Carmen."

"What? Who told—"

"Bye. Go away." She closed the door of the taxi. "Classes are over for you," Daniel heard through the window, as the cab buzzed off.

Daniel stayed there in the street. Two men passing by yelled, "You screwed it up, idiot." A woman looked at him, proud that another woman stood him up. Daniel turned and started walking, frustrated. Some bystanders made a nasty comment.

The thing came to nothing.

To make matters worse, the next day nothing happened either. *There it is. I screwed up. Now, I don't know, should I wait, should I do something. What?*

The next day he decided to go and meet Gina face to face. *If she's going to screw my plans, then let her do it and tell me and it's over.*

"Have you had a fight with anyone?" asked the taxi driver. "A woman, huh?"

He arrived at five forty-five.

"Apologize to her," the taxi driver told him.

He knew she'd be out by six. He set out to wait on the front door. He lit a cigarette, leaned over a parked car, and talked to the pigeons. Cars passed by. A peanuts street vendor looked at him.

At five past six he saw Lourdes, Rosario, and Gina coming out.

Time stopped, cars stopped, and even the peanut man kept quiet. The pigeons didn't even move. Rosario and Lourdes said goodbye to Gina, who slowly crossed the street to meet Daniel. She looked at him while approaching and kept looking at him. Daniel waited for her as she stopped in front of him. She seemed troubled, confused. Daniel seemed to understand.

She approached him, talked to him for a minute and said, "And we have nothing else to talk about," then turned around and left.

I really screwed this one up, he concluded, slumping into one of the benches.

"Yes, you did," hollered the hot peanuts guy. "Yes, you did screw this one up. Roasted peanuts! hot peanuts! Right here. The girl left you and you deserve it."

I don't like this guy, he told himself.

Chapter 17

Two days later his mother told him to call a woman called Berta. He did.

"Call Gina, Danny," she said and hung up.

He did.

He met Gina in a quiet coffee shop. She was dressed in a loose T-shirt, torn jean shorts, and her hair was all spread out. She looked like a lioness, a very attractive lioness. She also had a loose bra and Daniel made the effort to control his animal instincts.

"One flirty look at me and I am leaving," she warned him.

"Okay" he said. "Sure."

"I know you have your Dorita, little pig. Are you still seeing her too?"

"No, we just... she's... I mean... she..."

"Ah, ah, you don't want to talk about her. Why? Did she give you a hard time? Did she leave you?"

"Why are you so inquisitive now?"

"Are you with her and that prostitute too?"

"Oh, just stop with that."

"Hopefully, you all have been tested."

"Tell me, Gina—"

"STDs..."

"What do we do now? What do I do?"

"What? You don't want to talk about your Dorita and your Carmencita?"

He looked at her with surprise. Evidently, she was well connected and had done some investigation. *What's she trying to do?*

"You've done some research, Gina, hmm?"

She gave him a sarcastic gaze. He waited and then gave her a smile and looked at her up and down. *She looks good*, he thought.

"Behave, Danny boy. Control your wolf side. I just needed to know a bit more about you, but gee... everything I find is dirt, corpses, and trashy women. You are—"

"Shhh... Okay. Enough of that."

She waited and took a deep breath.

"Look Daniel," she said. "You're stuck in your business, we're stuck in our business, so we don't know how to go on."

"Who *are* you? How many are there?"

"That doesn't even matter now. What ideas do you have? What would you do?"

Daniel leaned on the chair, then looked at her. He thought a little. "I'm missing data," he finally said. "I don't know how many were killed like that. I know they asked for ransom, and I suspect you have some of that information but you're not sharing it."

"No. I don't," she said. "We don't have all the.... There are many cases—we're both missing data."

"Not just simple data. We are missing detailed information, and I found the place where we can get it."

"Yes, we do. And you do too. Hey, what place? Where? Yes. I may... I mean... I may be able to help."

"Ah, good," Daniel replied. "I need to know all of that, with ages and... and... the data about autopsies and... And... Hmm... data such as where they were found, how were they killed, possible torture, I mean detailed data, and information from... from... I don't know... what else?"

"You understand that there's risk."

"Yes. But I need that information... and I don't know what information might be relevant."

"Daniel, first of all, why are you in this? Why, I mean, why did you get into this?"

"Things developed that way."

She is really attractive in those slutty shorts, he thought.

"But why are you in the police headquarters? How come you got in there?"

"I just... I am trying to... hmm... not now, Gina. Why all this interrogation?"

"I want to know. The headquarters is a dangerous place for you to go into sniffing around.

"Sure."

"So... why?"

"Not now, Gina."

"Why? Did something bad happened to you that made you get in there?"

"Things... eh... there were... I got involved in certain things."

"Ah, I see you don't want to tell me. Okay. Why can't you tell me?"

"Stop this. I have my reasons, as you might have yours. This's not the time to address that."

She kept quiet. Daniel turned and placed his hand on her shoulder.

"Trust me, Gina. I am not the bad guy here."

"Well, well... okay, I'm going to see what I can get, Daniel."

They both kept silent, thinking. She had some sources, and she would try to access them.

Daniel noticed that her rigid and dry attitude was softening up.

Yes, she looks good, he thought.

He got closer to her, then held her hand. She held his. They looked at each other for a while. Something was happening. They exchanged phone numbers.

"I've got to go to class," he said. "Come with me to the bus stop."

As she got up, Daniel said, "Goodbye," and gave her a kiss on the cheek. Caught distracted, she didn't move her head on time and Daniel moved forward and kissed her on the lips. The short kiss startled her, and Daniel used that moment to give her a longer kiss. She separated and pushed him back, looking at him half upset and emotionally affected. They went out and started to walk. As they were approaching the bus stop, he got her in between two parked cars, turned her around and gave her a long kiss and then another one. She didn't reject him but kept silent until his bus came. Before getting on the bus, he kissed her again.

She stood there, at the bus stop, looking at him as he was leaving.

"You poisoned her," said the driver.

Daniel and Gina met the next day. She was in a hurry. He had to run to the hospital. They just had a few minutes, which they spent kissing each other under the tree at San Jose and Paraguay.

The next few days had him very busy with emergency and a surgical clinic exam. On the third afternoon he finally got free, left anatomy early and called Gina. "I would like to see you." She wanted to see him too, "I need to see you, Daniel." She'd come to pick him up at his house later.

At about ten o'clock at night, Daniel left his apartment on the seventh floor of 21 de Septiembre Street and went down to wait for her at the door of his building. The evening was fresh and pleasant. The breeze brought the smells of trees. The squadron was there: Marisa talking to Estela and the Spaniard lady of next door. The seamstress from around the corner had come too.

The Spaniard's husband was smoking by the door and shook his head when he saw Daniel all dressed up.

Geee... how many more people are going to be here? he thought.

"Hey, Daniel, you look good."

"Aaahh, aaah, well perfumed, your good shirt, and you even washed that squirrel's nest on top of your head," Marisa said. "I see you're going out for a kill. Poor victim."

"Is Dorita coming?"

"Holy Mary Manzanita! poor woman," added the Spaniard.

Estela lit one of her cigarettes.

Gina's Fiat stopped; she went down and came towards him walking slowly. She seemed emotionally affected by passion. After a hundred years of Christian, conservative and right-wing education, she had become leftist, deviating from her family's tradition. That had been a dramatic step and created conflicts and discussions. Thanks to her uncle Martinez she got the informatic technology job at the Judicial Center and had access to enormous amounts of information. However, socially she had remained withdrawn. Now, suddenly, she found herself involved and somehow attracted to a Jewish boy, atheist, an irreverent scoundrel who deals with dead bodies, slutty women, and even a prostitute, and she was straying even further from the sacred family line. That created conflict for her, but even knowing that she felt defenseless and at the mercy of a new feeling that devoured and carried her. Despite her resistance, Daniel had sparked an internal fire in her.

Daniel had already made peace with his ghosts and could see in her gaze that she was trying to make peace with hers. Gina's passion and inner fire were noticed as an aura of color emanating from an animal's body. Even Marisa noticed it and kept quiet. What was walking there was a woman overpowered by the simmer that was consuming her. The Spaniard stopped talking, which was a big deal, and just stared at her. Gina looked like another woman, groomed, and dressed, her hair pulled back, with heels and a dark dress. She walked slowly and looked beautiful and incredibly sexy, and it was clear she hadn't come to teach handbooks. She had come to look for that other animal whose passion had ignited her. She warmly greeted the Spaniard, then Marisa and Estela, who were left mute at what they realized. Then she greeted Daniel with a kiss and said, "Hello."

They left right away leaving their neighbors speechless. As she didn't know where to go, Daniel told her to go to the Punta Carretas lighthouse field. When they got there, they got out of the car, walked a little and started to chat. Her stern face indicated she may try to resist him when he turned around and kissed her. Taken again by surprise, she froze, unable to react. He then kissed her more, opened her mouth and poisoned her. There, facing the sea, feeling the noise of the waves, and with the complicity of the night, he embraced her, leaned her against the car, and devoured her face, neck, and shoulders. He kissed her slowly feeling Gina's heart beating like a drum from a fire that consumed her. As he kissed her, Daniel put his hands down and slowly opened her dress, button by button, and squeezed his hand under her bra. She embraced him sensually as he was slowly discovering her body. "No... not here," she said. "I'm not one of your tramps." He opened the back of the car, and they got in. He pulled her dress down and she helped him taking his shirt off. She was warm and could no longer contain herself. Daniel took his time to remove her bra in slow motion and took his jeans off. They let themselves be carried away by a new passion.

A while later, both calm, they stayed embraced, looking at each other. They had found something they did not expect.

"Animal," she said. "Pig."

The sea was in front of them, and a waning moon had begun to rise. A slight breeze was blowing into the car and carrying the scent of rough seas.

"Daniel," she said. "Daniel."

Calmed down, they began to chat. They got out of the car and leaned against the door, smoking, looking at the sea. A while later they got back in the car to love each other more.

They rested, ate some chocolate, got out and lit a cigarette.

"Let's talk."

"Yes."

"We must see how we do it, Daniel."

"Yes, I need... we need a plan."

"Well, you were told there were several factors, do you remember? It takes computer science but also curiosity and drive, or it comes to nothing. Do you remember...? Didn't Maggiolo and Etcheverry tell you?"

"Yes, no, I don't know, I don't know, I don't remember."

"Well, didn't you read it in the booklets?"

"Stop it with that training. Talk to me."

She fell silent and took him by the hand. "It is... it's that I know that what you must do is... is risky, do you understand? Do you understand the complexity of all this?"

"What? Understand what? What..."

"Don't you understand what's going on? They're killing boys and girls, Daniel. It's awful."

"Of course. I know, I know, we already talked about it, but... Why are you now talking about factors?"

"Because the main factor is power, do you get it? Power, little Danny visitor-of-whores. Power!"

"Don't call me that, Gina. Just enough of that."

"Power!" she answered. "Did you understand? Power. That's right. You need to have it clear. To advance you need informatics yes, drive yes, curiosity, yes, and power. With those four you advance. With them you make progress. Without them you don't. I'm telling it to you very clearly so that it is recorded in your head. Think about that. It's more what you must conclude in your mind than what I can tell you."

"What's the point?"

"That you need power and a team. Don't go alone! Don't even think about doing it alone. You need a team, and you need power. Work on that. Discover it."

"And if... I find it difficult to understand... you fool me with enigmatic words. Oh, Gina, explain a little."

"Well, you take a walk and think about it. I don't know what you are looking for and I don't know what secret plans you have, but you know what we are trying to find out. You only need to know that you are not powerful enough alone and you are not the only one on this mission."

Gina lit a cigarette and handed it to him. Daniel leaned against her, looked away and then looked at her.

"If you don't realize it, I'm not going to spoon-feed you. Don't you understand what I'm saying? You have been in the headquarters, but you haven't had access. You haven't been able to advance. If you can't find that source of power, you will not advance."

"I understand."

"Good," she said looking out to sea. "It's one thing to visit the headquarters and help, and another thing is to enter forbidden areas and access what you need, what the mission needs. If you find that source of power, you could have access to the informatics section, which is linked to that of the army and Interpol and to the whole center of the military Joint Forces."

"Ah."

"Yes. Let me give you an example. No matter how much you access the intelligence and informatics section, if you do not know what you are looking for and how to look for it, you will be like a monkey with a watch, unable to retrieve anything. You must chew on that well."

"I see. I agree. You are right. Yes, I accept that."

"That's good. Just like that. We will help you on the hunt because you are on the outside, and we cannot do it from the inside. It's a hunt using your brain."

"Hmm... I... but... yes, but why me? There are others who..."

"No. There are no others. What others? People from the headquarters, the Judiciary, policemen, detectives? No Daniel. It's not known who they are or where they are hiding. We are sure that it is a small group within the army or the Joint Forces or... or the police who are doing those killings. And even the police don't have some of the access you already got with your medical school creds, forensic photography skills, and silly boy charm."

"But Gina..."

"We're going through a dirty war, Daniel. Abductions, tortures, and assassinations, all done by the Joint Forces and their death squads."

"But—"

"It's done in secret. Nothing is known about them. It is not known which branch of the armed forces they are coming from or if they are from a police station or what. It is not known if they are policemen or technicians or if the Nubian is involved in this."

"Eh...? The Nubian...? Who?"

"The Nubian is a murderer who is based in the Capurro neighborhood. It is known that his group is connected to paramilitary groups."

"Hmm... Capurro."

"Yes, Capurro neighborhood," Gina said, lighting another cigarette. "These people may be sheltered behind the desks of the Judiciary or the headquarters. We do not know anything. Maybe they are private, maybe not. If an investigation is launched, they could hide and disappear. It was tried before, investigating, and they disappeared, and nothing was known. No. It must be someone special, someone from the outside." she blew smoke. "Someone from outside, Daniel."

"So, use people from the headquarters...? Yamandu...? MacLagan...? Inspectors?"

"It could not be done. Understand that well, it has not been possible. Many smart and dedicated people have been working on this, Danny, for longer than you know. It was tried and went nowhere. They would find out one way or another and hide. MacLagan couldn't stop something like this, even if he wanted to, and we don't even know if he wants to. No. It must be someone from outside, someone trustworthy. Those people need someone like you, someone who is motivated, someone half smart and half an idiot, half loving, and half brute, and... stealthy, and... whore's costumer, and... and... smooth talker, marginally immoral, and touched with evil and... and half a piece of shit... and... and..."

"OK. I got it."

Daniel looked at Gina then gazed out over the water.

He knew where to find information technology and he knew where to find power. He knew now he also needed a team.

Chapter 18

Two days later they met again in a pizza place.

"What have you been reading, Gina...? Don't get mad... tell me more of what you know. I want to immerse."

"Do you want to know? Well, don't bark at me. It's not that they just chose you. They needed someone and did not know who. There was no one who seemed suitable to them."

"*They*? They *who*...?"

"Does it matter now? They couldn't find anyone who would give any indication that he could. They searched in silence, tried in vain, but there was no one who would be smart and wicked, saint and scoundrel at the same time... and a... and a.... " She paused and took a bite of pie then waved her hand. "Meanwhile, you went into the morgue alone, and you stuck your nose into autopsies, and started with your damn photos and... and... gee, how daring you are. You started with pictures and one day you fell into the police headquarters. Well, talk about imprudent, gee! They were surprised by your audacity. *What is he doing here? Who is that Jew? What is he looking for*? they wondered."

"I don't think I'm special."

"No? Well, I wonder, would you have continued. Had you known the danger and the treacherous waters teaming with sharks all around you, would you have still bumbled your way into this mess...?? You alone started to relate to the people... But how nosy and... and... and insolent you were. You."

"How do you know that?"

"Don't forget that Martinez is my uncle. So, there you were. A daring unknown guy. Yamandu and Martinez wondered where you came from that you poked your nose everywhere without anyone slapping you.

"Yes. Good, is that..."

"I don't know how you did it, Daniel, you're like a rat. Well, shut up for a bit. You and only you were filling out reports, and... and giving statements to the judge. The judge! But by God! What an accidental hero! The judge! How the hell did you get in there? And the judge listened to you and paid attention to you and... and... they just couldn't believe it. How was it possible...? Ah, ah, and... then came the situation with that communist Jew, that... Hey..."

"Lewinsky. Did you know about that?"

"Ha! How can I not find out? Ha! Yamandu was left scratching his head thinking how the hell you managed to do such a thing. And... and I... and I thought, I thought *out of pure shitty and crazy luck, that's how.*"

"Don't tell me... don't talk like that. It was a very difficult time for me."

"I don't know how many things to tell you, Daniel. Well, the thing is that you got into this because you've already been getting into strange messes. Yourself. We did not know if you were innocent, mastermind, pure fool, or if you had a goal that no one knew about. Martinez, my uncle, suspected you were after something, but he didn't know what it was. He tried to corner you, but damn you're slippery."

"I didn't get involved, I felt carried away by... uh... hmm, what did you read about me?"

"It doesn't matter anymore, Daniel. Let me—"

"I do care about it, you see...?" he said. "You sound angry, such disdain describing me, assessing me. Why?" Daniel put his hand under her chin and raised her face to look at him. "Come, come here, tell me, what else have you been reading?"

"Of your exploits, animal! Yes, you're an animal. How you got into those parties at the Salvo Palace as the son of a consul with a friend and sat at the table with a stone face. You're crazy? That was a diplomatic private party."

"No. Wait. The real reason was that the dancing in those parties is excellent, and with orchestra."

"Dancing? Oh, come on. And... and of your smuggling ops. How you stole the war memories from that Nazi German. Do you want me to continue? You are insolent, Daniel! Disrespectful, you're a..."

"No. I'm not. That Nazi deserved it. He was a Nazi, Gina. The real deal. A Nazi with those who after the war got refuge in Uruguay, and I found out about—"

"Shut up... and how.... How did you sneak into that party at the palace? Silly boy with dumb luck."

"Right..."

"But how'd you get in there?"

"I promised not to tell."

"By the way, thief, did you make any money with the smuggling?

"A lot. Watches, fine Cuban cigars, jeans, and—"

"No, shut up. Don't tell me. Tell me, has your mother ever hugged you crying inconsolably, telling you that you are not very normal but that she loves you the same and everything will be fine?"

"Ah, don't say those things! I was a bit... eh... a bit... well, I did some crazy things but... they were the crazy stuff of a kid. Lighten up on me, Gina."

"Did a deputy commissar ever grab you and talk to you so you can start behaving well?"

"Three. Three spoke to me. But I was younger, I already told you."

"Yes, crazy young man."

"They were screw ups when I was younger. I already told you. It was before entering the School of Medicine. Leave it there in the past, huh. Years of that already passed, Gina, don't accuse me like that."

"As a young man...? I'm not stupid, Daniel! That was not so long ago, I tell you I read it and I was ashamed."

"Don't talk like that. I'm not like that anymore."

"Ah, no...? I tell you that when I read it, I even felt sorry for your mother. And a few days ago, I remembered what I had read about you, and I was ashamed to know that I was dating you, really. I said to myself, "*And this is the son of a bitch who pulls my panties down? How do I let myself be groped by a crazy and unconscious sinner like this*?" What a shame you gave me, Daniel! Shame!"

"They're things that happened! And I never did them meanly. Please, it was young things, Gina. I already told you that it was all over when I entered medicine. Can't you see that it's over. I'm normal now."

"Normal? ah!" Gina said with surprised eyes. "Normal *you*? ha."

"Please, Gina. How much research did you do about me?"

"And what is not understood," she said furiously. "What I could not understand is how you could get away with it each time... each time they let you go and not even your parents were told. Shit with you, Daniel, not even your parents were told. The policemen were terribly angry with you, they wrote reports, but they didn't arrest you... How the hell did you do that? You are sneaky, you are cheeky, you have three faces, five faces, the few times the inspectors grabbed you, God knows what you told them, why did they let you go... shit, they let you go... how the hell did they let you go? Now I can't make you let go of my tits. Did you bribe them or what?"

"No but... not so, it's because I'm nice."

"Ah, I know, yes, I know. It's because of what your daddy was. Yeah, sure. They knew who your dad was. Clear. And they forgave you out of respect for daddy. But... what a damn profiteer you are, Daniel. Perhaps worse than the capitali—"

"Don't talk... please, don't get mad at me... Everything is left behind, in the past, Gee. I already changed. I'm good now... look at me, can't you see I'm good?"

"Ha! *you*! *changed*! And how did you get rid of all that? *I'm good* ha! We couldn't understand it when we read your records, even though we knew about your father."

"Who? Who read my records?"

"Never mind."

"I do mind."

"The people who chose you for this. And I refuse to tell you more."

"Who, Gina?"

"I won't tell you. But I want you to know that these people needed someone like you."

"Where is that file? Where is it?"

"Somewhere in the headquarters. You're getting closer. Do you want to talk about it now?"

"Yes. And how do I destroy that file?"

"It's surely in the same place. The file must be in that special place where they keep all the files and I don't know where it is, but you apparently suspect where that place is. It's probably in that very large computer center where you can find other things. Important things. And to enter there you need the key to power, as we talked the other day. Remember what I told you? Power and a team."

"Yes. I'm figuring it out."

"They say that center is in the headquarters, and it's linked to the headquarters, armed forces, Interpol and the intelligence center of the Joint Forces, as well as to various ministries and government offices, and if you manage to stick your nose in there, maybe you can find out something about what we want to know."

"*We*? again, who are *we*?"

"Leave me with that question."

"No. This time you must tell me."

"No!"

"Yes! Who?"

She kept silence for a few minutes. Then she spoke. "Did you or did you not get some key with a special medallion, a cross and a special thread?"

Daniel got goose bumps. He understood. He didn't talk for a while. *So now I see.*

Finally, Daniel said, "Yes. I did. Now I understand all this a bit better.""

"Don't ask me anymore, please. Let's go."

Daniel tried to kiss her, but she said, "Don't touch me for a while, little pig."

When he got home, Gina spoke to him again. "Maybe I told you what I shouldn't tell you, but it didn't seem fair that you wouldn't know."

Daniel was silent, thinking. Gina was looking at him with concern.

He rubbed his hands through his hair, sighed and then relaxed. "And Gina... tell me, what is that Nubian thing you named?"

"You never heard his name?"

"No. Who?"

"I don't know well, but I know that this Nubian guy is a fierce criminal smuggler who deals in drugs, arms sales, and other things. You were probably working for him unknowingly you know, when you were uh... *younger.*"

"Very funny..."

"Our group thinks he had a lot to do with the murders. He operates mainly in the Capurro neighborhood."

"And?"

"We think he's involved in the kidnapping business and in the murders of those boys and girls. Him and his gang."

"Oh, so he must be the one."

"I don't know. I do not know any more. Take care, Daniel. You're going to enter a dangerous zone. I do not know much about that Nubian. He has connections with the Joint Forces."

"But—"

"You're going to be in *danger,*" she emphasized while taking his face in her hands and looking at him with teary eyes. "Take care. You do crazy things, but you can't do them against bullets."

Once back in his room he recalled the conversation. He went to bed and hoped to fall asleep quickly. But his visions disallowed that. He was already somnolent when the nebula appeared. This time he could see not one but several figures, blurred, as if several people wanted to get out through a narrow hole and say something to him.

Damn it with these visions, it's my imagination.

He rolled over in bed.

Go away, I want to sleep.

But the warm glow would not go away.

"What do you want?" he asked aloud, but he only got looks and gestures. "What do you want me to do? What?"

Several of those images were looking at him and moving arms and hands.

"What is it? What do you want?"

He looked at them for a while and thought he felt their warmth and that they wanted to communicate something. Tiredness overcame him and he fell asleep.

The next morning, he woke up with a clear mind, determined, and very sure of himself.

As he was leaving the medical school, a very pretty woman approached him absentmindedly and asked for directions on how to get to a pharmacy that was near there. Daniel explained to her and began to give her details when she interrupted him and scoffed, "Shut up, idiot, and listen." They had found out that the kidnappings were true, they were making a list of cases, they had spoken with several of the parents. "Now, you say absolutely nothing to anyone, and we will let you know shortly." Then she added in a low voice, "Ciao, stupid, take care of those buttocks!"

He was left thinking about what the woman told him. He was surprised and his heart was racing. *Oh, but who was that devil*? He kept walking. After a while he thought, "*Damn, they had started to investigate seriously...* But who? Who were they? Who were these people?

He went to the bus stop. *And now, what's going to happen*? He had no answer. There was nothing he could find out, nor was there anyone to talk to. He didn't know what to expect.

Chapter 19

Days later, he returned to the headquarters. The secretary was waiting for him and took him to the police command center, where a sergeant gave him a brief talk about horrible crimes that they had to investigate. Cabrera showed him more details of criminality techniques and evaluation of the crime scene and then gave him a book to read.

Throughout the days, at home or on the bus, he read chapter by chapter, going through the pages of methodology, analysis of reports, procedural prerogatives, Stockholm syndrome, fingerprints, forensic photography, and the dramatic concepts of Kinsey. The French Michenaux descriptions were terrifying."

"The fight against crime tolerates no failures, Daniel," Yamandu had said. "Planning each investigation requires concepts of criminology, technicalities, and criminal law. This other book will reveal the details of the crime scene that must be detected, the importance of the signs of the crime, and the exhaustive study of the scene. Remember, the dead speak, and you must know how to listen to them."

That phrase rumbled in his mind: *Remember that the dead speak.*

They took him along a couple of times to crime scenes, "That's how you learn," they told him. The first two or three times that they took him they realized that he was not a hindrance, but that he was careful not to alter evidence, and that his curiosity helped them to complete their task more effectively.

"Always remember the importance of protecting the scene of a crime," MacLagan told him, "Which are all those actions and measures adopted, tending to secure, protect, and preserve the place of the crime." Then MacLagan looked him dead in the eye and added, "Do not touch anything!"

"And look at the true extent of the scene, set up secondary scenarios, and determine the methodology to be used," Martinez continued, while they drank coffee, and while he gave him the notebooks: *Technical-Ocular Inspection, The Agent's Management of Evidence,* and *Technical-Legal Chain of Custody,* which Daniel later read at home and on the beach.

And remember that the dead speak came to his mind over and over.

They gave him free classes on photography fixation and forensic photography. They made him try various lenses and filters, and they gave him a special Russian camera to use, they explained how it worked and told him, "You must take great care of this Russian camera. It's to take certain photos in cases of assassinations." The Russian camera was a wonderful Kiev-88. A modular format SLR, with four types of Leica lenses and a fabulous 28-80 without distortion. A gem.

"You must consider the responsibility of each shot," said a sergeant. "Use the appropriate adapter, adjust the shutter, focus on the lighting, and always follow the rules of protocol. Remember that your photos can end up in a courtroom display and you don't want a judge to be unhappy."

Detectives sometimes called him in the middle of the night to escort them to a crime scene, usually a dark scene on a dark night, with a fresh corpse and relatives crying outside. Some of those moments were very difficult, because sometimes the children of the dead were there, going through horrible grief. Sometimes the amount of blood on the floor was astonishing. In some very unpleasant deaths, the detectives warned him not to enter, to stay outside, and they waited for the technicians to come, because they knew that he was very young and, above all, delicate. "There are things that you better not see yet," they told him. A couple of times he saw what he should not have and had to go out and vomit from so much shock. Domínguez and MacLagan would see him there, absorbed, possessed by an existential anguish, and would tell him, "We work in no-man's-land, Daniel. Between two worlds."

One time they took him to a house on a hill where two guys had been shot. They laid around for four days before someone from down the road detected the scent. Daniel got to the door, sniffed, turned, and left. He did not want to enter. Those smells were horrible.

"I'm staying outside," he said. "I already told you that rotting dead are not for me!"

The forbidden smell of death from several days earlier was something he couldn't bear. He would gag. Whether their brains or guts were scattered on the wall or there was a pool of blood, or the victim had been shot, he didn't care if the body was fresh.

"Don't let me see rotting corpses," he complained.

Whenever they could they showed him the Hoffman Sign and the important Benassi Sign of gun powder marks. On many occasions they taught him about the importance of splatter marks and the Mercaux Sign. "Don't forget those three signs."

"Always look for signs of violence."

Detective work was a bit difficult and complicated. First, they entered the house and then the scene of the crime itself. They took some photos with the Russian camera, with a wide-open lens but without an angle of distortion. The film stock Daniel used had silver polynitrate mixed with sulfite, perchlorate, and indigo salts from Peru, which gave a special image when they used a trimanganate flash, which produced a bluish-violet fire pit. That left marks on the film of where there had been a weapon flash in the last 24-48 hours. The brighter the image, the more recent the fired shot. Sometimes they used two simultaneous cameras, with a lowered filter, which recorded the photos in a rather complicated, three-dimensional way. Thus, with that technique, they could know if shots had been fired or not and how many. Daniel took photos with the Russian camera and with the Pentax, and he took photos of the whole house and where there was blood it was seen in orange. The photos with the Russian camera came out in a bluish black and white but the bloodstains were like orange, including the photos of the corpse. If there had been blood in a place but someone had cleaned it up, the stains would come out a bluish color. They took air samples by opening a small petri dish and circulating it through the house, and with this they could know what kind of sulfites the gun had, with which they were informed about the type of weapon that had been used. They knew that the bullets made in Brazil had a high concentration of phosphorus mixed with sulfite, while those from Argentina had trimanganate, and the American ones had a component that they call porlatt which is a smoke killer so that the bullets do not make so much noise. The percentage of nitrites and nitrates varied with the country of origin. The Belgian and French bullets also had their characteristics. All of that, Daniel learned in a couple of courses he had to study in detail. By analyzing the petri dishes, the technicians could know what type of bullet they had used and therefore, what type or types of weapons had been used. It was very interesting, and Daniel learned a lot. Once they found a guy in his 30s who had committed suicide. A typical suicide. There was nothing to attract attention. They did all this research work, but the box showed that there was no powder in the air, and the photos showed that there were no orange spots. The other pictures also showed nothing. There they determined that the poor guy was killed in some other place, then they brought him home when the parents were away, and they fixed everything as if it was a suicide. Then the detectives called the technicians, who took many fingerprints, and with that they caught the culprits. Another time a man killed a thief with two shots and said it was in self-defense, but when they later did their investigation, the photos, petri dishes, and data showed that the shots had occurred in the bedroom and that the thief that had been shot was actually the jealous husband of a neighbor who had come to complain to the guy.

"See! Remember that science and technology will help you hear and understand what a dead person wants to say," MacLagan told him. "But it's up to you to know how to listen."

Chapter 20

All these comings and goings with the headquarters were sometimes like an adventure.

One afternoon, taking advantage of the fact that he was leaving early, he went to the Department of Justice to see Gina. Lourdes came out and told him that Gina had left early because her mother was ill. Daniel saw that as an opportunity to speak with Berta alone and try to find certain answers.

"Hello... what's going on?" Berta asked when she saw him.

Her office was a large room with a huge table, old and polished. A smell of old paper and coffee hovered over the table. He had to close the door and told her, "Tell me now, what I need to know."

"You came with your fangs out, huh?" she told him.

"Yes. Enough of this crap. If you want me in, speak up. Who chose me and why?"

An argument between them followed.

"Oh, so they should blow their cover and expose themselves and their families to torture and murder because you, some crybaby brat who barely paid any dues wears his curiosity on his sleeve?"

"You too are a little witch," he yelled at her.

"Daniel, Daniel," Berta said, sighing a deep breath. "We don't know who these kidnappers are. Whether they are people from the armed forces, or from the Joint Forces, from the police leadership or elsewhere. They can be secretaries, policemen, and perhaps even one of the inspectors."

"Please just tell me who—"

"It could be people from the court, from a police station, from one of the ministries," cried Berta. "Believe me. There is so much corruption and this dictatorship and is so strong and spread out that it can be any group from any side. And if they find out that it is being investigated, they vanish and disappear. What? no, no, don't leave. Wait."

"You...you—"

"Oh, Daniel, there's danger!" said Berta. "Danger of being killed. Danger. We just... we are all afraid." She paused. "Go home, Daniel. Drop all this. This is unknown and dangerous. They are killing young men and women." She took out a handkerchief and wiped her eyes. "I see Gina happy now, happy, I don't want anything to happen to her. I... I... if something happens to you or her I..." She lowered her head and she started to cry.

"But Berta..."

"Daniel, others.... We are in the middle of a horrible, horrible dictatorship. We all have relatives or acquaintances who have disappeared, and nothing can be done."

She took another sip of her coffee with sugar. She cleared her voice and explained. "It's not a clear mission, Daniel," she said and coughed. "It's about helping you climb as high as possible so that you get closer to that computer center and other centers where the data of those who were murdered is collected. Somehow these information streams do not appear in the police stations and do not reach the Judiciary. Several judges tried to obtain those reports, but somehow, they disappear."

"But where...?"

"Shut up and listen," Berta pleaded. "Someone or some people move their influences in some way and the data and files are then not found. And it is not known who does it or how. The information centers of the armed forces are inaccessible, but... but... they seem to have their connection to the Interpol center or in that special room next to it."

"How can you be sure?"

"Because those are international regulations. Interesting, huh? The center is in the headquarters, but in a section guarded by a select group of the armed forces. The door's armored and has an antechamber with a grill and a military guard. They do it because there, or in the military center, are all the data of the revolutionary Tupamaros group, the living, the dead and the imprisoned. That's why no one can enter there. They have everything classified and filed there."

"Hmm..."

"Several operators can carry files and reports, documents which are passed through a shielded window, but the operators cannot enter. The employees who work there are army technicians, selected people, very aggressive, and they enter from that special gate or through a secretive basement entrance, which crosses a military garrison and has its own staircase. Not a fly passes by without being controlled."

"So...? Do you mean—"

"You're getting it, huh?" Berta chided with an affable nod. "That's your goal. There may or may not be a clue that clarifies the main problem: the disappearance and death of many young men and women, whose parents are desperate. It's a horrible situation, Daniel. Each person is the son, brother, cousin, boyfriend, or nephew of others, and thus each disappearance affects many people. There are hundreds and hundreds of people suffering from all of this. But the government denies it, the army denies it, and the Joint Forces do not accept it. People have no one to complain to and nothing can be done."

"And me, why did they give it to me? Why was *I* chosen?"

"Dummy!" Berta huffed. "No one gave it to you. You found it alone. You just fell through the crack. We only open the doors that you wanted to open yourself."

"And why isn't a strong group formed to investigate it?"

"Investigate what? By whom? It is all layered and intertwined and no clear culprit or savior can be seen. It is not known where, it is not known to whom, everything has been denied, nothing is known. Lawyers and consuls have tried to find out. Reporters and foreign ambassadors have tried to press for an investigation, there has been international pressure, but it was of no use. The problem does not exist and there is no way to do anything. So, we hoped and prayed for a smart and scoundrel fox that we could bring into the castle, and one day, suddenly, one fox showed up without even calling him. A smart asshole with a fool's face that misleads, elusive and shrewd, with a dirty past but who looks so innocent, who was suddenly awakened by a strong feeling, or hatred, or who knows what."

Daniel stared at her as amazement possessed him and his skin crawled.

He sat down and she sat next to him. They were silent for a long while. He understood.

"Where do I get help and obtain the power to achieve that?"

"From the darkness, Daniel. From people who are in the darkness and who are going to get close to you.

He stood up. Berta hugged him in silence.

As he was leaving, he asked, "Last question. Who is the Anubis?"

"Hmm... Anubis? no, no Anubis, is the Nubian.... Some people call him Anubis, others the Nubian. He is a... hmm... he's a *mercenary* from Belgium who's rolling around here. It is said that he provided weapons to the Tupamaros, to criminals, and those in the army. A merchant. A merchant of death. Nobody knows his face. He has his powerhouse somewhere in the Capurro neighborhood, but not even the police or the army go near there. Don't go near their area. They will kill you; just like they killed your dad."

"Will the Nubian be involved in all this?"

"There are people who say yes, there are people who say no. I don't know more."

"What if I need to contact him?"

"What!? are you crazy? This is beyond you. Go away."

"Yes, goodbye."

"Danny, Daniel, wait," she said and hugged him. "Be careful... and... and don't do bad things to Gina.... Pig!" she said and hugged him again and started to cry. "Love her. Love her, Daniel."

He left.

Chapter 21

The following Saturday he went to the street market in the Villa Biarritz, several square blocks of open market stocked with vegetables, fruits, flowers, and farm products. He liked to walk until tired in that sea of produce, so full of smells, colors, and well-known people. He crossed paths with several neighbors and two friends, greeted the parents of another friend, chatted with the greengrocers, and even met Pocho Pereyra, who invited him to come to his house during the week to talk about life. "And I'm not going to ask you anything," he told him. "I just have a new bottle of Gin and I need company to open it."

When he returned from the street, carrying fruits, onions and his favorite potatoes, his mother told him that he had a call from a rude woman, "Oh how aggressive, said you are a bad son, a pervert, and left her number. But... Who is that animal?"

"I don't know," said Daniel, dialing the number. A woman answered and said, "Luckily you called, eunuch, go to the corner of Roque Grasseras Street three blocks from 21."

"Ah, it was nothing, mom. I forgot something; I'll be back in a bit."

"But who is that woman?"

He walked down the street, went to the corner. The bitch he had seen on the street outside the medical school was waiting for him, leaning on the black Mercedes Benz with an aggressive face. She said, "Hurry up, idiot," and went for a walk.

What's wrong with this woman? Daniel wondered.

"Hi Daniel," said the gentleman of the Mercedes. They shook hands. The old man had the same green emerald on his lapel and his same ring with a large emerald. Same alpaca suit.

"Who is that woman who speaks badly to me?"

"Never mind. Never mind."

"Gave my poor mother a stroke," Daniel said, raising his voice so she could hear.

"What matters are other things."

They talked, and the subject was diverted towards current politics and other subjects. Daniel fell silent.

"What's wrong?"

"Nothing... it's that... it's that.... I still feel that I would be helping those above, the rich men, the strong, the elite... the..."

"The bad guys from above, eh? Do you feel that you are helping those from above, those who screw up the poor, eh?"

"Yes! that. Yes. I feel like I'm helping the oligarchs, the ruling class."

"Daniel, we are the true pillars of the economy," said the green old man "Yes, we helped evacuate your friend. Look Daniel, your brain is contaminated by leftist ideas, the slogans, and the Tupamaros ideas of this time. You are not objective."

"Yes, I am. If the poor want to eat every day and have a roof that does not leak, these are not leftist ideas, but humanitarian ones. The problem is that people like you, who have so much money and are so far to the right, see those in the center and humanitarians as people of the left and communists."

"Oh, shut up."

"I won't shut up!" yelled Daniel. "I feel I'm helping the same oligarchs, Colorados and Blancos, who sank the economy!"

"Oh, no you don't!" snapped back the man, in a rare moment of lowered poise. "Daniel, Daniel, you don't know anything. Listen to this and listen well. With the poor, a country does not rise, nor does the economy sustain itself. With poor people you don't go anywhere. Those of the lower class and the lower middle class are parasites of the country who neither build nor contribute anything. Basing the economy on them is to melt the country and just leave it in poverty, plowing a breeding ground for all sorts of strife and corruption. With the people of the upper middle class, the upper class itself, with those rich oligarchs who know how to be lucky and successful and make a fortune, with those the economy rises. With them, there is work, there are employees, there is production, and a country is built, and I am with them."

"Hmm..."

"Silly. With the humble men of this land, you get nowhere. The proletarians are not constructive because they have no head for it, they lack brains. The small farmer who complains so much that he has no more land would not contribute anything to the economy if he was given more land. Listen to this because it is a worldwide truth. Communist ideas are nothing but destructive."

"But... with those big businessmen and landowners who build the country, the worker and the peasant are crushed by great misery, without food, or shelter, or health care, or..."

"Ah, ay, Daniel, don't give me phrases made by others. You are spitting propaganda. You need a mental enema to get that shit out of your head."

"It's not shit! It's a... It's a—"

"Ah, shut up. You know nothing. You know a little about something narrow and myopic and you already think that's the whole truth. Say what you want, but it's a reality that the Uruguayan left, the socialists and communists, are dirty from the Russian Marxism they try to spread in Uruguay. That leftism that is spreading in Uruguay, those Marxist ideals, that urban guerrilla, are nothing more than reflections of an advancing Russian imperialism."

"It's not like that. No."

"You don't know anything, Daniel," he added. "You have a brain contaminated with anti-capitalism. You're stuck there, and you do not see the world reality or the geopolitical facets of the southern cone. Schmuck! You're mixing the real pain you feel and the legit humanism you have with reactionary anti-capitalism, and for that reason you think that the leftists are right. Like many, you have a mental mix up, a psychological salad. The left is not humanitarian, and capitalism is not necessarily anti-humanitarian."

Daniel couldn't answer immediately. He thought and grappled with the man's powerful rhetoric, then finally said, "Come on, sir, eh.... I cannot ignore the reality of Uruguay or all the abuse and impoverishment that has occurred, the country and its people have been dispossessed."

"Okay, I agree, yes," the man answered. "But that doesn't mean that the left is going to bring an improvement or put a solution on the table; neither them nor the Tupamaros, who by the way, I tell you they don't even know what they want."

"Of course, they know."

"They don't. They are just a bunch of communists and anarchist reactionaries who are not capable of being constructive. Morons."

"No. They do know. They do know."

"Ah, they don't even have good humanity to govern, and they have neither the conditions nor the quality to manage the economy and, far worse, they are shitty anti-Semites."

Daniel began to think about what he was saying.

"And I'm going to give you the key, Daniel, so you can see how shitty they are and how wrong they are," the emerald man continued. "The key is that the Montevideo leftists, be them students, workers, or communists, obeying

Russian directives, are pro-Arab, and anti-Semitic. If they were as original in their ideas, as independent as they claim to be, as liberal as they state, they would accept that Israel offers the best version of socialism. But no, no. They ignore the reality of the Israelis and cling to the lies cooked up by the Russians just because the Russians told them. Do you realize it or not? I repeat. They embrace the lie and reject the Israeli truth, just for licking the ass of the Russians. And you would give them the management of the country?"

Daniel listened without answering.

"I tell you more. If the leftist and pseudo-socialists of Uruguay accepted that Israel has the best socialism money can buy, and if the Tupamaros accepted that too, they would all be pro-Semitic, pro-Jewish, and very anti-Arab, instead of what they are."

"Which is...?"

"Assholes of the Russians, anti-Semites, and pro-Arab lackeys."

"Well, that's not—"

"Well nothing, you asked! That's the way they are. Israel has the best example of socialism, but have you ever heard of a Tupamaro praising Israel? Have you ever heard someone from the socialist or communist party of Uruguay crying out in favor of Israel? No! Because they are all ass-lickers of the Russian tsunami that seeks to advance in this country."

"Well, but... but..."

"But nothing. Everyone on the Uruguayan left... and every socialist or communist in all of South America, you hear me...? All anti-Semites. Including the Tupamaros, yes, and all those from the socialist and communist party of Uruguay. Everybody! And the only reason they are anti-Semitic, okay? it's because they are pro-Russian. Nothing more. That's what they are."

Daniel was still silent.

"You will see. I tell you. If one day... if one day the leftists or socialists or any of these Tupamaros come to power, you will see how they speak out against Israel, they befriend Russia and Cuba, and they lick hairy Arab ass. You'll see. They'll kiss the feet of the Russians and proclaim themselves anti-Israel with any excuse. I predict it. And even more. If one day they come to power, there you'll see what bad leaders they are. They will elect shameful and incompetent presidents, the economy will go down, and drugs and crime will increase. You'll see."

"What you're saying can't be."

"No...? The Leftists, the Socialists, the Communists, and the Tupamaros are all anti-Semites, although they call it anti-Zionist so it would sound more legit.

And if Russia told them to eat poop, they would go to the bathrooms, licking the toilets, but declaring that they do it because of their own original ideologies."

"No. Don't talk like that."

"Ah, no? And if the Russians or Cubans tell them to drink cow piss, there they will go kneeling behind cows, slurping urine, and shouting that they do it as part of the universal union of the left against imperialism. I tell you that the day Cuba and Russia tell those of the Uruguayan leftists to use dung to comb their hair instead of hair gel, you are going to see them all well combed and smelling of dung but proclaiming that they do it for their own ideas and blaming the ranchers and the corporations. And you will see them stealing. So, it will be.

"Ah, stop, you're just ranting now." Daniel couldn't argue with him. He knew it was true. The Uruguayan left *was* anti-Semitic, and the scar on his forehead, from the stone of a leftist Uruguayan at high school, was a beautiful proof.

"You're very local in your concepts and you don't see the entire party," he continued. "You tell me that the poor are cold and hungry, that the peasants suffer, that the workers suffer misery. And I answer that you're right. But what you don't see and prefer to ignore is globalism. And if you don't understand that, it's going to be extremely difficult for you to understand why an Inter-American plan like Operation Condor is so necessary and vital."

Gee, Daniel thought, *this guy has no shortage of arguments.*

"Yes, Daniel. With Paraguay and Brazil in the lead, thanks to the dear brothers Stroessner and Garrastazu Médici, South American militarism is organizing itself very well to defeat this attack by international communism. Do you realize that?"

Gee, that's...

"Pinochet, from Chile, is doing his part. Great guy! They're all united and well-organized on a common front. And that organization is the Condor Operation. A great plan. Weapons, money, training, coordination, mutual support, Uruguay has everything to face the problem. The Tupamaros of our country and similar groups in each country are going to be bullied, removed, and they'll be gone."

"Yes, I see. And in the middle, many innocents will be slaughtered and will be..."

"Ah, in every war there are innocent victims, Daniel. Look closely. Thanks to the fabulous logistical and military assistance, Brazil, Chile, and Paraguay have calmed down and entered a phase of economic progress. Hopefully, all Latin America will follow in their footsteps."

"But... the victims—"

"But nothing, Daniel. You must fight, and you must win. Or do you want another Cuba here, where we share all the grain but can't buy a loaf of bread? And yes, the Condor operation provides weapons, trains paramilitaries, teaches interrogation, brings specialists, and..."

"Well, well," Daniel spoke to him. "Now that... hey, don't get upset."

"First, I wanted to retort to your audacity to speak like that, ignorant!" he blurted out. "You're daring, but instead of raising my voice, I wanted to show you that you neither have the right nor the last word. Second, uh... well... something else... meh... let's leave it there."

Daniel shut up, then stood up and said: "What about my request? Of what I asked you, about the murders?"

"I didn't forget. Certain contacts of mine have found out that yes, there seems to be something to that. Hmm, that's very ugly. We'll find out more. It appears that there were several unjustified murders. And with ransom money involved. Ugly, ugly. I didn't know that, but we'll continue to investigate that."

"I need help with that," Daniel said. And he thought, *this emerald man is the representative of the power that I need.*

"Are you sticking your nose in the headquarters?" asked the Mercedes green man, "hmm?"

"Yes, on those walks. There's a secret room there, where there seems to be great information, but it's inaccessible and very well guarded. I want to get in there."

"Well, let me find out. As soon as I know something, I'll let you know."

"I'm just not going to be able to do it. There... eh... there is a secret staircase that allows you to reach that room from the basement but this..."

"Oh yeah?... hmm... I see you kept sniffing."

"Yes, I plan to continue. Yes. I need information. I just cannot... do it all alone."

"Hmm... I'll see."

"I need a hand in this," Daniel stressed.

The old man stared at him and nodded his head, letting him know that he understood. "Okay, you'll get it."

"What... will I?"

"Yes. You'll get the help you want, once you know what you want."

"Okay, thanks. And... and also... Who is this one that they call the Nubian?"

"Hmm... no... not Nubian. Anubis. They call him Anubis. Hmm... wait, you're right. Some people call him The Nubian, and others call him Anubis. I don't know why. He's a mercenary with roots in Europe. He's a guy who sometimes does a favor here and sometimes does it there, but overall, he's a dangerous SOB, an unaffiliated assassin. Why? Do you think he's involved?"

"I don't know. Possibly."

"Hmm... tread carefully there. He's part of a wider organization located in Europe, I think Switzerland, where he is connected to another criminal called The Belgian. Operation Condor has sourced weapons from them on several occasions. Don't even think about getting near The Nubian. They will cut you up alive before killing you. Your mother will find you eaten by rats."

"Yes, but what? Who *is* he?"

"Leave it there. Never mind. Why do you ask?"

"They told me that... that the Nubian... uh... Why...why do they call him that?"

"Hmm... it's Anubis, The Nubian, something like that. They call him that because he's the god of death. Would that give a clue? Whoever gets too close to him tends to die."

"Well... he might—"

"That's a difficult subject, Danny boy," said the old green emerald man. "Leave it there, I'll explain another day," he emphasized. "And something else, Daniel, and I know you're going to take this badly. We are in rough times, where unexpected bad things happen to people unexpectedly."

"Yeah. So?"

"Do you know how to use a weapon?"

Daniel's eyes answered before his mouth could.

"No?" said the old man. "Well, I think you should learn."

"No. Never."

"For protection. Just in case. For security."

"Danny Blum, agent collaborateur, armed agent? Forget it! I'm a student, not a guerrilla. No. And I'm leaving."

"Well, go away, but if you can learn, take advantage of it. Take care of yourself, take care of yourself a lot. Look Daniel, there are struggles between powers here in Uruguay, some you know, others you don't, be very careful. If you are caught in the middle, they will kill you."

"Yes. I understand, I know."

They said goodbye and Daniel got out of the car.

What should I call him? he wondered. *The man of the emerald? The old man of the green emerald? The green old man? We'll see.*

Daniel got out. He took three steps and saw the blonde woman approaching.

"Wipe your ass well before leaving your house next time, pig," she said aloud. "Now the car will stink because of you."

Daniel got scared. *She's coming to hit me,* he thought and walked away fast. He did not want problems, and he left quickly.

Beast... Beast bitch, he thought, *who is this blonde whore?*

He walked home chewing on his thoughts.

And so, knowing or not knowing, believing that he knew what he still did not understand, Daniel advanced in his attempt to be in the middle of the infernal conflict between opposing powers and not get burned on either side.

Chapter 22

One day Martinez saw him and told him, "The time has come for you to learn to handle various weapons. It's part of your training," and without further ado, they took him to the firing range.

He allowed himself to be convinced because the idea appealed to him. Guns were a horrible thing. But he had never been exposed to them and he didn't want to miss out on that opportunity. There's something that fascinated him about those instruments of death. So, they brought in a couple of instructors who had significant experience not only in shooting but also in teaching.

They measured his hand, to see which weapon would suit him. They taught him first how to grip the band, how to put the fingers and how to hold them, how to pose his arms, how to place his feet and balance his body. First, they used a heavy, empty pistol and taught him to balance and avoid being knocked back by the gun. They made him try various weapons.

"You're going to start with a 22, Daniel," the instructor told him.

He learned a lot. He tried a Glock 17, Austrian, hard, and heavy, and then the German Walther P99AS and the Walther PPK. The instructor showed him how to take it apart, put it back together, and lubricate it with a special oil while explaining how dependable, and powerful they were.

Later, Valdemar, the instructor, showed him the Swiss Sig Sauer pistol, which he didn't like, and then a Smith & Wesson American pistol, but they were very powerful and heavy. He learned how to disassemble and clean the pistols and separate the trigger, the firing pin, barrel, and the slide, and fit them on the frame. He assembled and disassembled various pistols, inserted magazines, retracted the slide without hurting his fine, delicate fingers, and learned how to cock the various weapons. He was taught everything related to the structure of the bullets, and was given a ballistics class, which studies the trajectory of the projectile and the elements that affect it.

An instructor named Matilde explained further.

"The recent use of a weapon is manifested by the presence in its interior of the Mendell-Koch Sign, which is the presence of semi-combusted powder residue, which gives the swab an orange color with the Griess reagent, which is an amine mixed with acetic acid," Matilde told him. "The dark orange or reddish color is due to nitrites. If you do it in the field and you want it to have legal force, you must use a sealed swab from the Judicial Power and you must have one or two witnesses, if not, even if it is incontrovertibly positive, it will have no value in court. Did you hear me, dummy? Or is this overly difficult for you?"

"Oh yeah, yes, a swab!," Daniel laughed. "Uuuuuhh... a swab."

"Pay attention!"

"Yes, Instructor Matilde."

She explained the interior ballistics and all the parts of the firearms. That bored Daniel.

"Pay attention," she said again. "Or I tell Yamandu and to the other Russian.

"What... you, Matilde?" Daniel said. "That MacLagan must have told you something about that guy, eh?"

"You are not the only one who does not like those two ripper-faced Russians"

Damn Russians, thought Daniel. *Jewish murderers They were born with antisemitism in their genes.*

The following week he had a class on ballistic microscopy, photographic devices, photograph analysis, and other things, and then he started shooting more weapons. With all that he was already bored, and he told Matilde.

"If you don't like it, at any moment you can go back to your whore of a mommy's house and forget about this whole thing. No drips outta my vodka glass."

"Wait a freaking min—"

"Nobody's training you for anything, hey, you are in the headquarters, and it would be almost immoral not to teach you to use a weapon. You can never go on a live call with the guys if you can't use a gun. It's the regulation."

Daniel decided to take it all as an interesting and educational adventure and continued testing weapons. He tried out a Bersa 22, then fired a Mauser C-96 pistol, then an Astra, another special Beretta, and a Remington.

In the classrooms of the polygon, they gave him more classes of all kinds on ballistics.

"The study of the effects of ballistics is complex," said one of the instructors. "The determination of the entry and exit holes is essential, as well as the angle of incidence. When the projectile, the bullet, hits the skin and muscles, a depression is first produced with stretching of the tissues, which, when their elasticity and resistance are overcome, are perforated, leaving a circular or ovoid wound according to the angle. The effect varies according to the type of tissue and the area of the body, and according to the nose, speed, rotation, orientation, position, and incidence.... "

He gave Daniel several examples on the blackboard and marked them in the notebook they gave him to study. He followed it with photos from a projector.

"Look, you see here? This is Fisch's Ring, which is the circular area of contusive characteristics that mark the entrance area. See here? That's Fisch's Ring, do you see it? They also call it a wiping ring, and it has its zone of attenuation as the projectile moves away... here... and here... do you see it?

"Yes, yes, I see it."

"Remember that the diameter and damage in the entrance hole does not by itself indicate the caliber of the weapon used," Matilde said later. "But you can calculate the angle with the Belaunde Sign, and you see them here... and... there, you see? The area of the Fisch's Ring may or may not be followed by the smoking area, if the shot was close, and the tattoo area, according to the distance at which the shot occurred."

"Yes, I see. Yes."

"Before I forget, Daniel," Matilde continued, "always remember to look for what is not seen."

"Right."

"This is a very important rule. Research exhaustively what you find, yes, but always think about what you haven't found, what's not seen."

They showed him several photos to give him examples.

"And also remember that other rule, that the dead talk to you. It is up to you to listen. Did you hear that before?"

"Yes, from MacLagan."

"Hmm...I figured."

"In point-blank shooting, from less than ten centimeters away, the fumes produce dirt on the skin, often washable, produced by burnt powder," explained an instructor. "That dirt or stain, known as the smoke stain, sets the distance according to how washable it is and how much it has burned the skin. It is also called a fake tattoo."

"Tattoo, yes."

"The real tattoo is made up of semi-combusted and unburned particles of powder and metal particles detached from the projectile," Matilde said, while she drew on the blackboard and showed several photos on the screen.

Daniel put the coffee aside. *This class is serious,* he thought. *This is important.*

They showed him many photos and made many diagrams to show him real tattoos, fake tattoos, traces of primer on the skin, forensic findings, Simonin's Cockade, Hoffman's Mine Blow, Benassi's Sign, how to diagnose a gunshot from point-blank shots. The Bourchett and Altoid signs impressed him greatly. He got drunk on so many details.

When the other instructor left and they were alone in the classroom, Matilde stood up, approached him, and said: "Remember this day well, dear Daniel. What you are being taught is for a reason. Daniel, I repeat, always remember to look for what is not seen." She stared at him with big eyes. "Investigate a lot what you find, yes, but always think about what is not seen. Do not be guided only by what you see and what you know. There are things you cannot talk about, but you can search in the silence of files and photos. The dead have a story to tell. Always."

"What?" Daniel said, startled by what she said. *Why is she telling me that?* he thought, with his skin full of goose bumps. Who is she? What does she know?

"As you go, sooner or later, you will face a source of information, where the pieces are not clear. Like with a big puzzle where many pieces are missing, but the picture on the box, the photo in your mind looks a certain way. Then remember this phrase that I tell you today: dig into what's not seen to string together the data."

The hairs on Daniel's neck stood on end. *What does this bitch know?* he thought, *Is there another message here?* Adrenaline rushed through his entire body, and in his gaze, he knew that Matilde knew he had gotten the message. *But who is this woman?* "... remember what she is going to teach you" Etcheverry had told him. *Oh, that explained it. How horrible. Who did she lose?* Daniel began to understand. That woman in front of him surely lost a son or a sister, and there was nothing she could do against that fact in this harsh dictatorship. She must be a relative of one or two of those who have disappeared, *The Missings*, as they were called, those taken by the army, never be seen again. *How atrocious.*

Daniel looked at her with big eyes and knew, through her wet eyes, that she knew he had understood. She approached him before leaving class, with teary eyes, and gave him a long hug and kissed him on the cheek. She held him tight for a moment, like hoping that Daniel could bring back whoever she had lost. He felt that feeling, understanding her pain, and came out wiping his eyes. *Shit, how many more tears I am going to shed?*

Then they explained and showed him the Gomez-Smith Destructive Sign, which was the zone of destruction exactly three centimeters from the entrance orifice and which varies from organ to organ and with the projectile features.

"That zone of destruction varies with the caliber and mass of the projectile, Daniel, and with its centrifugal force. A large caliber bullet, fired at close range, has impact but little centrifugal force, and a small bullet, say a lined 22, fired with a long-distance precision rifle, has little hit and a lot of centrifugal force, thus using Gomez-Smith, one can calculate mass, caliber, distance, and even type of weapon. The angle complements the information."

The next class was on types of gunpowder and its analysis in the crime zone and in the laboratory.

The following day they called him to class to tell him that three assailants had been very generous in donating their lives for him to learn. They had been shot. Matilde and one of the instructors were waiting for him at the morgue to show him shot by shot the forensic details of each one. There were the three corpses of the unfortunate men who until the day before were alive. Pale, lifeless dolls, like sleeping a long sleep, unperturbed now, exonerated from the misery that had led them to violence, they didn't protest. They had him take photos of each wound and told him to save them as part of his learning. Then they asked him questions about everything that had been explained to him and about things in the notebook. Matilde was surprised at what Daniel already knew.

"Perhaps you're not such a dummy after all," she said smiling. "Your ugliness misleads. Hmm... And maybe it's your innocent face that confuses. I hope you remember the most important thing."

"Yes," he said. "I'm going to remember the most important thing, that you only have nice words for me."

"Good luck... dummy!" she said, then approached and hugged him again, a hug like he was her savior, her only hope.

"Thank you, I had a good teacher," he said. "Not very hygienic, but very sweet and good."

"Hmm!" she said going out with him to the patio of the morgue and lighting a cigarette. She looked out at the sky and looked around to Daniel. "So, you fell in love with Gina, eh? Love her, Daniel, don't hurt her. I'm a friend of Berta and she told me about you. You devil."

"You know her? No, I'm not going to hurt her, Matilde."

"Good. And remember well what I taught you. Join the pieces."

"Yup. The pieces."

"Did you hear me?

"Hmm...?"

"Sooner or later, you will get to where you want to go," she said while smoking. "I saw it in your ugly face the moment you walked through the door.

That investigating face. That secret plan face. No. Don't tell me. Listen, the day will come in which you'll get whatever you are looking for. That day things are not going to be clear. You will have to think. Let this be clear to you, do you hear me? When you don't see what you get, you must know how to connect the dots. It's part of the criminal investigation."

"Explain."

"Record it in your memory. When one comes across a lot of information, it's difficult to know what is and what is not relevant. Therefore, one must find what is seen and at the same time search for what is not seen. Confusing? I will boil it down, so someone stupid can understand. You must search for what you cannot see. Then you must join the loose ends, between what you see and what you don't see, like putting together a puzzle where pieces are missing. That, yes, that example is good."

"Repeat it more clearly."

Matilde rolled her eyes and repeated it to him. They discussed it. She gave him other examples.

He then said goodbye and left.

He went outside but waited and was thinking about going back to the morgue. He lit a cigarette and walked a bit to clear his mind.

He kept walking.

Join the dots. Search for what is not seen. He began to think about everything that happened. Suddenly... could it be what he was thinking of? *Ay, ay, and if I study the data and reports of the other autopsies... can I find common clues and data? Is it possible?*

"The power, Daniel, the power."

"It's like I told you. The power, Daniel."

Chapter 23

They kept insisting on the weapons training. They made him shoot with a Colt 38 revolver, another H&K revolver, and another Smith & Wesson, but he didn't like any of them as they were too heavy. They brought him the semiautomatic P-64 9mm pistol, and then a Russian Tocarev, and a Makarov PM, also Russian. "These are combat weapons," the instructor told him, "And not for ordinary people."

Daniel finished his weapons and bullet's course having chosen the Remington 51 as his favorite and the Beretta 951 as his second choice. He was relieved that his weapons training was over, and considering all the atrocities he had endured, things hadn't gone badly.

He met Gina at the Expreso Pocitos café, and they enjoyed Frangelico liquor. Later they went for a walk.

Daniel asked her about the relationship between what was going on in Uruguay and the Fourth International. After calling him a stupid pig a couple times, she explained.

"The Fourth International is an international organization of communist parties that follows the ideas of Marx, Engels, Lenin, and Trotsky. Everything had started in the nineteenth century with the First International to organize the workers of the world into a common intellectual and active mass. A beautiful idea. The Second International congress was around the end of that century and was led by Engels himself. Do you know who he was?"

"Yes, I read about it. But why is it important in all this?"

"Shhh, Shhh, wait," she said while adjusting the napkin under her drink. If you want to understand what is happening in Uruguay and why, you must listen to this. The Third was the Bolshevik International and was soon discredited because it became a Stalinist Russian instrument with more imperialist than humanist intentions. Look Daniel, you must look at the International as an organization that tries and plans to organize all the groups and labor movements of the world into a great mass of thought. Then unite them all through similar actions, do you understand? It's the labor movement of each country uniting and adopting an international policy and controlling their governments. Hmm. See? So, are all the proletarians of the world united in a single entity and with a common goal."

"Yes Gina, but... and what about Trotsky?"

"I'll tell you, but first let's take a cab to the Montjui Hotel." They finished the Frangelico, got up, took a cab, and went straight to the hotel. She got undressed while he sat in bed.

"What about Trotsky?"

"Uh, Daniel. Okay. The Fourth International was the great heir to all workers' organizations, but that's where the mess started, because it was organized by Trotsky himself, who understood the International as a world party of the proletarian revolution. And he caused a mess because the guy proclaimed, and with good reason, that the third international had abandoned the flag of the international proletariat to dedicate itself to kissing Stalin's imperialist ass, you see? You must remember... the third had become a Stalinist instrument.

"Yes," said Daniel, taking his shirt off while she was pulling his pants down. I remember that. It was a very rough time."

"Yes, it was. As Stalinism spread throughout Europe, such as France, Germany, Lithuania, and other countries, the local working masses had become Stalinist in turn. Trotsky, a great intellectual, proclaimed that this was a betrayal, that Stalinism was a betrayal of the Workers of the World and that Stalin, a great opportunist brute, was a traitor. With that ideology and mentality, the Fourth International was founded. There you go. Indeed, the full name was the Communist Fourth International Congress."

Daniel was left thinking. They were both nude, sitting side by side, talking.

"Do you know anything about that Trotsky, Daniel?" she asked him.

"Nooo... not much."

"Well, you should, because he was like you, a non-religious Jew, atheist, nosy, troublemaker, and full of strange ideas. He was the fifth son of a Jewish family, and his real name was Lev Davidovich Bronstein. He was a little Jewish boy like you, and his little pee-pee was cut off like yours. Ha, like this one! Ha. Ha. Small and cut like yours, ha!"

"Gina! Small but effective!"

"Oh, prove it."

They jumped at each other. They made love in a hurry. Then lit a cigarette and continued talking.

She continued to explain. "Then Trotsky proclaimed himself anti-Stalinist, and that attitude cost him, because Stalin finally had him killed in 1940 to get rid of the hindrance. The Fourth proclaimed the theory of a permanent international revolution, and this is where the Trotskyists parted ways with the ass-licking Marxist-Leninists of Moscow."

"We're basically taught that all communists are cut from the same cloth—"

"Don't blame your stupidity on your teachers," Gina teased. "The problem was that the world began to modernize and complicate and the current of international communism divided between Stalin's ass kissers, that is, the Stalinists, and the Trotskyists, who were anti-Stalinists, and then came Mao, who began to export Maoism, then came Cuba, and already many communists changed course."

"Hmm... messy."

"You see Daniel?" Gina continued. "And so, we reached the sixties." She reached down and arched her back to pull on her panties "With a great mass of workers, students, peasants, and poor people scattered throughout Uruguay and all Latin America, being propagandized by the international Trotskyists, by the Maoists, by the centrist Stalinists, by the pro-Castro fans, and by other groups, liberals, and others more orthodox, and each one of those lions wants to be the lion-king of the savanna. That explains the mess and confusion you see in Uruguay, Argentina, Brazil, and other countries."

"Yes, a tangle, a mixture of leftist ideologies," said Daniel, caressing her shoulders and her breasts. "A violent mess."

"Oh, you finally see now?" she scoffed. "A whole nation of little-dicked morons like you is so easily controlled," she continued. "You are a shortsighted, little-Danny-breast-baby. You see only the injustice of the worker, the hunger of the peasants, and the local inequality. That squeezes your narrow heart and fills you with sorrow and your ignorant tears do not allow you see the whole global concept. It's not about hugging the left because that is going to feed little Johnny or make Madam Susan get more pay. No. It is about organizing all the Johnnies, all the Susans, all the Josephs, and the Marias, of all the Latin countries in a common organization, in an awakened, active, powerful, and proclaiming front so that all of them, all, have a better time and improved lifestyle. Are you glimpsing this, dummy, or did you just shoot what was left of your brain between my legs? That's what the Fourth International is all about, silly, or maybe your head doesn't let you see the global table? Eh...? Maybe between the dead and sex your mind has degenerated, my baby?"

Daniel was mesmerized by her dialogue.

"And there's something else, Daniel, and I'm done," Gina continued, standing up and walking in the room. "Latin American governments and dictatorships are trying to stop the armed advance of all those leftists by organizing themselves in a fighting association called Operation Condor, where they obtain logistics, money and weapons for a common battle."

"How do you know that?"

"Because I don't wander around thinking with tiny balls all day."

"Which side are you on?"

"I am on the side of Uruguay, as Uruguayan I am. I want you to know this. The left or communism are divided into various factions, as I told you, Marxists, Trotskyists, Maoists, Castroists, etc., and they all seek to conquer the minds and attitudes of workers, students, the poor, day laborers, and others. They don't do it to help them improve their lifestyle or to be better off, but to conquer them and be able to advance their imperialist plans in that country. They will seduce them with lies, promises, and ideology to gain their favor and fight for them. Don't be misled."

"Hey, but they... wait, let's take a shower."

"Why? No amount of water in the world will cleanse you."

"I want to soap all your body."

"Shhh, listen, pervert. This is important. The left is a human mass, with many different faces, many different policies, and strategies that advance and conquer."

"Yes, but what about poverty, the peasants? That is real too."

"Oh, shut up, you and the poverty, you whining simpleton. Christ I could conquer a whole continent of idiots like you without firing a single shot. They know that there is poverty and disadvantage, and they use it as propaganda and as a means of infiltration. They do it in Uruguay, Argentina, Brazil, Chile, Paraguay, etc. They make you believe that it is social justice that is advancing when it is an imperialist infiltration of the left, with Russian Stalinism in disguise. The only way to stop it is by the South American countries joining and fighting this wave off. However, the governments of all those countries are commanded by corrupt, ignorant, and demagogic politicians, incapable of doing something in their own country, much less joining with other countries, their lands also full of whining Dannys, and their useless politicians, to create a front and a common struggle. Just look here, in Uruguay, how ineffective they were."

"Yes, I know," said Daniel.

"And in Argentina, Paraguay, and Brazil it's all the same. The same political-economic degeneration disorganizing society and allowing the imperialist advance of the Russians, ah, and the Chinese as well."

"I realize. Yes."

"Then what?" Gina continued. "The big corporations, the high-ranking military and the Americans saw that the only solution in all these countries was to overthrow those political governments with military coups, kick out the politicians and send them home, impose brutal dictatorships and unite in a common front. All this with information, training, data, and weapons that the Americans provide. And that common organization, that operation, is called Operation Condor. So that's what happens. You see?"

"Yes. But are you agreeing with the Condor?"

"Yes and no. No and yes. I hate them for what they are, and for their support and organization of dictatorships, and for the brutality, the dead, the social injustice, and all the crap they brought upon us. You need to know about this Operation Condor. It is a secret pact between the dictators of our country and Bolivia, Brazil, Argentina, Chile, and Paraguay to exchange information, weapons, money, detainees, and even heavy artillery. It's a trans-border diabolic pact. They have all created special detention centers for torture and executions of any dissident and even opponents from other countries."

"Oh, Gina."

"They use violent death squads to arrest and kill people and to create terror. Right here in our country. Horrible. And those death squads are comprised of Uruguayans themselves. Imagine that. Uruguayans killing Uruguayans. They are animals. Hyenas. Hundreds of people have been abducted and made to disappear.

"Hundreds!?"

"That we know of. The detention center called Libertad is just one of those centers. Operation Condor has a dark and sadistic agenda. I hate them."

"I see," Daniel said, standing nude in front of her. "Come on, let's take a shower."

"Not yet, wait. Listen, it *is* horrible, but on the other hand The Condor is needed to cleanse and clean our country, and the other countries, and immunize them against the invading communist wave. Otherwise... can you imagine a Uruguay-Cuba, with a pro-Russian demagogue general as a president? Can you imagine a Castro-like Uruguayan president becoming a dictator? Can you imagine Uruguay under an economic blockade full of hunger and misery? Can you imagine a civil war?"

"Gee... I see, we are in between two evil and bloody giants."

"Yes, we are, in between two monsters. I don't like those South American dictatorships, I hate them, but they are the lions you bring to kill the hyenas in your backyard."

"Hmm... yes, I see."

"And so, in Uruguayan land, you have the struggle of the military front fighting against the leftist front. But in the middle of this, the freedoms are annulled, there are many prisoners, and countless deaths. There is a struggle between powers, a battle with many innocent victims."

"Horrible," he said and turned the water on. "Come on, get in the shower, I want to soap and enjoy your body."

"Yes, horrible, but I can't figure out why I expect a fiend like you to comprehend. And I... and I... what is it with you and the shower today? Hold on. I worry that you are slipping into the middle of that fight. Two very strong groups, visible and not visible, are fighting and little Danny empty-headed goes and gets in the middle."

Daniel was kept thinking.

She got in the shower, and he followed. They talked a little more while under the spray of water. Daniel was silent.

"So? What about soaping me up?"

Daniel took the soap but didn't do much. He was worried.

She grabbed the soap. "Pathetic liar..." She started to soap him. "Ah, you are worried, you little shit?"

"Yes."

"Mm... well... listen, learn. In addition, you have a hidden morbid interest, and you are getting into a dangerous game. You are getting into things of crimes in the police headquarters itself, in things that you should not get involved, that you know well that you should not get involved, but you get involved anyway. I'm warning you."

"No Gina... it's not like that. It's just..."

"You know what? You're not a humanist, no. You are an existentialist and that's why your mind is a salad of things, and passions, and frustrations, and tits, and politics, and blood, and women, and cadavers, and besides..."

"Yes, enough already, Gina."

They rinsed and got out.

She kept silent for a while, and then she took him home. Her long black hair was all fluffed up, her shirt half open, her jeans all cut. She had the look of an animal man-eater. Daniel got down from the cab; they talked a little bit. Daniel was worried about all the things she told him. She kissed him, patted his butt, gave him a hug, "We'll sit down and talk about it calmly." She gave him another big kiss. "Once you grow a brain," she added and left. Daniel turned around to enter his home and there he saw the military squadron: his mother, Marisa, Estela, Zulema, the Spaniard lady from next door, with her two daughters. Estela looked at him, smoking, like one looks at a fugitive killer. They were in the middle of a late-night chat, there on the walkway, without expecting something like this to happen. They were all surprised, quiet, staring at him.

"Holy Mary Manzanita..." sighed out the Spaniard lady.

His mother managed to say, "But... yes... but... but..."

"What about that wild aborigine ?" Estela told him. "Is she going to be behind bars again? They just let her free to go out with you, eh?"

"Oh, oh, where did that wild aborigine escape from, Daniel?" yelled Marisa. "Dorita will find out."

"Oh, Lila," said the Spaniard. "How horrible. Dorita, ay, she's going to leave him."

As he walked past them, his mother said, "What are you transforming yourself into? What if poor Dorita finds out...? What about..."

"Who was that disgusting wild woman, Daniel?"

"You came with that erotic Indian to your neighborhood, but... How? Aren't you a little embarrassed? Exposing yourself like this."

Within two days a very sweet voice of a woman called him and asked if he could be on the corner of Boulevard España and Roque Grasseras in an hour.

He left and before arriving he met the old green man of the Mercedes, leaning on the car, smoking, and chatting with the driver. He told him that they had found out that there were more kidnappings than they thought and did not understand who they were or why they did it, but that the high command of the Joint Forces and the officers of the armed forces had no idea that was happening even though many gave their approval anyway. This situation had to be examined and an investigation had to be initiated. But the investigation should be secret, with no one knowing and that in that process, perhaps the cooperation of some civilians would be needed.

"Would you get into that? Would you participate? And if you had that power? Huh? Will you advance?"

"You know I will."

"Look Daniel, let's put some cards on the table. I know you're involved in this; do you hear me? I know you've made progress. And you've made it on your own decision. What? Don't be surprised. Yes, I already talked to Maggiolo and Etcheverry, what do you think?"

So, there's a connection between him and Etcheverry and Maggiolo?

"Why do you think they showed you their keys?

Oh, of course, the old green man is part of the Condor and at the same time it's connected to that Sephardic-Mason-Catholic group or whatever.......... gee, damn! He's in everything.

Daniel kept thinking about all that. *Who are they?*

"And tell me, do you think I don't know Yamandu and the others, and Rosario, and Gina, and that... as she's called? Ah, Berta? And don't you think I talk to them? By the way, this cute Gina, uh, is she or isn't she such a loving creature? Doesn't she give you—?

"What? Eh... please. I just..."

"Let's get back to our business. We're facing a field with lots of burrows. In one of them lies what we need, I can't dig without being detected, and so many others can't do it either, undetected. We need a fox, half son of a bitch, half silent and slippery, who can sneak in and find what we need...."

"Yes, I've been told all that, thanks. I've already been given a lot of adjectives. I know that. I'm working on... eh... I'm thinking on how to do it."

"Good. But I want... hmm... eh... but we can make the fox strong and empowered."

"Okay, I want that," said Daniel while thinking, *all right, all right, we're getting close. Yes.* "But what do you mean by giving me the power? How?"

"I'll tell you later, when I clear up a few more things, but I'm pretty sure, my fox, that you understand what I'm saying."

"But, well, what about it? What power will you give me? How...? For what?"

"You'll see. Take it easy, Danny boy."

"What about the guns?" Daniel continued, taking advantage of the issue of weapons, which he suspected had a purpose that hadn't been disclosed to him. "How does that get hooked into the story?"

"Do you want one? I'll get you one."

"Aren't you going to tell me now? Give me details, that sort of thing."

"No. And don't pull my tongue. Well, I wanted to tell you this, and tell you we're going to take it to higher levels and we're going to start a process. I'll keep you posted. Mm, yes, a little power wouldn't hurt...."

"Okay, okay, I see you won't give me details."

"You'll get the details, foxy-Danny, in its time."

"Okay, all right. And... wait, what do you know about the Nubian or Anubis?"

"Ah, the Nubian? Yes, we still don't know if... yea, they call him Anubis, yes... he's... hmm..."

"What? What if he was the one we're looking for?"

"Hmm... I don't smell that he's the one," he said. "Anyway, that mercenary is untouchable. He hides in his Capurro fortification which is somehow connected to the harbor and a pier in the west side of the Capurro neighborhood. They tried to catch him on several occasions, but he just vanished."

"Ah, I see you know more than you were telling me. What else do you know? Did anyone try to contact him?"

"Don't you get smart with me. And don't get in that deadly field. You could end up.... "

"I know, amputated, and then executed. But it intrigues me, so I explore the territory."

"You're not allowed in that neighborhood. The Nubian is a merchant of death. It's a nest of rats and snakes. Your father found out too many things, and that's why he's not here with us to high-five all your sleazy affairs. They won't do anything to you because you are young, and as long as you don't stick your nose in there."

"And how would you know those things, eh? How'd you find out all that?"

The green man became irritated, took a few steps, then stopped. He glared at Daniel, lit a cigarette, and leaned on the car again.

"You... you're making me talk about things we shouldn't be discussing," he said with a red face.

"I've heard that before. Come on. Tell me."

"I won't. Shut up."

"Okay, I may find out by myself, and later, perhaps, they will bring my amputated body to your doorstep. Let's see how you feel then."

The green old man opened his arms and closed them fast against his body. He threw the cigarette, took more steps, he was upset. He stared at Daniel for a while and said: "People in my group, people I work with, deal with the officers and deputies of Capurro. That's how I know. They still remember what your father did and how you helped him. They won't forget. They will not touch you, if you stay away. Stay away, little piece of man-whoring dung."

"Sure. Too late."

"What? What? What did you do? Don't tell me you—"

"Yes."

"Give it to me you child."

"I already stuck my nose there."

"How? How?"

"I asked Berta and Gomez to share some of their connections in that police department that—"

"Crazy fool! You're going to get yourself killed. You can get them killed too. Ay, ay, why I am even talking to you? You're not allowed in the Capurro neighborhood. Your father should have told you of the danger before he was killed."

"He did. I knew it then, and I know it now."

"So, what are you doing then?"

"Playing my game."

"You know that the Nubian or one of his guys probably shot your dad, don't you?"

"I have my thoughts about that."

"Hmm.... But you need to know that there is much more than that. The Nubian is connected to Operation Condor. I didn't tell you this. You're not supposed to know any of this. Condor operatives use the Nubian to bring weapons, ammunition, money, and even abducted prisoners into the country. He is therefore untouchable."

"I see. So, this is one of the ways this right-wing dictatorship gets support to fight its dirty wars."

"What? It's not a dirty war, it is a necessary cleansing."

"Sure... with human rights violations, murderous death squads, and street terror?" asked Daniel.

"Again, I tell you that your mind is dirty with communist propaganda. Operation Condor is a very necessary coordinated effort uniting Uruguay with Pinochet in Chile, Stroessner in Paraguay, the commanders of Bolivia, and the other countries in a very needed battle against Russian and Cuban imperial plans."

"A bloody plan. Horrible. But tell me again, remind me, who am I helping here? Am I helping the Condor?"

"Fool! It was you who wanted to find out. It was you who asked me for help. It is your search; it is your plan. Condor, whether you like it or not, is a separate thing that has nothing to do with you. Don't get into it. Stick to your goals."

"Yes, but what if I—"

"Crazy. Idiot! Just stop that!"

"I've been told that before. "

Silence.

Chapter 24

Here and there, Daniel began to feel a sense of unease. There was something that worried him, and he didn't know what.

As he had done before, one afternoon upon returning from anatomy he went for a walk in the park near his house. He sat on the bench to distract himself by watching people play tennis. He lit a cigarette and was thinking about Gina, when he heard the voice of Pereyra, his ex-professor of literature.

"Look Quique, look," Pereyra told his dog, pointing at Daniel. "Here's the delegate of humanism, Mr. Daniel Blum himself, the one with the heavy balls, who's going to screw around with human values, the equality of the idiots, the spirituality of the hens, and the misery of the cows. Only manure will come out of his mouth. God free us from this infamous one who embraces the madness."

"Hello, Pereyra."

"Did you bring cigarettes?" he asked.

"Yes. How are you doing?"

"I'm fine. I see you've got a conflicted ass face."

Daniel told him a little of his news.

"Ha! Didn't I tell you...? Didn't I tell you before you messed with the corpses?"

"But if you don't know what I'm going to tell you."

"I can see the worry and the anguish in your ugly face from half a block away, Daniel, and it's enough to see the girl you were hanging out with the other day to know that for lack of love and flesh is not the problem. What happened?

They both lit a cigarette and Daniel told him a limited version of his experiences since they had last seen each other. He told him about the morgue, about his work at headquarters, about guns, and the judiciary. By the time they lit the third cigarette, he was going to tell him about how the boy was taken out of the country, but he decided to put it aside for the time being.

Pocho Pereyra crouched down and grabbed his head with his hands, saying, "Oh Daniel, Daniel, screw you, man, you get into things like that? Yes! I know! Those things just come along, don't they?

"Yes. I don't… I don't…"

"Ah, no?"

"No, Pereyra!"

"And here you are. I told you, remember, when you were going into anatomy, that you were going to be meeting death and that something was going to happen. And you with your twisted little brain to begin with. And when you were thinking of entering the morgue, I also told you that you were entering an unknown dimension, where unusual things happen. Do you remember our talk? You got into the red circle, man."

"Yes. I remember."

"I told you; I told you, stay out of death because you can be left at the mercy of spirits. And here you are. You went even deeper into the red circle, and you know it well. But what the hell is a humanist like you doing among the dead? What do you want to do? To talk to them and explain to them to see if they recover?"

"I… it's not that bad…."

Pereyra was silent, astonished. Worried. Finally, he said, "People like you have a tendency to disappear, you know. But… you're going to become an *agent collaborateur*, Daniel. No, you are one already. Those kinds of people are found shot dead in garbage dumpsters eaten by rats. Rats! Daniel, please, realize that!"

"I don't care…"

"Hence your conflict, eh…? You don't care about the rats, do you? Or to get killed either. Oh, oh, Daniel."

"Yes, I think so… and no, I don't care about rats, I mean, yes, I do, but…"

"It is a problem of conscience. It's that human consciousness that doesn't leave men alone. What makes an intellectual a Tupamaro? What makes a teacher a soldier? What makes a nun a missionary? Culture? Love of danger? No, what…? Itch in the tail? Craziness? Neither. These are acts of conscience. That's what it is, Daniel, your conscience guides you."

"Hmm… Yes. Maybe that's right."

"Yes, Daniel, didn't you read Schopenhauer like I told you?"

"No, I felt like you were…"

"Well, the thing is, there you are, nailed with your own nails. People like you fight in strange battles and in distant countries, like Americans in the Spanish Civil War, like missionaries in Africa, and you wonder what the hell are they doing there, and I see you, and I hear you talking about corpses, morgues, guns, gun training, going to crime scenes with detectives, and I ask myself the same question: What the hell are you doing there?"

"I try to—"

"No! Don't tell me! I know the answer. I saw it in the spark of your eyes before you entered the morgue, and I told you that you were entering the dimension of the dead, where untold things happen to people like you."

"Hmm! But....and now? what do I do?

"Whatever," Pereyra answered. "Good luck. Again, I tell you, think about what I told you, before you are found in the garbage eaten by rats. Let's go Quique, this guy is lost."

"Thank you."

"And something else, and you're not going to like it. The red circles of death end up in death, it'll be good for you to know that."

Daniel just sat there a little longer, thoughtfully. He lit another cigarette and looked around, meditating. Villa Biarritz's Park was always nice. It had beautiful trees, was full of birds and flowers, and had a pleasant aroma. In the distance you could see people happily playing tennis. The breeze brought smells of the garbage left by the street market of the day before.

Chapter 25

On Tuesday he went to the hospital in the morning and then to anatomy in the afternoon. When he was leaving and as he was heading toward the bus stop, that same woman that he had seen on the street passed by and told him "Squeeze your buttocks, dirty, stinking scum; and walk two blocks there, they are waiting for you," and left. *Crap with this mean-looking bitch,* he thought, *one day she will catch me in a bad mood and I will... I will... I better not do anything because she will hit me back, that stupid mare.*

He walked to where he was told and got in the Mercedes.

"Remember?" said the green-emerald man. "Remember I told you to be careful with what you wish for because you may get it?"

"Yeah... so?"

"You're going to have to put yourself on the floor because I neither want you to see where you are going, and I don't want them to see you," said the old man.

He obeyed. *Now things are going to be bad,* he thought. *Here I slide from the frying pan into the fire*, and he also thought, *Oh, will this car have a bathroom?*

"Ay, does this car have a bathroom?"

"Shhh, shut up, dirty ass dipshit."

"But who is that bitch of a woman who speaks so badly to me?"

"I will tell you some other time."

"Damn it. Why can't you tell me now?"

"Shhhh..."

"But.... what does that woman have? What's her problem?"

"Just shut up. I'll tell you later."

The car drove on for a long time and then entered a place. When Daniel got out, he realized that it was an army unit. *Holy crap! I am in a battalion*!

"You got me... you brought me here to be executed? And... and I trusted you."

"Oh, shut up, pansy, you wanted something and here I begin to give it to you. I told you. He who favors others, favors receive."

They entered a building and after a corridor they went into a room. *I'm going to jail here, it's all over.* The room was half dark. There were two officers there, but Daniel couldn't see them well. They were standing in front of a desk. There was little light. *Oh, right, the Gestapo interrogation before the torture.* A good time passed, and they still didn't say anything. *And these? Who are they? Why don't they speak?* Daniel's lip trembled and his palms sweated. The old man with the green emerald looked at him in silence.

In the end Daniel spoke: "So...? What happens now?"

"We are waiting to see your reaction."

Somebody turned the lights on.

"Quiet, Daniel, take it easy."

"Hmm, alright..." said one of the officers. "You can see us now, but it's important that you don't know where you are nor who we are. Well, look Daniel, we have here a folder showing... containing what you wanted."

"Yes," said the other officer. "This folder contains what you asked for. The description of the cases you wanted to know. The murders."

Daniel was numb, surprised, and opened his eyes wide. *It can't be.* He got goose bumps.

"What?" he said, without being able to believe it. "You have what? The folder?"

"Yes. You wanted data, and here's your data. In this folder."

"There's what you asked for, Daniel," said the Mercedes man.

"This affects us all."

"How? Do you—"

"Look, Daniel," an officer told him, calmer. "I'm going to tell you something. My two daughters are socialists and very left-wingers. It's a constant problem for me to keep them from getting into trouble, and one of the reasons I'm in this is for fear something like this will happen to them."

"Oh..." Daniel replied. "Uh, you?"

"I told you," said the Mercedes guy.

"If... uh...it's a problem... eh..." said the other officer. "From the moment girls like that, leftists, communists, Tupamaros, put the security of the country at risk, they're a problem for us. But when they are family members, we don't always know what to do."

"Ah yes, you're right," said Daniel. "Those liberal girls..."

"Ssshhh, ssshhh, don't jump with your tongue," said the old green man. "Calm down."

"Look Daniel, what you discovered we've known for a few months now. There's a kidnapping problem and we don't know how it happens or what to do about it."

"I know. I know you're not doing anything about it. You just—"

"Shut up, Danny boy."

"Wait, Daniel," followed the officer. "Within the general context there are many men and women who are communists and Tupamaros and we in the army, along with joint armed forces, are dedicated to neutralizing that problem. Whether you agree or not, we consider our task very important. But several problems have arisen."

"We're not all the same," spoke the other officer. "Many officers like us believe that it is true that there are many injustices in our country and that perhaps leftism is a response to the socioeconomic injustices that began long ago Do you realize that?"

"Yes, yes."

"The solution would be to improve the very roots that have caused all this," continued the officer. "Make a socio-political-economic reform and at the same time starting a legal process. Then, arresting and prosecuting the left-wing elements that go over the line and are violent to society might be needed. It's not about arresting everyone who we think is crooked, but only, *only* those who truly break the law. Do you understand? We must clean up the country, yes, but kidnappings, demanding ransom, and executing is unacceptable."

Daniel was very surprised. *What craziness is this?*

"Are you getting it? We're Uruguayans and we want our Uruguay, but things are going the wrong way. Now they are arresting every citizen under suspicion, and sometimes with minimal suspicion, and without suspicion as well. They are taken to detention centers where they are subjected to torture. This should not, under any circumstances, be happening on Uruguayan soil."

"Yes. I know. But you—"

"Wait. Hey, hey. It's cheesy, it's horrible, it shouldn't happen. A lot of officers like us don't agree. It is very difficult for us, however, from our position to fight openly against that higher force, you see. We can't run down every personal rabbit hole; we are part of a larger nation."

"Seeing what?"

"That we need someone from outside. We cannot address and attack the whole problem altogether, but we can, from the shadows, try to improve or eliminate several of the problems into which all this has degenerated. Are you watching or not watching, Danny boy? Torture is a problem that's getting out of hand and we're planning to do something about it. We're going to create a situation where torture is eliminated. We're evaluating several plans."

There was silence for a while.

"And then?," Daniel said. "What do I do?"

"Then we need to investigate it," the officer explained. "We need data on that whole thing. Not just conjecture and suspicions, but real evidence. But it can't be investigated by us or our subordinates or those of the police or anyone in the government. We don't know who they are, or where their base is, what their connections are, and let us ask who we ask, and as we ask, the culprits will vanish. They could be civilians, or navy, or judicial, or commissars' people, who knows? We would never know anything. Do you understand that? We can't trust anyone."

"I see. I've been told that."

"We need someone from outside. Someone unknown and unrelated and... and without ties to any organization. Someone free to act and to whom we can give power and bring closer to the sources of information and data."

"Yes, I understand very well."

"Yes, Daniel. We found you thanks to your friend here."

"Everything must be done in secret; do you hear me? You are getting this and whatever else you need. We're going to protect you a lot more than you think. By the time you open this folder, you're going to realize that the chosen person is going to have to face the family of the apprehended, who in their suspicion and pain don't trust anyone and wouldn't talk to any detectives, police, or someone in the government. But they'd trust you."

"Daniel, the press and international community is looking at us, and we are looking at our people."

"We're going to protect you from afar. We're going to protect you more than you can even imagine. We're going to know where you are for anything that happens. We will give you the documentation, identity, and access necessary for you to carry out this task. In addition, we will plan a way to pay you that you might find suitable."

"Pay me? Sounds good."

"Good. Take this folder and go. We'll help you. We'll meet again."

"Something else. May I ask?"

"Sure, what?"

"Who is the Nubian? or Anubis? Who is he?"

"It's the Nubian, although some call him Anubis, the god of death, because anyone who gets close to him tends to die. He's a criminal who trades in drugs, weapons, medicine, whatever comes. His organization is headquartered in the Capurro area and has connections with Belgium and other European countries. Why are you asking?"

"Because maybe he's one of the culprits. I've heard his name from some sources."

"I am not surprised. His cronies have been seen by the Capurro neighborhood involved in a large smuggling of weapons and drugs for certain police units, but also for the Tupamaros. They're very dangerous."

"Yes. It's possible he's involved. He and his cronies are very bad people, people who murder first, ask questions later. Don't even get near there."

"He's got connections in Madrid, Lisbon, and Rio, you never know where he is," followed the officer. "There are no pictures of him. We know that he relates to several embassies at the same time as with Russia and the weapons factories of Poland and Italy. He gets and sells diplomatic information to whoever pays him."

"Yes. There is information linking him to arms sales in Uruguay. Looks like they're being brought on a freighter boat and then smuggled across the beach and Port of Capurro."

"That area is crawling with criminals."

"Yes. I already knew that. Do you think they could have killed those boys and girls?"

"They'd kill anyone."

"Completely amoral, Danny."

"Maybe several of those kids were part of something, I don't know, some organization that's sticking its nose in that... And that's why they were killed. Whoever approaches the Nubian dies. Did you ever hear the story of the Sandman?"

"That's a European myth," answered Daniel. "What is that?"

"The Sandman is a figure of northern Europe folklore. They say that whoever gets too close to him falls asleep. Some people call the Nubian with the nickname Sandman. Be very careful, little Daniel."

"I will."

"We need you awake."

"Take care."

"Yes. Take good care of yourself."

"Yes. But if you know anything about that man, send me a message."

"Yes, kid. You're going to hear from us. You can go."

Daniel got up, still nervous, with the folder in his hand, but didn't move. He had more questions.

"What's up with you?"

Daniel tried to organize his thoughts and said, "What's Operation Condor really?"

"Let's go, Daniel."

"No! What is it?" demanded Daniel aloud.

Silence followed. They all looked at each other.

"You can't talk about it," yelled one of the officers.

"Yes, I can," dared Daniel.

Another electrifying silence. The green old man's face looked like a pressure cooker.

"I'm going to give you an idea," said the other officer. "But be extremely careful to not to repeat this. Operation Condor is part of an international effort uniting our country with Paraguay, Chile, Bolivia, and Brazil in a—"

"And Argentina."

"Oh yes, Argentina too. Uniting those countries in a fight against the invading communism. It's a coordinated effort, a transborder network between governments to help each other in this difficult struggle."

"What about the abductions, tortures and..."

"Shut up, Daniel, you little shit," screamed the green man, holding him by the arm and taking him outside. "Don't you know where you are? Idiot!"

"I want to know who I am helping here?"

"No one here answers to you!"

"I have a right to—"

"You are helping with what we talked about initially. We can't solve all the world's problems, but we can kick Russian communism out of Uruguay. Stay out of the other stuff."

"I just want..."

"You just nothing! Shut up."

They got into the Mercedes and the green old man took him back towards the hospital.

Chapter 26

Daniel hardly slept that night. The folder revealed horrible events. He read things that brought tears to his eyes. He saw the pictures and data of young people and could not contain his silent cry. Quite past midnight he laid down and closed his eyes, but the glare of the nebula made him open them. "No. Not now. I want to sleep." It was like a round cloud, as he had seen before, almost like a window. One figure slid around, then another, and another. There were both women and men, gesticulating, signaling, all in a strange motion. *Are they like... like trying to speak*? There was a man too, young, and tall. An echo in his ears suggested a voice coming out of those figures. *What do these visions mean to me*?

"What do you want to tell me?" he asked.

Three of the figures moved slowly and seemed to point at something to the right and down where the folder was.

"What?"

The strange voice continued in his ears like a whisper of several people. *They can't be...*

"What?" he said. "What do you want?"

He sat on the bed. The figures gesticulated again. The air in the room got colder. He looked back at where the figures were signaling and saw the folder in that direction. He slowly took it in his hands and immediately the murmur changed, and became more intense, like a faraway noisy river. The room got warmer, then colder again. His hair felt strange, and he felt that those figures had something to do with the dead in the folder.

"What do I do?" he whispered.

He opened the folder again, he read a few more details. *No. It can't be.*

He laid the folder down. What he saw there was just too much.

In the morning, his mother found him sleeping on the floor, his face in the folder.

"Why did you sleep on the floor?"

"I... I... don't—"

He got some coffee, ate some, took a shower, then kept studying the folder. That whole thing was bigger than he thought. He stopped, looked out the window. He hadn't wanted this mission, *but for my sins they gave it to me and now I'm in trouble. This is just horrendous.*

He sat on the armchair in his room to analyze the data in the folder.

There they were. There had been many kidnappings and several other cases that were unclear. They added up to forty-four, and had occurred within two, no, three years. There were some other cases, unclear, with no precise information or data, but if they were added they would increase the numbers even more, and to a range of four years. *No, I can't take those in....*

Whoa... forty-four! Forty-four clear cases, he thought. *How dreadful.*

But how did... how's this not known? How has nobody published it?

Forty-four!

It was all mixed up with the dirty war against the Tupamaros, the Communists, and the arrests and attacks. Kidnappings and arrests look the same on the street. And the dictatorship doesn't allow anything to be published. *But... forty-four gee? What madness.*

How can it be? Forty-four, forty-four that they know of. Or more? Probably more.

But of all of them, thirty-eight kidnappings were clear and documented cases, thirty-eight. Of those, eighteen were returned alive after the ransom payment, and fourteen were delivered dead, killed. Nothing was known about the others. *Hmm, but was it thirty-eight? Was it more?*

If I personally know of five killings, there must have been more than forty-four... many more.

However, the dead had not been tortured. Those who came back alive hadn't been tortured either. Nobody wanted to talk. Those who came back didn't want to talk. Parents didn't want to talk.

He read the autopsy reports. All the deceased victims had been shot in the head. He examined the pictures. On every corpse the autopsy had been thorough. There were photos and documentation of many bodies, but not everyone had been kidnapped. There was also the picture of the boy he had seen in the hospital that night, poor guy, he remembered him. And there was the picture of the girl they had brought to the morgue when he was there. A huge sadness came to him. He always had such sadness when he saw the cadaver of young women, perhaps because each woman's life is a beautiful one, perhaps because it was not just a beautiful life that was lost but also the possible lives that that body could have procreated. This was brutal. He never understood that feeling well, it was something that came out of him from the inside. Perhaps because of the love that the body of a woman could have given and received and now could never do so because her existence had already been extinguished and it was horribly unfair that only a cadaveric decomposition was ahead of that divine body. He tried to imagine the woman in one of those pictures holding her baby and kissing it with affection. He started to cry, put his hands on his face, and stopped reading for a while. *Enough is enough. Control yourself and stay cool.*

He knew he was losing focus. In addition to the victims in question, there were bodies of people who were shot in the head but had not been kidnapped or were too old. Then there were those who were kidnapped and set free after payment. It was maddening to envision. *Where am I going?*

Chapter 27

He got up. He couldn't go on. He went to the balcony to calm down. Then he came back and went on again.

The folder had a lot of data, however, many of the reports were missing. The information was not complete. In most of the photos they had shaved the bullet area to better see the wound and the entry of the projectile. In twelve of the victims, he clearly saw the sign of Trimber-Gomez, the crescent opening backwards and the fan of dust expanding towards the nape. Forensic doctors had done detailed work, and even more detailed analysis than usual, perhaps intuiting that it would be useful one day in the event of a thorough investigation, but many of the reports were incomplete. Moreover, some of the pictures were missing as well. *Why?*

This is not complete. Where would the rest of the information be? They had done a thorough toxicological and biochemical analysis of the tissues, but none of those reports were there. Several cuts of each victim had been sent with a sealed envelope to pathological anatomy, but they used private numbers to keep the names hidden, and the data was missing. *How? why?* he wondered. If data is missing, then information about the number of deaths is missing too.

He began to study the scattering and tattooing of the dust, which looked good in twenty of the several dozen groups of photos, although some had not been kidnapped. On all the bullet impacts, the cleaning collar caused by the projectile had the same pattern and was not circular. There was more. The Fisch's Ring was oblique. Forensics had done a good job and the Belaunde's sign had been studied even under a microscope. *My god, yes.* Those who did the autopsy knew what they were looking for and had used the polarized green filter camera to get more data.

Mmm... would the technicians suspect anything?

In many of the pictures, the image looked good, especially in the middle section of the projectile's hole.

The technicians had made incisions in different angles, showing the characteristics of the traumatic necrosis caused by the debris from the shot.

Hmm, yes, thankfully, the technicians were suspicious.

He remembered Matilde's teachings. "Daniel, remember what I told you."

The metal remains of the wound had been analyzed. There was no doubt, it had been a revolver and not a semiautomatic, and the bullets were not armored. *Ha! Interesting.* They had not been parabellum bullets. *Hmm...*

He scanned the reports. No. It hadn't been a parabellum. *Hmm... good job.*

The type of lead was studied under microscopy, and a chemical analysis had even been done in each case. Reviewing each case, he could not find the characteristics of the lead in each bullet. Where would that data be? All the victims had a strong and deep tattoo caused by gunpowder, suggesting an execution at close range, perhaps at point-blank range. The areas that had suffered from the Simonín Cockade and the effect of gases from the deflagration of the Hoffman Coup had been studied more closely. *Very good.* The technicians were excellent. Studies of the brain mass had been done. That girl and many of the others had a piece of primer embedded in their brains. *Shit.* The primer was analyzed in one of the departments of the chemistry college, but the results were not there. *Hey, why not?* He did not know.

After a while he pulled himself out of there and went to the balcony again to clear his mind.

"You're good?" asked his mother.

"Yes, yes, I got an allergy."

He made himself some coffee with sugar. He washed his face. *Enough. Hold on. Stay cool.*

Before entering his room again, he said to himself: Who killed them? *Help me.*

He sat down, opened a magazine, and spent a few minutes clearing his mind.

But... data is missing, he told himself. There was a lack of data on those in the folder, and there was no data on others that were not in the folder.

Calmer, he opened the folder and continued reading. There were grains of gunpowder embedded in the deep part of the wounds and even in the brain, confirming in six of the victims that the shot had been made at point-blank range and even pushing the barrel against the temple. *Whoa!* In two of the pictures, he could see the mark of the muzzle. *What an assassin, what an animal.*

The chromatographic analysis of the powder was nowhere to be found. Twelve of the bodies had their skull bones blown away by the gases of the deflagration. Tissue remains had been sent to pathology, to the military engineering division, and to the chemistry department. The percentages and types of nitrites and nitrates in the gunpowder were studied in each case, a brilliant idea, but the reports were missing. *Where are those reports?*

The forensics in charge had done an excellent job. Over the hours, analyzing this data, the data from the determination of metallic particles, the study of the remains of the primer, and comparing the analysis of the gunpowder, he was able to realize something that froze his blood. It seemed that all the fatal shots had been made with the same weapon and using the same type of bullet, but those details had to be confirmed with the missing studies. Where were they? All the victims had a single entry.

Where are the missing reports?

Studies had even been done with red scanning spectral photometry and the studies had been evaluated with a chemical analysis of antimony and boron, but the results were not there.

Yes, the technicians suspected something and followed the leads.

Suddenly he woke up. He had fallen asleep on the folder. *Did I dream that data or did I read it?* He checked the folder again. He examined the photos again and read the detail of what was found in the brain. He studied again the photos that showed the Fisch's fake tattoo sign. The bullet hole was always on the left side, the trajectory in the brain mass was ten to twenty degrees to the right, and the weapon was always. 38 caliber. Traces of lead mixed with other metals could perhaps indicate whether the bullets were of a common type, and whether those bullets were sold in armories to civilians or not. Was it the same person, one who always performed with the same style and with the victim sitting still? It looked like it, *I'm going to catch you, son of a thousand whores.*

He reexamined the trajectory of the projectile. It showed a slightly ascending line, suggesting, according to the angle, that the hand holding the weapon was from a person approximately five feet tall. He examined the angle variations and saw they changed proportionally according to the height of the victim. *Yes! It's the same hand, probably the same man!*

He examined the ballistics evidence. It had been a revolver, yes, and not an automatic. A revolver, always the *same* revolver. And always. 38 caliber. Maybe always the same type of bullet? No victim was shot by a. 32 or a. 44 automatic, or by a. 45, as used by officers, inspectors at headquarters, and powerful joint force officers. Those bullets had a jacket, hollow point or not, but they had a jacket and... *there is no sign of any jacket in any report.*

Hmm... no jacket. The flattening effect confirmed it.

A. 38 caliber revolver. Shot by someone who is not an officer. *An enforcer for that Nubian?*

Hmm... that Nubian. *If I were the Nubian and I sent one of my assassins to kill someone, I would make sure he carried a fine weapon, a. 38 automatic and with jacketed bullets. I would want him to carry that revolver just in case he has to defend me. I would not give him a six-shot revolver.* No.

How do I get to that man? he wondered. Sure, to end up amputated.

I'm going to catch you, son of a thousand whores.

He took a deep breath, got a flash of memories.

But... why would Anubis kill them?

Hmm... for the money. All that money, multiplied by forty-four or fifty or whatever, it's a lot of cash.

The trajectories of the projectiles were similar in nineteen of the twenty-eight victims, even in no-kidnapping cases. What? no kidnapping? *So, why were they shot?*

Perhaps some of the cases were political. Why did some of them look just like such cases?

After a brief review, he realized that neither the forty-four nor the twenty-eight were accurate because lots of data was missing.

Then he found that some victims were shot in the head with a rifle, while other were downed with a parabellum. *Well, looks like some unrelated assassinations are mixed with all these: but... but then, the cases of murder are more.*

Those who were shot with a rifle or gunned down with a bullet in the forehead or in the chest were confusing the panorama, increasing the numbers, so he had to review and reclassify the data again.

However, it was clear that the executioner appeared to be the same person in most cases when the shot was on the side of the head, and was of medium height, right-handed, and using a revolver for the fatal shot. Markings on the wrists indicated that they had all been tied up, but those shot in the chest didn't have such marks. There were no signs of sexual abuse or violence. Examination of the perineum in the women showed incontinence. *Son of a bitch.* The victims knew they were going to be killed, they saw the murderer and they pissed themselves. *Poor girls.* The men had incontinence too. Therefore, this had not been an accident, but a cold, slow, calculated action.

Daniel checked everything again. No. It was more than nineteen, and maybe many more. Yes, many more.

So, the victims were neither lying down nor on their back nor escaping nor standing. It had not been a rifle shot fired in an ill-calculated attempt to stop the escape, nor was it an accident or in the heat of the moment. No. It had been a well thought out, cold event, with the victim always sitting and tied up. Yes, an execution. And apparently, always with a. 38 caliber revolver.

But why? The ransom had been paid. Why kill those and not the others? What did those nineteen or twenty-four or more have? The total and partial numbers were confusing. He didn't have many answers and was getting confused with all the data. He meditated, his head felt heavier, the ideas were not flowing right when he decided on something crazy. He invoked his visions. He asked them to come. "Talk to me, give me a signal," he whispered. He waited. "Come. Show me." He shook his head and tried the get out of those thoughts. *Don't be ridiculous*.

He was falling asleep when a brightness formed on one side of his room. As figures advanced, he couldn't resist the cool relaxation he was feeling and closed his eyes and fell asleep while small fingers of brightness caressed his scalp. The figures were not agitated but moved in slow motion, floating in and out of the brightness, approaching in intervals.

He woke up. *What was that? A dream. Yes.*

He examined the toxicology reports, they were all incomplete. Nothing. He checked the nail and hair reports, but the clues were missing. The internal examination of the victims had been done systematically but had not yielded valuable clues. The stomachs had been emptied. One of the stomachs had a crumpled piece of paper with the number 91, which looked like the corner of a book. In another stomach, a ring was found that was not the victim's, but it was a common ring without any details. A paper was also found where it said, "Marta 91." Three victims had tattooed a number, one with something metallic got the number 16 tattooed on the calf, and the other two got the number 91 tattooed, in ink, on the thigh. *Hmm, will it be 16 or a 91 flipped? What's 91 mean?*" In three stomachs, remains of meat were found. Two of the girls were named Marta.

Point blank, point blank. Why? Why the number?

Three of the dead were found in the same garbage dump at Durazno and Ejido, and another was found two blocks away. *Why? What's there?*

Number 91, Durazno and Ejido.... *What does it indicate?*

The medical examination of those who returned alive did not indicate anything. He compared the ages of the two groups, the colors of their hair, but nothing.

"Daniel, it's Gina on the phone."

He talked to her. He told her he had to study. He will call her later. Yes... yes.

He went back to the folder.

Gee... twenty-eight! There were more, but twenty-eight were clear cases.

Several representatives of the armed forces contacted the survivors and the relatives of the dead and could not find out anything. Headquarters detectives were unable to investigate either. Perhaps there was great fear of speaking. *Everyone was afraid?* Nobody said anything. The fear of possible reprisals was great. *Eh? Would it be the same bastard that stopped me in the street?* A female detective posed as a social worker but could not find out any details. Nothing was advanced. Nothing was known. They tried through relatives, but nothing. No details were known, and the reports were incomplete. Where the hell were the reports and missing data?

Crap, nothing was known. He spent the whole day in his room. He left only to eat lunch and later for dinner. Sleep came to him, he leaned back. The night images came and were whispering something to him. "I'm tired. Leave. I need to sleep."

He closed the folder. But wait, had he called them this time? *No, I imagined that.*

However, the images made signals for him to open the folder. The images kept pointing at the folder. It felt cool and relaxing.

He woke up. He did not know if his ideas were his or the images had been given to him. *Are they giving me information while I sleep?*

He got dressed. It was Saturday, and he went to the street market to walk and think. It was the Villa Biarritz fair that he liked so much, but that now seemed different. There was death in the environment. The opened watermelons were the color of blood. He saw one of the dead boys lying on one of the vegetable tables. A dead woman was laying with the oranges. *No.* People looked at him as if they knew what he had gotten himself into. The three criminals he had seen in the morgue were there, selling celery and peppers, and they looked at him with a warning. The florist guarded the entrance to the cemetery. The fish lady crossed herself when she saw him. *She knows.* He thought he saw a dead woman on the apple stand. There were blood and dead people under the fruits. The vendors were screaming, "Do it, Daniel, do it!"

"*I have apples and pears... special!* shouted one, "with a bullet in each one."

"Daniel," screamed a body under the pile of sweet potatoes, "find out who killed us!!"

"Come, come, see the grapes bleed. Ahhh ha, ha, ha."

He leaned against a bench and came out of his abstraction. He felt disturbed and sat down. The bench was next to where they sold bloody strawberries freshly removed from one of the corpses. *No, no, nooo!*

What should I do? he thought. *What? How did I not... I just can't....*

"Apples, the best bananas," shouted a vendor.

I'm a student, why the hell did he have to get involved in a case like this?

"There are tomatoes... tomatoes!" shouted someone.

Two women passed by and looked at him with accusing eyes. *They know.*

The street market was full of people. Many of them looked at him with pain in their eyes.

A man came by, told him, "Yeah, keep walking with the dead, Danny boy," and kept walking.

"This is not real. No."

He had to talk to someone about it. His own humanism told him that such a nightmare could not be left undiscovered, although the documentation indicated that the cases had been shelved and there was no intention of further investigation. The claims of the relatives had been silenced, and the dead had remained underground without being able to tell anything.

Where would the missing reports be?

The breeze shook the branches of the trees and carried the smell of the cart of farm products. A delicious aroma of salami and cheese seduced him and improved his morale. He got up, went to the cart, and bought himself half a sliced salami.

"A bit of cheese? Dry sausage?"

"No thanks."

He began to eat the salami. Daniel's morale always rose when he ate salami. It cooled his brain. He turned to the bench. A puppy barked at him. A fat woman passed near him wearing jewelry and said hello. *Oops, does she know me?*

I can't get into something like this, he thought, *that's way too many deaths. I just can't do this.*

However, something was calling him into this, as he was trying to resist it.

They killed a lot of people already. Curiosity and indignation were asking him to do something and were making his salami bitter.

"I have saffron! Saffron and nutmeg." shouted the poor old boy he always saw in the market. "Saffroooon!"

Daniel looked at him. *Does he ever sell anything else?* he wondered as he bought some saffron from the guy. *He's been selling the same things for years.* Daniel liked to eat lentils with saffron and butter.

He kept talking to himself. But... why did they kill those twenty and not the others? And there were twenty or...? No, what? There were more; there were twenty-four, no, no, the cases were... how many? Forty-four? *I'm already dizzy with the numbers.* But why did he kill them, that same person, that son of a bitch, why did he kill them? *And for what?* If they already had the money.

He tried to focus. *There were over sixty cases of... of... sixty deaths*? No, no... there were... uh, this was getting confusing. *And the girls*? If he already had them in front of him, tied up, and was armed, why didn't he rape them? Well, maybe he wouldn't like one of them, but they were pretty, yes, why not abuse each one? *Why not, miserable piece of shit, why didn't you rape them*?

The bustle of the street fair was already dying down, but the smells of fruits and vegetables still filled the air. He thought that with his eyes closed he could tell in which part of the fair he was simply by the smell and the typical noise. He loved that fair, and he loved the park. All Villa Biarritz was beautiful and pleasant and all Pocitos too, where each area had its typical smell and its houses and its trees all different.

Daniel went home for lunch. At night he went out with Gina to the movies and to eat a lot of pizza. But he ate too much and drank a lot of beer as if desperate to calm his anxiety.

"Calm down, Daniel," said Gina, "You're killing the pizza!"

He said nothing.

"You gonna tell me what's wrong?"

"Nothing."

"It shows, eh, don't start with that *It's nothing* thing when I see that there is a cuckoo chasing you."

"I can't... I shouldn't tell you. Give me some time."

"Why? You always ask for more time to explain things and then you don't explain anything."

"Wait Gina, give me a little time."

"Look Daniel, I'm very worried, I—"

"Something happened a few days ago, and I..." He didn't want to talk; he didn't know what to do. "I just didn't want to tell you about it—I just... I couldn't... I didn't want you to know of those things."

They had arrived at a small square and they sat down on one of the benches.

He then told her about how the green old man took him to the military barracks and told her what had happened and about the folder. Then he described some of the things he had found through the contents of that folder. Gina grabbed hold of her head and started to cry.

"It's horrible, Gina," he said, covering his face.

"Forty-four?" she yelled and threw herself on the bed.

For half an hour they both cried and moaned. Then she remained silent, crying in silence.

"I told you, Danny. I told you that the day would come when the dead would come to you, do you remember?"

"Yes."

"Daniel, listen to me well. You can't do this alone. You need people to help you. I told you this before."

Daniel stared at her, remembering that conversation.

They talked a bit and said goodbye.

He went to buy cigarettes, grabbed a bit of lunch, and then went to Pocho Pereyra's home.

Chapter 28

"Hi Pereyra."

"I saw you in the park next to that tree and I already knew you were going to call me."

"Yeah."

"Tell me. What's up?"

"Murder." And then he told him about his interview with the officers, what they had asked of him, and how that added to what the teachers at the morgue had asked him. He told him the details of the folder they had given him. He made him see how what the two officers asked him coincided with what Maggiolo and Etcheverry had told him. When finished, he was silent. Pereyra was silent as well and lit another cigarette. He got up without saying anything and stood in front of the window. He then sat down on the couch for a long while. He stood up, gave some gin to Daniel, and poured some for himself.

"This is already too serious."

He pushed open a chair in front of the window, grabbed an ashtray, and sat down. He was thinking for a long time.

"Damn you, Daniel! I see that you are progressing. Before you went to where the dead and crimes were, now they come to you. I close my eyes and I see you lying in a wasteland, without eyes or ears, eaten by rats."

"Yeah, I know. I don't know what to do, I don't know what to think, and I don't know how to even be ready to decide what to do."

"This goes beyond the murders and your situation with respect to the officers or that old emerald man with the Mercedes. This is a confrontation with the struggle between good and evil. This is complex. How.... But... How do you make this shit fall on you? What in the hell are you doing, Daniel?"

Daniel didn't say anything.

Pereyra was silent for a long time, then he spoke. "This is going to make us examine the depths of our human condition. Neither you nor I are going to be the same when this is over, it would be better for you to realize this."

"I am not ready for this."

"Not ready? Look, how many soldiers were super ready and trained for battle and were killed on the first day? Huh? How ready and prepared is a physician his first night on call? You see? How much can one prepare himself to face the diabolical? Did you understand the tongue twister? One is never ready. Not for something like this. Never!"

"Thanks for the encouragement. And so...?"

Pereyra thought a bit. He lit another cigarette. "Oh, Daniel, you have the conflict," he finally said. "But you don't have the answer. There is no such thing as being ready for someone like you or the assurance that you need help. It does not exist for you because you are an existentialist and doomed to be immature."

"But I just—"

"For people like you, there's no clear exit, but rather an advance and a progression full of doubts and ambiguous thoughts. You're gonna be a storm of meditations that advances and acts and meditates again and attacks again and so on. But don't worry so much."

Daniel returned home. At night he opened the folder and examined the data again. "Daniel, dive into what is not seen," Matilde had said. "Look for what is not seen."

"They blew his head off with a bullet."

"They will find you in a wasteland eaten by rats."

"You can't do it alone," Gina had told him.

"The dead talk to you," MacLagan said.

"Daniel, remember to connect the dots," Matilde had said. "Connect the dots."

But... what dots?

Join what?

"Matilde, unite what?" he asked aloud.

"Focus on what is not seen."

"The dead talk to you and it's up to you to listen."

I have to get help. I need someone to help me see things better.

At night he read the reports again, but they were not complete, he lacked details. He kept realizing that he just couldn't do it alone. *I have to put together my little trustworthy crew to help me.*

Who?

At night, the images he saw or thought he saw made gestures to him. He communicated with them. "Talk to me, give a signal." But nothing came in return, just a whisper. "Who killed them?" The whispering came and went, the figures seemed to gesticulate more quickly and pointed back to the folder repeatedly. A slim, flat female figure made gestures to him, and he seemed to feel a voice. *It cannot be, it cannot be.* "Marta?"... There was another woman behind, and he seemed to recognize her. "Is she... is she... no, it can't be."

"Dive... dig into what is not seen... search what you don't see and then join the loose ends!"

Yes, Matilde, I'm going to do that.

"Search for the factors and the number... number 91? Or is it 16? With four of the bodies found at Durazno and Ejido. Is it 1691?"

He found more data. The markings on the wrists indicated that they were handcuffed, and not tied, and certain markings and positions confirmed that they had all been seated when they were shot. He studied the chemical findings again, but they weren't complete. "Remember to search..." Matilde had told him.

What is it that I don't see, damn it! he said to himself? *Or I don't see it because it's not here, because they have taken it out*?

He went to bed at night and thought he saw the hazy images that pointed to the folder. *They know.* Or only he knew and imagined the rest. *This can't be... it can't be.*

"Talk to me, say who killed you."

The visions seemed to alter. They shook their heads.

"Talk to me! Tell me," he called out in whispers into the darkness, seeing that the images were getting agitated. "Just... just give me a clue. Who killed you?"

Only stares returned.

"I cannot continue like this.... Show me."

He got up, opened the folder. The light from the nebula was more intense, it was like there were more people. The arms of those images moved with greater excitation. He contemplated what they indicated: the folder. And then he realized. It had been there, in front of him, in sight, and he hadn't seen it because he couldn't see it. "See what is not seen," Matilde told him, and she was right. Several things were missing. The biochemical analysis of the tissues that had been sent to the chemistry faculty was not complete. In many reports there was a page one that offered preliminary data and it looked like everything was in it, but at the bottom right it read, *Continues on Page 2.* All those second pages of the reports were missing. Second, the analysis of the type of lead had been studied in spectroscopy in the college of chemistry and in all twenty cases it came back as an analysis of figures but without the final report. Those reports were missing. Third, the analysis of the powder was done at the headquarters, but the analysis of the percentage of nitrites, nitrates, sulfates, and pollutants had also been done at the chemistry college and the final report was never obtained in any of the cases. There it read, in several places *SEE PAGE 3B*, but no 3B pages were there. *The data is missing*! It's not that they were incomplete reports, but rather someone took them out, they made them disappear. He checked again. Many of the reports indicated a next page that was missing.

"There! There was the thing! Just like the woman told him. "Dig into what is not seen."

Shit! and he had not understood her, he had not glimpsed it. Now he realized, not looking at what is seen but looking for data that is not seen because it is not there because someone hid it. Very good!

That, yes! Search the data that is not seen because it is not there. Search where they are.

Daniel knew from experience that the college of chemistry was required by law to send reports to the police headquarters. They could send a duplicate to the morgue if someone asked for it, but that was no longer an obligation. Here there was omission, error, complicity, or some other problem, but it gave food for thought and needed to be investigated. What's more, there could be vital information and even data on a possible accomplice. That didn't smell good. That shit was going to be investigated no matter what happened, and he was going to do it no matter what.

Probably all that information should have been in a place reserved for data storage and retrieval where all the information is kept, and access is restricted: *the headquarters information center*. And to get there he needed power, a vile power, a power that was above the Joint Forces and chief of police, a strong, secret, and almost diabolical power. He needed... he needed the Condor. He needed the power that had already been offered to him. He did not know what it was, he did not understand it well, but the lord of the Mercedes, the man with the green emerald, was his representative, and therefore he represented the power to be able to enter there. Would that be the meaning of the key that had been given to him? Did that key symbolize the fact that he could have access to whatever he wanted if he knew what he was diving for? *Well, now I know what I'm looking for and Operation Condor is going to give it to me*."

He sat in his chair. He felt better. He went to class, more relieved, and even walked lighter. In the middle of the morning, he went down to the public telephone and called the number they had given to him. He gave a specific message.

"Yes, of course," he was told.

He returned to class and at recess, as he walked down the corridor between the rooms, a doctor from the cardiology ward approached him and asked him about what he would need.

"What's your menu?" he said in a whisper.

He told him to get him six maps of the city of Montevideo, money for taxis and expenses, a false ID, and a credential with his photo and with the name of Alberto Battle Herrera, Special Services, Ministry of something, so that it inspired fear or respect to whoever would stop him.

"Hmm, what else?"

"I also need you to notify the two officers so that they would be ready to give me a hand as soon as I need it. I would need a ghost to follow me when he can, from afar, to eliminate possible complications and notify Martinez to give me a hand if I need it."

"Don't worry. Martinez is well aware, and we'll talk to him."

"Thanks. Ah, also the telephone numbers of all the homes where a boy or girl died."

"Yes, telephone numbers," the doctor said. "Anything else, Daniel? A grenade launcher, three machetes, a silencer, your Remington 51, hmm?"

"Enough of this Remington, I don't..." said Daniel, taking the joke with a smile. "No. Nothing else."

He walked into the hospital cafeteria feeling good and celebrated his decision with a good espresso.

He finished in anatomy early and went home to study. The exams were coming up. He had dinner with his parents in peace, then Gina came, ate cake, and left because she had to study too. Nothing else happened that day.

Two days passed, and they did not notify him of anything. On the third day, when he left anatomy, he went to the morgue, but there was nothing interesting. The crows were not there, so Domínguez is not here.

He went to the back room for coffee. Skinny Pranchin and Detective Cabrera were there finishing a report, having coffee, and talking about weapons with the sub-commissar, Castro-Aronceda, chief investigator of department number eight of the headquarters, who was filling out another report. Unshaven, with half a cigar hanging from his lips, Castro-Aronceda gave him a yellow-toothed smile, "Hi, Danny." They greeted each other cordially and he served himself a coffee. They asked him about his studies and classes and about the brunette with the scooter.

"Eh, do you want some? We have cheesecake that Gomes brought. He makes delicious cakes."

"Hmm... no thanks."

"And Daniel? Did you decide? Do you want the Remington?"

"I already told you that I'm not going to carry weapons."

"Well, whatever you want, my love. A doctor and a woman are looking for you. They told me they would be in the college; I don't know, didn't you see them?"

"No, I'm going there. Bye, see you."

They were not upstairs, so he went out. Around the corner he found the same ill-mannered woman as always. *Mare, she-dog, animal*, he thought.

The woman told him that the doctor had to leave, but that he was leaving Daniel a book as a gift, and she gave it to him.

"And do you know what hygiene is?"

Daniel looked at her, looked at the book and looked at her again. She just turned around. *But... who is she*?

The book was tied with a string like what is usually given to a student when he asks for a book from another library.

"You know who sends it to you," she said, as she turned around and stared at him with a mean face. "The rest of the things arrive at your house today... Degenerate."

She took two steps toward him, and he took a few steps back.

"Coward," she said and left quickly before he could answer the insolence.

But what a damn mean mare is this chick, he thought. *Bad mare*. She left him frozen again with her evil speaking. She always said something to him that left him off balance. *One day I'm going to tell her something and... and... and she's still going to hit me.*

It was a book by Isaac Asimov, with nothing, but with a note inside that read, *Very good*. It was a way of telling him that his message had been welcomed.

When he got home, he greeted his mother and Marisa, ate, and began to study. At about nine o'clock, they called from downstairs, his mother went down to open the door and came back with a closed box of Garoto Brazilian chocolates that a messenger gave her. She loved them and opened the box and was eating one of the bonbons when she found the documents, maps, and money. There was a note with two phone numbers, and it read, *You are independent but not alone, if you need money, help, or the Remington, let me know.*

"What? All this money!" said his mother. "They mean a Remington electric shaver?" She swallowed a chocolate. "Are you going to buy one?"

While reading the note, his mother checked the box and kept eating the chocolate.

"Who is this Alberto Battle...?" she asked as she opened the credential. Isn't that... oh Daniel, it's your photo! Oh, oh, it's your photo, Daniel! And... what's this? Oh, and this money? Lots of money! Nothing! I didn't see anything, no, do not tell me anything! I'm going to sleep. I didn't see anything." And she went to the kitchen and spat out the chocolate. "I don't want to know."

"But mom..."

"You're going to kill me, Daniel. You are my son, but... nothing. Nothing." She came, hugged him, and said, "Don't worry, I love you anyway, even if you are wrong and naïve, you are going to be alright... someday... I hope."

Daniel called Pocho Pereyra, who told him to unfold the map and put it on the back side of the door and to buy two boxes of colored tacks and a couple of notebooks.

"And Daniel, you need more people. You need to enter a restricted information and data center, Daniel. You need to get more people on this."

"I know, yes. And I think I know where to find them."

"And you need someone of super-confidence to help you. You need Gina. I know it is at risk, but you need it if you want to progress in this. You're going to have to interview people and you just won't be able to do it. Gina must help you. I can help you, but you need more people."

"Yes."

"Well, but look," said Pereyra. "Listen, there's another problem that you must face. Even if you manage to enter, even if you have the freedom to inquire, are you listening to me? Even if you could stick your nose in at ease, you would not know where to start in there... nor how to retrieve the data. You need a computer guy, and you need a data expert... and you will need to know what file or section to search, and how to use the computer, do you see? You would not know the way to find the data, do you see?"

"Yes, you're right. So?"

"That before entering you need someone who knows how to search files, who knows how to find things on the computer, who knows how to use files and the computer, both, and who is on your side. Think about it. Who? Who could that person be? See? It's not just about entering; you need someone who knows how to search. What's more, listen, you need at least two people, one an expert in computers and another expert in files and sections and pages and things like that."

"And one that helps me get in, that makes three."
"And with you there are four."
"And someone armed, for protection, too. Better two, so it's going to be at least five or six."
"Yes, two armed. Seven? If you want to go faster, you're going to need another expert in archives, communications, and things like that. Seven, no, wait, eight. And with me, that's... eh... eight or nine? Better if you..."
"Uuuuffff, eight. Shit. No. I don't know how many. And that place is not easy to enter."
They said goodbye. Daniel was left thinking about how to solve what Pereyra told him.
He talked to Gina, met her, and shared his ideas with her. "It's risky, Gina."
"I must help you, Daniel, for you and for those people. I'm afraid for you because I got you into this, knowing what a moron you are. But I know I am dying to help you."
He called Urine Gomez, and they met in a bar and then walked while Daniel explained the situation.
"I knew it! Yes, I knew that you had something up your sleeve when you started to come. You misled everyone, but I realized you were coming with a mission. Ah! I knew it, you foxy rascal."
"Yes."
"I didn't ask you why. I knew you weren't going to tell me anyway, but I knew that it wasn't bad."
"Thanks for understanding."
"Daniel. You can count on me one hundred percent. I'm a brain for hire."
"Thank you, Gomes."
"Ah, and what did you think of the cheesecake?"
"Very rich, Gomes. Yes."
"If you want, I will make a special one for you. From poppy seeds. I have a Polish recipe. Yes? Your mom is going to like it."
"I would love it to."
That afternoon the three of them went to the house of the boy he had seen in the emergency room that night. Daniel wanted to be able to comfort the parents, but there was no comfort. They all took a sip of white wine and said, "Cheers."
They stayed there for a while until the alcohol took effect, then they went to the living room where they were waiting with a coffee. They all hugged for a while and then started talking. The payment was made between two cars that crossed in the Allies Park. The other car was a light brown Renault. He didn't

know anything else. Daniel gave him the phone numbers of the other families and asked the parents to call everyone and give them his fictitious name, and that of Gina.

They went to his home and into his room. They had sad hearts for what they heard at the victim's house. They sat on the bed and took the folder. They decided to number each case according to the date they were released or killed, but when Daniel called Pereyra the next day he told him to do so according to when they were kidnapped. He decided to do both.

They reviewed the list of those who were released alive, and went to see person number five, a certain Carlos, a medical student who did not remember anything. When Daniel began to intensify his questions, Carlos remembered noises and smells on certain days. Gina asked details of smells and foods, voices, and uniforms, and wrote everything down.

Pereyra called him later. Gomez had come to his house, and they were chatting and eating cake. Daniel and Gina went there and chatted for a while.

"Hey, try, try the cake that Gomez made. It's strawberries with cream."

"You and your cakes, Gomes. I can't stop eating them."

Gina said that Lourdes was going to help in the interviews, and one of her friends too. Gomez had a niece that would help as well. The work had to be divided.

The next afternoon Gina went alone to the house of one of the families. Later she met a certain Alberto Guzman in the living room of his house, who was case number nine. The call from one of the parents facilitated the encounter. She also asked him about voices, uniforms, foods, smells, events. He gave her some information, but it was all very vague. Gina wrote down everything in her notebook.

Maria de las Mercedes Yanipietro, the daughter of Dr. Yanipietro, had been the first to be kidnapped and lived nearby, so Daniel called her and went to see her. Cute girl, a chemistry student. She had not been tortured or even groped. It attracted attention. Mercedes was a pretty woman, with latte hair, thin eyebrows, wide lips and moderately busty. She was sexy and, above all, interesting, so why not sexually abuse her having the opportunity? Why not drug her, undress her, and do everything to her, keeping her locked there?

That's weird. Had she been kidnapped by women?

The ransom was paid the same way, through two cars that crossed in the same park, and the father remembered the same light brown Renault. They talked about foods, smells, perfumes, parental occupation, voices, coughs? And various other details. He went home.

No, he thought, *if she had been kidnapped by women she would have remembered. That's weird.*

In the following days Daniel and Gina, separately, went to see a couple more boys thanks to the calls of the parents of the others. For their part, Gomez and Pereyra spoke with the parents of other boys, asked many questions, and collected data.

The two met with Pereyra and Gomez and discussed the possibility of using the municipality and the police to search for a brown Renault, but that would have alerted the murderer and he would know that they were looking for him.

"Agreed. Now... what ideas do you have about recovering the missing reports?"

"Look, Daniel, if you go to the chemistry college and ask for them, or if you go with a friendly policeman and demand them, or you ask for them through a friendly professor, in one way or another you will be alerting the possible accomplices of the murderer. Forget it. The little information you would garner would screw up all the research. Remember that it's not known who they are. What if it was a group with branches in the morgue or chemistry college? Eh? You never know."

"It must be that Nubian."

"We don't know."

"Then what?"

"Hmm... you would need..." said Pereyra. "You need to get there without anyone knowing it and you would have to do it with the same types of people who will help you later in the computer center, let's call that kind of person an investigator, no, no, better let's call that person a *finder*. And... uh... you need someone who knows how to operate computers."

"I don't know who," said Gina.

"And then?" Gomez asked.

"Hmm I don't know."

"But... hey, don't you go to the movies?" Pereyra said suddenly. "Don't you read fiction books, Daniel? If we remember movies, maybe we'll get some ideas."

"I don't know Pereyra."

"Think. Let's see, where can those reports be? In a drawer? Interspersed with other papers? Who can have access? Will they be on the computer? Which one? Who from the outside could access that computer?"

"But who could be the investigator, eh, the finder, eh?" Gomez added. "Who are the brightest computer experts in our country?"

"I don't know..."

"Me neither. Ah! wait!" Gomes spoke excitedly. "Ahhhh... of course... those who teach computing in the engineering college. That's it, that's it! Go first to the chemistry place and put on a stupid face—"

"He's great at that," Gina injected.

"Ha yeah... and see on which floor and in which office, where are the computers and electronic files that handle this type of information. But do not say anything. Then think about who in the headquarters or in the Judiciary can connect you with the computer brains in the engineering school. It must be a special person, someone who is not very fond of the government, who knows how to shut up, who either does it out of love or for the pleasure of hurting the government. Think about it. A seeker in that field. And then we plan the coup there."

"I know," said Gina. "The people from Engineering helped us with our IT section and we know who to contact. I know quite a few of them."

"Probably screwed quite a few too," Daniel quipped.

"Bright, yes!" said Pereyra.

A year earlier there had been a problem in the engineering school, and they had tried to keep it as a private matter. It was a crime related to drugs and money, and the professors involved in the problem asked the inspectors of the headquarters for maximum discretion. MacLagan and Domínguez solved the problem, and nothing else was known. Now it was time to return the favor.

"Yes, it will be a pleasure," said the engineer Passogui Prieto, professor of civil engineering at the college, while they chatted in his office. "The man you need is the engineer Dr. Ramos. His wife is a political prisoner, and he will be very happy to help. Wait a bit."

He picked up the phone and called. In five minutes, the engineer appeared. Daniel took him aside and explained what he needed, but without giving many explanations or details. Ramos loved the idea. He knew very well how to help them and was salivating out of excitement. "Whenever and however you want," he said.

Daniel still needed someone who was an expert in files and data. He decided to ask Gina, who took him to Berta, from the Judicial Office, and they asked her if there would be someone trustworthy there. Berta hugged and kissed them and saw in their eyes that they were planning something.

"Your man, Daniel, is Deputy Commissar Alfredo Perez Gomez of the narcotics division."

"What!? Urine Gomez?"

"Nobody like him. Smart, he's an encyclopedia. He knows how to keep secrets; he knows about murders, and he hates those in the army since his niece and neighbor were tortured."

"Ah good. He is already in the group."

It took Daniel a couple of days to contact the people he needed. There was no way to tell Pocho not to come. "I'm not going to miss this one."

Chapter 29

Three nights later, after dinner, the whole crew met in a cafe on Rivera Street with a certain Doctor Ramos, a computer genius from the engineering school, who liked adventure. Urine Gomez came in sportswear, with a gun on his hip, and another on his ankle. All the others were there, well disposed. They walked around, smoked to kill time, and around midnight they all found themselves at the entrance to the chemistry college.

The night was calm, good for some action. Pocho Pereyra, Daniel, Doctor Ramos and a theft expert in keys and locks, a friend of Daniel from the good old days. Gomez had come with one of his friends, who he trusted a great deal, an alarm and surveillance expert. Also, there were three personal police friends of Martinez, well-armed, including "El Pancho," a six-foot beast, scar-faced brute with whom no one would ever argue. They entered and the police officers spoke to the night guards warning them. They went straight to the second floor, to the office containing the data that Daniel sought. In front of the door, there stood a blue beret policeman. Two of the officers went to talk to him and left with him, going out through one of the doors. They opened the lock and padlock and entered the chamber where the computer was. It took Ramos barely twenty minutes to find the source of the data they were looking for, but it was not complete. A note on the same computer said that they had been sent to the headquarters, and after the delivery confirmation, the data had been erased. There was the source of the reports of those who were executed, but the information on the biochemical analysis of the tissues of each one, the analysis of the type of lead of each bullet, the results of the spectroscopy, the Shiogram Graphs, and the other reports, they were all gone. "Sons of bad bitches!"

To make matters worse, the data in the computer described ninety-eight deaths, for which Ramos had to apply several criteria to select the appropriate ones. It ended up with sixty-four clear cases of deaths that corresponded to what they were looking for. "You were close, little Danny, but looks like there were more," Ramos remarked.

Minutes passed.

"Hey... wait, the numbers..." Ramos said. "Hey, look here, looks like over forty-six, perhaps, not what you said. They're probably... corresponding to those for whom we are searching. Uuuuuhh, brother, crap! Danny, they killed even more. But... such animals."

Ramos got tears in his eyes. "I didn't... I didn't know there could be so many."

They were all saddened.

Ramos dried his tears and continued. "To hell with you, Danny. It's true what they say about you."

"What? What do they say about me?"

"That anyone who gets too close to you ends up crying."

Daniel kept silent.

"Ha, from boredom!" said Pocho, and they all started to laugh. "Bored to tears."

They all laughed in silence. Except Daniel.

Only a minute passed when Ramos interrupted them.

"Yes, the reports of the analysis of the powder with the percentage of nitrites, nitrates, sulfates, and pollutants were missing as well. They were probably done by spectro-magnetic and electrophoretic examination. I'm sure each one had its own report. You agree, Gomez?"

"Yup. And it's the law that the results would be sent to police headquarters with a sealed envelope. The originals are usually thrown away after they get confirmation of their arrival at the headquarters. They usually arrive in two to three days unless they use a courier."

"What do you think?"

"Well, perhaps there was an error, some problem with the messenger, complicity, or who knows. We would have known. I know that for sure."

"Who oversees the reception of that kind of correspondence at the headquarters?"

"Hmm... it is usually the Russian... "

"It had to be!" said Daniel. "It *had* to be him. Now we know of one rotten apple."

"That creep! So, he's involved, for sure."

"I guess we're starting to see something."

They all started to think about possibilities.

Ramos continued. They did not find any data that would serve to advance the investigation, since everything had been sent to the information center to become archives of the blessed police headquarters. Hardly the names and identification of each one remained. Ramos printed out everything he could, including information on the thirty-four dead, but took the information of thirty more people who had been shot. "I don't know what else I'm taking," he said, "I...I...I never imagined something so horrible." Daniel and Gomez gave him each half a hug and they continued.

"Daniel, here was an unholy hand," said Ramos. "These reports did not disappear because of magic. Someone made them disappear, someone from here, do you understand?"

"Yes, I understand."

"Your friend Pereyra is right," Ramos continued. "The one who deleted this is someone who operates this computer, this *same* computer. It's someone from here, from this floor of the chemistry college."

"Yes, apparently. The two ends are corrupted."

"Can you copy the memory?" Gomez asked.

"Sure, but there isn't much. Look, do you see?"

"Hmm yes. Well, Daniel, do you understand that?"

"Hmm, not really."

"Well, Daniel, when we bounce out of here, we must leave everything as it was, and we must make sure that nobody knows we were here."

They came out with the reports in hand. The officers took the guards aside to warn them again and took their names. They gave them a little money and at the same time they threatened them. They indicated that if their entry became known, they would return for them. El Pancho greeted the blue beret and then the two policemen at the entrance. He talked to them a bit. None of them had any doubts about what might happen to them if they opened their mouths; they had already heard about El Pancho before.

Daniel thanked everyone, they all said goodbye with a sincere, "At your service, whenever you want," to each other, and left.

Pereyra and Daniel were in their car, spitting bad words. Pereyra was hot with anger. The fear and grief over the murders was turning to rage. They stopped at a late-night bar for a gin and had a conversation about it.

"At least now you know where you must go," Pereyra said with stern eyes. "There's no return."

"Yes," Daniel said. "And with you and with Ramos and with everyone else."

"And with two special guards, very special," Pereyra said, while savoring his gin. "This is no longer going to be a little glimpse or a casual glance, this is going to be an operation, a real operation, and you must find someone who knows about special operations to help you plan it well. I don't know about those things, get someone much smarter. Ramos may or may not serve you well. You must take someone who knows how to search archives with you, which is not so easy. I think that Gomez can help you. Why do they call him *Urine*?"

"Another day I'll tell you. I don't know who to ask who knows about operations."

"Well, hey, think about it. Who can be thirsty for revenge and would give anything to help you? Think."

They finished the drink, paid, and left.

"Think, Carmencito, think."

"Hey, hey, who told you they call me that?"

"Gina and Gomez."

"Well, I don't know, I don't know, Pocho."

"Shit, I told you not to call me Pocho."

"Uuuuuhh, sorry, sorry, uh... as soon as I know, I'll let you know, Pereyra. Thank you."

Daniel walked home.

The next day he went to see kidnapped number two, a mathematics teacher, whom he met in a bar on Sierra Street and asked the same questions. As they always said, he said he did not remember anything. He asked to see his ID and asked him a few questions. He told him about the smells of fruit and vegetables on certain days, of voices, the noises of pipes, how the showers and meals were. As with the previous ones, Daniel asked him about his and his parents' occupation, about number 91 or 16, and many more details that he was writing down.

Gina went to see two more cases, numbers seven and thirty-two, one that was alive and gave her information like the previous one, and another that had been killed, where she had to face the horrible pain of her parents and aunts. After that, Gina looked bad, and she didn't want to do any more interviews that day or the next. Anyway, he had to interrupt things for several days to prepare for an exam. Pereyra and Gomez interviewed others.

After the exam, the two of them began to put colored tacks on the map, but they had no idea. They met with Pereyra to discuss the cases. It was at one of those meetings where they handed out gin, cigarettes, and comments on movies they'd seen, that they came up with the next step: entering the information center.

"Why not?" said Pereyra. "It's such madness that nobody expects it. No one would expect someone like you to dare to enter there. Much less in broad daylight."

"But... it's crazy, also it's... it's... me? Go in alone? I'm not a digger in these sorts of things."

"We already talked about it. Go with Ramos, and—"

"No, I need more people. I need another digger, a finder, a... two is better than one, like last time."

"Gomez. You told me yourself. He seems to know about it."

"But if they find out, they kill him."

"And they'll kill you and Ramos too, idiot. Ay Daniel, open that mind. You need help. Go talk to the green old man."

"Is that... you must understand..."

"But loosen up, silly Philosopher! Pocket Schopenhauer! Go talk to the old man. If you know that he wants to help you, just do it."

"Yes. You're right. Very good."

"But when you go," said Pereyra, "think of a plan... hmm... maybe a movie will give you an idea, I don't know."

Thereafter he could hardly sleep anymore, thinking what to do, how to do it. To make matters worse, his nocturnal images were a swarm of people gesturing. "Let me sleep," he begged them.

In the morning he went to class, at noon he went to eat with Gina and in the afternoon, he went to anatomy.

He then remembered something one of his friends had said to him: "When you find yourself in an unusual situation, put aside your conscience and take advantage of the situation."

He called by phone. He told them he already had a plan. He met the green man two hours later. He greeted him, they exchanged a few words, and Daniel told him about his plan.

"The great chief director of the police headquarters is part of the system of the Ministry of the Interior, which suggests that if the minister gives him an order or makes a request, that would have to be fulfilled. Don't you think?"

"What did get into your head?"

Then Daniel explained. "We need to find someone who no one will argue with, an aggressive guy. If someone, somehow, could be asked for something special, something like a moral favor, a secret favor, that..."

"What? What are you talking about?"

"Well, a very particular favor, like perhaps asking the minister himself to suggest to the chief of police a little cooperation."

"Cooperation? But are you—?"

"Ssshhh, wait. I mean a little cooperation, without anyone knowing, to allow a small group of well-behaved, extremely discreet individuals, to secretly enter the information center to silently retrieve the data they need."

The green old man opened his eyes in astonishment. "Oh, oh. Where did you get that madness from? What data? What data are you talking about?"

Then Daniel told him how he got into the chemistry college and why, and what they found.

"You? But you continue with your adventures, man, I cannot.... "

"Shhh, wait, don't grumble," Daniel said and told him how they got into the computer room, but how the details of the data and several reports were missing, which had been done on purpose. He explained why they were so important and why he suspected they should be there.

"And there was nothing in the chemistry college? But... but that suggests that there is an accomplice there in that college, don't you think?"

"Yes. We found out, but we'll find out more later. We are going to get it."

"Well, Daniel, do you know what you are asking me?"

"Yes," he answered. "But I need more. I need eight mid-adult size IBM uniforms to..."

"What!? What the hell are you...? *Uniforms*? But what are you going to—"

"And several IBM ID cards with fictitious names," Daniel continued. "Any name. And I also need two men who know how to use weapons and who are not shy about using them, armed and in uniform, and wearing a blue beret, to protect us."

"*Beret*? Oh! *ID cards* and... *guns!*? You... you're stone cold crazy. You're going to cause a political-military conflict!"

"No. Listen. Shut up and listen."

"But what did you eat last night?"

"Listen, listen. I also need an officer that you might know, who is highly trusted, someone from the army or the navy, who knows how to plan operations, to help us plan what we want to do. Someone who is very trustworthy, very reliable, and at the same time intelligent."

The old man with the green emerald looked at him with big eyes and without speaking. In his gaze, Daniel could see how his imagination showed him his plans.

"Now I see that all those things that are described in your folder are true, you have been doing this kind of... you were really involved in the Capurro..."

"Yeah. So what?"

"Oh, now I understand why you are not allowed in that Capurro neighborhood, hmm..."

"Leave this subject now."

"Okay, don't be mad, dusty," the old man said. "I see you know things that you won't talk about. Okay. Well, very well tell me more."

"Look. We don't have time to bring you up to speed."

"*Up to spe—*"

"And I don't like to reveal my things. People are programmed to expect the expected, but they do not expect the unexpected. How do you think I slipped into the palace? Through a broken back window under the cover of darkness? No, through the front door, walking slowly in front of the guards with a glass of champagne in hand. And I did it several times, yes. Everyone believed that I was one of the guests and no one asked me anything. They did not expect the unexpected."

"And what did you do it for?"

"You may not understand that, but I'll tell you a bit. The dancing with a big orchestra is fabulous. I love to dance that way. The food was incredible. However, the curiosity and the temptation of the challenge were intoxicating. Besides, the main reason was... ah, it doesn't matter now."

Daniel told him what his plan was and shared a few details and alternatives. They talked about it for a while.

"But... you watch a lot of movies, Daniel.... You got this out of the movies."

"Yeah, yeah, if you want to believe that, okay. I got the idea from several movies, yes, and it entered my head that it is so ridiculous that nobody will think of it. And this time I go with guards, and no one takes me out until I finish."

"Oh, I'm going to light a candle for you."

"Better say a "Baruch atah Adonai."

"Do not be daring."

The old man took him home. Before getting out of the car, Daniel asked him again about the Nubian.

"That Nubian, or Anubis..." said the old green man. "Hmm... his hands are dirty in all this. They told me in the high command. His associates have been selling weapons, medicines, and drugs to army officers but also to the Tupamaros. They are very aggressive people and there have already been several shootings with them... and several deaths. You wanted to know, so yes, they do execute people. Don't go near there. Don't tell Domínguez or Berta to contact anybody in Capurro. Danger, Daniel, *mortal* danger."

"Gee... but he's in that same Capurro area. I need to contact..."

"No. You don't need to contact anybody there. This assassin is thought to have dealings with people... with powerful people. And...well...you are not going to like this."

"What?"

"And it's thought he's got one or two contacts in the leadership at police headquarters. With the Russian That Statchenko."

"Aaahh... that figures. That explains a lot. Look, my impression is that the Nubian, and his contacts, for money or some other reason, could be at the very root of the executions. I need to find more. I need to..."

"Don't go near there."

"Hmm... well..."

"Look Daniel, that Nubian and his people are very dangerous, and it's known that they have murdered several men. If Statchenko is in with them, it's more dangerous than you thought. Maybe... I don't know... maybe he's related to the executor. But there is something else. It seems that whoever the executors are, they have contacts too. They'll see you coming before you know it. You can't get close to that Anubis. The guy kills."

"And why not suck it up and kill him?"

"Ah so now who's talking about killing without a trial or jury..."

"Yes, just like you tried to convince me to be part of."

"I don't even know where he is. Nobody knows for sure. His face is not known. It is also known that he has connections with the Russians, with the Brazilians, the Chinese, and the Americans. In a way, his connections protect him. Whoever gets close to him is killed."

"Oh. But... so there are... army and police officers dealing with this guy, huh? And possibly linked to the murderers?"

"It looks like. We don't know well. That's why I warn you. We can't protect you everywhere. Once you advance in what you seek, you'll have to leave the area because they can kill you. In what you are doing you won't be able to continue until the end. It's going to get too dangerous."

"Yes. I get it. You are right."

"Did you understand? Before the end you should quit the game. And don't be infatuated with it."

"It's okay."

For several days, Daniel dedicated himself to his studies and his work and did not want to think about what he had discussed with the green-emerald man. On the fifth day, when leaving anatomy and going to the bus stop, the same ill-mannered woman stopped her car and told him that they were waiting for him on San Martin Avenue, and added "Go straight there, your putrid filth. I'm not taking you there because you're an unpleasant stinky guy," and spat on the floor in disgust and left.

But... what's wrong with that mare? Why? Daniel said to himself. *This bad-looking she-animal... she's... she's such a... and if I yell something at her, she might stop the car, get out and... and... beat me with whatevver ugly stick hit her own face... or shoot me... or....* He just didn't really know who she was. He had asked the green-emerald man a few times but got no answer. He was a little scared to think that the chick might turn around and pull out a gun and yell, "Here, stupid!" and leave him there, hurt, wounded, bleeding. *One day she will catch me on a bad day, and I will teach her a lesson or turn her in to answer ugly charges at the wart-face tribunal.*

He ran to the Mercedes and got in. The green-emerald man explained.

"In this package is everything you asked for and what you asked for is already fixed."

There, at the time, it was even clearer that what was in front of him was the representative of the power. But... *how powerful was he?*

"But... how'd you do it?" Daniel asked him.

"Courtesy of my charm and my good looks," he said and began to laugh sarcastically. "I'm going to tell you one day, if you're good. In the meantime, is there anything you want to know?"

"Come on, tell me... How could you fix all that?"

"Look, Mister *Up to Speed*," the old man smirked. "There are things in your limited world that you don't know. I did all this with the help of General Pedro Minart Blum, a member of the Ministry of the Interior. Only someone like him could give you the white card and the key to the plan you need. The general's name is Minart from his father and grandfather, all Spaniards, and Minart comes from Minaret, and it's a Sephardic surname. The last name Blum comes from somewhere else. His mother was Blumstein, but he changed it when his father started making his fortune and did not want conservative Uruguayan society to know he was Jewish."

"*Jew*? The? But no—"

"That's right, Moishe Blumstein became Juan Carlos Blum, and his beautiful daughter went from being Shoshana Blumstein to being called Susana Blum. Later, at a party, she met the young Doctor Minart who would later become her husband. Her second son was Peter, who would later become a general. I had a little private dialogue with him in which we talked about our origins. I then asked him for an incredibly special favor, to which he did not wish to refuse."

"Hmm."

Now, Daniel-mess-up, don't go messing up. All that I told you is super-secret. Ah, by the way, I tell you, the keys to the center, the top door, and the basement, are in a small plastic box inside the package. The names and phone numbers of the two assistants you need are also there. They await your call. When you finish, either destroy it all—well destroyed—or give it back to me for me to do it. If they catch you, don't go and say who you are, do you hear me correctly? Don't let it escape you, don't say your name and tell the others not to say their names, you must tell them to call Garrido Lopes, the undersecretary General Minart, in a hurry. Did you understand well? Don't say anything else. Garrido Lopes. Garrido Lopes. Repeat."

"Yes, yes, Garrido Lopes," answered Daniel, already half worried. "Will you say the Baruch atah Adonai for me?"

"I already told you not to be audacious nor daring with me. Get down. The hell with you, Daniel, you're impossible. We're already by your house. Off you go.

"But—"

"Bye!"

Daniel went home to have a quiet dinner and talk with his mother, just in case there would not be another family moment like that.

He spent the next day making phone calls and meeting with some individuals to talk about the plan. Ramos and Urine Gomez were available and eager to participate. At one point he felt that it was very naïve to accept that an inexperienced student like him, who did not know anything about these kinds of operations, would be planning something like that. *What am I doing? I don't know how to arrange and plan all that.* He called Martinez and met him in a cafe. "Stay home, Daniel, I will have somebody call you."

At around six, he got the phone call and was given a phone number. The call connected him with an army lieutenant colonel who met with him and Pereyra the next day. He was an operations expert, a man known by the old green man, who listened to them and met again with them the next day. He analyzed the situation and devised a plan. He did some diagrams, evaluated options, and gave them operational details with backup plans. When he said goodbye, he told them that he had orders to accompany them to ensure the success of the mission and to be able to provide protection in case of problems. He would come with his friend Walter, the silent one.

"Who?" Pereyra asked.

"I call it that. It's my favorite pistol, a Walther, and I bring it with a silencer."

"Ah, have you ever used it," asked Daniel, amazed.

"Yeah, sure. And I never fail. Should I bring one for you too?"

"No! No, thanks."

"Very well. I might bring another friend with me."

Daniel and Pereyra were amazed. They did not know whether to be scared or glad that someone like that protected them. They looked at each other concerned. They knew that the risk was great, and the possible mistakes were many. What the officer had just said was suddenly a mental slap that made them see a reality they did not see earlier. The danger was going to be real.

However, the invitation to that kind of risk and the anxiety to discover the data ate Daniel alive, and the idea of getting into such a forbidden place was captivating. Even knowing the danger, he was dying to get in there. "I don't care. I am going to catch you, son of thousands of whores."

When the officer left, Pocho Pereyra told him: "I think the danger we are going to run into is greater than we thought, Daniel. Why don't you stay at home?"

"No, I must go, I have to be there to make sure we find what I'm looking for. Yes, I know. The danger will be greater than I assumed. This is not going to be an adventure. I want to be there. I will be there."

When the officer left, Pocho Pereyra told him: "Daniel, I want to be there. I will be there, too."

The next morning, he went to the bar on the corner, made a couple of calls, and arranged for the operation to happen on Sunday, when everything would be quiet.

Chapter 30

That Sunday was indeed a quiet Sunday. A cloudless day, slightly cool. A nice day for soccer and a good walk in the park with the family. The street was quiet, and the weather was encouraging. Nothing important happened at the headquarters. There was a good soccer game and that was going to be the event of the day. On Saturday night the guard office had been notified by the chief of police that there was a malfunction in the computers of the information center, but not to worry, the IBM technicians had been notified, and as soon as the technicians show up, to open the door to the central area so they can do their job. The guards asked if they were going to cut the power, so they were promised that the technicians would bring an auxiliary television and connect it to another electrical source in case that happens. No problem, you will not miss the match. "Oh, thank you, sir."

That morning, seven IBM technicians escorted by two ministry guards and an army lieutenant colonel, all armed, arrived at headquarters and showed their credentials. Everything seemed in order. The agents from the guard office were notified and took them to the information center. There was a cordial greeting and the door was opened for them. They were all very nice. The two guards stayed outside ensuring that the technicians were not disturbed. There was no reason to worry.

A few minutes later, two of the technicians went to their truck, brought in a battery-operated television, and took it to the room of the police on duty. The soccer game was underway.

Once inside the computer room, the engineer Ramos and his assistant took care of the computers, while Pereyra and Daniel tried to guess the order in that disorder. Urine Gomez and another technician, knowledgeable about the file system, friends of Berta and Gina, helped them search and investigate the data. As the data was found, it was copied on a photocopier, and photographed. The information found in the computers was not complete so, a couple of hours later, they decided to go down to find the other files using the stairs to the basement. When they got there, they found that the staircase led upward to a second computer room, but it also led downward to a large room. They spent a good while in each of those places, retrieving information.

A sign with red letters at the foot of the stairs announced that only people from Interpol could descend into the basement room. "No Trespassing. Stop: only INTERPOL," read the notice.

They descended in silence, and reached the large room, where a notice read, "INTERPOL Only." The door was closed and locked with two locks, but Daniel opened it with his keys. Once in the large room they began to search. Daniel took a side corridor, found the door that led to the prison corridors, and saw that it had an alarm device and two small windows with covers. The halls outside were continuously patrolled by blue berets with dogs and armed with machine guns.

Technicians opened files and gathered data. Suddenly, in a rush, one of the technicians pushed a box and a tool fell to the ground. They were silent, still. Daniel approached the window and ran the viewer very slowly. He found himself squarely in the face of a blue beret, who, machine gun in hand and a dog at his side, had approached.

"Anyone there?" he yelled. "Who's there?"

Silence. Nobody inside moved.

"Who's there? Hello?" he shouted again "Open the door! I am armed and ready to shoot."

Silence. They were all holding their breath.

The steel *click* of a cocking rifle pierced the stillness. Daniel froze. Then he moved slowly to the side of the door in case he was hit by the blast. He has seen those assault rifles some time ago. They were designed to chop people up.

"Raul! Raul! come!" the armed guard shouted again. "Someone's here."

They felt footsteps approaching. Another dog. They heard key noises. The guards were going to enter. The door was to be opened and the two blue berets were preparing to enter with their weapons ready.

Daniel flattened himself against the wall. He couldn't move. His heart pounded. He heard another click. They were getting ready.

"There's going to be a shootout."

"Answer, answer," shouted the other guard. "Who is there?"

More noise of keys. They were going to come in and Daniel was in the line of fire. He looked around, no place to hide against the caliber of those bullets.

Suddenly he saw a shadow. The lieutenant colonel had approached him, he was about five or six feet away and he was waving his hand for him to crouch and stay down. At the same time, he had his weapon at the ready, with a silencer, 'Walter-the-silent', with an extended barrel and ten-round magazine. He crouched down, knelt one knee on the floor, held his weapon with both hands and prepared to fire. Whoever entered through that door will never tell the story.

Daniel's heart stopped and he could see that Pereyra was hiding behind a box, white and pale. Urine Gomez noticed what was happening and from his waist he took out his pistol, a Browning, onto which he screwed a silencer, and showed a face like he wanted to shoot someone. He just wanted them to try to enter to enjoy the opportunity of unloading his gun. *Is this the same nice guy and cake baker I know*? His hulky Browning pistol looked like it was about to spit fire.

Daniel told himself, *Alas, he's going to use it at any moment.* Then, very quietly, Gomez opened a case he had in his bag and took out an automatic pistol which he then handed to Daniel. It was a Remington 51, same one he trained with. He cocked the weapon in silence, while Daniel tried to refuse it, and whispered in his ear "Be ready, lie down on the floor, point to the door, and whoever enters just shoot."

Daniel freaked out and his heart leapt out of his mouth. He looked at the gun in his hand. *They'll kill us here*, he thought and crushed to the ground, and then, *Am I going to shoot somebody*?

"Open, open or I shoot," the policeman shouted again.

One more noise and two silencers were going to spew fire. The seconds stretched. The earth stopped.

Beads of sweat were pouring from Daniel and falling to the floor. His hand was sweating, and the Remington was slipping. "Oh."

"Wait Pedro, wait. Do *not* shoot. I'm going to call upstairs, see what they know. Wait, don't open fire."

Daniel tried to hold the Remington without shaking. He saw the officer crouched; he saw Gomez behind some metal file cabinets ready to shoot. *This Gomes is going to kill someone,* he thought. The others were hiding nowhere to be seen.

They heard footsteps moving away. The panting and sniffing of the dogs were heard on the edge of the door.

"Come on, Raul, the dogs are nervous. Something's happening here."

Daniel had already crouched down and very carefully he laid down and flattened himself even more against the floor. His belly was full of noises. If they entered, everything would be very fast. The lieutenant colonel signaled him to be ready. Daniel was sweating.

The seconds passed.

Again, he heard the sound of the keys. A key was stealthily entering the lock. The blue beret was preparing to open the door.

Time stopped. The lieutenant colonel's hands were steady. One shot was going to fly at any moment.

"Wait Pedro!" shouted a distant voice. "There are some IBM technicians upstairs fixing something. They were sent from the ministry. They are supposedly going up and down the stairs."

"Ah, well," said the blue beret and began to walk away. "Come on, come on Cheecho," he said to the dog.

They felt footsteps moving away.

The lieutenant colonel got up, lowered his weapon, and put it away. Daniel rolled over on the floor and rolled onto his back. He tried to get his pulse back and swore he will never get into something like that again. He laid there for a while until a hand helped him up.

"Do you want me to change your diaper?" Ramos said.

Daniel smiled at him, stood up and they gave each other a silent wet hug. They were both sweaty.

They kept searching. What they were interested in was all on paper and scattered in several drawers, and it took them a long time to find it. They photocopied what they could, printed a good part and took pictures of the rest. Upon leaving, with a handkerchief, they cleaned and tidied up everything they touched to prevent anyone from noticing anything. Bursting with new data, they went back up to the computer room and searched and found even more missing data.

Daniel searched the files for his folder, to destroy it, but could not find it. "You won't find her here, Daniel," Urine told him. "You're not that important and you're not a criminal. Yours is in the general file."

Hours later, with the task accomplished, the technicians left the area and thanked the guard agents telling them that everything was ready for Monday. Daniel was wearing a wig, though it wasn't noticeable, to hide his long wavy hair. He had put on a brown-haired mustache and wore thick glasses so his silly Jewish face wouldn't give him away. He did not attract attention.

There was nothing to comment on. The two vans left and on Monday there was nothing that would have been irregular in the areas that were visited. Nobody knew anything. There was nothing to take notice of.

When Daniel got home, he put the uniforms and the rest of the stuff in a bag and took out all the photocopies and reports from the IBM suitcase.

He arranged them in numbered folders corresponding to each case. The next day he developed the photos and began to study everything.

"Daniel," his mother asked, "why was there an IBM card in your room with a... uh— no, nothing."

"What, mom?"

"Nothing. I did not see anything."

It was too much information, complicated, with details that he did not understand. Many of the missing second and third pages were there, filling in gaps of records he already reviewed. But he was going to need help.

Regarding the chemical results, Berta and Gina collected the books that Daniel had requested and took them to the technical division of the judicial where they had a meeting with three of the most informed guys who helped him review the data. Two of the technicians advised Daniel to ask Deputy Commissar Gomez for help, "The guy is an encyclopedia," So Urine joined the group. The information was now much more complete, the characteristics of the lead of each bullet and the types of caps were there.

"The chromatographic analysis, the nitrite report, the antimony and boron studies, and even the details of the remains of the powder are all there, Daniel." one of the technical guys said, lighting a cigarette. "Gas chromatography and mass spectrometry were done in each case and that part is complete. Wanna see?"

"Yes."

Daniel knew it, when a firearm is fired at a human body, gases are generated containing incinerated and non-incinerated components mixed with shell and propellant residues, and analytical chemical analysis combined in tandem with a scattering spectrometer can find and classify the projectile, the make and origin of the casing, and even the details of the weapon used.

"Many of the pages two and three that were missing are here, Carmencito. And they shed a lot of light into these events."

"Yes. Look at this and look here."

"Daniel, it was all there," Gomez told him. "We used the Grill-Swetsky technique properly, so we know even what type of ammunition was used. They had deleted everything so that the details could not be found, but here they are."

They reviewed the spectroscopy, the molecular symmetry, the electrophoretic chromatography, and everything was confirmed. With that, Urine and three experts worked evaluating the results of the chemical analysis of the tissues, with which they obtained information on the primer of each shot.

Then they went on to the lead reports, then to the percentage of nitrites, nitrates, and sulfates.

"Look here, see?" They showed him.

"The first part showed that the primer was based on gelinite, and not nitrotoluene," said Gomez. "Therefore, they were revolver bullets and not automatic ones."

"And now... look here... see? There. The second part showed that the lead was not from commercial bullets but from lead with alloy. This is not for sale to the public but is only distributed to police stations and barracks, therefore these bullets are only used by the police, private soldiers, corporals, and sergeants, but no officers. The rest use jacketed bullets."

"Hmm... they had figured that out right."

"Look, Daniel, the soldiers and officers of the armed forces do not use revolvers at this time," said one of the officers. "They've been dispatched semi-automatic pistols with armored bullets. Most of the officers use parabellum projectiles, and those who do not use either, used. 44 caliber semi-armored projectiles. Even the ones using. 38s have semi-armored bullets."

"Daniel, Daniel, these kids haven't been killed by someone in the army nor by someone with a rifle or automatic weapon," Martinez told him when he read several of the reports. "It was not a rifle bullet, or a shrapnel shot in an escape attempt, nor was it a firing squad against the wall. It was a revolver execution with the victim seated. The evidence is there."

Martinez and Gomez explained. The public does not have access to those bullets, and they were much more expensive. However, the remittances to the police and the army came from two special places. They received the bullets from Argentina and Brazil, the ones from Brazil going to the army units. The nitrite and nitrate analysis showed that in all cases the bullets had been Brazilian, and always the same bullets, and from the same weapon. When they put all the graphs together and crossed the derivatives, and compared with publications and reports, they had the final conclusion before them.

"Oh, oops, shit, look at this, Daniel," noted one of the officers "All the fatal shots were made with the same 38 revolver, not a pistol, by a uniformed person, not a policeman, not an officer, and from a barracks in Montevideo and not from the interior of the country. Therefore, police stations and police are excluded. According to this information, those of the air force and those of the navy are excluded. Do you understand why?"

They agreed that given all the information in the folder and the details they had compiled, it was about an army barracks or battalion that would be in Montevideo, east of the Agraciada-General Flore line. This man, 'the X-man,' was not an officer, nor was he a civilian, nor was he a policeman. He was someone of low rank in the army. They called him 'the executor X.' He was right-handed, not left; and he was about five feet tall.

Daniel was left brooding over what he already knew, *I'm going to catch you, son of a thousand whores*, he declared to himself.

"Well, very good, Daniel, but listen to me well. After investigating all this, you are going to have to exit the game. It seems clear to me that the Nubian murderer is involved and if there is a spy of his at the headquarters, it's certain that he will try to liquidate those who are investigating this."

"No, wait," Daniel jumped. "I don't agree. This was not the Nubian's doing."

"What?"

Then Daniel explained his theory.

"Yes. I realize that. Mmm..."

"Anyway, set yourself a limit and get out of this soon," stressed the agent, patting Daniel on the back "We don't want anything to happen to you."

They finished after midnight. They felt good; they had advanced on the case. He thanked them very much. They chatted a while longer and Daniel got up to leave.

"Wait, wait, Danny boy," Gomez said and gave him a package. "Here, take this to your mother."

"What is it?"

"A poppy seed roll. Yes. My Polish recipe. She'll like it, you will see."

"Thank you," said Daniel, giving him a half hug. "Thank you very much."

He found Gina and Martinez sleeping on some chairs at the exit of the technical section. He woke them up. "What are you doing here?" he asked them.

They had waited in case Daniel needed something urgent and to coordinate whatever, they told him.

"Thank you."

"Did everything go well, Daniel?"

"Yes."

Chapter 31

Daniel and Pereyra decided to consolidate the data, so Daniel took his maps to Pereyra's home. They compared and studied the data of the cases they already had but found no details that could give them a solid clue. They concluded that they needed another brain to collaborate on this and possibly find some relationship between the data.

The next day, after anatomy, Daniel bought cigarettes and went to Pocho's house. They reviewed all the cases and reviewed the responses and the interview data. They reviewed the map where they had all the addresses of the kidnapped, then they made another map separating men from women with different colored tacks. They made several maps, until suddenly Pereyra noticed that all the directions were east of the Boulevard España-Soca line, west of Carrasco and south of Avenida Italia Highway. Why would it be? They went through everything again, digging for something that would indicate a clue.

The next day Gomez, Pereyra, and Daniel reviewed everything again.

And suddenly, a light went on. They looked at each other with wide-open eyes. They were astonished.

They had found the clue.

The surprise was tremendous. They stared at the map with excitement. Most of the parents' business addresses were on Rivera Street or one of its collaterals, but no more than one or two blocks away, and they were all located near the intersection with Larraniaga Street. There was a concentration of colored tacks near the intersection of Rivera and Larraniaga. The parents of almost all the cases had their business or their offices near that intersection. They had finally found a relationship between the victims, although they did not know what to do with it.

But why those businesses and not others in the same area? Would they all be from the same phone directory? No.

Would they be from the same club? No. Did they belong to the same society, or were they from the same high school class? No, but why? Or, why not?

They decided to go exploring. They went into some of the businesses and looked around. Nothing, there was nothing to give a clue.

Why those businesses and not others that were next door? What did the other businesses have that were not touched? What protected them? They couldn't find anything. They went through their questions and answers, went through the folder, getting nowhere. A study had to be made of the businesses whose owners had not been touched by kidnapping to try to understand why. And it was necessary to study the folder and the answers again to see if there was any clue.

Daniel decided to call some of those parents on the phone and ask a few final questions, but it didn't help. An hour later he called on the phone and requested a meeting at the hospital. Once in the Hospital de Clinicas, in the cardiology division, he explained to a doctor what he needed.

Two days later, when he returned home, he met the foul-mouthed woman who was waiting for him, and who got out and approached him with an inquisitive face. *Oh, she's going to yell at me again*, he thought and stood still.

"Where were you, stinking idiot?" she said approaching. "What? You're afraid of me?

That's it, thought Daniel, *she's going to hit me, here, in front of the neighbors*, and he started walking to the side.

"But don't be scared, she said. "Haven't you asked a certain person for something special? Eh, lady ladybug? Here is what you wanted. "And she gave him a thick folder.

She told him that she had taken the folder from the census office and other information centers and to review it and call her if he needed more information or if he drew any conclusions, but to study it well. Daniel asked her what was inside because the folder was thick. She replied that it was demographic information about the businesses and offices of the parents of the abductees, plus the information of many other merchants and offices within a radius of two hundred meters from each business. "It's what you requested, just like you requested." She told him to call her as soon as he discovered anything and left him several numbers.

"And study all that well, and don't get distracted by that indecent busty whore. Did you hear me, immoral shit stick?" She turned around and got into the car. She spat on the ground from the window as a sign of contempt.

But what a mare! Daniel said to himself. *How aggressive is she? Who is this woman?*

He kept walking. *Well, at least she didn't hit me, and no one saw me.*

He turned around. *Ah, but one of these days she is going to hit me... and on the street.*

He stopped and thought. He turned around, went back to Pocho's house, told him the score, and left him the folder. They met the next day.

"Well, what about the folder? Did it show anything?"

"Look kid, I've been studying it and studying it and... well ..."

"Do you know what the "Friends of Rivera Society" is, huh?" Pocho asked.

"No, no idea."

"It is a very good society. It will interest you."

"Friends of Rivera? What? *Society*?"

They chatted for a while, Pocho described what he knew.

He stood up, amazed.

"Oh," Daniel said to Pocho, "it's a lot of manure together and more than I thought."

They shook hands and Daniel left, thinking about everything they had talked about.

The next day he made some calls, said he had found some clues, and a few hours later he received the place and time of the appointment.

There he was sitting in a cafe at the crossing of General Flores and Domingo Aramburu, in the middle of the Goes neighborhood, enjoying his espresso and his ham-and-cheese croissant after leaving anatomy. He had a bag full of papers and data and was thinking that his interview was not going to be very nice. He was nervous.

He lit a cigarette, wondering if the Mercedes would come with the green man or would it be just the driver, when a Citroen honked its horn and the unfriendly animal-woman that always made him feel like his spleen burst in a vice signaled him to come with her. "I screwed myself up." Daniel didn't move, he didn't feel safe. She kept waving at him and eventually Daniel got up and came toward her with hard buttocks, bracing himself for verbal aggression. The nasty woman told him to get in the car.

"No. I don't want to go with you!" And he went back to his table.

He paid the bill and started to go half scared to the other side. She honked at him again, "Get in, come here, don't let mama scare you."

"No."

"Will you get in the car?"

"No. Leave me alone, mule. What are you going to do to me?"

"Get in. Hey, come here."

He turned around and started to walk in the opposite direction.

"Get in the car. Or do you want me to get out and get you in myself?"

"No. You are unfriendly and mean. I'm leaving."

She made a move to open the car door and get out. Daniel hesitated. *Oh, if she gets out, she hits me here in the street. What a shame."* Daniel knew he was going to have a hard time. He stopped, calculated. Things weren't going to go well. He turned and began to walk quickly to the other side of the street. She reversed the car and yelled at him, "The old man wants to see you, snake turd" He stopped. Several people had already looked at him, and he felt unpleasant. *What to do?*

"Okay," he said nervously. *I'm not going to do well here.*

He got into the chariot of death, expecting a punch. She said, "Mama really dug her claws into you, huh?" Then didn't say anything during the rest of the trip. He was going in fear, expecting a blow. *What are you going to do to me?*

The car drove into the Prado area until it came to a huge house with a rose garden and massive ivy vines in front. Two policemen were guarding the entrance and let her pass. Daniel was already nervous and even more anxious when the woman told him: "Get ready for the beating of your life. Now you'll see, idiot."

This is going to be horrible, Daniel thought, and his blood stopped flowing. It felt even worse. He did not dare to tell her anything because he knew that the woman's hand would transform into an animal claw and destroy his face. He got scared. He couldn't answer anything. *What did I come for?*

She drove all the way back to a large private parking lot, where three Mercedes Benz and several other European cars were parked. A man the size of a mountainside, ugly and armed to the teeth, opened the door for him and Daniel got out of the car, nervous. She stayed but told the officer, "Take him to the bathroom to clean himself a little because he's scared and dirty, poor thing, and then take him to where they are waiting... without his pants, with just a towel." And she closed the door. Daniel gasped from the bad feeling he was getting. What a shame. He did not know whether to walk weak or hard. He looked at the guy, feeling tiny and embarrassed.

The guy, hiding a smirk, led him straight into the living room.

"Don't worry, I'm not going to take you to the bathroom," he said reassuring him. "She always makes those horrible jokes. She likes to play games and mortify people. She is bad. She's a bad broad. If you could hear what she told me the day I met her when she first came here with her father. She's a bastard. Don't worry, I'm taking you to her father."

"Thank you," Daniel said as he walked half nervous, and half scared. "Eh? eh... who's the father?"

"The owner of this home, Mr. Saravia-Cohen, you don't know him. The one who is all gummed up, with the green emerald on his lapel. Now you'll see. He's waiting for you with the others."

Ahh! Saravia-Cohen... so this mare is the daughter of Saravia-Cohen, the old green man with the emerald. Daniel surmised.

"And my name's Anselmo," mister Daniel," said mountainside man. "Colonel Anselmo Arellanes but call me Anselmo. Yes?"

"Pleasure."

The house was bigger inside than it looked. The entrance had very nice furniture. Through a window he could see some large dogs in one of the courtyards. *A mistake here and they throw me to the dogs,* he told himself, making jokes with himself to calm down.

He kept thinking about the woman and started to get irritated. *So, this wretched woman hides herself behind the power of her father to talk to me like that! Manipulator!* His irritation increased, remembering the times she had spoken badly to him. *But... how abusive and bad.*

"Through here," said the big man. "And don't worry, everything is fine."

"Thank you," said Daniel, who felt a growing anger. *But what a bitch.* The times she left him boiling in the street, hiding behind her father's pants... and just for fun. *Bad mare.*

They turned around the next corridor and the guy opened a large door that led into the living room. There was the gentleman of the Mercedes, Mr. Saravia-Cohen in person, with his herringbone suit and his very green emerald on the lapel. There were also the two officers he had met that afternoon at the barracks, and two other officers from some branch of the army, all wearing that dark green jacket with gold studs attached with which they tried to improve their disgusting images. *Hmm...they also wear those little shitty colored flags...* stuck to the chest which the army bosses like so much. *To remind people how they crushed innocents with their boots*, snarled Daniel to himself.

There were also two other people in suits, with serious faces, probably civilians of high position. They all looked at Daniel anxiously, stone-faced.

Daniel, irritated by the trip and by the woman, stood at the door, thinking and already angry. *I had to face that mean woman and now I must face these creepers.* He wasn't sure if he wanted to enter or not.

"Yes, go ahead, Mr. Daniel."

Daniel entered the officers' room, saying, "Thanks for waiting, excuse me..."

"Okay. Can we start?"

"Well," said one of the officers, "let's leave family issues for later." He looked at Daniel and held his arm out toward a chair. "Sit down, take your time and tell us what you found."

"Coffee, you?"

"Yes please."

"Tea anybody?"

Daniel asked that they bring a large map of the city and colored tacks. When they brought it in, he pinned the map to the wall and first showed them the linear area of the kidnappings, as they had happened around Rivera Street, progressing from left to right in a linear fashion, suggesting that the kidnappers were using a map and had a master plan.

"Here there was no coincidence," he told them. "They didn't choose them randomly or for political reasons. These were not kidnappings brought by complaints or for being seditious or suspects. Here was a kidnapping plan in progress. The kidnappers had a profit-making plan, and the alleged ideology of the kidnapped had nothing to do with it."

They all looked at the map carefully. They were surprised.

"Let's see, show me the data," Saravia-Cohen said.

Daniel went through it and the other various documents.

"And those numbers?" said an officer.

Daniel explained to him about the numbers and then told them about the fact that all the affected parents had college-age children. After discussing that for a while and drawing various conclusions, the old green man asked for some further details.

"I see. Hmm... that's Larraniaga Street, right?"

Curiosity stung them. They went on to other details and then entered the field of the *Friends of Rivera Society*. He did an analysis of that society and its members.

"You know what the Rivera Friends is, huh?"

"No, I have no idea."

"A very good society, comprised of good people, friendly, well-educated, great traders. They're good."

"Well, and what about it?'

"Notice that many years ago," Daniel continued, "several traders and professionals from the Rivera and Larraniaga areas came together and decided to form this society to do common marketing, share in promotional activities, and in turn obtain certain benefits from the Municipality, and reciprocate by making campaigns and donations in common. Good idea. Over time, the society expanded into more territory, number of members, and became more influential."

"Yes, yes, but why do you tell me this?"

"Wait, please... over time, other traders from other areas wanted to join and become members," he explained. "But they were not accepted because the most important members decided to maintain the society exclusively for traders in the areas of Rivera and Larraniaga. Do you hear me well? The members are only merchants and traders from that area."

"And what?"

"And... and... mister official, more than forty of the fathers of the abducted are members of that society. What does it look like?"

"Pa! to the...!" another officer said, astonished, standing up. "Whoa, Daniel!"

"Shaking, eh?"

"Ha, very interesting. Yes."

"And now?" asked Saravia-Cohen, as he sipped some of his tea.

"Now we must unite our brains."

"What?"

"Well, this one will make you burst. Forty-four parents, possibly even forty-eight, whose kids were abducted are members of that society, and they all had a son or daughter of twenty to twenty-nine years old, who is or was recently a student. That's one thing you can't let go of."

"Holy... gee..."

"Yes. Hey, that indicates several things to focus on. You must think about it."

"Did they have any military relationships, divorces, marital status, parents ages, things like that?" asked an officer.

"No."

They all kept quiet, and Daniel waited for the information to sink in their minds.

"Bank accounts?" said one officer.

"Of course!" replied Daniel. "The next step is to investigate the bank accounts of each business of the affected parents and the personal accounts of each of those parents, although it would be necessary to search in several banks."

"It seems to make sense, but what would you look for? Sounds... complicated."

"I don't know, I would look for many things at once," Daniel stated. "I suppose there will be several things to check. I suppose that all personal accounts should show an expense at the time of the ransom payment, but what would you think if a certain account, personal or business, shows earnings every time there was a ransom payment, eh?"

"How?"

"Yes, yes, imagine if a certain account receives a similar large entry within a few days of each ransom, and that this happens thirty or more times. You wouldn't have to be Sherlock Holmes to become suspicious."

"That... eh, is the executor... the executor X, or... or an accomplice!" he said. "Uuuuuuuyyy! This step is brave. Are you sure about that?"

"Hey, let him—"

"So what? Yes, I know, it's a rough step, and no, I'm not sure, it's just a theory. However, it smells to me that perhaps it is a step in the right direction."

He waited a bit and spoke again about the companies, businesses, and the society. This time with more details and with what he found out about the banking relationship. There he stopped again and waited for the idea to settle in their minds. Slowly everyone stopped commenting and started looking at Daniel. Their eyes widened.

"What did you say?" shouted a certain Goicochea. "Did I hear you right?"

"What? You... do you know what you're saying?"

"But—How? Wait—"

"But you... Did you say well? Are you sure?"

Everyone was amazed. The explanation was clear, and there was no longer a coincidence.

"You realize that... that... then the kidnappers..."

"Yes, that's what I mean," he said. "There might be other partners, yes, but somehow the kidnappers either live or work in the area. I think this is an important concept and we must think along those lines. The kidnappers are either members of that society or they are related to someone in the society, and that someone is a partner."

"Wow" said a general. "And now?"

"Aaaahhhh... This's valuable information. Very good, Daniel."

"I already knew, I knew it," said old Saravia-Cohen, like a proud father. "I knew that if we let you loose in the Roman circus in front of the lions, you would find a way around it."

"And now?" said someone.

"Yes... what happens?" asked one of the officers.

Following the data from another map, Daniel put black tacks on each residence of those affected. He explained that sooner or later the accomplice should use a bank to deposit what he earned, therefore he had to search all the banks in the area for deposits of a similar amount that had been made within the days following the payment of a ransom. If that fails, perhaps because the culprit or culprits have converted the money to foreign currency and put it in a safety deposit box, it would be necessary to check each bank for periodic visits after each payment, foreign currency transactions, purchases of gold, visits to the safety deposit boxes, and things like that. He put tacks on the banks that he most suspected. He shuffled other theories but told them that the next step should be bank exploration.

"And you... how did you manage to find all that? You?"

"No. Not only me. The four of us thought about it, and we also—"

"What four? Who... exactly?

"I will let you know in time, General."

"Good. Let me know, Daniel. I want to know those names."

"Sure, I will," he mumbled. "My ass."

"What?"

"Shut up, Daniel, don't start."

"Well, the next step is to explore local banking activities," Daniel said.

"Mmm.... yes," said one of the officers. "Yes. I'm with you."

"Yes. What did you eat, Daniel? What did you eat to make these things come to your mind?"

"Again, I wasn't alone," he said. "It was thanks to the group. I insist that there is a connection between this one particular bank and the society. Most of the parents of the kidnapped belong to the society and all have their money in this one bank. Do you see it there in the photo? That's the root of the thread, and from there we must search and pull until we reach the skein.

"What if your theory fails, mister Daniel?" said one of the officers.

"So then, mister General," Daniel replied, raising his voice. "You go and try to—"

"Shut up, Daniel," said Saravia-Cohen again.

"Okay! Then let's get into this. That the parents all have a bank in common, without knowing it, perhaps the Commercial Bank that is three blocks from the crossing, or another local bank, and that perhaps within the bank there is an accomplice who knows which are the big fish to catch, and he makes arrangements with an outside fisherman, perhaps a military fisherman."

"Hmm... yes," said an officer.

"And? And?"

"The one or two partners are either related to the society or work in that bank or both."

"Pa! Talk about a plot, gee Daniel."

"Very good, young man."

They discussed it for a while, and all agreed to mobilize their group of researchers to see what they could find.

"What? No, wait," warned Daniel. "Cool off. You just can't have too many people investigating this. The culprits will catch wind and for sure they will scatter and vanish."

"He's right."

"So...?"

"So, we silently search keeping in mind the two theories, simultaneously," Daniel added. "Yes, we must get into that bank without anyone noticing. In the society too, and in the other local banks as well."

"We must have a plan."

"Whatever you do, do it in silence, and in a very discreet way. The culprits are sure to be on the alert. Do not share information with anyone. Don't talk to anybody!"

"Yeah, sure."

"Don't tell me *yeah, sure* when I know that you—"

"Shut up, Daniel."

"No. Don't shut me up, Saravia," said Daniel, raising his voice with a red face and quivering lip. "None of you, none! should involve more than one very reliable person. Just one. No words to your own family and friends either. This needs to be kept secret."

"Ha, you are not going to come and tell us what we should do o—"

"General Goicochea," said the green Saravia-Cohen raising his voice above the others and showing clear signs of being upset—you are wrong. Daniel here will tell you what to do and what not to do, and you will do what he says."

"Well, you are..."

"What? Are you actually arguing? I represent Condor here, and you will listen. We are all involved with this situation, which has become an international concern. If we don't find a solution, we may end up with United Nations forces here in Uruguay and a blockade at the port and airport."

"Well, I—"

"So far, neither of you have been able to provide even a slight idea of what to do about it. Therefore, you will do what Daniel says, and I will make sure you do it."

"Okay. Okay. I get you. I'll get just one or two persons. Yes, silently."

"Yes."

"Yes, yes, very discreetly."

Daniel gave them some more ideas and told them that he had finished. They congratulated him, and since everyone had something to do, they said goodbye very cordially. They all gave half a hug to Daniel and congratulated him for what he found out. Before leaving, in the courtyard, he approached the bad woman to call her on her nonsense, but Anselmo saw him and told him that it was not worth it. He looked at him and made a gesture with his face.

Tabeiras, a driver, took him home. "Mister Saravia-Cohen asked me to take you home before you get in trouble, Mister Daniel."

"Thanks."

"You... you don't get along with that woman, no?"

"No."

The next day nobody called him or surprised him. He had just a normal day and felt very well and calm. He liked days like that.

Chapter 32

Life in Montevideo kept passing by. The city, under the military dictatorship, was getting worse. There were no personal freedoms or freedom of the press. Army vehicles, soldiers, and military men pushing people were daily scenes throughout the city.

It was no longer about eliminating the Tupamaros group; it was about scaring, controlling, mistreating, running over, and even imprisoning anyone who raised his head. Yet, amid that full social harassment, during that shameful totalitarian regime, many Uruguayans agreed with what the dictatorship was doing. Citizens of Montevideo applauded the fact that other citizens of Montevideo were imprisoned, tortured, and even killed. Many Uruguayans, falsely proud of their great culture, hailed the military, while ignoring the historical events and the political corruption that had led to that phase. "Praise the military!" they shouted in the street when they saw a convoy or a jeep.

The army and the Joint Forces, owners and lords of the land and life of the Uruguayans, dedicated themselves to keeping the population frightened. Many people were surprisingly visited by soldiers, then hooded and taken to detention centers where they were tortured.

One of the very common tortures of those times was the electric cattle prod, in which the victim was tied up, then wet down, and subjected to electric shocks on different parts of the body. The favorite places of those who used the prod were, of course, the genitals and breasts, extremely painful points. The pain was enough to break down the victims, and sometimes killed them.

The torturers were Uruguayans from Montevideo. They were Montevideans torturing fellow Montevideans. Horrible. And when they got bored, they changed their torture, and gave them punches, or submitted them to waterboarding. Or drowned them while laughing at human suffering.

However, it was not a foreign attack. It was not Europeans or Asians who were invading and torturing Uruguayan men and women. They were the same people from Montevideo, people from "around the corner," people from the neighborhood, who did horrible things to their own neighbors and compatriots, beat them up without mercy and even executed them without regret. Many Uruguayan women were raped, raped by Uruguayans. Who were those animals?

Chapter 33

Montevideo was going from bad to worse. The number of detainees, political prisoners, and tortured was on the rise, and an adverse social climate was growing. The cost of living was rising and poverty, now silenced by the butt of a rifle, was expanding.

In the midst of this panorama, of this daily reality of lack of freedom and of financial difficulties, those who couldn't leave the country and could not hide, suffered the uncertainty of living under the boots of those modern Nazis who, with blood in their clutches, self-declared themselves as liberators. Jews and historians, more sensitive to those events, recalled the horrors of World War II, and saw in the statements and deeds of the dictatorship a clear resemblance to Nazism and its Gestapo. What was the abrupt entry into homes and the hooded arrest of suspected dissidents if not a direct copy of Nazi brutality? What were these deadly tortures and executions in the hands of uniformed men if not a copy of the Gestapo and the SS of Nazi Europe?

The winds of atrocious fascism smothered the country. A Uruguayan fascism, dictated by Uruguayans, executed by Uruguayans, and designed to destroy Uruguayans, spread through the country. A social cannibalism.

A brutality, primitive and military, cruel and uniformed, closed the spirits and bit the bodies of the Uruguayans. The bewilderment was such that many people no longer expected better times.

"And during all that, here I am," Daniel said, "with my family, hoping nothing will happen to us."

It was a very difficult time. Human rights violations were a daily thing. The military had firmly decided that they would do their best to provide security for this national development and participate in the country's moral and material organization. Paraguay's animal dictator Stroessner, a cruel killer, an indescribable beast, came to visit them and felt so at ease in that Uruguayan fascism that it was said that he was as comfortable as a pig in the mud. In the following month, the gorilla Pinochet, the savage dictator of Chile, came to visit glorious Uruguay. A ruthless ape, a neo-Hitler, a horrible human being, who felt very comfortable surrounded by jailers and torturers.

This was all clear to Daniel. All of that was part of Operation Condor, and those visits were to confirm and seal the pacts of that operation. He was disgusted to think that somehow, he had been, and he was still, part of that operation. He lived debating himself, knowing on one hand that he was participating in an operation of synchronized slaughter and coordinated cruelty which he rejected, but on the other it offered a secret viaduct to rescue and save at least some of the unfortunate. It was paradoxical, and he knew it. He didn't want to continue with this, but he knew he had no choice. *It's the only way I will accomplish what I want.*

There, standing during all that, he questioned his own morals and saw himself in an increasingly uncomfortable position. "What to do? Separate myself from everything? Go my own way?" There were times when he felt trapped and slowly going into a funnel where sooner or later things were going to get critical. Those were occasions when he caressed the possibility of continuing his career abroad... *And what do I do with Gina?* he wondered.

That's how things went on, quietly.

Monday. Walking down the street, he came up with an idea about the banks. He didn't go to class. He went to visit two businesses on Rivera Street and then walked into the Commercial Bank and asked a couple of questions using his fictitious name. *Hmm...I'll call one of the numbers from a café later and ask for a meeting.* They asked him for details. He told them he wanted a meeting with everyone, Pereyra and two experts in bank accounting and computers. The meeting happened the following day in a judiciary room, with Pereyra, the officers, Saravia-Cohen, his daughter, Gomez, and the specialists he asked for. They had brought information from the banks of the affected cases, and coffee and cake from the Hamburg Confectionary.

"They all used the Commercial Bank in the area, yes, every last one. Many of them used another bank for other transactions, but those were several different banks and in several areas."

"Yes, I studied it," Pereyra said, eating cake non-stop. "The common factor is the Commercial Bank. We analyzed the data and agreed. We've got to get somebody in there. Hey, who made this cake?"

"Me.

"Yes, we've already placed someone there," one of the officers replied. "Two commercial employees moved through the undersecretary to the headquarters in the Old City creating two empty posts that were filled by two accountants from the police headquarters."

They had a long conversation about possibilities, and Gomez and Pereyra brought several ideas. Transactions in current account boxes would be analyzed retroactively. They considered marking the money, but they concluded that it could be dangerous. It was planned to make a detective pass as a new merchant in the area and deposit a large sum of money. Banking experts provided the idea of giving each section of the bank a different code to be able to enter into the computer and make a program. They weren't sure about that; it could make the culprit suspicious. Gomez said that if they put in a second fake trader, they'd increase the chances of finding a vein, and they argued for a while about how to do that. The other banks were faced with further investigation. The meeting ended, and Daniel left after shaking hands.

The damn bitch waited for her father at the white Mercedes and Daniel noticed she was dressed better. Her hair was loose, she had some make up, and her bra... *Hmm, she had more than I thought.*

"Have a good time, you bad bitch," he said. "Try talking to me the wrong way again and you'll see... rotten mare!"

"But—hey— I mean..."

"But? Yeah, *butt* face!"

"I'm... my name is Ines," she told him with sadness, looking at the floor.

"Yes, Ines the mare," he answered. "I am guessing your dad talked to you. Witch!"

"Yes... he did."

Her father, the very serious old green man, seemed to try to keep himself separated from the friction between the two of them, but it was clear that he was worried about her, and he made him some signals with his hands as if apologizing.

Pereyra took him home. When they got there, chatting, Pereyra told him: "A demon is waiting for you."

Ines, the bitch, was there, leaning on her car.

"Ah, but what does she want now? What the hell with this one?"

"Bye, dummy," Pereyra said and left. "May death be mild to you."

Daniel got out and headed to his building door. Ines came walking towards him.

"Hi... eh, hi... um... Daniel."

He turned around, silent, suspicious.

"Hi, Daniel. I wanted... I just wanted..." She hesitated. "My dad told me about your... eh...I'm sorry."

He just looked at her, half angry, half bored, and prayed for God to sweep her away from Earth right then.

"Daniel, I wanted... just... I wanted you to know..."

"I don't want to know anything from you."

She stayed there, looking at him.

"It is not... well... I just... it's not easy to say that... eh, I'm sorry, I was..."

"I don't want your *sorry*."

"It's... I'm sorry. I was mean. You made me see that... uh... I... Uh... I don't know, I didn't know that. I don't know why...."

"Okay. Sure. Good night."

"No. No. Wait. Please. It is... it was that I was... it's like I didn't realize that—"

"You didn't know you're a piece of shit?"

"No. I mean, yes. It is that... I don't know how to say." She tried to explain, already with tears in her eyes. "I'm truly sorry, I was... what happened was...."

Daniel looked at her with a lack of patience.

"Sorry, Daniel. I was..." and she went back to her car.

Angry as he had been, upset with her as he was, Daniel felt compelled to understand the situation knowing that it would alleviate her father's concern. *I do it for you, green old man.* He took a deep breath and went to her car. He made a sign with his hands for her to get out. He leaned himself on one of the doors of her Citroen.

"Alright, Ines," he said, swallowing his bitterness. "It's okay."

"What you told me... you had... You're right. I know there's nothing to justify that I've talked to you like this, but... no, it... what you did and... what you did... made me think. Yes. I'm a bitch. I came to apologize, but I know well that..." Then she stood and said, "I'm here to apologize."

"It's okay. Well, I wonder why... why would a woman like you, pretty, smart, treat me like that? You didn't see how you scared me?"

She just looked at the floor.

"Why did you have to be like that?"

"I can't talk... I can't explain it standing here. Can we get in the car?"

"Well, Ines, tell me. What's the matter with you?"

They got in the car, and she started to explain what he already knew, her husband's death, her accident, her struggle with her pregnancy, her losing the baby, her horrible depression and more. He took the time to listen to her while she was sobbing and tearing. Then he talked to her, calmed her down. He waited and then made her cry again by bringing up her painful memories. *Maybe she might get a bit of peace,* he thought, *if I make her bring her pain to the surface.* Somehow it worked, and she started to cry even more. He waited, caressing her shoulder and her hair.

After a while, she calmed down.

"Thank you. I'm sorry. Thank you, Daniel."

They hugged and Ines said goodbye and galloped away with her Citroen.

Daniel stayed there, thinking.

As he turned around, he saw the Galician neighbor with her two daughters at the door of their house. They looked at him worriedly.

"She's a friend in pain," he told them. "What can I do?"

The women looked at him and didn't move their lips. Then she spoke: "You bring them here to break their hearts at your doorstep?"

He bid them goodnight and went home.

Later he thought a little more about the whole thing.

He woke up the next day thinking, *There I am, tucked in the middle between several powerful and antagonistic groups, yes, and I stand in the middle.*

He realized that his intention to solve the problem and get out unscratched might not have a good chance of success. *But if I don't, I'll never forgive myself.* He also realized that leaving the country would be necessary, "before the red circles of death loom with you inside," and "they find you eaten by rats."

He went to class. He examined the prostate of three sick people, with whom he discharged his nerves by messing with their rectums and left them sweating.

"Ay, Daniel, please, are you examining them or are you taking revenge on someone?" Claudia, his companion, told him.

Then he gave an injection and went to surgery to help in a mastectomy. He dialogued with two professors, argued with a surgeon, changed clothes, and entered the other surgery room to attend an appendectomy. He left there and was in a hurry to get to the "F" ward of the hospital where he had a medical clinic class. After the class, he went out the front door of the Hospital de Clinicas, and took a taxi to headquarters, where he went to the third floor, greeted Cecilia, went into the office, finished the report on the dead woman he had photographed about two days earlier, went to Urine Gomez's office and gave him a copy of the report, "Hey Gomes," "Hello Daniel," then took another copy to Martinez, "Are you behaving well, Daniel?" "Yes, Martinez, yes," and gave him the pictures of the two bullets he needed, grabbed two cookies, and ran down the steps while eating them, greeting Yamandu and Castro-Aronceda who just walked in. He took another cab to the medical school, where he went down to the anatomy room, put on his coat, and began to teach his class. He opened a knee and slit a throat, smoked a cigarette, and drew pictures on the board explaining things to the students. He advised one of the students, ate chocolate cake from another, and after three hours went down to the morgue, had a coffee, and ate a piece of sponge cake. Luckily there was no dead body, so he hung up his robe, and sat down to smoke a cigarette, enjoying a quiet moment. *Here, among the dead, I can rest easy.* It had been a regular day.

He finished smoking and left the school through the very back door, which only a few knew about. He got into a police car that was waiting for him. The agent took him three blocks away, where the inevitable Citroen was waiting. "Good luck, Danny, looks like you are going to need it." There was Ines, in a green-striped dress.

"What is it?"

"They're waiting for us."

They got in the car and went to Punta Carretas where the old man was waiting. On the road, she said, "Thank you, Daniel," and "I'm sorry for what I did," three times and he answered, "It's okay, Ines," three times as well.

They got inside the Mercedes Benz. There sat old green Saravia-Cohen. He greeted him.

"Did you come to tell me why you are called Cohen?" he asked him."

"Don't be impolite, I told you."

"I thought, well, how would Saravia have joined Cohen? You wouldn't want to—"

"Don't be rude, Daniel. Don't flaunt your well-known impertinence or start warming me up again."

"Uuuuuhh... we are getting upset, aren't we?"

"Daniel!"

"Leave him alone, Daniel. He's been nervous."

"Alright. I hear you. What?"

The old man spoke for a while. Daniel listened, serious.

After that, Ines took him home. He had to lay down after that dialogue. *Shit!*

He had fallen into a life with a lot of dead people, and he knew it.

"The red circle has only death inside," Rabbi Bernstein had told him.

"Your path, Daniel, your path is not right." Pereyra had warned him. "You're going deeper into the kingdom of death."

"You're walking with the dead. Stop!" Marisa and Estela pointed out.

He sighed.

I must keep going. I must find out, he told himself.

"Daniel, Daniel, change course before they find you in a garbage dump, half eaten by rats... without ears, without eyes."

"I know."

That day he knew he was leaving the country.

The next day Ines invited him to the house to discuss some details, to try to make amends, and to eat paella. *Yes, paella with meat,* thought Daniel. She invited Martinez, an attorney, Berta, and the officer who had helped him in the operation at the headquarters. The house smelled of saffron rice and after greeting each other they began to eat and chat. Ines was unusually charming and shortly after she started eating the paella she began to talk about her personal life and thanked Daniel for helping her but without going into details.

They talked a while about the legalities of what they did and about some of the plans they had in mind.

"To all of you," said the attorney, "I tell you the same: be careful."

Upon leaving, in the street, when the lawyer had already left, Ines said to Daniel from the door, "Again, I am sorry."

"Yes. It's okay, Ines."

Martinez took him home. He drove all the way in silence, as if angry.

When they got to Daniel's place, Martinez was still quiet, serious.

"What is it, Martinez?"

Martinez got out of the car, leaned on one side, and lit a cigarette.

"These things... Hmm... these things that are happening... never... never... eh, I didn't think that you were who I later discovered that you were... and... and..."

"Yeah?"

"And... who are you, Daniel? What are you?"

"Huh?"

"And well, now that I see... I wonder.... Hmm... I mean, I asked you once again why you got into the headquarters. It is something that... that I'm not very clear about. What was your real reason?" He took a puff and continued. "From the beginning I realized there was something else. Didn't kick you out because... because... I don't know why. MacLagan and Pranchin wondered as well. They knew you were coming for something."

"Leave it, Martinez. I don't want to—"

"Danny, listen, it smelled like you had something... that... you had something like a mission. What is it?"

"I just can't tell."

"Danny boy, we talked to Yamandu, and he said to not kick you out. Why? Who are you?"

People passed down the street in slow motion. A taxi stopped and left. A dog barked in the distance.

"No Martinez. Please. Don't."

"Something ate you, Daniel, right? But... but I didn't realize what it was. What was it?"

"But you did realize that it was something not bad," Daniel told him, already with tears in his eyes, that there was a valid reason.

"Yes. And what is the truth?"

Daniel was silent. He didn't want to get into the topic. It had been hard for him to keep a shell over his feelings. He got more tears.

"Martinez..."

"Oh, come on, Danny. Look at what we've been through so far."

"Martinez, I.... There's a lot of pain behind that. I—"

"Daniel, Daniel, listen to me. Look at me, who I am, you already know that you can trust me. What was it that got you into the headquarters like that?"

Daniel was silent for a while. He tried to remember, but without bringing the pain. He wiped his tears and tried to control himself. However, the feeling was very strong, and a flare of pain, sadness, and anger came over him.

"Revenge!" he finally said, with tears in his eyes. "Yes. That! Revenge, Martinez. It was devouring me."

"What? What revenge? What was. . .? Tell me."

"Revenge, yes. They murdered the woman I loved. It was when..."

"Carmen? But if she..."

"No, my passion, my forbidden love..." he explained, looking at the floor. "Tamara. They killed her."

He then told him about his relationship with her and his comings and goings. Tears welled up in his eyes then streaked his cheeks and dropped to the floor. He had to stop several times because his voice was cutting off. He told him how they met and who and how she was.

"When? When did—"

Daniel continued to tell him about his tumultuous relationship with Tamara and how it had been. They lit another cigarette. "I... I loved her so much."

Few people passed by, so they were able to speak calmly. Luckily, the neighbors were not there.

They waited a few minutes for Daniel to catch his breath.

"I loved her madly," he spoke with a wet face. "She had certain shady activities with the Tupamaros, so I knew it, but I couldn't leave her. She was even armed. She was walking around with a gun in her purse."

"What? Why didn't you just leave her, man?"

"I...I...I couldn't. I just loved her. I was just..."

"Uuuuuhh... that was dangerous, Danny boy," Martinez emphasized, smoothing his mustache. "Tamara, eh? Tamara the Tupamara, you do know how—"

"I know, yes, I knew, but.... "

Daniel kept silent for a few moments, trying to dry his tears.

"But I was like..." he continued, "Well, the thing was that one morning they found her dead.... In a garbage dump." Daniel had more tears in his eyes. "Naked, dead, in a dump! Tamara."

"How... horrible."

Daniel put his hands on his face and started to sob.

"Dirty, in the trash. Imagine that. Some cats found her. Cats, Martinez! She had a hole in her head."

Daniel let his head hang and whimpered. Martinez, surprised, kept silent and waited.

"She was shot. Executed."

"But why...? Why? And why naked...?"

"I don't know. I did not know."

"Was she raped? Eh... abused?"

"No. No."

Martinez was silent for a while and then asked: "When? When was it?"

"Three weeks before I showed up in your office to be an assistant," Daniel answered, while he was sniffling.

The two were silent. They watched the cars go by. Daniel turned around so that some passing ladies would not see him. They both lit another cigarette.

"Hmm... but you came as an auxiliary, and there were other auxiliaries before you. They sent you from the Forensic Institute as an assistant. How are you mixing it with Tamara's murder?"

"It's just that... after they killed Tamara, I was in a lot of pain. And... and... I was going through bad times, Martinez. I had no one to talk to. I tried to tell my friends, but they didn't understand and... and... they just felt sorry for me, that's all. I just... had no one to talk to. I couldn't focus in class. I was... I was in... so much pain. She was dead. Dead. I felt so lost."

"And then?"

"And one day... uh... one day Maggiolo saw me like this and asked me. Then he took me to his office, and I told him what had happened. He listened to me, advised me, and I felt better. He talked to me like an uncle. Several days later, Maggiolo and Etcheverry invited me to have coffee at their desk and spoke to me. They explained to me what I already knew... in part."

"What?"

"That there were other Tamaras murdered, and boys too, and that it was not known who did it. That perhaps the army, that perhaps the Nubian, that perhaps someone from the police headquarters, maybe the Joint Forces, but they just didn't know who was doing those horrible murders. Yes, they knew that people of the dictatorship were involved. But how can we ever prove that? No, they just did not know who. They told me that the assassins were asking for ransom, that it was horrible. They said that there were desperate parents, that I could help them."

"Help them? How?"

Daniel waited.

"Sticking my nose into the headquarters. Yes. They told me that if they helped me get into the headquarters, I could look for some indication, something, I don't know, some clue that would suggest who was committing those murders. And incidentally... and incidentally—"

"Yes?"

"And by the way, perhaps, find out who killed Tamara. That they were going to help me, but they asked me to help them."

Daniel stopped to catch his breath.

"Then I felt... I felt my pain converting into anger. An incredible rage got in me thinking that the killer of Tamara could be found and... and... The pain became ire because suddenly... suddenly I could go from just accepting her inexorable death to actually have the assassin in front of me and... and... and make him pay, yes, beat him, cut him in a hundred pieces, burn him alive, I don't know, something to make him pay for the horrible things he did."

"Gee...is that you talking?"

"Yes. It's me, Martinez. A part of me. Now you know. Now you understand what I did."

"But... *they*... who are the people helping you?" asked Martinez. "Surely, it's not just the two of them."

"No. There are many, and they do everything in secret. It took me a while to realize that. But I know. The two of them are part of a secret society where there are Jews and Christians. It is more than anything a society for the study of history and culture, and they are all descendants of the escapees of the

Spanish Inquisition. They use old keys as symbols of their union, and the keys have gold filigree to remember Toledo. The keys are attached to a metal ring from which hangs a small shield bearing the image of the Masons.

"Masons? Freemasons with the Jews?"

"Yes. It seems that many of the Freemasons are Jews, and others, being Christians, had ancestors in the same Spain of those times. That is why they are united in it."

"And do you know who they are?"

"Vaguely. They stay hidden away and in secret. They dedicate themselves to study, to review old texts, to unite the past with the present, and things like that. And it seems that several of them lost children in a similar way."

"And how did you bond with them?"

"Well, it's not that *I* linked up with them, more than anything *they* linked up with *me*. They saw in me an opportunity I guess... eh... an opportunity to find out something, I don't know, something. So, they gave me.... They told me about... what to do to get into the headquarters. Me... I was in pain and anger because of what happened, and I couldn't... I couldn't... I don't know... I saw the opportunity to... to get into the cave of the wolves for... you know."

Daniel grabbed his head with his hands. "Vengeance," he mumbled.

Martinez was silent for a while, then sighed and said: "So that was it. And you already came with plans."

"Yes."

"Double plans. Triple plans."

"Yes."

"And Doctors Etcheverry and Maggiolo helped you get in, eh?"

"Yes. They helped me; they knew. And then they helped me with information. But they had that other plan, too."

"I suspected that there was a fundamental reason. It showed on your face. But you didn't give away anything. When you want to be, you are a manipulative liar. MacLagan and I thought we would kick you out, but on the one hand we thought there was a strong reason behind all that and that the reason was neither unfair nor wrong, so out of curiosity we let you stay."

"Yes, Martinez."

"I see. But there was another reason. You didn't know, but when we were in doubt and we thought we'd kick you out, Dr. Maggiolo came to see me at my house and explained certain things that left me worried. That you had to figure out something too important for him to tell me what it was. He asked me to give you a hand. It was... it was like... like a request out of conscience."

"Yes. Thank you."

"And what plans did you have? What were you going to do?

"I didn't know. I didn't know what to do. Like a dog doesn't know what to do with a car when he catches it. But I suspected something at headquarters could give me an indication, an idea... something to find out why she was killed... and... and... and who killed her."

"And what were you going to do with that information? Go out and kill? Grab a revolver and shoot the culprit? You don't strike me as a killer, even out of revenge."

"I don't know. I do not know. I... I wanted to... maybe just walk up and piss on their tires a little."

"Did you want that? What if it was the Nubian who killed her for money, then what? Were you going to attack him?"

"I don't know. Yes, yes, I don't know. No."

"Didn't you realize what you were planning? I mean, you didn't even know what you were planning. You didn't know what you were up to. You could have—"

"Yes. I know I didn't know... but the pain tortured me, Martinez. The pain... and... and besides... hmm... the feeling that I had lost her, and... hmm... in addition, she... Tamara... it seemed to me she comes to me at night, sometimes."

"Did you think of... eh... as visions?"

"Yes. I... For a long time, sometimes, at night, she would come to visit some—"

"Visions? Already enough, leave me with that madness. They could have killed you, Daniel. If you had been discovered or suspected by someone, someone might have shot you. Didn't you think about that?"

"No. I mean, yes. But they already killed me, Martinez, they killed me by killing her."

Martinez was silent. He looked up, looked at Daniel, then looked at the street.

"I want to ask you something now, Daniel, but inside the car. Come in before one of your neighbors comes."

They got in the car, closed the windows so the noise wouldn't come in.

"When you entered headquarters as an assistant, we soon realized that you had knowledge of criminal investigation and police techniques. We were amazed."

"Yes. You know why and from where. My dad's... He was—"

"Yes. I know who your dad was. Commissar investigator, inspector of the seventh section, always chasing criminals who got into the Capurro neighborhood. That coastal area, near the pier, is a constant inlet of smugglers and crap."

"Yes, I do know."

"They killed him, huh? And what happened?"

"When he was active there, from his comments, notes, and books, I was soaking up detective arts from an early age. Argentine Vignalli's book *Criminal Research* was very didactic."

"Yes. It's very good."

"Yes, well, Dad worked in the tough area of the Capurro neighborhood, a very difficult area, with many smugglers and criminals of all kinds. He also secretly investigated the comings and goings of several officers of the seventh, including the corrupt commissar and several of his friends. Well, the thing was, I learned a lot of interesting things about crime investigation. It was there that I was interested in continuing medical studies and diverting myself to the forensic field in the future.

"I see."

"Yes. I read other books and publications, and sometimes we talked about his notes. On more than one occasion, we analyzed together a whole investigation. That's when I discovered things I shouldn't have found about certain people and cops in that area, where corruption and illicit sales came hand-in-hand. I had been given a small job, fifteen hours a week, as a technical photography assistant, but as soon as they realized my curiosity and the things I was asking, they got me out of there. Soon after, my father was killed."

"Why are? Who did you want to—"

"It was not known, but it had something to do with my dad's investigation into money management between several sub-commissars and criminals in the area. He was very curious and stuck his nose where he shouldn't have, and that's why..."

"I see who you're out to get, Danny-the-nosy."

"Yes. That's right. The thing is, he got shot."

"Has it been... hmm... did it have to do with police officers?"

"I don't know. I don't think so. I didn't know anything about it. There was a break-in, or something related to a big smuggler, and there was a shooting where three criminals died, and a cop and my dad were killed. Looks like the sheriff and deputy commissars were involved. To this day, I think the one who shot him was a cop. There was interest in getting my father out of there."

"Oh, that's serious, Daniel."

And did you report that or consult with someone about it?

"Report who? Consult with whom? You know the code, the big blue wall. There are strong relationships between these commissars, police, army officers, and Joint Forces. There are links, dollars, arrangements, things that are neither known nor discovered. No. Nothing could be done. Thanks to my uncle my mom got a place in the Pocitos neighborhood, and an agency emptied our former home and moved everything here, to Pocitos."

"Pa, shit!"

"We never went there again. And I'm not going to go there either. They know my face. I know there's more than one who knows this."

"And what are you going to do about it?"

"Nothing. There's nothing I can do. If I tried to do something, it could have severe consequences against someone in the family."

"What about the shooting? Did you hear anything?"

"Not much, but one of the criminals was poor Carmen's husband. She was a teacher and suffered living with that delinquent animal. When he died, however, she could no longer pay the rent and moved with her daughter to her mother's house. She was in ruins. She didn't know what to do. Teacher's salary wasn't enough for her. She was trying hard to get another job, but nothing. In the end, together with a lot of bravery, she started working as a prostitute, first on the street, and then she walked into the brothel on Convention Street and asked to work there."

"Poor woman. Is that the little Carmencita? Is that the brothel El Ensuenio?"

"Yes. That's where I met her. I felt very sorry for her, and she... well... she became my friend. That's why I'm helping her."

Martinez was silent. He started pinching his mustache. He looked to his side, seeing cars and people passing by.

"You could have talked to me. I would have—"

"No, Martinez. I couldn't. When I got into headquarters, I didn't know who was good and who was bad. I had to lie. I had to be very careful. I felt very insecure."

"But—"

"Martinez, please. I had entered the wolf's cave and didn't know how I was going to leave."

"But you knew what you were looking for, didn't you?"

"Yes, but I didn't know *who*, or *what* to look for, or *where*. I didn't know how to do it."

"Gina, my niece, does she know anything about this?"

"Something. Pieces."

"To hell with you, Daniel. Your complicated life is now going to complicate her life."

"I hope not."

"Did you tell your friends about this?

"Pieces. Pieces. I've been trying to put all that aside and dedicate myself to who I am, a student, a medical student. Being a student and nothing else. But you see."

"Yes. I see. The dead are after you. They're coming at you."

"Yes. I don't know why. There I got into the morgue, there I got in with the inspectors and with the police people, there they killed my Tamara, and they killed others and... and... then came more things, and more, and the escapes of the boys and the old man from the Mercedes and... and..." Daniel cringed his face as he whined. "I don't know what to do! Martinez, I don't know what to do."

Daniel got out of the car. Martinez came out and held him in a half-hug.

"I don't know what to do. I don't know how to get out of all this and get back to normal. I want a normal life. Normal. A student life, with love and without the dead. And not like my neighbors tell me."

"What do they tell you?"

"They say to me, 'Oh, there you are walking through life with lots of dead and little love.' And they're right. They're right."

"And... well... Daniel, they're right."

They stayed there for a while. Without talking.

"Daniel, do you understand that the danger to you has increased? They must know about you and what you've done."

"Yes. Martinez. I can see that."

"And what are you going to do?"

"I don't know. I do not know."

Daniel lit another cigarette. Martinez kept silent and waited a while.

"Well, I'm leaving, Martinez. Thanks for listening."

"I hope you keep telling me things. You can talk to me. And I hope... I hope you find peace, son."

"Thank you, Martinez. Thanks for letting me talk."

Martinez patted him in the face. "Ciao, Daniel."

"Ciao."

Martinez was gone. Daniel stayed downstairs for a while until the Galician came with her daughter.

"Are you making other people cry?" she asked him.

Daniel looked at them and left. He went to bed to meet his ghosts and tell them what his feelings were.

Chapter 34

"Daniel, come over," screamed Pereyra over the phone. "Martinez talked to Gina, and she called me and Manuel. We know. Come over. Now."

Daniel showed up there. Pepe, Manuel, and Carlos were there too. Pablo showed up a few minutes later, shaking their heads. Gina was there and Dorita too; his friends had introduced them to one another. They all asked him about Tamara's death.

"Well, what do you want me to tell you? Things just happened that way."

"Crazy."

"You should have told us."

"Things just... just wrapped around me that way," said Daniel.

"I told you! I told you that diabolic woman would involve you in something deadly. And you..."

"Shut up, Pablo. Let him talk."

"Look what happened to you!"

"Just leave him alone, Pablo."

"Ruined for life..." slipped in Pablo before clamming up.

"Tell us."

He, sipped on his gin.

"Just... just start where you left at that time. You said you separated but later got together again, eh?"

"Yes, but it was not the same. It was...it was..."

"It was more stupid, Danny boy!"

"Enough, Pablo. Shhh..."

"Don't laugh, Manuel," said Pereyra.

"I already knew that she was linked to the Tupamaros—half the people are in one capacity or another—but that reality hit me head on when, once, in a motel, while she was in the shower, I could see that she was carrying an automatic pistol in her purse and a grenade. I took the gun out carefully. It was a Colt 38. *Gee...you have to train to know how to use this,* I thought.

"Oh, Daniel, oh, Daniel. What madness!"

"You should have run away. Running."

"Ah yeah, running?" said Daniel. "One does not run away from a woman like that. Things got complicated."

"How crazy, Daniel."

"I know. I know. I realized that and at the same time I began to see in my mind that my own activities, together with my relationship with this woman, were not going to lead me to anything good and that my risk was evident."

"That it was no longer an adventure, hey, how crazy," Pepe yelled at him. "You're an irresponsible fool. Didn't you think about your mother?"

Daniel continued. Time passed and Tamara had begun to worry him. He knew he was taking a risk walking with her in times when military forces increased their power and took away hooded people. But what to do? She loved him and he loved her and could not leave her, especially intuiting, as she herself intuited, that one day they were going to take her away because she was already marked. Thus, the weeks passed, and more weeks, and Daniel and Tamara were carried away by that fiery relationship combined with a great companionship, although, inside, Daniel felt that she was getting up the courage to make the decision to separate from him once more.

"Well, that day finally arrived," continued Daniel after drinking some gin. "And standing on the sidewalk at Colonia and Paraguay, crying, she told me that she was leaving me for another, that she had met a man, an architect who was a professor of something or other. I knew it was not true, but I did not want to insist, knowing well that she deserved someone better, and I needed to get out of that dangerous relationship. Standing on that corner, I endured my pain because I knew that she was very hurt, and I did not want to make her hurt anymore. Without kissing her, I thanked her for all the affection she had given me and let her take a taxi. She got into the taxi crying and left. I watched her wipe her eyes with a handkerchief as the taxi drove away. *It's better this way, Tamara,* I thought, *it's for your own good.*

"And yes, for your sake, too, silly," said Manuel. "But what an obsession. A busty obsession of a very obsessed man. Luckily, she didn't pull the revolver and shoot you."

Daniel was silent and could not speak.

"Well, Daniel. What happened? Hmm?"

Daniel wiped his eyes and said, "It was the last time I saw her. A few weeks later, they found her in the dump."

"What? They took her...."

"To where? What?"

"Did they take her?" jumped Pepe, "But why didn't you tell us?"

"Hey! How did they take her? Daniel!"

"They took her. I did not know where. I could not know."

"Did they take her prisoner?"

"Yes. Hooded and... handcuffed and... and shackled."

"Damn!!" Pereyra said, standing up. "Damn this to hell!"

"Did you not know where?"

"No. You know how it works. They come and go in the shadows. One day Chiqui, her neighbor, called me and told me over the phone: *Daniel, Daniel... they took Tamara, they took her hooded! Hooded and cuffed.*"

There was silence. All four were silent. Daniel was on the couch, staring at his knees, tears falling, while the others were standing, upset, in front of him. Daniel couldn't speak.

After a while Pereyra spoke and said, "And what happened? What happened after that?"

"Tell us. Keep telling us."

"They killed her."

"What?"

"Oh, what a... gee.... "

"Oh, what do you mean...?"

"They killed her with a bullet to the head. In jail."

He was silent, bent at his knees. Quiet.

"They shot her in the head," he continued. "And then... they threw her in a garbage dump. Naked. Some feral cats found her."

Daniel told some more and then leaned back on the couch. He couldn't talk anymore. He became frozen and overwhelmed by tiredness and gin. He leaned on the couch and fell asleep, possessed by pain, alcohol, and simultaneous feelings of guilt and sadness. The last thing he said before giving himself up to sleep was "She was... Tamara... she.... " Pereyra left him there on the couch. His friends decided to leave him alone. Gina decided to stay.

Daniel slept for an hour and woke up, drank some coffee, and washed his face. "Sorry, I fell asleep."

"Give him some more coffee, Pocho," said Gina. "Hey... doing okay?"

"Yeah, I'll be alright."

"Well, so, what happened then?"

He continued his story.

After he was told about the cats, he had gone to the hospital, but they had already taken her to the morgue. He arrived there to face a drama.

The funeral company had already pulled out the coffin while parents, relatives and friends were hugging as if trying to resurrect her. They clung to each other as if with that last desperate effort, they could work a miracle and bring her back to life. No, she couldn't be dead. They loaded the coffin into the truck and at that moment everyone felt the absolute and irreversible harshness of death and burst into tears.

It was at that moment that the parents said that everything had been going well, they could not understand what happened, they had paid what was asked of them and had been told that she would be released in two days. They were already happy because they were clearly told that she would be released without major problems.

Daniel was curious and asked them how much they paid, and how they had paid it. The mother told him the amount; it had been a lot of money... too much money. It was supposed to pay for attorney, processing, and paperwork fees, but they had demanded a lot more.

"Do you realize? They asked for ransom. It looks like it was a kidnapping."

"A kidnapping...? *Kidnapping*?"

"Yes. I stayed in the yard watching the hearse drive away. The parents and Chiqui came, hugged me while crying. I hugged all of them and Chiqui and the others. Everybody was crying. It was a horrible moment. I tried to keep my cool, but I couldn't. I... I had loved her very much and... I would not see her anymore."

"Oh, Danny boy."

"I was... I was standing there, in the Courtyard of Sorrows, accompanied by the dead, feeling horrible." *How hard death is*, I thought, *and how irreversible.* So many nights. So much love we gave to each other." Everything went away with death.

"But... what a tragedy," said Pepe.

"So, what did you do?"

Daniel said that, standing there in the middle of the patio, without consolation and without relief, feeling a new kind of pain against which he had no defense. He put a hand on his face, began to sob, and sank into sorrow. Suddenly the blackness and absoluteness of death, the definitive and irreversible nature of Tamara's disappearance, became real to him and the grief struck him too hard.

"It was horrible. Someone came, hugged me, and took me to a car. I just cried all the way to the cemetery. There were a lot of people there. I wanted to stay there, keeping her company, but a friend of the family took me to his car and took me home. Pranchin and MacLagan were there, with my mom, and they all hugged me and... and..."

"Take a deep breath, Daniel," said Pereyra. "Tell us what happened."

"Just that. They killed her, murdered her, and then threw her in a garbage dump like... like she was garbage, like some dictator's table scraps."

Pereyra and Gina fell silent.

"And so, what did you do?"

"It took me several days to... to climb out of the horrible pain I had, but I was recovering little by little. I whimpered when I was alone and cried in the shower. As the pain deepened, I was getting used to living with it, until I slowly normalized. I threw myself into my routine of studies, hospital, anatomy, and books. With a clearer mind, I began to think about what her parents had told me, and I was intrigued by the payment and even more by the way it was paid. It had been a prearranged meeting between two cars in the Parque de los Aliados, a minimal contact with a man without a uniform in an unofficial car. How weird. Had it been a kidnapping? No. It couldn't be but *whoa,* I thought, *that really sounded like a kidnapping.*"

"Did you talk to anyone?"

"Who? I didn't do anything about it and couldn't talk about it with anyone because there was no one to talk to."

"Well, you could—"

"Nothing! Of those things, nothing is published, and nothing can be commented on. This did not appear in the newspaper because these things are not published in these times of dictatorship in which the military does horrible things to the population."

"But something... do something."

"I couldn't even think of whom to talk to, and even if I did, I had no idea what to do about it. This goes on all the time and cops like Martinez and MacLagan don't do anything, they can't, and they have the power. I am just one poor student. No, I couldn't find out or discuss it with anyone. This is how things are in this era without freedom."

"But... and what can one do? Just stand still."

"Nothing. Cry, as many do."

"But you, you, Daniel, you must... you must have done something, right?"

Daniel was silent for a while, then wiped away his tears. He took a deep breath and stood up. He walked to the window and stared to the outside.

"Yes, maybe I'll recover," he said with a hard voice and firm body as he turned around and looked at them with eyes clouded over by hatred. "And maybe I will not. In the meantime... in the meantime, I'm going to do something about it."

"What are you going to do?" Pereyra asked aloud, knowing that he had seen that look before. "What are you planning to do?"

Daniel didn't answer.

"Daniel!" yelled Gina.

"What's in your crazy mind, Danny?" demanded Pablo.

"I am going to get them."

"*Get them*? Are you nuts?"

"No. Well, maybe. But they will pay for this and for the many others they murdered."

Chapter 35

Something came to his mind. He met with the detectives.

"Even with an *empty* gun a normal person would hesitate before aiming it at another person. A normal person or soldier could shoot and kill from a distance or in case of fear, or assault, or any specific situation, but it would do so in the front of the head or in the chest. But shooting a young person, tied up, possibly crying, and pissing in fear, for no reason, and from the side, only a true murderer who had killed before could do that, see? Therefore, it was possible that executor-X had a criminal record, or at least was a suspect in one or more deaths."

"That's it," said Pranchin. "The X is surely an assassin, and is probably someone who has killed before, at least twice, and then came to Montevideo and joined the army by changing his name."

"Yeah!"

Daniel discussed that with Yamandu, Martinez, and Pranchin. They needed to have another roundtable.

"The executor, *X*, or whatever we call him," continued Pranchin, "was already a murderer before this began, so he must have a criminal record and we must look for it." Pranchin looked around the table. "Yamandu is going to oversee that," he explained. "Moreover, X must have killed before the same way and the files of the morgue and police stations throughout the country need to be reviewed."

"I agree, yes, one does not go and kill pretty girls and young boys, sitting and tied, without reason, unless one is already without conscience from previous murders."

"If you want to hire a butcher, do you recruit at the flower shop or at the slaughterhouse?" Yamandu said.

"Very good. Yes."

"Shocking!"

Yamandu added that surely, after previous murders, that murderer X, with the change of regime, saw the opportunity to join the Joint Forces or the army and hide in a military barracks. So, someone should go from barracks to barracks, checking files on every soldier. From the data that Daniel had found, only the barracks in the eastern half of the city should be studied and he explained why. He also explained why he thought X should be between thirty and fifty years old.

"Okay, I agree," said one of the accountants. "About the bank, I am convinced that Commercial Bank is the key."

"There must be some detectable funds in that branch, with abnormal profits coinciding with the events," said another of the accountants."

"They say: *follow the money*," noted Ines.

"The bank also has a financial section on the second floor that must be investigated because they maintain separate files. There must be a person who coordinates the activities in the two branches. The central agency's computer would probably show which activities were recorded, so place a man, preferably a bank accountant, in that section of the Old City."

"Hmm, it makes sense," said one of the officers.

"Yes."

"But then... it may be necessary to review the family group of each employee of the bank in question and find who had relatives in the army or in the Joint Forces," said Martinez. "Or follow the most suspicious to see who they are related to."

"Let's do it."

"But that research work must be done by you," added Daniel. "It's not something I can do."

"We got this!"

"Don't worry, you've done enough."

"Bearing this in mind, the urgency of the situation demands that the plan should be started very soon," said Yamandu.

"And the plan requires an official in charge of controlling the economic team to infiltrate and study the bank transactions," added an accountant.

"Very good, yes."

"I have resolved to modify the moment of the beginning of the bank infiltration to within 48 hours, if you accept it," said Bauza, one of the officers. "It's time to start laying the network."

"Yes! Let's go for it."

"Go ahead! Yes!"

"Yes, man, yes!"

The three accountants then stood up and started explaining some details.

"Please listen to this," said the first one. Suppose two or three people employed by the Commercial Bank are related, either because they are friends, brothers, or cousins, and that the wife of one of them is the sister or cousin of a military officer. And assume they meet successively in family gatherings and from that a friendship is born and later some form of complicity develops to join in a secret plan for profit."

"Yeah... so?"

"Well... *so*..." said the second accountant. "Maybe they tried some fishy businesses without success, until one day, in a family reunion, word goes, word comes, the idea of kidnapping was born. They do the first one, everything is fine, and then they do the second one, but maybe then things get complicated. They have a taste of the money now and don't want to stop. But they need help, they need a strong hand to help them control the boys, and they get more people, and then... perhaps..."

"Go on."

"Perhaps that's how they get the wrong people involved. Maybe that is how they got someone who was a killer."

"Someone from a slaughterhouse, not a barbershop."

"From the barracks?"

"I don't know. I assume... *We* must assume that they got someone who was unstable and kills for fun, and then things got really complicated."

"The ante was officially upped."

"Where did you get that idea?

"I am... we are assuming that this could—"

"Makes sense. How can we—"

"Hey, wait. Okay, but it is just a theory."

"More than that," said Daniel. "It is a very interesting idea."

"A working idea. Yes. To start with. We'll change it as we go along."

"For sure."

"Could that strongman from the slaughterhouse be the Nubian?"

"I see. Interesting. And what about that Nubian? Maybe he was the one they got involved with."

"Or one of his men."

"Yes. Perhaps that murderer, that unstable, is the Nubian himself or... or one of his associates. Yes. We'll have to be careful."

"And you, Daniel, stay out of this."

"Wait a minute! I am the one who—"

"Oh, shut up. It's for your own protection."

"No. I won't. You are—"

"You'd shoot yourself in the foot just to prove you had good aim."

"Shhhh... shut up," Saravia-Cohen's daughter said. "There is real danger now."

"So what? And you know what? I've been thinking about what Fonseca and the accountants said. You need to find out, through the people you placed in the bank, which two or three are buddies, or brothers, or cousins, bridge partners, something... and of those see if any of their wives have close family that lives in the Capurro neighborhood, or is related to policemen, or someone in the army."

"Okay Daniel," said Fonseca.

"Moreover," continued Daniel. "Search the family of each employee... find out about those possible connections, and look among the—"

"Okay, okay, Danny boy, don't get excited."

"What did you eat last night, Daniel, that you are so inspired?" asked one of the officers.

"Soup."

"What did they put in your soup, man?" asked another. "Some of that new stuff in the US they call *crack*?"

Some chuckles of levity circled the room, except from Martinez, who knew a bit about the growing crack epidemic.

Daniel took a quick look at Martinez, who was looking at him with killer's eyes, and took a deep breath.

With this Daniel calmed down. A bit.

The third accountant added: "We would look for the characteristics and personal data of each employee of the Commercial, using the central accounting office to find out about the electricity, gas, and telephone payments of each one to see what checks they wrote, then that they would look in the same banks to see if there were deposits more than thirty times a few days after each ransom payment."

"Yes. We'll do it quietly. I assume that those deposits would all be similar. We have made a probability matrix and applied the triangle rule in each case and, according to that, Montevideo Bank, by Rivera and Propios were found statistically interesting, so we already placed two researchers there and started an investigation into their accounting. And nothing more."

"Yes, very good," said one of the officers. "We've already placed a man there, armed, and we are going to place another. We're already studying all the personnel of the Commercial."

"And if everything fails?" asked the undersecretary."

"We play it by ear."

"Other possibilities will occur to us, or to this supposedly just-a-student, Daniel."

"Hey!"

"But it smells to me that something fat is going to appear in one of those corners," continued the officer.

"It must appear!"

"Okay. We are going for it."

"But... at the end of the day," Daniel started to tell them, "There is something I also have to say." He stood and addressed the room. "It smells to me that at the end of our search we may find one or two officers of the army or of the Joint Forces, someone of high rank, who may be untouchable. Or we might find that the Nubian is the culprit, and who is going to accuse or catch *him*, eh? The thing is, that in the end it might be either a strong officer or the Nubian himself at the root of the assassinations. If we get to that, it might be a difficult time. And there will be blood, one way or another."

"You know what, Danny boy? We should not let you talk again."

"Yeah, you sound like a bearer of bad omens."

"The bad omen is here, Fonseca!"

"Okay, Okay, Daniel."

"Yes. You are quite right, Daniel."

The meeting ended with jokes from all sides. They all said goodbye in a very friendly way.

They continued saying goodbye for a while and Daniel left. At the exit, Martinez was waiting for him, he took him home and they hardly spoke. They were both very nervous.

Chapter 36

Two days later, Daniel's mother woke him up early. He had a phone call.

"Daniel, they call you," his mother yelled at him. "It's that Martinez."

"Hi? Yes."

"Daniel. Did Domínguez call you?"

"No. Why?"

"He doesn't answer. We don't know where he is. I'm going to his home. Pranchin is going to pick you up. Be ready. Be ready downstairs."

Daniel got dressed, went downstairs, and Pranchin picked him up quickly to look for Domínguez.

"What happened?"

"I don't know. I guess nothing. We pick up Domínguez and from there you and I and Martinez are going back to your business. Why did Martinez call you?"

"I don't know. He just said to be ready."

Pranchin drove fast. They went up Boulevard Artigas and headed towards the Prado. Before he could say anything, they broke into the Capurro neighborhood, Daniel noticed. "Crap!"

"Pranchin, this is Capurro," Daniel said, worried. "You know that I—"

"Yes, I know. But let's go fast."

"Pranchin, please, it's the Capurro neighborhood. I'm not allowed in this area. They know my face."

"It is just to get Domínguez. It will take a few seconds."

Shit, it's Capurro, thought Daniel and slumped down in his seat. "There are eyes in every corner."

"You know that here I can—"

"Enough. Enough already. We go in and we leave fast."

After a few quick turns, they arrived at Domínguez's house. Martinez, two agents, and two patrolmen were there, outside. They had not entered. The two trees in front of the house were full of crows. *Fucking crows*, thought Daniel, *Ah, but that indicates that Domínguez is inside.*

"Domínguez! Eh, Domínguez!" they yelled.

They waited. There was no answer.

"Hey, Domínguez! We have a young grieving widow out here for you to... *interrogate*."

"Domínguez!"

"Domínguez doesn't answer, and we hear noises inside. What are those crows?"

"They are the ones who follow him because... nothing. It is a signal that he is inside."

"What are you talking about, those crows?"

"Just nothing. Go on."

"Pranchin, a neighbor says he heard two shots."

"Domínguez!," shouted another agent. "Domínguez!"

"Oh, maybe..."

"Stay outside, Daniel," Martinez said, and he and the others drew their pistols.

"Go over there. Go ahead."

"Go behind the car, Danny boy."

They came in half crouched and the doors slammed. Daniel heard furniture noises, a couple of shots, silence, three more shots, screams, and more shots. Suddenly, out of nowhere, a bullet flew into Daniel's arm. He fell backwards to the ground while seeing how a policeman turned around and was attempting to flee when his chest blew out from the blast of the weapon of one of the agents. One of the agents had shot him.

Wounded, Daniel couldn't move. The pain was overwhelming. Two agents came, wrapped his arm tight and got him up, his face white.

There were more shots inside the house.

Then silence. Several crows flew out the door.

After a while, Martinez and all the others came out, arms in hand. One of the policemen was injured, and they propped him against the wall. They called for the ambulance.

"You are wounded. I don't know if you should go in, Daniel. Wait."

"Why? Is it safe inside?"

"Yes, but that's not... wait, wait... Daniel!

Daniel had already entered with the support of one of the agents. His bleeding was dwindling.

Inside everything was in disarray, with broken glass and pieces of furniture everywhere. Domínguez's naked and lifeless body was terrifying. He was sitting and tied to a chair. Semi-reclined. His body had holes and marks made with some instrument.

"Is that Domínguez?"

"What's left of him."

"He was beaten very badly. Those marks are from an electric prod, Daniel. They tortured him."

"Oh, Domínguez, Domínguez. No. No."

"Poor man."

There were several crows walking on the floor or standing on the furniture. One of them and then another jumped and flew up to Domínguez's body and pecked at his eyes. The agents watched it in disbelief. Pranchin and an officer batted at them using chair pieces.

"But what the hell are these crows doing here?"

"They came to take revenge," said Daniel, astonished. "It was true. They followed him."

"You're saying stupid things, Daniel," Martinez said. "Fucking crows."

"No. They have been following him for a long time. They knew him. They were waiting for their moment."

"Shut up."

"It's Domínguez, our friend, don't talk like that."

Daniel shook off several of the crows with his hands. Then he looked at Domínguez. It hurt so much to see him like that. "Ay, Domínguez." He had been hacked from several sides. The eyes were in bad shape. There was blood on the walls. His arms twisted; his fingers busted. "He must have suffered so much."

"But why?"

"Yes. Why? What were they looking for?"

"This is awful."

Tied, tortured, beaten. It was horrible to see this friend who had been so good. Daniel froze. The horror at that image was hypnotizing.

The whole scene was gruesome.

"Come and see this," Martinez said "Hey, here. Come. See! Here are the culprits. They were crouching when we entered and they managed to shoot Jose, but we caught them with crossfire, and they fell."

"Sons of bitches," mumbled an agent and kicked one of them. Pranchin kicked them too and spat at them.

There, on the ground, in the middle of pools of blood, were two immobile bodies. The smell of gunpowder and blood filled the air. Disgusting.

"Too bad they weren't left alive to question them," said Pranchin, as another agent began to search the bodies.

They called others. The ambulance came. The coroner came. They stood aside. They sat on a chair and from a distance they observed the body of their good friend. Their brother. With teary eyes, they said goodbye to him as they remembered the moments they spent together. They said to each other, "Do you remember that time when...?" and there were cases in which Domínguez had stood out. They grabbed each other's faces and whimpered.

"Martinez! Martinez, come!" shouted an agent. "Here. You gotta see this."

Everyone wiped their faces and went to see. The agent showed them the weapons that the criminals used, the wallets, and....

"And this... See? They both had these papers in their pockets."

"They look like—"

"They're photos. Photos taken of the faces of Domínguez and Daniel."

"These people had orders to catch you. To catch both. To kill you."

"Shit."

"Damn, you were... you're next, little Carmen kid."

"They were going to kill both of you."

Who are they?

"Daniel, they're out to kill you, whoever they are."

"Let's see. Yes. Shit, whoa. They've already killed Domínguez and... and this should indicate that there must be other criminals with your photo, ready to kill you. Daniel, you are in danger!"

"Oh, what do I do? What do I do?"

"You can't stay. You can't stay here in the city."

"But—"

"No."

"No? But I'm—"

"Danny, Danny, they're out to kill you and we don't even know how many of them there are."

"There could be a sniper anywhere."

"If they were able to grab Domínguez, that means they are well capable of grabbing you. You must go."

"You must get away now."

"First Domínguez, they plan to grab one at a time... and the next one is you, Daniel."

"Martinez, tell him he has to go... and that's it."

"How? But no!" Daniel protested. "Where to? My mother. Me..."

"Daniel, there's no time to plan anything. Go with Martinez and Ines. They will protect you. You'll be safer. And you can't think about it."

"But I didn't want to go with..."

"There's no time, no time."

"You must go. This has spread out and now who knows how many know."

"My mother. Gina, I—"

"Daniel, Daniel, listen to me," Pranchin said grabbing him by the lapel. "You must go now. Immediately! We'll take care of your mother, your brother, and Gina. With guards, with hiding places, with whatever, they'll be in my custody, and nothing will happen to them. I promise. But you, you must survive this. Go away!" Pranchin hugged him and yelled at him while shaking his neck.

Martinez agreed. "You have to go; you have to survive," he said. "No matter what happens, you are already part of us. Survive, Daniel, survive."

Daniel was in a stupor. Martinez grabbed Daniel by the arm and took him away, scared and groaning as he was. Wounded, in a state of confusion, he let himself be taken to the car. The pain and the shock were overwhelming.

The car drove fast while Martinez said something on the radio. They stopped somewhere, and a woman got in. It was Ines, and she had a box and a small suitcase with her. They drove east, fast, while Daniel was slowly losing consciousness.

Chapter 37
PIRIÁPOLIS

Daniel awoke the next day. His arm was all wrapped up and a bag of fluids dripped into his vein. He was in a room, alone. He had a fever, his arm ached a lot, he tried to talk. He fell asleep.

Later he woke again, a woman was sitting next to him and saying something. He had a bad taste in his mouth. The light of the room was strange. The woman kept talking.

"...but the weather is better today, and we are getting for you an..."

"What? Who are you? Where—"

"It's me. Ines. How do you feel? You are still feverish."

"Me... why... uh, my arm," Daniel said. "What...?"

He fell asleep again. He was awakened later, and some pillows were stuck under his back. As he opened his eyes, the woman placed a spoon with something sweet in his mouth. Peach jelly. Then he got a sip of something bitter and more jelly.

"Swallow," she said.

After the jelly came something pasty and rich, then pieces of chicken, and some more food. Another woman came in and gave him a shot. He fell asleep.

He woke up the next day, feeling stronger. He sat on the side of the bed. The woman came, gave him some coffee and something to eat. The intravenous solution was disconnected. His arm, stiff and aching, unwrapped and wrapped again. Another woman helped him to the bathroom. He was very weak. Two large women sat him in a chair and gave him a sponge bath. "You stink," one said.

"Where am I?"

"You're in a clinic in the Piriápolis resort, a hundred kilometers from Montevideo. You were shot."

He spent the day dozing on and off, eating, drinking, resting. A doctor came twice, checked him out. A nurse came several times. He got injections of something. Ines came to see him several times.

"You lost blood."

A few days later he had a full meal, took a bath, sat outside on the balcony, and started to remember. Ines helped him to come back to reality and recall the events.

"They killed Domínguez," he said. "It was horrible."

"I know."

"Hey, and... and who shot me? Did they find out?"

"He was dead. Had a uniform and he was part of the police department. We think the Nubian sent him."

"So why don't they go and kill him."

"The Nubian and his men vanished. We... they couldn't find a clue."

"What about the other stuff? What we were searching for."

"You are out of the game. You're staying here, protected, recovering, healing yourself... and nothing else."

"Protected?"

"Yes, there are men outside, some of them well hidden. They are there for your protection and to make sure you won't leave. Nobody but me and they know where you are."

"But where am I?"

"I told you. In a private clinic outside Piriápolis. That's all you need to know. You're not leaving anytime soon."

"But my mother, and Gina?"

"All protected. All safe."

"But who—"

"No more questions, Daniel," she said and left.

"Wait. What's going on, Ines? Come on, tell me."

"I can't tell you much. You need rest. What you started, the plan that you and the others talked about in the last two or three meetings..."

"Yes, what about it?"

"It's in progress. The whole plan is in progress. We need to be sure you are not going to stick your nose in or interfere."

The nurse came, gave him two injections and some pills.

"It's bigger than you now, Danny."

He fell asleep.

He woke up the next day.

As the days passed, he continued to recover. His arm got a lot better. "Oh, you are a good healer," said the nurse.

He started to walk and later jog around the clinic. He talked to himself. Talked to the guards.

"I need to go back, Ines. My life, my family, my studies."

"Things are taken care of. You are not ready yet."

Two days later they transferred him to a nearby hotel.

They brought his mother and his brother in. There were lots of tears and hugs. He told them what he knew, but they were already told. "We know." They were all staying in another hotel nearby.

"And Gina? Where is she?"

His mother told him the truth. Gina was gone.

"What? Gone where?"

"Yes, Daniel, she's gone." his mother told him. "She had to run away with her family."

"They escaped."

"No! no!" he groaned. "Gina... Gina... How... what...?

"We don't know. She escaped."

"They found out that they were looking for them," said his mother. "A man friend of yours will come today or tomorrow and will explain."

"No! no!"

The green old man, Saravia-Cohen himself, came the next day to see him. They hugged each other.

"Look Daniel, I feel sorry for what happened to you. I came to..."

"Gina... Gina..." he said. "What happened to her?"

"Look Daniel... you must know... she had to... Gina... had to go," he said. "She had to escape."

"But... did they hurt her? She's okay? How do you know?"

"While you were out, our section chief received a call from the section chief of the Joint Forces and... and... things were complicated, Daniel," the old green man began to explain. "Three or four days after you left it seems that a notification got to her family that they were going to be searched and taken away. They packed up some things and went to wait elsewhere. It seems that that night or the next their house was raided and, when they were not found, the armed forces announced on television and radio that they were wanted. The rest you can imagine."

"Imagine what?"

"You know how it works. That they fled. As you can imagine."

"But how? How did they run away, Saravia? Tell me what happened."

"When I found out, I proceeded to do immediately as you said. I located them at an aunt's house in Punta del Este, and from there I personally took them to a small airport on the outskirts of town. They flew to Rivera and from there to Brazil, and from there to somewhere. I understand they are fine, and nothing happened to the four of them. We followed your instructions, so I know they are safe."

"And where are they? For what country did they leave?"

"We don't know, they didn't tell us.... for their safety. You know how it works, right?"

Daniel was engulfed in great sadness. As Saravia-Cohen kept talking, his mind escaped in images of the love that went away.

Gina.

Slowly, the old man stopped talking, and they stared at each other, silently. Daniel was distressed by the sadness of losing Gina and felt his strength crumble. The old man was distraught by everything Daniel had gone through, which he had learned through his daughter and what others had told him. He felt guilty.

Daniel sat on the couch. "Gina..." Sitting there, her image came toward him and her memory had him engrossed. Her eyes, her smile. Gina eating pizza, Gina laughing. . . Gina... Gina taking off her towel and telling him about the Fourth International, naked, in front of him... Gina at home having dinner...

"No!"

Saravia sat next to him, bewildered. Daniel asked him again. He didn't know anything else.

He had a strong suspicion that Gina's association with Daniel had generated a chain of events, but he couldn't tell him why or how, he wasn't sure. Maybe all the reasons together, maybe none, but they probably saw in Gina an accomplice that had to be gotten out of the way.

"But I saw it coming, Daniel," said the green man. "After you left, I knew she'd be vulnerable, so I asked some friends to raise their antennae. And when the warning came, I wasn't surprised. When I was notified of the complaint and the immediate request, then I made those calls and proceeded as you would have wanted me to proceed."

"Thank you...," said Daniel. "Thank you very much... I wouldn't have—"

"It's part of our responsibility, when we send friends abroad, to make sure that the people who stay behind do not go through problems. And no, I don't know what name they used or what country they went to. It is extremely important that these things are not recorded or known, both for fear of reprisals and for not disturbing Interpol's friends."

"I see."

"Anything inside you can be squeezed out of you."

"Can you at least—"

"I don't know more, Daniel," he added. "I can't tell you more. At least she wasn't killed, or caught in the street making her disappear, as happened with others."

"Thank you."

"Daniel, you mustn't talk about it with anyone. You must suffer all this alone and wait for... maybe one day you'll meet again. I'm so sorry, Daniel. I'm sorry about what you went through, about what happened, I'm sorry about Gina. But you know I needed you, and you know you had to do it. Yes. Just like I must keep doing what I do. We'll talk later. In the meantime, heal and get better. You survived, Daniel."

The eyes of both started to drip. The old man hugged Daniel and left.

Daniel was assaulted by memories. A mixture of love and hatred flowed through his mind. Gina. He didn't know until that day how much he had started to love her. At night, memories of the shooting and the death of Domínguez came to him like nightmares, dancing around the nebula.

Dreams would come to him with images of guns and the dead, and he would wake up agitated and sweaty. Sometimes he moaned, sometimes sobbed, feeling like things would never be the same again.

He saw himself grabbing a gun while swearing revenge. The Remington. A sudden gunshot. The smoke. The bullet in the arm. The wound, the pain.

Some nights he slept with Gina next to him, looking at her long black hair as he squeezed her ribs and pinched her shoulders. He told Gina once again that he loved her. She spoke to him but without a voice and smiled at him and said things, silent things that made him laugh. They fell asleep, hugged.

He was never going to see her again. Never again her voice, never again her breath.

Officers Cabrera and Herrera came to see him several times, along with other agents. MacLagan and Gomez came several times also and brought him pastries and cakes. Yamandu came twice.

He continued to recover and was back to normal, but he was still told to stay in Piriápolis.

"Why do I have to stay?"

"You are going to find out soon."

Chapter 38

As for the kidnappings, they didn't tell him anything until he was back to normal. One of the officers came to his hotel with Gomez and MacLagan to have some tea. They got some cake. They greeted him with great emotion and told him everything they regretted about what had happened to him, but then told him that they were happy about the result. The story had been like how Daniel had suggested it, but not exactly.

Two middle-aged ladies worked at that Commercial Bank, one in the checking accounts section and the other in the deposits section, and they had access to all kinds of information. The husband of one of them had two brothers who were in the army, and the husband of the other was a financier. Of the two brothers in the army was a friend of a certain Colonel Pedraza.

"Listen..." started Gomez. "The thing was that these two women, encouraged by their husbands, had quietly removed a certain amount of money from the bank, diverting funds from various accounts, calculating that they would refund everything without anyone noticing. They used the money to make investments with an investor they knew, but things went wrong. They lost every penny. Then this investor, who had already been in jail for fraud, was left owing money to several clients, his family, and two other officers. To make matters worse, things were pressing, because if the bank realized that the funds had disappeared, the two women, their husbands, and other members of the family, would go to jail.

"They couldn't just return the money?"

"No. They had no way to return that money and things got hot at a family reunion, where accusations and threats rained down. The two women with their husbands, the two soldiers, and other members of the family concluded that there was no way to obtain that money given the poor socio-economic circumstances the country was experiencing. Finally, after a long discussion, and pressed for time, they decided to proceed in carrying out a criminal act that could provide the money. Various possibilities were considered, including a bank robbery, house robberies, and even street assaults.

"Gee... a criminal act."

"Yes. However, knowing the risk they were taking, they were afraid of being captured and perhaps even shot. Somehow they got the idea of concocting a kidnapping as if it was a political event, which everyone would expect in these times, but they realized that they could not do it alone."

"Ah," said Daniel. "Then they—"

"Wait, wait, and listen. Then the two soldiers went to speak to Colonel Pedraza, an army commander based in Montevideo. They already knew the tastes and the soft side of the colonel, and so they raised the possibility of doing something together that would be beneficial for both sides. Pedraza was already a veteran of abuse, extortion, and expropriation, and it was already known that his hands were stained, and his conscience compromised from the blood and money of certain previous events. They talked about the abduction idea and the colonel liked it. He helped arrange the general plan and many of the operations. Cars and some uniforms would be used and even personnel from the barracks and cells would be available.

Gomez took a sip of water and continued.

The plan was in motion. There was enthusiasm among the people. It was decided to do it with someone wealthy. The women reviewed the accounts of merchants in the area, and reviewed data on family, children, and residence. They found the ideal candidate, a businessman who made good money and who had a son or daughter in the university. They knew it would not be unusual if they kidnapped him or her pretending to be an arrest. That was common at that time, and still is. The first kidnapping was carried out using an army jeep and was done by the two soldiers and a friend from the same barracks as that colonel. They invaded the merchant's house at night as in a classic operation and took the hooded boy. A later call demanded a certain sum, which the desperate parents paid. However, perhaps due to nervousness and inexperience, things did not go well, and the boy died, they killed him; it is not known if on purpose or what. They buried the poor guy in a little field on the Carrasco Road, and the parents were told that they sent him to the Freedom Prison.

The money was paid off, and the colonel got his cut, but it seems that the women didn't like that the victim had died; they were good Christians and there was tension in the group. The money obtained was used to pay the debts, and that was to be the end of it, nothing more. However, sweetened by the large amount of easy money, and excited by the colonel who was attracted to the idea of receiving more money, they got together again to make their second kidnapping. This time it was decided to do it with more care to ensure that the person returned alive. The money was also very good, and it didn't take long to make a third and fourth kidnapping. As someone in the barracks smelled something, others found out and demanded to participate, they had to let them enter the plot, although in any case the large amount of easy money was enough for everyone. The colonel helped organize each kidnapping and provided jeeps and cars for transportation and, of course, got his big cut.

"Some of them were shot. Why some and not others?"

"We don't... eh... just wait."

"And that was the main team, Daniel, see?" continued the officer. "The two women, their husbands, the two military men, those of the family, and Colonel Pedraza. That was the core. Yes. But later more people from the barracks were added. Of the three soldiers who joined the group, one of them had been in prison in Salto for killing his wife and lover in a fit of jealousy, and later killed two more people. He had come to Montevideo and had changed his name to enter the army. They had to watch him so that he did not kill the hostages. A real killer."

"Yeah. Apparently, a few times he managed to kill a hostage."

"Oh."

"And Pedraza was around on some of those occasions. He knew."

Gomez continued. "Thus, the abductions kept going, guided by the information that the women brought from the bank about those who had good money in the area and had children who could be kidnapped making it seem like a political issue. That is why they did not use children, because if they had, the case would have gone straight to the police and perhaps to Interpol."

"The friends were careful in choosing each case, being sure that the funds were available. On several occasions, as you said, the murderer had the opportunity to be alone with the victim and had the pleasure of shooting him or her with his weapon, yes, always the same weapon, always in the same way, always in the same position and at the same angle, just as you, Daniel, had said. Yes, always the same killer, Daniel. You were right."

"They proposed to bury the corpse and make it disappear, but the friends were good Christians and demanded that the body be given to the parents for a moral and Christian burial so that it would have a proper rest in a tomb blessed by a priest. That is why the bodies were delivered to the hospital, taken to the morgue, or dumped in a garbage dump."

"How dreadful. But how did they discover all this?"

"Following your idea, Daniel," said the officer.

They brought in more staff and followed up on all those who left in groups of two or more. They followed them for several days, to see where they were going. So it was that they noticed that the two women always went back and forth together, and that was noted in the file. Later, the minister contributed six or seven bank accountants who reviewed the deposit accounts of the five or six banks that were in an area of two kilometers from the Commercial Bank. It was calculated that the money would always be divided in the same way, so they were working on the theory that the same amount would have been deposited more than thirty times within the five days following the payment of the ransom, or that, alternatively, someone would visit the security box of one or more of those banks the same number of times.

"Do you realize it? It was considered that one or more of the culprits would surely try to hide their deposit by changing it to foreign currency and securing it in a bank safe. The accounts of all the banks were reviewed and specialists in current accounts were installed in each of the banks. Addresses were reviewed, payments were compared, and a very thorough job was done."

"Yes. Yes."

"Thus, three suspects were found, one of the women, who each time made a deposit in the same bank eight blocks from her work, and two of the men, who did the same in other banks. A common pattern was found. They were followed and their address was confirmed with the other data and thus the soldiers were located. The soldiers were followed to the barracks and all the data was put together. Many other tracking, accounting, and filing data were added, and the criminal picture began to become clear. The accounts were investigated. Some boxes were secretly opened. More follow-up was done."

"And? And?"

"Listen. Pieces of the puzzle were still missing. We needed one of them to confess. Then a ruse was planned. The two women were detained stealthily, without anyone noticing on one occasion when they went to the street market, and they were taken to a barracks, a different barracks where a double mirror and hidden microphones were placed.

"Those from the headquarters and the officers were put in the hidden room and the women were interrogated in separate rooms. They denied everything and were even surprised to have been accused. They did not understand what the investigators wanted. Nothing was advanced. It was tried in various ways without success; the women were still amazed that there was such an accusation, until Yamandu went to his church and brought the clothes of his priest friend and asked an actor who sometimes helped the police to talk to the women. The more religious of the two was pressured with descriptions of how horrible it had all been, from the Christian and church point of view. She was told that those young people had been murdered, and that her spirit was stained with their blood. Her sins had been capital and her soul would no longer have peace. The lady listened to the false priest and began to break down. Using his skills, the actor continued talking to her about issues of God, Jesus, and the Holy Spirit, and the woman could not take much more. In tears she confessed everything. Kneeling and mortified, she explained and gave details, asking for divine forgiveness and crossing herself every minute. That recording was played to the other woman, and she was given a shovel and told that in a little while she was going to go out to dig a grave, her grave, in the little field behind. She was told that she will not go to jail for what she did. *You can't be left alive after what you've done*, she was told. At the same time, an officer began to slowly remove his clothes while two of the detectives undressed the woman, saying they were Jews and made evil jokes. They both had placed on themselves a necklace with the Star of David. They told her that she was going to be penetrated by two Jews and then killed and buried forever with the semen of the two Jews inside her for all eternity. She will never reach heaven. That destroyed her emotionally..."

"Especially when she saw agent Berkowitz with his pants and underwear down."

"Yes. Yes. And listen to this. When her underwear was pulled down, and she saw what was coming, subjugated by remorse, faced with the evidence, and horrified at being raped by two impure Jews, she threw herself to the floor, burst into tears and chanted everything she knew in precious details. The masterminds kept a lot of details from her. But she had enough to connect the dots. She was able to explain even more of what had happened. The two women were arrested and kept in separate cells. Statements were recorded. The men were captured and the first, after making him listen to the two recordings, was told that the two women accused him of having been the murderer and it was explained that given the country's situation it was necessary to end his existence, but they gave him the opportunity to execute himself. He was given a revolver with a single bullet and after a quarter of an hour of deliberation he confessed all the details. The officers prepared their soldiers and the barracks in question was seized. The soldiers resisted, two were killed, and two were wounded in the shooting. Five soldiers and two officers were imprisoned in the same battalion that you visited. There they were asked very delicately if they wanted to confess anything. In full agony they sang what they knew. They described the kidnappings, money details, the two infiltrators at the police headquarters, and others."

"They told us how they grabbed, tortured, and killed Domínguez afterwards."
"But I thought the two attackers were killed."
"We thought so too, but there were more."
"But why did they kill him?"
"That's what we... they wanted to know how much he knew. Awful."
"And who was in the headquarters?"
"Yes, yes, you were right. The Russian Statchenko was one of those."
"Damn Russian !"
"You won't have to worry about him. He's gone."
"Gone? Where?"
"Escaped to Paraguay."
"And the Nubian? That Anubis guy?"
"The Nubian, yes, well, he had nothing to do with it. He was just our working theory, remember? That Nubian and his people weren't in Uruguay, and they weren't involved in this, as far as we know."
"Aaahh..."
"This was too small time for him," said MacLagan.
"About the two spies at the headquarters... Statchenko and the other guy... well, Yamandu, who was badly hurt by Domínguez's death, apprehended the other guy. He took him in a car, and he didn't come back until the next day, in a trance of excitation. No one bothered to ask the Russian what he did with him, but the one who saw him said he had bloodstains on his hands and didn't want to wash them. And he didn't wash them for three days, they say, as if to keep savoring his revenge. Nobody dared to make a comment about that or ask any questions."
"Gee...what do you think he did with him?"
"Don't even want to imagine," he said, straightening his mustache and drying a couple of tears. "Domínguez was like a brother to him."
"And the executing killer?"
"Ah, with that devil we went to talk," MacLagan said. "We talked with lead and very slowly we thought we'd bring Tamara's parents or the parents of the others who died to give them a chance to *say a few words*, but that could have opened their wounds and leave witnesses."
"Yes, yes."
"We thought we'd bring you, my little Carmencito, so that it would be you, the father of the investigation, who would have given him the death shot. But we thought that you've already had enough, that you were trying to heal and that you've already seen too much shit and death, and we shouldn't stain your life with what technically, after all, would be murder. Did we do well?"

Daniel kept thinking. The images were blowing around his head and his eyes filled with tears.

"Calm down, Daniel. Take it easy."

"Yes. Yes. You did well, but... and what did they do? How?"

"Look, Daniel, we have our style, so don't feel bad," continued MacLagan. "That man did horrible things and a quick death, or a cushy cage with free meals, wouldn't have been fair. See?"

"Yes, yes."

"We knew that sooner or later, before, during, and after the trial of the women, several parents would ask us about the matter, and we should give them an answer that would satisfy them. But we couldn't use an option that could give us problems in the future, after all, rightly and for no reason, it was an execution."

"And what? What about_"

"It would have been horrible for Tamara's parents and for some other parents, do you understand? But we felt, however, it was necessary and good for others... and for you. Brought... well... no, I don't know if you're going to like this... but, look, life isn't a movie, and sometimes you must do things that aren't so..."

"Yes, yes, what? Tell me. What have you done with him?"

"Well, but maybe that doesn't—"

"Oh, come on."

"Well, it was all done behind the polygon stadium, where there's a field, see? It is an area surrounded by trees. The killer was brought in, and he was given a shovel and told to start digging. Pranchin brought with him two guys, not very holy people, dudes who owe us favors. They brought their own tools. In that area the earth is hard and difficult to dig, so the guy was digging his pit with difficulty as he cried and begged for his life, under the watchful eye of those boys. I had a gun loaded, just in case."

Daniel looked at him dumbfounded.

"Look, Daniel, I had to be sure, I... uh... I brought with me the pictures. Yes, the pictures of those executed, yes, including Tamara's, and well, eh... I showed them to him one by one, while giving him false promises."

"And?"

"Daniel, my friend, perhaps I should not go on. You are—"

"No. Tell me. What?"

MacLagan kept silent for a while. Gomez felt uneasy.

"Well, he didn't recognize several of the photos, but... but..."

"Yes, what? What did you do? Hurry!"

"He recognized Tamara's, Daniel, and... and..." the detective passed a handkerchief through his eyes. "And yes... he remembered that she was one who was tall and had freckles... and... that... yes, he recognized her."

Daniel was silent, remembering her. *Tamara.* His face wrinkled and his eyes filled with tears. He turned around and covered himself with a pillow and began to cry. MacLagan and the officer looked at him worried. They left him alone and went outside for a smoke. They waited for him to calm down. After a while, when he calmed down, they went back in.

"Then what?" asked Daniel, controlling himself.

"And... as the pit formed, things became more dramatic. Until the moment came when neither I nor Pranchin could keep looking. In addition, given our position... we should not have been there. We turned around and went to smoke behind a tree. The other men stayed there. We heard some drowning screams and then silence. We waited a moment and went to see. His head was between his feet, and the boys were throwing lime and plugging the pit. They stepped firmly on the ground later, threw twigs and straws, and nothing happened there."

The agent was silent.

"Tell him, MacLagan," said Gomez.

"I... maybe... you may not agree... but—"

"What? What?"

"I don't know... maybe... you may not agree on how—"

"I do. Thank you. Yes, I agree."

They gave each other a hug, and they were silent for a while, as Daniel stopped whining and dried his eyes.

"And then?"

"And then nothing. That's where that killer's life ended. The trial of all the others is still ahead. And... And... there's Colonel Pedraza's business. And... this... I do not know."

"What to do? Is the Colonel free?"

"Yes."

"Yes, he's free," MacLagan said. "He's untouchable, Danny."

"What do you mean, untouchable?" Daniel asked.

"Just like you heard it," remarked Gomez.

"But... but he knew of every kidnapping and knew of the deaths, and he knew—"

"Yes, Daniel, he knew everything," MacLagan said. "And he was involved in all that and there's more. The kidnapping thing would have been over after the second or third case, but Pedraza encouraged and pushed them and even threatened them to do more and more. He got rich. He made a lot of money.

"So...so he helped organize everything."

"Yup."

"Oh, oh. But how can that Pedraza be free?"

"He's from the Joint Forces," answered Gomez.

"But you are officers of the law," he said. "You could—"

"What law?" Gomez added. "I cannot do anything. Some of our people are linked to the army and the Joint Forces, we got them involved and they even agreed with us. However, because of hierarchy, status, and other issues, they couldn't do anything."

"Don't tell me that. It can't be."

"Yes, I tell you that. That's the way things are. The Joint Forces are all powerful and control this country, and Pedraza is part of them."

Daniel stared at him with big eyes, amazed. Not being able to believe or accept that Pedraza was so untouchable.

"There's more," Gomez said. "He was the one who had brought the murderer into the abduction business, because he already knew him. He used him at times as part of his personal guard, and at times for certain dirty jobs."

"After the first two cases, that Pedraza became the main leader of everything, and... well... eh... he was in command when Tamara was killed. He... I... look Daniel, the X told us that... hmm... I don't know how to tell you... I..."

"Yeah? What!?"

"Daniel... that Pedraza saw Tamara in the barracks. Do you realize it? He saw her and could have said to deliver her alive. Alive! But he didn't.... "

Daniel froze in amazement. "Alive! One word from that animal and she could be alive." He tilted his head down trying to control a gasp of pain. For an instant he saw her in the street, in bed, in the tango cafe, *her hair, her scent, never again*. He felt a void in his chest, an emptiness, and his throat knotted. The tears came to him. *Tamara*. He stayed like that for a while. *Never again her scent, never again her voice*."

"Daniel, Daniel."

He stayed like that for a while. They didn't want to interrupt him.

"Daniel .... Yes? Daniel.... "

"Yes. It's— I'm fine."

"Should I keep telling you, yes?"

"Yes. Okay," he answered. "Ah. So, the assassin had no problem killing the hostages because he knew he was protected by the colonel, eh?"

"That's how it went. This is not the only dirty thing this colonel has been involved in."

"Hmm... so... so..." stammered Daniel and had to hold back his tears again. "So, if this colonel... if this Colonel Pedraza had done something after the first murder, then... So maybe Tamara would never have been killed, huh?"

"Yes. I believe that," said Gomez. "And the others. Yes. Many of those would have been saved."

"I know that this is just plain horrible, Daniel," the agent declared. "He was killing them, that is, letting his lackeys kill them, one by one, without even considering the pain that each of those deaths would cause."

MacLagan took him by the hand.

Sitting up, Daniel tilted his face down again, and let sadness wash over him. Suddenly, all that pain he had felt came back to him. He felt himself in a well, in a horrible cold darkness, possessed by a deep pain.

He stayed like that for a while until the others were silent.

"And why...? And why do they say that he is so untouchable?"

"As I told you, he is now a colonel in the Joint Forces. And he's very smart and powerful. A strong officer. He was trained in the Navy, where he quickly obtained decorations, medals, and special mentions. He was shaping up to be a captain, and his path to be an admiral shortened. However, he asked to be transferred to the army."

"The army?" said Daniel. "What the hell did he do that for?"

"He had plans, I guess. Power plans. He asked many times to be transferred and was denied, until he threatened to leave the country, then they gave it to him, but they made him undergo rigorous training, which he passed in eighteen months. They made him a colonel and from there he began to grow. He joined the Joint Forces, he networked a lot, and now he is part of the strong military gear of the dictatorship. That gave him the power to dive in on any opportunity to get into highly-profitable shady deals. Drugs, smuggling, arms sales, he likes everything. The kidnapping thing is just one more of his chores."

"Hmm... a real son of a bitch of great caliber."

"Yes. And *untouchable*."

"But... there's going to be a trial," Daniel said. "There will be a court."

"The court and the judges who are going to try the kidnappers is a closed military court, with specific objectives and determined to clean things up without staining the good name or the glorious work of the Joint Forces. Nothing is going to be published. Nothing will be known. Nothing will go abroad. Pedraza is not going to be involved.

"But... but... something must happen... Something must be done."

"Calm down, my little Carmen kid, and listen."

They told him that a long and detailed report was made. That report was then raised to the minister and from there to the great General 'Beto' Garrido Alavart, who used that opportunity to show the photos of all of them and show that "those are the bad guys, not us." He spoke on radio and TV and said, "Those were the culprits of the disappeared and the injustices, and not our glorious joint armed forces."

Nothing was said about Colonel Esteban Carlos Pedraza and his licensed assassins. Nothing. They used the kidnappers to clean up the bad name of the great Joint Forces, and everything ended even better when "Beto," with the help of the team that did the investigation, managed to obtain part of the ransom money, to which he added some money that he got from retirees and municipal expenses. Good little bit of money. Then, in sensational acts, part of that money was returned to each of the parents, just about half of what they paid, with a special letter from his office, the national flag, a medal for courage, and a colorful picture. The enormous profits of Pedraza were not touched. Parents whose children had been murdered also received special recognition, an official salute, a tribute, and a large sum of extra money drained from an Inter-American Development Bank loan.

Of Operation Condor, of Domínguez's death and some other events, nothing was said.

"But... what the hell!"

That's how it went.

"And Tamara's parents...? What'd they say?"

"They took all their things and money and went to Spain."

"Hmm...case closed then."

"Case almost closed, Daniel, thanks to you," said MacLagan. "And I want you to know that when I introduced the murderer to the two friends who came to *talk* to him, I said, 'I leave you in the hands of my three friends, but only two came, the third, a certain Daniel, sends you his greetings.' I did it thinking of you."

Daniel got excited again and tears came back. He started to cry. "You told him my name... thank you!" he whimpered.

Gomez gave him a hug.

"Oh, oh, don't squeeze me so tight. My arm."

"Oh sorry."

"And now?" he said, running his finger over his eyes.

"Now nothing. Recover! While you're recovering better think that there are some powerful people who are eager to reward you for what you have done.... Ponder what you want. The world suddenly opens in front of you."

"Yes, thank you," he said while he was thinking. "Thank you, all of you, very much. And... And how are those of Domínguez's family?"

"They are relieved. The money they received as compensation from the headquarters and the Department of Justice, plus the pension, plus a little money that the chief of the Joint Forces sent them, and some other things, helped them a lot. They grabbed their things and left for Portugal."

"Well... well... at least. And what else?"

"That's all. However, there's something strange... regarding the death of Domínguez. I don't know... what to think."

MacLagan explained that Domínguez died, tied in a chair, yes, but that his face and eyes were bitten and pecked by those crows. Horrible. The autopsy showed no bullet holes or stabbings, no heart attack, no stroke, no infection, or suffocation.

"So, what was the cause of death?"

"Well, that's the question," said Gomez. "Strange question. What they did find was a couple of toxins, kind of strong toxins. Then they analyzed the bodies of some of the crows that were killed during the firefight and guess what? Those toxins were found to be more concentrated in the beaks of the crows. It didn't make sense. Were they extracting toxins out of him or were they injecting them in him? See? Impossible."

"That's not possible," claimed Gomez.

"Daniel, it's like the crows had pecked him with something toxic," said MacLagan. "But that theory is impossible to believe. What are we going to say? That the crows found him and killed him? It just can't be. They are birds."

"I do believe it," Daniel stressed. "Yes, it can be. Finally, the souls of the women he abused came together, and they did it."

"What are you talking about?"

"I understood it thanks to One-eye Juan," said Daniel. "He did with wives and daughters what should not be done with grieving women. And... and sometimes nature does strange things to avenge itself. I think the wounded souls of those women somehow got linked with the crows or the spirit of one with the spirit of another, and... I am guessing... I think nature exacted vengeance through the crows. I don't know. It's not possible, but what other—"

"What are you talking about? The *souls of women* interacting with... with the *spirits of birds*. Please. You know it can't be."

"Listen to what..."

"No. You listen! Are you mixing reality with your fantasies?"

"Look. If you didn't know before, if you hadn't noticed, now you will have to accept it. Domínguez was followed by crows for certain things he did, things a little immoral, even he knew it, and those crows—"

"Ahhh.... Leave it there. Don't start with those things."

"Okay. Don't believe me."

He stayed for a while thinking, remembering. He lit a cigarette, looked out the window.

"What's wrong, Daniel?" asked MacLagan.

"Nothing. Well, it's just that... that colonel remains free. That Colonel Pedraza. And he remains—"

"Shut up, Daniel. Whatever you must think and say, leave it now. Face it later when your body and your mind are better."

"Okay, okay, MacLagan, you're a man of honor and justice; but... what about him... will he ever receive punishment?"

"No. Again, he is untouchable."

"Don't you want justice?"

"Of course. But it's part of the dictatorial system. It is undeniable. He cannot be accused. You must leave it there."

"But hell, it's not fair that—"

"Did you hear what I said? Nothing! You can't do anything."

"Yes, I heard."

They talked a little more and decided to leave. They gave him pats and big hugs, and to his mother, and even to Marisa who was just coming.

The kidnapping problem was over. Almost.

And they had almost finished him. Almost.

Chapter 39

Colonel Esteban Carlos Pedraza was neither accused nor named at all. The guy was free and clear. Daniel was very upset and vocal about it.

One day a man came to his hotel dressed in an armed forces uniform, smelling of cheap cologne. It was nighttime. He introduced himself and spoke to Daniel in a very polite way. He spoke to him clearly, saying that things had gone wrong, but he had to understand that certain people, civilians, and military, performed certain jobs necessary for the dictatorship for which they were and would be untouchable. That even if he managed to know who they were, there would be nothing he could do. The situation was regrettable, but Daniel had to accept things the way they were. The officer greeted him politely and before leaving he told him that what he had said did not indicate that certain people in the Uruguayan government would not be willing to give him a hand in other things. "Perhaps pertinent to your studies, Mr. Daniel, or your future, perhaps... hmm... from a financial point of view."

"Okay..."

"You know Mr. Daniel, if you are interested in knowing more, just call me." And he left his card, Lieutenant General Engineer Mario Robledo Sosa.

A few nights later, Saravia-Cohen came to see him.

"Listen to this," Saravia-Cohen said. "I can't fix that disaster that happened, some things don't heal like wounded arms do. But I want you to know that, well... in a broad sense, we will compensate you in the way that you prefer, money, tickets, I do not know, whatever."

"There are grateful people behind the curtains. Take advantage of that."

Daniel looked at him and said the words that he knew would change his life and future: "A visa and studies abroad."

"For wherever you want, and whenever you want, and with the help you need."

"Thank you."

"Go gathering your blessings and putting your prayers to the Holy Lord in order," he said, and then explained that he would arrange the visa to where Daniel wanted, the United States, France, Sweden, Spain, wherever he wanted. Condor would provide certain funds and perhaps even a scholarship. The people of Uruguay and the undersecretary of the minister were very grateful. It was time for them to show how grateful they were. In the embassies of each country there were books that described their universities in detail and what the embassy itself could not find out; he would find out. In each embassy there were also recognized translators who could translate and certify what Daniel wanted.

"Nice."

"That's right, Danny. Operation Condor knows how to be thankful. How to return favors. With letters of recommendation from the dean, one or two ministers, and the consul, you can go wherever you want."

"Thank you. Thank you so much."

They talked a bit more and then he left.

Daniel had other plans. He was building something in his mind.

He called Pereyra and told him, "But you see? In the meantime, that officer, Colonel Esteban Carlos Pedraza, continues with his hands filthy from the blood of the kidnapped. And he is free."

"Listen to me," Pereyra answered. "They told you he's untouchable, Daniel. Get it out of your head."

"But he is guilty of Tamara's death and..."

"You think he's only guilty of *her* death? There is nothing that either you or anyone can do."

Several of the abductees' parents began visiting Daniel to thank him and to recognize him as the one who had resolved the matter. Whether their child had died or not, everyone was relieved by how things had been resolved, many were happy and almost everyone had been glad to have received back some of the money and extra compensation. Knowing that justice had been done with those who abducted or murdered their son or daughter gave these families a final mental relief, answered their questions, and gave them the strength to move on.

What better way for those families than to come visit, thank him in person, and show their appreciation with a cash envelope. At first, Daniel didn't want to take the money, but seeing tears in these people's eyes and listening to Marisa, who was very religious, say, "God said that from my garden you can eat what I have given to you, so you can't deny what you're given from the heart." He then decided to accept the envelopes with great gratitude.

The good thing about it was that, from envelope to envelope, he was accumulating good money, but what was even better was that several of those families who came to see him had a daughter of deserving age, with whom he did not delay in exchanging words and getting their phone number.

But his hate persisted. That was something he chewed night and day, and although he tried to forget, he couldn't.

The memories, the knowledge, the flashbacks, all combined to keep a hot pain inside of him and the growing deep desire for revenge.

Chapter 40

At night he rested well, but the heat of revenge was growing on him. How could he leave the country knowing that the murderer of Tamara is enjoying a good life? *Her body is underground, together with all the affection we gave to each other. While the colonel is having fun.*

"The desire for revenge is very difficult to carry," he had been warned. "It will make you sick."

"Ah, see, it's like I told you," the trainer had said. "The Remington 51 looks good in your hand."

"Don't do it!"

"Daniel, revenge enslaves a human being and makes him sick."

I'm already sick, he told himself. *I'm already a slave.*

"If you need anything, whatever you want, let me know," was the common farewell of many parents.

Yes, he told himself, *Yes*!

He developed a plan and asked to be taken back to his home. Once there, in his apartment at 21 De Septiembre Street, he planned a move. Very risky.

He made some phone calls, did some research, and located Pedraza. He found out that he was always hanging out with his two bodyguards.

He had no other option than asking for helpful information. He decided to talk to Ines about it.

"What are you planning on doing?" she asked him in the car. "Don't! Whatever it is, don't! Take those crazy thoughts out of your mind."

"Nothing. I just wanted to be sure."

"Daniel, revenge poisons the heart, even as you smite your enemy. The grudge will make your life sour. You may end up in a grave or in jail.

"No!" he yelled at her.

"Shhh... don't yell at me," she replied. "See the poison's already taking effect. Come, sit quietly, tell me what you want."

"I don't. I don't want to talk to you."

"Idiot," she said. "Crazy stinking fool."

But three days later she showed up at his house. Ines took him to his room and talked to him.

"Yes. Pedraza was involved in all that. He helped plan the actions; he helped select the candidates; he was even in the barracks when more than one was killed. He provided intelligence and support. He made a lot of money. But you are going to leave the country and live your new life somewhere else."

"I can't."

"What's the matter with you?"

"Nothing, Ines."

"Ah, you don't want to talk, are you planning something?"

"Nothing, Ines."

"I'm sorry! Talk to me, you idiot! What are you thinking?"

"Leave me now."

But she didn't give up. She knew that his mind was harboring something, and she didn't leave it alone until Daniel agreed to go to dinner and walk with her the next day. He knew she wanted to get him to talk, but he needed to talk to someone anyway. She came to get him one stormy night, took him straight to a tango bar where he ate half a sandwich, had a whiskey, and danced some tangos with her. She had come dressed very sexy, in a low-cut black dress, a loose bra, with a good perfume, and bad intentions. They danced and warmed their blood. By the time she suggested they go eat paella at her house, Daniel already had his blood warmed and did not refuse. They entered her home, she took off her dress, undressed him and finished undressing, then took him slowly to her bed and did with him what she wanted. Her breasts made Daniel forget the rest of the world for a while. Then, once they calmed down and in privacy, sheltered in her cave, they began to eat and talk.

"Look, Daniel. Revenge is treacherous and can leave you ill. Don't you remember Rhamnousia? With taste only for revenge. Forever carrying a whip and dagger?"

"I read about her."

"They called her *Nemesis*, Daniel."

"Actually, they called her *Adrasteia*, Daughter of Justice, dedicated to bringing men fortune and balance of life."

"That was earlier," said Ines. "Later she was feared and hated, because she traveled the world with a death cult, killing men."

Daniel looked out the window at the rain.

Ines moved in to nuzzle him. "Open up to me. Tell me what's going on and what you're thinking."

"I just don't know... I don't know if you're going to understand me."

"Look at everything I already know about you. The Tamara thing, the things you did in the past, your stupid things, the Isabel thing, and that Gina who is a double woman, the things we shared, many things, Daniel. I don't want anything to happen to you."

"Is that... look Ines. I've been thinking about it since my mind improved after the wound. The memory of Tamara... eh....

"I'll have the memory of Tamara for my whole life. The pain that she was murdered, and how, will haunt me for many years. Ines, it was horrible what they did to her. I'm going to have to live with it.

"I hear you."

"But I want the balance of justice."

"Even if it means only carrying a sharp dagger...?" she asked, bringing his hand up to her breast. "Never touching anything else?" she whispered in his ear.

"A hundred times—" Daniel pulled away. He walked to the other side of the room and turned to face her. "A hundred times I promised myself and promised to heaven that I was going to catch the son of a bitch who killed her. The count of sands on the beach are the tears I cried for what they did to her. And now I'm faced with two options. Continue living with that pain, but leaving the thirst for revenge aside, or not to leave the revenge aside. And why? Why... who cares if revenge makes the heart sick? My heart is already sick."

Ines tried to reassure him.

"And why also?" Daniel continued. "Why will revenge hurt me? What? Still more damage? Do you see what I'm telling you? If I do nothing, if I simply continue living my life, am I going to live many more years, years of hurt knowing that those who did that barbaric murder are alive?"

"But some have already been killed and others are in jail, Daniel."

"But that guy is alive! Alive!"

"Don't let Perfect be the *nemesis* of Pretty Good."

"No. I can't accept it. I can't live with it. And why? Why do I have to base myself on what others say about revenge? Revenge this, revenge that, you don't have to take revenge, and things like that. Those charlatans. If everything works out kinda okay for them, they just let all the imbalance of life stand. Let's hear what they would say over one of their loved ones eaten by rats."

"So what?"

"Ines. These things are waking me up at night. I wake up some mornings thinking about it. What they did to Tamara was horrible, she was... divine... I loved her very much... even though I knew..."

"That she wasn't for you," she said. "You let her go without a word so she could get someone better than you, huh? Take my handkerchief."

"Thank you. Yes."

"I know, Daniel. Well, tell me more."

"The second option. Remembering for many years that I tormented and killed the guilty one."

"Uuuuuuuffffffff, Daniel, do you know what you're saying? You're no murderer, Daniel."

"Yes, I know very well... No, I don't know what to do."

"They can kill you, Daniel."

"I know. To reunite my body with my soul."

"You can end up in jail."

"I don `t believe it. I will go into hiding and escape, yes, but not to jail. I have friends in high places now."

"Hmm... I see. You would use Condor to escape the country."

"Yup.."

They continued talking until he fell asleep.

In the morning she made him a coffee, took a bath with him, they made love, and then she took him home and said nothing more.

That same day he started with his plan.

He began to plan everything in his mind and even made a secondary plan and an optional one. The second plan would be better. Some of the parents would help him. He discussed it with Tamara's father and with four other parents. They gave him suggestions. They came up with something even better.

He talked about it with other parents. Some did not want to get involved, but many were thirsty for the blood on Nemesis' dagger. "Yes, we'll help."

He felt safe.

"I am going to get you... son of thousands of whores... and the crack of a whip will be the final thing you hear."

Chapter 41

He was there, in his revenge world, when late one afternoon Pranchin called him and told him that he was going to pick him up to take him somewhere.

He came to get him with MacLagan, and two other officers, and they drove away.

"Look, Daniel, you're about to make a big crappy mistake, way too big, and that's why we came."

"What are you talking about?" he said as they continued driving east through the shore of Pocitos.

"We know, Daniel."

"But—"

"Ines told! Several parents of the abductees too!" said one of the agents.

"Sons of a bad bitches..."

"No! No, you are wrong," said Pranchin. "Children of good mothers. But are you drunk? Don't you realize?"

"Realize what?'

"Dummy... but just how stupid are you?" said MacLagan. "You're planning the murder of a high-ranking colonel like someone plans a family barbecue. Are you stupid? What the hell do you have in your head? To begin with, the thirst for revenge does not let you see. You are making mistakes and you are going to make more. We cannot allow it. You will be disgraced, and you will..."

"Leave me alone!"

"No!"

"No! we won't leave you alone," Pranchin shouted. "You made it to medical school, but are you half a moron? You can't... if I leave you alone and you either kill somebody, or you get killed, or I will end up with your ass in jail. Not that I feel sorry for you..."

"Thanks."

"Don't you see it?" MacLagan said. "You're talking about taking up arms and killing somebody. And in cold blood!

"Someone guilty as hell!"

"Doesn't matter."

"Don't you see? Do you think that because you know how to defend yourself and you handled a gun a few times in a classroom, that you are already a man of arms? Wake up!"

"Hey, killing a man in self-defense or in war is already mentally damaging," added the other agent. "Killing in cold blood will damage your soul and your brain for years to come."

"Don't you know what this man did?" protested Daniel. "He... he—"

"We know!"

"We *all* know."

"Enough of this. He is, for you, untouchable."

"He won't."

"Drop it, Danny boy."

"You are going to be disgraced, Daniel," said the first agent. "You are planning a crime in a stupid way, and you will be disgraced."

"And disgrace others," Pranchin added.

"Leave me," shouted Daniel.

"You're out of your mind *and* out of your league!"

"Take me home. You... you didn't have to go through that pain. I loved her, and... and... and seeing her coffin... dead was... And the parents of the others, they... It was horrible... I—"

"I know it was horrible, okay. But... that's not what I am talking about here."

"Okay," said Daniel, more calmly.

"Are you going to give up? Are you going to leave the matter?"

"That's my thing. My revenge."

"Yes or no??"

"Take me home," shouted Daniel. "It's something I must do... I can't live knowing that Pedraza is still—"

"I give up, Daniel!" MacLagan yelled. "There's no reasoning with you."

"No!"

"Hmm, Pranchin, let's go to the second plan. Go ahead. Put them on and that's it."

"Put what on?"

MacLagan stopped the car. He turned around and grabbed Daniel's hand. In the same instant, Pranchin grabbed Daniel's neck and flattened himself against his body. He couldn't move or breathe. They put handcuffs on him and then tape over his mouth to keep him quiet. He tried to protest, but they ignored him. The handcuffs were attached to a seat bar and there was nothing he could do; he tried to fight them, but to no avail. He was very surprised.

They reported something on the radio. MacLagan drove fast down the boulevard towards the Malvin neighborhood.

"You little chunk of manure," said one of the agents.

"We do this for you, because we see that we have no other choice, stupid," said MacLagan. "But also, for the parents of the men and women whom you, idiot, almost implicated in a crime. Or didn't you realize that? You were going to.... ah, why am I still trying to talk to you?"

Daniel tried to mumble something. He just couldn't say anything. The tape covering his mouth was wide and thick.

"Dummy! mindless! stubborn !...you were going to bathe in a tub of murder," MacLagan yelled at him, grabbing his neck, and shaking him. "And with that you were soiling and disgracing your family. Moron!"

"And we also do this for Ines," Pranchin said angrily and gave him a hard slap in the face. "And for us."

Daniel had no idea what they were saying to him, but it was clear that they knew most of his plans. He was very scared.

They stopped the car near the entrance of a sprawling house, protected by a large fence and a towering gate. They said something on the radio.

"Look and shut up."

The five of them stayed in the car, while two officers approached the door and rang the bell. One of the bodyguards came out. They told him something. There was a silence, and a short argument. The bodyguard left, entered the house, and returned with the other bodyguard, who was armed with a machine gun. There was an exchange of words. The two bodyguards left their guns leaning by the gate, then received what looked like money, went out into the street, and hurried away. They didn't even look back. In the car, one of the two agents said something on the radio. They unhooked Daniel from the bar and got him out. They approached the gate. They were joined by two other men, and then another came from the shadows. It was El Pancho, that marked face that had helped them in the chemistry college.

Shit, thought Daniel.

They went to the door and rang the bell. After a while, Colonel Pedraza himself opened the door.

"Here he is," said MacLagan, as they all entered the house. "This is the Daniel Blum who ruined your cake."

"Ah, that's him... good... this is going to be just great," said Pedraza, wringing his hands with delight. "So, this is the lover of that big girl, eh?" And turning to Daniel gave him a pinch in the side. "So, you wanted to kill me? And for that big useless pig lady?" he said, grabbing his hair and giving him a slap.

Daniel couldn't speak and just managed to squeeze out, "Mmm MMmmm MMmmm..." He had the handcuffs behind his back and Pranchin had him by the arm. Something had been arranged beforehand.

"Do you want us to leave him here or would you need some assistance to take care of him?"

"Yes, yes, of course," Pedraza said. "Very good. You'll save me the work, yes... and the mess." And speaking to Daniel he said, "So the big bad student looking to fight me, eh? Well, I was already thinking of looking for you. Lately, I've been eager to make you disappear. But I was a little concerned that just a simple cap in the head like that fat pig-whore would be too quick. You deserve more."

"Hmm!" That's all Daniel could say.

"We have a pending matter... because of you my business was fucked up," continued Pedraza. "I lost a lot of money, and my nephew was killed."

Daniel kept with the "MMmmm MMmmm" and tried to shake the arms that held him. Suddenly he realized that they all had plotted something, and he had fallen into a trap. Handcuffed and grabbed. Other than shaking there was nothing he could do.

"Here's your money, boys. Thanks for dropping off the trash. Let's see, let's see, take off the tape, let's see what this little shit wants to say before he leaves us for good."

They had sold him. For money. ***Traitors***!

While Pancho and Pranchin held him, another of the agents ripped the tape from his mouth. Daniel was already crying with fear and indignation, but he was also walking with a lot of hatred.

"Murderer! Son of a whore!" he screamed and spat. "You killed my Tamara. Y— and— the others—"

"Uuuuuhh... this boy's upset."

Daniel tried to reach him with a kick but couldn't. They had a strong hold on him.

"Ah, shut up, you immature idiot. That hog Tamara was a good deal. I got good money. What do you care anyway about that communist? What? Did you have a student fever with her? Moron!"

Then the colonel shook him by the ear. "Ah, you were hot with that big momma, eh pervert?"

"I—I—"

"What? Did you love that cow? Oh, poor thing. Listen to me dummy, she was worth nothing. Nothing! Did you hear me? Just the money I got from her. Like livestock. She had more value dead than alive."

"Murderer! you got your money; you could have let her live."

"Oh, but she had seen me, you see. Anyway, ha! you should have seen her miserable naked body tied up. She was ready."

"Animal!

Daniel had to take a deep breath. He didn't want to whine in front of him.

"And why.... " he said while the tears ran. "And why did you have to kill the others? They were young kids. Why...?"

"Business is business," he said. "Those are things that you don't understand, and you won't understand because time is running out." He gave MacLagan and Pranchin a nod to take Daniel to the back. "Take him to the room next to the garage."

Daniel realized even more that they had betrayed him and that he had no escape.

"Yes, of course, sir," said MacLagan. "Let's see if this little whining prick will finally shut up."

"So, in love with that big girl?" Pedraza chuckled. "Well, I'm happy to know that you're going to be together... in the bellies of rats."

They all headed to the back room. It looked like they were going to leave him there. The situation was horrible.

"Assassin! killer of innocents," Daniel shouted. "You murdered my Tamara."

"Ah, don't keep saying that... none of those were innocent," he replied. "They were a good deal, yes, they were, and you had to come to spoil it. What do you know?"

"You not only killed them; you destroyed those families," Daniel said as they pushed him to the wall of the back room. "You.... "

"Ah," said the colonel hitting him in the face and splitting his lip. "Don't give me sentimentality and go prepare yourself for your departure. Do you like that sink? Well, there you are going to bleed out like others bled before you. Like a chicken in the street market."

Daniel saw the sink and a big knife on the side table. Two boxes rested in the corner, with a machete and a saw on top of them.

"Don't worry," said Pedraza. "Death comes fast. You'll see. Dying takes just a few seconds."

Pranchin put the tape back on him. A horrible fright came to Daniel suddenly. *My poor mother,* he thought, *she'll never know.*

Things happened very fast. Daniel began to think about his life and his family while he was being pushed to the sink. MacLagan and one of the officers were pushing him, and there was nothing he could do. They held him there, against the sink. Daniel kept seeing the knife that was on the side. They were going to cut his throat. *Oh, my mother.* They held him there as Pedraza approached, smiling. He was enjoying the moment.

"Oh, this is going to be good," he said.

Suddenly the detectives turned, pulling Daniel aside and pushing him away. Pranchin and MacLagan each drew their pistols and pointed them at Pedraza with clear intention to shoot. Daniel leaned against the wall, scared, and confused. There was going to be a shootout and he might be shot. Pedraza stood still, without understanding. As the slow seconds went by neither Pedraza nor Daniel knew what was going on. An agent moved to the back of Pranchin, turned around and pulled his gun pointing it to the patio, protecting the two detectives. There was a violent electricity in the air.

In that confusing moment, Pancho took a few steps forward and gave Pedraza a shove. The colonel pulled himself together and yelled at him. Pancho gave him a bigger push towards the sink.

"Hey, what's up?" complained Pedraza. "What's up? Wait! Wait!"

Pancho hit him hard in the face and the colonel fell to the ground, where he stayed, with his lip cut off. He looked up and saw the huge Pancho holding him against the floor and the two detectives pointing their guns at him.

"Son of a bitch, what are you doing? Hey, Hey!"

He saw MacLagan and Pranchin pointing their weapons at him and about to shoot.

"Hey, wait, wait. What are you doing? What are you *doing*?"

Daniel was watching, astonished, not understanding.

"Stay against the wall, Danny boy," yelled Pranchin.

The colonel tried to get up.

"This is for you, Daniel," said MacLagan, kicking Pedraza hard in the stomach.

The colonel bent over in pain.

Pancho grabbed him, lifted him from the floor, pushed him to the sink, twisted his arm and held him while Pedraza shouted, "Nooo! nooo! An arrangement! We had an arrangement!"

The colonel was bent over the sink. Pancho held his head and body, then pushed his body to keep the colonel firmly against the sink. Daniel flattened himself even more against the wall. Pranchin was nervous and looking for an angle to shoot Pedraza.

"Wait, Pranchinnetti."

In an instant, Pancho squeezed a hand in his pocket and pulled a Sicilian folding-blade knife. He unfolded the silver blade while Daniel could not believe what his eyes were seeing. The glow and sharpness of that blade announced what was coming. He held Pedraza a bit better, supporting his back with his body, and then bent his head with his hand.

"No... no!!" the colonel shouted, throwing his fist backwards. "No, wait... no, please!"

One of the agents stepped forward and held Pedraza's other hand.

Without hesitation, in an act that showed the dexterity of someone who had done it before, Pancho put the knife against the front of Pedraza's neck, pressed it against the skin, and in a quick movement from left to right made a deep cut. Pedraza shook as blood sprayed in various directions. Pancho held him tight, and the agent held his hand. The colonel shook and attempted to pull his hands while streams of blood were leaving his neck. Daniel was astonished; he knew what was cut—he sliced jugulars, carotids, and tracheas in less than a second.

The seconds lasted forever while spurts of blood continued and the air was filled with the noise of harsh breathing and the sounds of bubbling through the blood. The body was crumbling as it spasmed and the agent helped support it. They removed Daniel's handcuffs, but warned him to "Stay put," with a finger pointed straight at his face.

Pedraza's body went into tremors and then into contractions, until he was still, motionless, leaning over the sink. Daniel approached. The pool of blood made a red mirror across half the floor.

It was not the first time Daniel had seen someone die. His sense of dread and satisfaction mingled with curiosity, morbidity, and wonder.

"Watch out," said Pancho, opening the tap so that the water would run. "Move out!"

Blood began to run down the drain.

Daniel couldn't say anything. His surprise was enormous. There was a big gash in Pedraza's neck. Everything had been quick and awful. There, in front of him, the life of a despicable human being ended. He didn't deserve anything else.

Pancho washed his hands, then washed and folded the knife, and placed it back in his pocket. He took off his jacket and put it in a plastic bag. It was not the first time he had done this kind of job. He nodded to the detectives, who nodded back and placed their guns back in their holsters.

"Good work, Pancho," said one of the detectives.

"You did good, brother," said Pranchin.

Pancho turned his head meeting Daniel's eyes, frozen in amazement, and said "Thank you, mister Daniel."

"Thank you? why do you...?"

"Shut up, Danny," ordered MacLagan. "For once in your life, just try to understand and keep quiet."

Daniel looked at Pancho again. There were memories of pain and hate in his eyes and a slow incoming peace. It was like Pancho was feeling better after what he did. Daniel understood. *Who knows what the colonel did to his family and friends*? They both looked at each other in relief and understanding.

"Thank you, again, mister Daniel," Pancho added, and walked away.

"Raul, Jose, you know what to do," said Pranchin. "You, Daniel, stay aside."

The two men put on gloves. They took the watch and the ring from the dead man. They returned to the living room and listened as other men who had entered opened all the drawers and cabinets. They were bringing everything to the kitchen. Gold watches, leggings, rings, fine clothing, travel souvenirs, coin collections, various handguns, a set of ceramic pipes, silver cutlery, gold coins, and money in large quantities."

"Very well," said MacLagan. "Do you see Daniel? Everything will look as if it was a break-in, a robbery."

"Wait, hey MacLagan," – said Jose, an agent. "Go there.

"What?"

"Look, Raul is at the safe."

"You stay still, little Carmen kid, don't touch anything."

Dumbfounded, Daniel couldn't speak.

"He called you Carmen?" asked one of the agents.

Daniel couldn't answer.

After a while Raul came back and said, "We got a big one this time, man, go up carefully, you gotta see this."

They went upstairs and entered one of the bedrooms. There, in one of the wide-open wardrobes, with the clothes removed and scattered on the floor, stood the unlocked safe. Stack after stack of bills, all in dollars and euros, was piled up there, together with little bags of gold coins. A huge fortune.

"Get going, pack it all up and we're off. You know where it goes."

"Yes, MacLagan."

"Break the window and some furniture before we leave."

"Yep, I'm going. And the body?"

"Leave it. Hey, make sure you don't leave your gloves here. Come on."

"Give Pancho what we promised," said Pranchin to one of the agents, "take him home and get him drunk."

"Sure."

Everything was carefully bagged. Several packages were made. A couple of suitcases that were there were used to carry everything. One of the cars came in from the back and everything was taken over to the car, which then left. With a hammer they broke the lock at the bottom of the door and a second window, to make it look like the force of more than one person. Daniel was still numb with the horror of what had happened and did not speak. They took him to the car, got him in, and left.

"Now, do you see how things are, Daniel?"

"You could barely stand to watch; you really think you were up to doing it yourself?"

Daniel couldn't answer. He had a lump in his chest and another in his throat, and he was in a stupor. After a while he managed to speak and said: "I... I thought that... I thought that... eh..."

"What?" said an agent. "That we betrayed you? That we sold you? But who is going to want to buy you?"

"Only a mother can want someone as ugly and stupid as you, Danny boy," said Pranchin, hugging him.

"You are such a piece of shit, Daniel, but we don't dislike you *that* much."

"And not for the little bit of money he offered," said MacLagan, and they all started to laugh.

Daniel began to whimper. They stopped the car, Daniel got out, he felt bad and threw up. He leaned back on the car. Pranchin gave him whiskey from a purse he was carrying, and some tonic water.

"Have a good drink," he said, leaning back against the car, next to him. "Sorry I hit you."

They opened a bottle of tonic water and poured a good amount of whiskey into it.

"Here, have a whiskey tonic, it will help you feel better."

Daniel had a few good sips. He sat on the ground. Pranchin picked him up and hugged him again.

"Take more, you must erase what you saw with alcohol. And it must be well-erased because from now on this will never be talked about, and you will never talk about it with anyone."

"You just forgot anything you saw."

"Understand?"

"I do. Yes, I didn't see anything. I will never speak about it."

"It had to be done like that, Daniel," MacLagan continued. "On the one hand, we had to stop you before you did something wrong and disgraced yourself and others. And on the other hand, this guy had to be stopped. This ends here."

"It's balance."

"You understand, Daniel? Prachín said. "This ends here, now. And you end it here. Right now."

"And the two women?"

"Daniel!" shouted MacLagan. "Did you hear me? It's over! No more questions. No more conversation. No more endless arguing! Enough! No need to talk about that anymore. This all ends today, now, did you hear me? You did a good job. You did what was asked of you. You knew how to grow in the system and get into where you shouldn't have, but now this is over."

"It's over, Daniel. Already! No more talking."

"But what about—"

"Quit!"

"I'm only wondering what they're going to do with that money?" he asked. "And... with that gold and the rest.

"What we've done before," the agent said. "That goes to half a dozen schools in the periphery of the city. Food, school supplies and utensils are bought for the kids. We buy blankets, clothing, and even add heating systems to those schools. We get people to do repairs and fix the walls, and the ceilings. Sometimes we buy books. We have two people who are in charge. Drink more whiskey, Daniel, that will erase things."

"Ah, yes, it's finally over," Daniel answered. "The whiskey tonic was good. Yes."

"Do you have any questions?"

"No," said Daniel, who was beginning to be much less affected by fright and more affected by alcohol. He was slowly entering a more comfortable state. "All I remember is that you guys drove me out for a drink. Nothing more."

"Very good."

"Yes. Thanks for the ride."

They drove slowly and for a long time. Daniel had more whiskey tonic. They took him to Ines' house. They got him out of the car, rang the bell. Daniel was already dizzy from alcohol and was walking, leaning on Pranchin.

"That's it, Ines," said MacLagan. "It's done. We're leaving this fool here. He's half drunk and half in a stupor, so be careful."

"Yeah, yeah, goodbye."

They left. Daniel just stood there, inside the house. Ines led him into the kitchen and gave him whiskey. He took a drink and went to the bathroom to vomit. He sat on the bathroom floor. Ines covered him with a blanket and gave him something bitter greenish. "You idiot. You don't know your soul?" He stayed there for a while, whimpered a little, drank a little, stuttered a little. Slowly the alcohol began to make his mind cloudier. He tried to explain, but Ines cut it short.

"Erase it from your mind. Do not dwell on it."

He could not push it away. With the effect of the alcohol, he began to sob, while Ines gave him another bitter drink and another sip of something very sweet. He was becoming drowsy, so she left him there, then brought him a pillow, a blanket, and laid him there in the bathroom. He fell asleep.

A sip of sugary coffee woke him up in the morning, he had a headache, she gave him two aspirins, helped him get undressed, and got him into the shower. She helped him wash, then took him to bed, and washed off his pain with breast sweat.

Then, having more coffee, she told him, "This is the last time we talk about it. It's over, Daniel. It's over. The kidnapping thing, your supposed mission, it's over. Do you understand me? It's gone."

"Yes. Yes, Ines."

"And with that the Judicial, and the police headquarters and those damn cameras, and...and the morgue also must end. You must pull yourself out of it. Okay?"

"Okay."

"You must go. You have lost a lot, the danger is not over, you must leave. Redo your life. With help, with a well-planned path, but you must go, and you cannot think about it much."

"Yes, Ines. I already know it."

They began to discuss possible plans. She gave him a few ideas.

"Yes. Thanks, Ines.

"There are many grateful people. Take the opportunity."

She took him home. He got out of the car and watched her go. He stayed in the street for a while. Thinking. He knew he had to draw a line in his mind and leave many things behind. This game was over. He had won, but did he?

Did I win? Did I?

END

FINAL NOTE FROM THE AUTHOR

The manuscript ended here since by the time of its publication the whereabouts of Daniel Blum were unknown. Three days after Pedraza was killed, Daniel disappeared. He was nowhere to be found. His mother apparently knew where he went but refused to talk. His money, his clothes and his Remington 51 were all gone. Nobody knew what had happened, neither Pereyra nor his friends. Deputies of the police center inspected his usual haunts and asked some of his relatives, but there was no clue of his whereabouts. A police officer of the Capurro neighborhood reported he saw him driving around the area. It was thought that the Nubian had found him and murdered him. However, a neighbor of Domínguez saw him entering the house and leaving carrying a package, and what looked like a rifle case.

The search led to no clues.

A few days later, an Interpol search found him in São Paulo, Brazil, where he had a reservation to board a plane to Miami, but he never boarded it. He vanished. Condor officers ordered a search of the area but with no success.

Two weeks later, a report from the Brazil border showed he had re-entered Uruguay. When the information arrived at Police Headquarters, Pranchin notified Martinez who scratched his mustache and said: "He's coming back. He's got a score to settle."

LATE NOTE FROM THE AUTHOR

The dramatic events that followed Daniel Blum's return to Montevideo were not available by the time this second book was written. We knew at that time of some violent events against the Nubian and the discord among CONDOR operatives, but nothing more. Several violent deaths occurred in the Capurro neighborhood, including some police officers. No clues were found, but the investigations uncovered extensive archives, documents, names, pictures of execution centers, etc., which had to be processed and analyzed. As I reviewed them, I wrote a second manuscript: OPERATION CONDOR: ESCAPING FROM A DICTATORSHIP. This second book, not finished yet, will describe real and unpublished events that occurred in Uruguay, Brazil, and Argentina, and is being written using information and data provided by officers of the Justice Department and by Mr. Pereyra, by interviews with officers Pranchin, Dr. Maggiolo, newspapers and archival data, and some statements of the deputies of the police. Documents and Internet information support the manuscript reports.

If YOU have any additional information about the events of this book or Dr. Blum's whereabouts, or any other major event that could be added to the next edition or to the second book, please write to the publisher to get my e-mail address.

I am particularly thankful to Officer Martinez, Berta Ramirez, Dr. Etcheverry, and to Dr. Susana Bassilek (Chief Librarian of the University) for assistance in data collection and connecting dots in the narrative. I also thank the cooperation of some former Condor operatives and of some undisclosed sources which I can't reveal.

I apologize to many of those I interviewed in whom I refreshed the pain that they have learned to keep deep inside. I am sorry I reopened your veins, but I felt the need to write about it and to keep fresh in our community the pain we all went through at that time. We can't forget.

As part of my research, I contacted Gina in Barcelona, and we met in a coffee shop. She was still very distraught and refused to talk about 'her Daniel.' I couldn't get much information from her, but it was clear that she was still emotionally affected by the events described in this book. While in tears, she gave me a long statement and provided me with a folder full of important information, which was added to the manuscript. Still heartbroken by the events, she got up and left without saying anything else. The pain I saw in her eyes was too deep.

June 24, 2021